Past Present Future

Between greed, love and obsession
there is the truth we would rather
not see

Past Present Future

Between greed, love and obsession
there is the truth we would rather
not see

NJ Alexander

Winchester, UK
Washington, USA

First published by Roundfire Books, 2012
Roundfire Books is an imprint of John Hunt Publishing Ltd., Laurel House, Station Approach,
Alresford, Hants, SO24 9JH, UK
office1@jhpbooks.net
www.johnhuntpublishing.com
www.roundfire-books.com

For distributor details and how to order please visit the 'Ordering' section on our website.

Text copyright: NJ Alexander 2012

ISBN: 978 1 84694 970 8

A CIP catalogue record for this book is available from the British Library.

Design: Stuart Davies

Cover photography copyright: Michael Llori

Printed and bound by CPI Group (UK) Ltd, Croydon, CR0 4YY

We operate a distinctive and ethical publishing philosophy in all
areas of our business, from our global network of authors to
production and worldwide distribution.

Acknowledgements

Dedicated to my children XOX
When I first set about writing this novel, it never occurred to me
how much of a team effort the final book would be.
So a big thank you to…
My family and close friends for loving me, supporting me and
humouring me no matter what. Love you all.
My local police for agreeing to role-play with me: a fun but
unnerving experience on so many levels. A specific thank you to
Alison Jones. I could not have written some of the later chapters
without your help - the cursor would still be flashing at the top
of a blank page. I hope this mention is better than the offering
of burnt crumpets! Any legal inaccuracies will be down entirely
to my poetic licence and not your expertise.
Ajda for taking me seriously as a writer and prompting me to
take the story/events much further than I had originally dared
to venture. It was the first glimpse of an olive branch I'd seen in
a long time.
Tania for encouragement when I need it the most, and finding
10,000 unnecessary words!
Gareth Carrol for clarifying things that had me scratching my
head.
The team at John Hunt Publishing for their no nonsense
approach to publishing.

Prologue

N.b Transcript fallen loose from Nicole's file.

JD: Tell me something interesting about yourself Nicole, something I don't already know, that made you feel good.

Nicole: Interesting and good? I'm stumped. *(Noted that interviewee started doodling flowers on the paper in front of her.)*

JD: There must be something. Your book covers such a short period of your life.

Nicole: I once won a competition for designing a charity card for old people. My picture was in the paper and I was given a set of oil paints.

JD: When was that?

Nicole: When I was seven.

JD: Oh...right. Anything else charitable? When you were older perhaps.

Nicole: A sixteen-mile bike ride, or was it eighteen? But that's the whole point – I am boringly ordinary. What happened was extraordinary. But I am normal.

JD: Normal?

Nicole: You sound like Maddy now.

JD: Your best friend? I was merely going to ask your definition of normal. Okay... Try outrageous then.

Nicole: Arrested for shoplifting.

JD: I meant outrageously funny. Are you trying to sound bad?

Nicole: I was fourteen. It was a game with a group of friends. Badly influenced.

JD: Your games seem to have a habit of backfiring on you.

Nicole: I'm not bad enough to justify someone preferring me dead. I know I'm far from perfect. But then who is? I used to enter beauty pageants...is that any use?

JD: I want to come back to someone wanting you dead later.

But did you win any of the pageants?

Nicole: Runner-up to the girl who went on to win Miss UK. Suppose that makes her interesting and not me.

JD: You must have been sure of yourself to parade around in a swimsuit?

Nicole: I guess I was more like the pony stood in a line of thoroughbreds. These days beauty pageants aren't worth the effort are they? It was different in the 80s though.

JD: Why do you say that?

Nicole: *(Note that interviewee started doodling bees around the flowers.)* Do you think therapy works?

JD: You're answering a question with a question. Why do you ask that?

(Noted that interviewee raised her eyebrows.)

Nicole: I spent a fortune sitting on cheap bean bags trying to rationalise a fear of failure.

JD: Are you saying you think therapy is a waste of time and money?

Nicole: I'm saying I was right to have the fear.

JD: Tell me why.

Nicole: If you treated a man for a fear of bees only to find later that he'd died from a single sting, would you not conclude that he was right to feel afraid? His instincts were right.

JD: Or he was unlucky.

Nicole: Unlucky is a convenient explanation.

JD: I'm not sure where you ar—

Nicole: I should have been saved from the sting, and not the fear of it. I was right to feel afraid of failure because something, somewhere deep inside me knew what was to follow failure would be painful. What I mean is, even if it makes me insane to say it – this was always going to happen the way it did.

JD: You could have destroyed the book.

Nicole: Why on earth would I do that? It was the most challenging thing I've ever done – it did my head in some days trying to get it right. And even if I did burn it, it would still exist in me – it wouldn't disappear. At least this way I have a remote chance... *(Interviewee stopped speaking.)*

JD: A remote chance of what Nicole? The truth?

Nicole: If only. The path to truth is riddled with lies we can't get through. Can we take a break?

CHAPTER ONE

February 2008

I felt Richard looking over my shoulder and I shuffled in my seat. As I did, I caught a glimpse of the inappropriate skinny jeans I was wearing with a tan leather jacket; the magazine I was reading wasn't big enough to block my legs. This had to be the worst Valentine's Day ever.

I sighed, cursing the fact that I hadn't had time to get changed. The elegant decor could have almost fooled me into thinking I was sat in some posh hotel reception. But this was no holiday. At least Richard was wearing an expensive handmade suit – one of us being respectably presented was marginally better.

'What are you reading?' he asked.

'It's an article about stalking.'

'Stalking?

'Couldn't really stomach the *Business Matters* magazines, and there's no *Cosmo* knocking around. This psychology journal was the most removed I could fi—'

'So what does it say?'

'You don't want to think about *it* either then,' I said, raising my eyebrows.

He never showed nerves. His nickname at work was the unoriginal, lack of creative input – *Iceman*.

'No... not really,' he admitted.

I didn't know whether his admission made me feel better or worse. Probably worse – it made it right for me to feel unsafe. I sighed again. 'It's talking about all of the different types of stalkers. Apparently, there's the love obsessed, simple obsessed, the delusional erotomanic, even the borderline erotomanic.'

I took a breath. At least this stopped me from thinking about *it*, '...the vengeful, resentful and rejected. The narcissistic, psychopathic, sociopathic and the schizoid.'

'They've got a lot of options then,' Richard said, flippantly.

'A police detective is going on about them not really having a clear profile for cyberstalkers, and the problem is, they can be living anywhere...as in you don't know where they are. Did you know the average stalker's a 38-year-old male, no job, bit of a loner?'

'No.'

'Look – they've even drawn a photo-fit of one – don't you think he looks evil? You'd spot one a mile off.' I turned the magazine in Richard's direction, forcing his attention.

'Yeah, suppose he does look a bit weird.'

'They reckon stalkers have usually suffered an emotional loss about six months before they start doing it. It is stuff like relationship breakups, people dying or basically losing anything important to them that can trigger it. Don't you think that's quite sad? ... Richard...you're not listening to me.'

'Mmmm. You need to put that magazine down... David and James are heading this way.'

We all stood in silence.

The only noise came from the mechanics of the lift as it made its way to the third floor. We'd got the pleasantries over and done with downstairs and I was already missing the magazine I'd been clinging to.

David and James both stood a whole head above Richard. They made me feel small. And like Richard, they were wearing suits. The discomfort of my clothes was increasing by the minute: they definitely smacked of loser in this place. Then my memory reminded me of a harsh fact: I'd managed to lose one million pounds. In a solitary pile of twenty pound notes this was about the height of a double-decker bus. That would also be twice the height of the lift space we were standing in. Whatever it amounted to placed end to end or in a pile it was one hell of a lot of money to a working-class girl like me.

I grew up in an industrial and mining community where career choices back in the 80s amounted to not much more than shop assistant, typist, or spending your days sewing gussets onto tights in a factory.

One million pounds is life-changing money, and I'd lost it.

I forced my head to stay down.

We made our way into a small meeting room with a round mahogany table at its centre. Just like the foyer it had a sense of class with all of the messy paperwork from the previous tragedy tastefully hidden from our view. It was the type of room expected from a company connected to the law.

'Sit down and make yourselves comfortable while I buzz through to Andrea to bring in the papers,' David said, in his quiet, but self-assured manner; he had an air of intelligence that unnerved me. 'I appreciate that this is very emotional for you both, these are always difficult situations, but I think you've made the right decision,' he continued gently, as though we'd declined chemotherapy, after being told we were terminally ill. As partner of his firm, he'd probably delivered those words many times over.

'Well, it could be worse. At least it's only a secondary business that's going down,' Richard said.

I too was so thankful that Richard still had his other company in financial services – people have to have insurance.

'This must be hard for you, Nicole. Richard has told me how much effort you have put in over the last six or seven years.'

'Yes it is very hard,' I agreed, but I didn't want to elaborate any further.

I didn't need sympathy. Sympathy wasn't going to help me stay strong in the meeting.

I forced a smile but quickly lowered my eyes – I could feel all three of them staring at me, as if to measure my emotional response.

I will not cry, I told myself and dug my fingers into the palms of my hands to distract me whilst I blinked hard.

'Would you like me to request tea or coffee for you both?' David continued, in an attempt to fill the awkwardness until Andrea came back with the papers.

'No, I'm fine, thank you.'

Richard declined too.

Andrea, a twenty-something, with her whole career still ahead of her, entered the room. She was dressed head-to-toe in black with her dark hair pulled sleekly back. She swiftly handed the papers to David – the papers which were within minutes going to be terminating my career. I shuffled uncomfortably in my seat. David took a minute to read through them, double-checking his assistant's work, before allowing her to leave. She closed the door quietly behind her.

'Okay, Nicole as director and main shareholder, I need to run through these with you and explain exactly what you can and can't do from this point onwards. These are the legal documents assigning control of your company over to us. As you already know, any money paid into *Ilex Drapes* and the second company, as of today, has to be paid into the Client Holding Account – which has been set up this afternoon. Any previously ordered goods, which come through the door, cannot be accepted. We are now acting in the interest of the creditors, and our job is to not make their position any worse. Do you understand?'

'Yes,' I confirmed. He'd made me sound like a criminal, and my memory, once again, reminded me that I'd lost one million pounds.

'Over the next few weeks we need to work out which curtains and soft-furnishings have already been manufactured and are waiting to be fitted, and which orders can still be made. We also need to work out the costs involved, like staff wages, to again make sure that we are not further jeopardising creditors. The factory will remain open until we know your exact position, but the showroom will have to close immediately. I plan to send James in to work with you again for a few weeks. Are you happy with that arrangement?'

'Yes,' I said, silently glad it was James. I'd got quite used to having him around in the past week, and at least I didn't have to get to know another stranger. James smiled politely, acknowledging his delegated role. I quickly looked away so not to catch his eyes.

David continued to talk. 'We need to get the debtors' money in, then go through all the assets and get things sold off – do you both understand all of that?'

We nodded and I was amazed that my brain was actually taking in everything he was saying.

He then went on about the sale of the fixed and floating assets and relinquishing the lease on the showroom – the lease issue being aimed more at Richard than me.

'And another thing…we need to get these documents down to court tomorrow, first thing. We have to get appointed as the Official Administrator, before the bank appoints their own – it's really a race against time. Can you meet us at the court first thing tomorrow?' David asked me.

'No I can't – I'm in London with Mum and Dad,' and I turned helplessly to Richard. 'I have to go to London, it's William's birthday treat, I can't not go with him – he's going to be all of seven for God's sake.'

'It's fine – I'll do it,' Richard offered.

'I'm off tomorrow, too.'

'Are you? Have you booked some time off then, James?' questioned David in a – *this is news to me* tone.

'Only tomorrow, I'm going to Leeds for the weekend,' he confirmed. *With his girlfriend? I wondered.*

'Oh right – that's fine. I'll get someone else to run down to the court with Richard then and it means that Nicole, you will have to speak to all of the *Ilex Drapes* staff on Monday. Is that okay with you?'

'Yes, that's going to be fine,' I lied. The thought of telling all the staff they were soon to be out of a job pricked my eyes, more so than the thought of the customers who would lose their deposits.

Images flashed before me: staff busy cutting fabrics, sawing head rails, drilling into window frames, helping customers browse through sample books – people going about their day, oblivious to what was about to come; I was playing a futile God.

I dug my fingers into my palms. Any harder and I would fetch blood. I knew that I only had to hold myself together for a few more minutes.

'Okay, that's good,' David said, after taking a slow glance at the papers. 'One final thing, all the company records will need boxing up and inventories carried out. Now…we can get someone else to do that, but it is expensive. Are you able to do that, Nicole?'

Am I able to do that? My head repeated his words. *Of course I'm going to be able to do that. It's not like I've got any other bloody thing to do now is it? Not now you're taking my company, my third child, my baby…that you are going to rip apart and destroy,* my inner voice screamed, but one simple word fell from my mouth:

'Yes,' I said quietly.

'Right, so if you could sign here…' and he slid the papers in my direction, passing the pen to my right hand.

I hesitated, switched it to my left and signed my name.

Outside, the air in the city felt heavy. I had taken my turn in the rotating doors to emerge into a world that looked the same: people rushing about, buildings towering and cars fighting for limited parking imposed by the council. It was exactly how it was when I had entered the offices an hour before. But my world was different now and there was no spinning back through those doors. I wanted to sob, but now that I was free to do so, the tears wouldn't come.

Over one hundred cardboard boxes were stacked against the far wall of the factory.

I placed the remaining payroll documents into the last one but held a file back for a second or so, leafing through it. My name wasn't listed in it – I'd never even been paid for all my efforts. That was supposed to happen later.

I stood up and stretched out. The place felt so empty and cold – the heating was barely ticking over. The administrators had already sold off some of the assets: cutting tables, fabrics, components, all gone for peanuts to our local competitors; they'd descended on the place like vultures, delighted by our misfortune. My ten thousand customer database was gone as well; someone even bought our telephone number and gaps were starting to appear in the floor space.

Bitterness hit me: if only the other director hadn't blocked me from moving his machinery and staff into ours as soon as we'd bought his company, and if only Richard had backed me instead of trusting a man to know better. After the director left I did move to one factory – I spent New Year's Day dismantling machinery with my dad so it could all be transported here. But it was too late by then.

As I looked around me I could hear the ghostly memory of laugher, shouting, swearing and the constant buzz of sewing machines and saws. Of course, everyone had been gone for over six weeks now. It should have been the tears of their last day that I could hear – but I couldn't. I wanted to blank them out, but every now and then those images would feverishly strike like the bolt of lightning that leaves you running for cover.

If I looked closely at the far wall I could still see the outline of stone fighting its way through the paint. It must have been a magnificent stained glass window when the building had been a chapel years before, but other than the high arched ceiling, that was the only trace of its past.

Perhaps that was the problem – we'd tried to gain profit from a sacred place.

There was a loud knocking and tugging on the main door.

I'd locked it because customers were still coming to the building, not realising we'd closed down. They'd obviously missed the tiny piece in the local gazette called "The Mystery of Ilex Drapes" – I had refused to speak to anyone at the paper after they discovered we'd gone. But I knew this knock would be the administrators – they had come to take the boxes away. I opened the door and let two young men in.

'They're over there, you can't miss them,' I said. 'And I think you need these keys to lock up when you've finished. You can let me have them back later.'

'What happened,' asked the taller of the two.

'Happened?'

'I mean, what went wrong...with the company?'

I laughed at this directness. 'Bad luck,' I said. I couldn't really be bothered to tell him everything. 'Doesn't your company fill you in on the small details?'

'No...we're trainees – the dogsbodies.'

There was a pause. He had a searching expression on his face. His colleague was already busy going through the boxes.

'Okay, I'll tell you. The bank wanted us to put another forty thousand into the business to remove a director from his portion of the bank guarantee. They'd given us two weeks to do it; otherwise they were calling the whole overdraft in. We'd already chucked too much at it...as in four *hundred* thousand.'

His eyebrows raised and he did a faint whistle.

'Well – we didn't put it in – which is why you're here now. As I said...it's all due to bad luck. That freak rain last summer – it killed off the conservatory market, which was big for us. Then *Northern Rock* went and bloody well crashed in November didn't it? Just as people were coming off their fixed rates. People suddenly stopped spending and our sales practically halved overnight. It was scary how quickly it happened and I had a feeling that things weren't going to get any better.'

'That certainly was unlucky,'

'Yep, as things stood we were never going to make the big profits like the accountants and so-called business experts said we would – they'd become an impossible dream.

'So…what are you going to do now?'

'Dunno. But not waste my time working stupid hours for nothing – that's for sure.

'At least it's all over for you.'

'Over? Are you kidding? There's still a load of shit flying around. It's far from over for us.'

'I'm sorry I didn't…'

'No it's fine…but I'm off now. I'll leave you boys to it. Have fun – or at least try to.'

I took one last walk through the showroom. It looked drab without the lights on, but still elegant.

I ran my hands down the curtains and blinds that sat in their separate compartments. They were the only remaining evidence of all the hours of work and creativity I'd put in. I pulled the cord on one of the Venetian blinds, closing the slats. It was like lowering the eyelids on the dead.

Moments later, I threw the completed Statement of Affairs on the passenger seat of my car. Another gentle reminder that I'd lost one million – give or take a few pence.

Why hadn't they just rounded it up?

I took one last look at the sign writing – *Ilex Drapes* – the first two letters were made to look like a pair of curtains with a slight wave. Ilex is Latin pronounced Eilex. Soon, no one would again ask me why I had chosen that name. With a shake of the head, I switched thoughts and cursed myself that it wasn't Richard I was thinking about.

CHAPTER TWO

Three months later

'You should sign up to *Facebook* – you'd love it! Honest.'

'It really isn't my thing. I'm not that sociable,' I disputed.

I didn't really know much about *Facebook* at that point in my life, other than that it was a social networking site. Back then I could easily have mistaken *MySpace* for a storage company and *Twitter* hadn't even made a tweet on my radar in 2008. I'd only signed up to *Friends Reunited* because I'd lost a friend's telephone number and, once I'd got it, I never returned to the site.

'But that's why you'd love *Facebook*,' Maddy said. 'You can be nosey and look at what people are up to, but you don't have to be sociable. It's so funny seeing how people have turned out; it's amazing how many of the boys from my schooldays have gone downhill.' She clipped her hair out of the way. I noticed the cool April sunshine was bringing out the red tones of her otherwise brown hair.

'Social networking sites are full of psychopathic weirdos,' I said, remembering the article I read in the Administrator's offices.

'Are you calling me a weirdo?' she mocked, deliberately ignoring the psychopathic part.

We laughed, all three of us sitting round the table.

'Okay, I might join – I'll see.'

I was saved by the waitress who came to take our order. She took mine first and while she spoke to Maddy and Lorna I became aware of the goose bumps on my arms. I glanced enviably at the fellow diners who'd opted to eat inside the trendy restaurant on soft, cushioned chairs. That's where I wanted to be; surrounded by sleek decor and photos of beautiful actresses and models – not looking at passing overweight shoppers with their heavy bags smashing against their thighs.

Maddy and Lorna's bloody cigarettes, I silently cursed, wafting away the smoke that was heading in my direction, as they attempted to keep it away from the waitress. I scraped my metal chair across the cobbled stone, sending further shivers down my spine. This was my futile attempt to get closer to the patio heater; which would surely have failed to melt clingfilm if it had been lobbed in its direction.

Smoking wasn't the only thing that made me the odd one out. Maddy and Lorna preferred not to work; they were happy to be stay-at-home mothers. Which, actually, I was thankful for, because, without my business, at least I had some friends to socialise with during the week. And there was a part of me – despite being reluctant to admit it – that was quite enjoying the time I spent with Maddy and Lorna, without having the pressure of work hanging over me, or our kids under our feet, which was how it usually was.

'God, I love Steve. Who else would put up with me?' Maddy said as she switched her phone off and dropped it into her *Prada* bag. I hadn't bothered listening to her call, so I didn't know what had provoked her comment.

Probably got him to leave a job and drive back from Glasgow or somewhere equally ridiculous for the school run.

I watched her slide her cigarettes out of the way as the waitress placed the food on the table. I wasted no time digging my fork into the buttered potatoes, surprised by how hungry I actually was.

'You're both really lucky. You've both got it much easier than me,' Lorna managed, after elegantly guiding a piece of salmon down her throat.

Neither Maddy nor I would even attempt to argue this one with Lorna; we would fail miserably: Lorna's millionaire lifestyle had been whipped from under her feet after her husband's company collapsed and the house repossessed.

Still not knowing what to say, I turned my attention back to Maddy. 'Well…Steve's not going to go off with someone younger is he?' This was my pretend bitchy tone because I knew what her comeback would be. It's something Maddy and I had always done to entertain each other and Lorna sometimes looked horrified by the mock offensive remarks we made.

'No, because I *am* the younger model,' Maddy fired back, even though she was adamant that aging didn't bother her.

This confirmed yet again my long-held suspicion that she was bothered, but it would be literally over her dead wrinkled body before she'd ever admit it. Eighteen years younger than Steve, she was officially the younger model, like I with Richard, who was twenty-four years my senior.

'I do know what you mean though, Lorna,' I softened my voice. 'I'm a disorganised pain in the ass and drive Richard mad, but he would do anything for me,' and I said it as though it was the first time I'd ever stated this fact.

'Anyway, how did you two get together? You've never told me, not properly,' Lorna asked, in a more serious manner.

Lorna, out of the three of us, acted like a *grown-up* woman. She was a stunning-looking woman with chiselled bone structure, but she once said that having hit forty she was too old to pull off the girly thing.

That meant I had three years left to nail the maturity issue.

I slowly chewed on a piece of bread in an attempt to buy some time, while I thought through the best way to explain Richard to Lorna. What she really wanted to know was how I had made the transition from working for him, to shagging him, to living with him.

'He approached me at the work's Christmas party,' I started off nice and easy. 'I did know he was married.' There was no point in denying that bit; I think she already knew that much from the way Maddy had always sounded off about it. 'But he said he wanted me, and that he had wanted me since he saw me training in the gym. That's why he'd given me a job.' I was fully aware that it was no excuse, and I felt Maddy's disapproving blue eyes on me but I ignored her and carried on. 'I was really attracted to him, it was the ex-RAF pilot thing, plus his brain – he finished the FCII in half the required seven years and still came top in the country, and the fact that he'd built up a business off his own back. Oh…and he did have a very nice red two-seater sports car at the time with cream leather seats, it was gorgeous.' It would have been daft to deny the lure of a Mercedes SL that was probably worth more than my parents' house at the time, and there was a playful part of me that wanted to throw it in for Maddy's benefit.

'Gold digger…' Maddy delivered on cue. It was a term we'd thrown at each other many times before, so there was no malice behind her words. She carried on eating – she heard it all before anyway.

'I suppose that, as an employee, I was slightly in awe of him. It's that power thing, isn't it?' I offered this as both an attempt to defend my weakness and because the things that attracted me to him are the very same things that now make me proud of him. I shifted uncomfortably; I could feel myself shrinking into my chair as though trying to disappear leaving only my voice behind. I hated telling the story because it always made me feel like the scheming bitch from hell. 'The worse thing is, having a relationship with him, with no commitment, suited me at the time. I was planning to give up my job, return to full-time study, and was sick of relationships getting in the way of plans.'

Although I said 'relationships' that was a slight exaggeration – there had been a few men before Richard, but was only really referring to one previously screwed-up relationship that I'd been in when I'd started working for him.

'I suppose at twenty-two I was naive enough to think that we would have a bit of sexual fun, I'd go off to university and he would stay with his wife. Everyone knows that married men never leave their wives - so no harm done…right? Wroooong! Five per cent do leave their wives.' I said it as though I was acting as my own prosecution and defence. 'Anyway, he told me he wanted to leave her – to be with me – so I chose a university where I could commute and still be with him. He did go back to her a couple of times. But anyway the rest is, well just is...'

I had cut my story short – conscious that I was the one doing all the talking, which was unusual for me. I was usually quiet, which was sometimes misconstrued as my being aloof rather than shy – according to Lorna.

Before they could criticise me, I started again; talking about my affair with Richard had reminded me of my recent secret crush on someone. It wasn't that I'd been thinking much about the man in question anymore, but controlling my feelings over the crush had made me start to think a lot about the only other time in mine and Richard's history where I had secretly been attracted to someone else and spent several years hiding how I felt. It was life's events, which helped him simply drift further into my past. He was like the unopened box of chocolates that sits at the back of the cupboard fleetingly popping up on occasions when you're not even looking for them and, somehow, this box of chocolates had managed to make its way to the front of my cupboard again.

'Do you know when I worked for *Opus* on that year placement,' I said, as a statement, not a question.

'*Opus*? Ahhh…the job with the wanker boss – the nightclub owner, the band man – that job?' Maddy asked with her fork held in the air like a child's hand raised in a classroom.

'That's the one,' I said.

I'd often told her about Alf; a big fat lump of lard and the most arrogant bloody pig on the planet that I had to work for as part of my degree. I'd been placed in the marketing department, which was situated at the back of one of his clubs, and I still felt claustrophobic when I thought of that drab, windowless office.

But, strangely, I had loved the job and the people. It also had the buzz of occasionally meeting a new star, old star or fading star at the bigger events. But there was someone I liked in particular...

'There was a guy there who I was really attracted to. He was the lead singer of one of the bands that Alf managed. He was from New York.'

My tone was resigned and Lorna's eyes flashed, while Maddy perched herself in her chair in anticipation of what was about to fall from my mouth next. This was a story that she hadn't heard before.

The man in question was Anthony Hope, and I'd never uttered his name to either of them or to anyone in recent years for that matter. I was attracted to him from the very first moment I saw him, which had been when I was sitting in the back of one of the company "people carriers" with two other colleagues. We were on our way to a promotional event and he just happened to be walking down the road. The driver pulled over to introduce us all to the new band member. *Boyz2Blues*, as they were called, were not big time pop stars – they were cover artists and played at various venues up and down the country.

The blacked-out window came down and there he was, standing there like he'd been framed. He probably couldn't even see me squashed in the middle seat. He was tall, very slim, with good square shoulders and edgy-looking; dressed head-to-toe in black with skinny jeans. I think he had an earring, or male jewellery of some sort. His dark eyes were piercing and his shoulder-length, bobbed hair was tied back in a ponytail. Up until that point I would have always said that I hated men with longer hair; but it looked good on him. He was the opposite of Richard, who had been silver-haired since his twenties and looked distinguished, and he wasn't like the clean-cut pretty boys – as my mum always called them – that I had always gone for before Richard either.

There was just something about Anthony Hope – he looked

like the ultimate bad boy.

'Go on then,' Lorna urged.

'He had plenty of girlfriends – though he did stick with one for a while. But he once had a conversation about me with Richard at one of Alf's mansion-based parties. I was leaning on one of the French doors in Alf's kitchen and Richard and Anthony were side-by-side on the terrace; just outside my earshot. But then Richard shouted over to me that Anthony had said he was a lucky man.' I felt silly even saying that to Maddy and Lorna. 'Anthony was grinning at me,' I added.

I remembered grinning back at him, feeling myself falling into one of those prolonged eye-locks, staring into unfulfilled expectation. Even now, all these years on, I recall having to reluctantly pull myself out of it, hoping that Richard didn't suspect I was attracted to Anthony. I didn't say it to Maddy and Lorna, but I did remember Richard saying to me: 'He fancies you. You *don't* fancy him do you? He *is* an attractive guy, I could understand it if you did.' Richard went on to ask me the same trick question several times that night.

The waitress placed the tray of extra tea we'd ordered onto the table and briefly broke my confession. Lorna started sorting out the milk and sugar and her blonde hair fell forward, hiding her facial expression from my view, which was probably just as well. Then the waitress left.

'He was grinning at you...so what?' Maddy asked.

'I am trying to explain. Anthony used to have to come in and rehearse with the rest of the band a couple of times a week and it was my job to take refreshments to them. I was forever trying to be dismissive of him; trying to kid myself that I didn't find him attractive... I always ended up tongue-tied when I spoke to him.'

'You mean you wanted to be tongue-tied with him,' Maddy said and then laughed with Lorna.

'Ha, ha...but there was just something about his voice, his

smile and the way that he spoke to me that made me melt.'

Maddy nearly choked on her tea.

'It was like I knew him, yet I didn't really know anything about him.' I was conscious that I was sounding really dreamy which was why Maddy was struggling to take me seriously.

But that's how it was, although I didn't say it to Lorna and Maddy; for some reason I felt connected to Anthony. He always managed to make me smile.

I also felt protective of him, which was not a role I usually took in relationships.

Most of what I knew about him had been learned from others, but I hated it when people made snide remarks about him. Behind his confident exterior I could see glimpses of someone who seemed lost and not really sure where he was going and yet he also appeared to be a deep, literate, thinker. Occasionally I would see him sitting alone, reading a novel of some sort an hour or so before he was due to start rehearsing. The erudite titles would always catch me by surprise. Maybe my instinct to protect was simply because he'd not long arrived in the UK and was such a long way from home – I didn't know. Richard certainly didn't need me to protect him – Richard was the one who made me feel safe, *until recently.*

I sighed. 'Anyway since I left the job I've no idea what happened to him. I presume his Visa ran out and he went back home. Thing is, because I never got involved with him, I would still want him, even if I saw him today. It's weird isn't it, that once you break up with someone you look at them and wonder what attracted you to them in the first place. But with him it will never be like that, because it never got off the ground.'

'But why?' Lorna said it as though it should have been the easiest thing in the world to have done back then.

'There were loads of reasons why I didn't and couldn't pursue him, Lorna. He would have hurt me for sure. I think I was always the one he couldn't have because I was with Richard. If he'd had me at the time, I'm sure I'd have been like the others: dumped and heartbroken. Even in his late twenties, he'd still got a lot of living to do before settling down. It's all hypothetical anyway, *even* if he had had a thing for me, he would have moved on and long forgotten me – I was always going to be the loser out of the two of us.'

Maddy and Lorna looked slightly shocked or surprised by my confession – I couldn't decide which. But they hadn't seen it coming. With a shake of the head Maddy brought us back to reality.

'You see, that's what I mean about Steve and Richard,' she said in her singsong voice, spoken at her usual higher than average speed. 'We know that we can trust them and that they're not going to hurt us; they will always be there for us... I need a cigarette.'

'I do know what she means though. I think there is the "what if" in everyone's past,' Lorna politely defended.

But having had a severe case of verbal diarrhoea, I wasn't sure the Anthony Hope confession was such a good idea.

At least I'd had the sense to keep my mouth shut about my other crush.

CHAPTER THREE

Blue, our weimaraner was digging around in the soil surrounding the evergreen shrubs. I put my pen down and stared out of the window into the June sunshine; the gaps in the ivory shutters meant that I could see most of the garden and our field beyond. The expanse of mature trees, hawthorn hedges and the sound of birds singing reminded me how lucky we were to live in the English countryside. Our home was a three-storey new build, but it was unusual because of all the land that came with it.

The parasol was still out from Elyse's third birthday a couple of Sundays ago, and was gently flapping in the breeze. The wooden chairs were still in a state of disarray on the patio area; staring at them reminded me that they needed sanding down again – something I always did because Richard could never be bothered with it. Even the parasol has spun a hole this year which dad said looked like the work of mice.

I called Blue back to the house before he wrecked any more plants then turned my attention to my studies glancing miserably at the pile of accountancy books to my right. This was my new work alternative until I could think of what I did want to do career wise. It wasn't like I hadn't done my share of exams in my time either: I already had a performing arts degree and a masters in journalism. To call me lost was probably more accurate than to say that I was well on my way to becoming a professional student, but the mountain of mundane study felt overwhelming as I'd wrongly surmised that getting the first exam out of the way would spur me to knuckle down to the next one.

Facebook was open on the Log In page, but since signing up to the site, I vowed it wouldn't detract from my studies.

Normally the light, colonial feel of the room made me feel fresh and alive, but it wasn't working today; instead it felt oppressive and isolating. I contemplated taking a break and doing something else constructive like tidying up, but then glanced around at the vast stone floor, the dining chairs covered in un-ironed shirts, and the dusty paw prints on the leather sofas and changed my mind.

I looked at the time on the laptop; it said 13:01 – that meant I had a good few hours before Richard was home to cram in some decent study. I thought about opening the windows to let a breeze into the garden room but couldn't think where Richard had moved the tiny keys for the safety locks, so instead I opened the lounge window. While I was in there I plumped up a few cushions on the sofa, another diversion tactic.

Several hours later after being engrossed in my studies I felt warm again and noticed the breeze had stopped filtering through. The time on the laptop said 16:00. That meant the day was past peak heat, so I went to check the lounge window. It was closed again.

I studied the window. It wasn't possible it could close and the catch be firmly back in place. I opened and closed it several times over as though to prove my theory. If a strong breeze had forced it closed, the long metal catch would still be sticking out.

I looked round the lounge. Blue was on the sofa watching me with intrigue – his head was cocked on one side. I thought back to when we were burgled a few years earlier, the whole reason we'd got a dog, even if he was useless. But this was the opposite way round – back then the burglars had opened the window; not closed it. They didn't even shut any of the drawers they had gone through. In fact, the house had looked like a poltergeist had been through it at the time.

I checked around downstairs: the TVs were still all in their place and nothing had moved. There was no evidence of burglary or even entry of any sort. I was baffled and ran my hands through my hair, pulling it away from my face and sighed. I called Richard.

'Have you been back to the house, creeping around and

closing the lounge window without telling me?' I asked.

'No. I'm on my way back from work and going to get the kids from school like I said I would. Why?'

'It's most likely nothing, but I opened the lounge window earlier and now it's closed.'

'Perhaps the wind blew it shut.'

'No. Not possible.'

'Has the gardener or window cleaner been, or Mick-The-Cleaner, has he done it?'

'No, of course not – it's not any of their days to be here, and besides you can't close the window properly from the outside.'

'You must have dreamt that you opened it.'

'I haven't been to sleep; I've been studying all afternoon.'

'Well I don't know then.'

'Me neither, but I can't see any evidence of anyone being in the house.' I looked round uneasily as I said it.

'I'll be home soon. Relax. I definitely think you've fallen asleep and dreamt you opened it. You are studying too much. You could have got over tired.'

He was probably right, I was just being silly. I let him go so he could focus on driving while I walked back in to the lounge for a final look. It was then that I remembered that I also plumped up the cushions after I opened the window. The cushions were still plump.

Despite my initial good intentions with *Facebook* I noticed that Maddy and I were increasingly substituting texts, for *Facebook* messages. This morning, whilst still damp from my early shower, I double-checked that she hadn't posted anything first thing which altered arrangements for meeting up for breakfast. While I was on, I quickly accepted a few more friend requests from old school friends I hadn't seen in two decades, but I didn't have time to look at what they'd been up to. It seemed like the whole world had cottoned on to this thing while I'd been oblivious. If it wasn't for Maddy I'm pretty sure it would still be missing my radar. Considering some of the people who had signed up, it still seemed strange to me that James Darnell and Anthony Hope hadn't joined as far as I could see.

I switched the laptop off, re-adjusted my towel and headed upstairs to finish getting ready.

The bed was still unmade, and my damp towel soon lay crumpled on the floor, blending into the pale cream carpet. I stood in front of the wardrobes in a dilemma – they were full of clothes but I had nothing to wear. I cursed myself for falling into this so-common female trap. When I was small I would watch Mum get herself in a state over her clothes. I vowed back then that it would be something I would never do as an adult; whatever I put on, I would wear with confidence. Now I wasn't working I'd got used to not having to think about what to wear: jeans, combats and vest top, hair back and be done with it.

But today I was feeling the pressure to make a little more effort, which had no logic to it either – it was only breakfast, I reminded myself.

I pulled on my high-waisted, straight-leg jeans, grabbed a white shirt and dressed it up with a long sleeveless cardigan; one I'd bought and never worn. I grabbed some matching grey beads and I stood in front of the tall mirror that was fixed to the inside of the wardrobe door. I turned to the left, then right, glanced over my shoulder and concluded it wasn't working; the look wasn't me. It worked well with my blondish hair, but it looked smart, too smart as in well-dressed 50-year-old, even when I removed the beads! The problem was the weather – despite the June heat wave, we were back to a cool July.

I know…where's that little dogtooth, charcoal skirt?

I wanted to get at least one wear out of the cardigan to justify its purchase. I knew that it was in there somewhere. I made my way through the hangers, thinking I really needed to sort my wardrobe out. It seemed ridiculous that we had a bedroom the size of a double garage with fitted wardrobes all down one side and it was still a disorganised mess; but I had things in there from when I was eighteen.

Aaargh that bloody phone, I cursed before picking it up to hear Richard's voice.

'The kids went in okay,' he said chirpily. Richard always did the morning school-run because it was on his way to the office.

'That's good...' I waited for him to explain why he was calling.

'Don't you want to talk to me?' his voice was still calm. Richard's voice was always calm. He had a quiet, authoritative voice, typical of a barrister or surgeon and perfect for his job. Even in an argument his voice remained quiet but in firm control, whereas as mine always lost it – along with my head.

'Yes, errr...no – I'm trying to find a skirt,' I continued, as I rattled through the hangers with the phone balanced against my shoulder. 'Ha – I've found it but I haven't got time to talk... I'm meeting Maddy in a minute...you know that I am.'

'Okay, I'll go then, see you later and...enjoy your breakfast,' Richard had now gone from calm chirpy to calm dejected.

'Will do. Thanks, see you later.'

'Love you.'

'Yeah, love you too. Bye,' I said, feeling bad that I'd cut him short. Richard always phoned me, he probably phoned me three or four times a day, always had done. But he was calling now because he was trying to gauge me. A few nights before, he started discussing things that filled me with shear dread. I recalled the tail end of a conversation I'd caught in Maddy's kitchen recently. It had been between Richard and Lorna's husband Bruce, but I'd listened in after having a playroom door slammed in my face after the kids' game of dob had got way out of hand. But he'd said then: *'Lawyers are still running up ridiculous legal fees for the sixty thousand balance payment for that company we bought back in July, we all lost out, but they still want my blood, and the bank want the hundred grand overdraft paying off; there are still issues with relinquishing the lease on the showroom...they're all still on my back.'* I knew about the financial bits and pieces, it was the 'want my blood' and 'all still on my back' that had bothered me. Obviously everything was getting on top of him. But I couldn't tell him how I felt about his latest suggestion. I certainly didn't want to start another argument over why he'd bought that second company – what was done, was done.

I still couldn't get my head around the fact that someone in Richard's position; working in financial services, had no knowledge of the financial storm that was coming. He had access to insider financial journals that the rest of us don't get to see. So I knew I was being a bit quiet about it all, and I knew that it was bothering him. But I felt that explaining how I felt was only going to make things worse.

I did one final check on my reflection, with the skirt on I'd gone from fifty, to borderline schoolgirl, but I didn't think the skirt was too short, not with my knee-high boots. Anyway, I was going to be late, so it had to do. I fluffed up my hair to get some bounce in my bob, then left.

I parked my car in the lay-by that was supposedly for drop-offs only and took my chance on a ticket to save time. St. Byrke-Crale was a tiny picture-postcard tourist trap and most of the residents went back generations. I walked past the quaint gift shops, chocolate shops and boutiques before getting to *Gossips* that stood right in the heart of our town. The smell of coffee, cakes and fresh pastries hit me the second I opened the tiny door.

I ordered myself some tea, sat at one of the pine tables dressed in white linen. *Gossips* was slightly old-fashioned, but charming. I slid the wild flowers and china salt 'n' pepper pots out of the way and got myself comfortable with an old edition of *Heat* magazine; the choice of available magazines had always puzzled me on the basis that most of its customers, apart from us two, were elderly or recently retired – which is probably why it was so relaxing. It was free from career-bragging social climbers who were only interested in what people can do for them and every conversation requiring an ego filter.

I sat and waited for Maddy to arrive, desperately trying to prevent my skirt from riding up my thighs and disappearing altogether. When she eventually turned up she said that her morning had been chaotic and as she talked to me her mobile was still firmly clamped to her ear.

Maddy was permanently stressed these days because of her own legal mess. She and Steve were subjected to a dawn raid about a year or so after I met her. But one morning I received a phone call from a clearly distraught Maddy. I thought she was going to say something had happened to Henry, her son. In between sobs, I managed to decipher that she and Steve had both been arrested. She had been released on bail and Steve, twenty-four hours later, was still being questioned.

The day it happened she'd opened her door to be greeted by uniformed police officers with a warrant. I didn't really understand all the charges, but the police document was about a centimetre thick and listed a load of companies I'd never heard of. It also made references to the Proceeds of Crime Act, fraud, money laundering and frozen assets. Steve had got himself involved with a gang who had all been simultaneously arrested. Maddy and Steve in a state of paranoia even had their house swept to see if any bugs were present.

Even months after the arrest, we still didn't dare say much in their kitchen because she was convinced that the cooker extractor fan was bugged. But there was still no clear date for a trial. It felt like Maddy's charges would eventually be dropped and that her arrest just happened so that Steve could not move his assets around.

'What's up with you?' Maddy said, finally letting go of her mobile. Her narrow, heart-shaped face looked more strained than usual and I didn't really want to burden her with my crap.

'Nothing,' the false spring in my voice pinged in my ears and her eyebrows raised – evidence that she heard it ping too.

'Aargh. Okay! Richard says he's thinking about retiring,' I could feel my eyes rapidly welling up. I closed the magazine, placing it back on the side as a means of distracting myself and hiding my expression.

'I know, he's told me.'

'Told you?'

'Yeah, because he says you won't talk about it.'

'I can't,' and I headed straight for the sugar packets in the centre of the table, twiddling them through my fingers to avoid meeting her eyes.

'Why can't you?'

'I just can't.'

'Of course you can.'

'I can't.' This time I stared at her defiantly but the terrier had its rat, and it was slowly but surely going to torture it, whether it liked it or not! That was the problem, that despite only knowing each other for four years, we had become very close as friends after William and her son Henry became best friends. They were both at the same private school. But Maddy and I pretty much hit it off when we found out that we had both been driving round in our twenties in Mercedes SLK sports cars. But Maddy knew better than anyone else how to work me.

'All right, I had a crush on James; our Administrator.'

'Yeah, I know you did.'

'What do you mean, you know I did, I never told you?'

'I could tell, the way you just dropped his name into every conversation.'

'God…this gets worse.' I felt my face flush.

'Anyway, what's that got to do with Richard retiring?'

'Everything.'

'Everything? '

'All right…if Richard retires, although I'm very much over the James thing and…I didn't realise he was only twenty-one!' I'd now gone from stubborn silence to rambling. 'Anyway...I don't know if he fancied me, it wasn't like he could have ever got involved with me, as it would be unprofessional and compromising. He was the oldest-looking 21-year-old I'd come across anyway. He had a girlfriend and was really bright and focused on his exams and career. Most 21-year-olds are out getting hammered all week aren't they?'

'Nicole – I don't really see you running off with a 21-year-old, it was just one of those things and you didn't do anything did you? Please tell me you didn't do anything?'

'Lord no, he's only a few years older than Richard's grandson and to be honest I started to think of him as more of a precious gift that made closing the place down easier. But I haven't really spoken to Richard much since *Ilex* closed, actually I think our only conversations the last year or so have been about *Ilex Drapes*, William and Elyse. I can't talk to him about having a crush on James and I'm scared...' I could feel my eyes fill again, so I went for the paper napkin as my emotional pendulum forcefully swung back to Richard.

'Of what?'

'That if Richard retires he'll say that he can take over the main childcare role and then I can go back to work full time.'

'Which is what you want? Don't you?'

'Yes...but no. I want to be at work but I want to be the one who is there during school holidays too. But it would mean that Richard would no longer be the Alpha male.'

'What the fuck do you mean – Alpha male?'

'Well...I'm scared that if he is at home, and I'm at work, that I'll be attracted to someone else but in an environment where my emotions won't be protected by circumstances...as with James. Okay – I am worried that I will fall into having an affair – that's it, I have said it now.'

On the word 'affair' the tears went into freefall down my cheeks. The paper napkin was rapidly disintegrating between my fingers as I thought about the fear of managing to land myself into any more explosive situations.

'But you can't be with someone of sixty and expect them to not want to slow down?'

'I know that. But retiring! That's a word that takes away the hope. Does that make sense? Being together and building things together gives hope. But retiring – it's like saying this is our life, and that's it, we climb no higher – there's no more fight left and life is about the fight.'

Despite my heightened emotion and tears, I was acutely aware that I was in a tiny confined space surrounded by elderly retired people, who would probably liked to have taken every last bit of strength in their failing limbs and give me a damn good punch.

'I need a cigarette, let's get some fresh air,' Maddy said, whilst texting.

'Okay, I just need to be a bit careful getting out of this chair, my skirt keeps disappearing.'

'What? Let's see?' and her head dropped under the table.

'Wow...that is short – hope you're wearing pants?'

'Of course, I'm wearing pants!'

I was grateful for fresh air. It would have been better without the cigarette smoke. But I was mostly grateful for being out of earshot of the fellow diners. I gathered myself a little, as I stood looking down at the back-door steps in the tiny stone courtyard. I rocked the sole of my feet against the edge of the step; feeling the pressure against it seemed to help somehow. Maddy inhaled her cigarette and exhaled as she adjusted her *Gucci* shoulder bag that matched her *Gucci* ballet pumps. 'You're right, you can't tell Richard – but I know what you mean about hope and building things together.'

'See, I told you.'

'But you need to talk to him. There must be a tactful why of explaining how you feel? You don't have to mention James. So what are you going to do?'

'What can I do?' I didn't mean to be churlish with her – this wasn't her fault.

'I don't know? Do you fancy a browse round the shops instead of breakfast?'

'I'll pay for the tea,' Maddy offered as usual.

'No...I'll pay,' we both hurled notes over the counter.

A few seconds out of the door and Maddy bumped into someone she knew but hadn't seen for ages. This always happened because she'd lived most of her life here. I was still a stranger to the place and had so far made no attempt to get to know people. I said a polite 'hello' and then stood idly kicking my feet against the pavement, waiting for them to finish their small talk. Then a driver in a passing car beeped his horn at me a couple of times.

'That skirt is way too short,' said Maddy as she crossed over to me.

'I know.'

'I just want to go home.'

'You promise to talk to him.'

'I promise,' I said. Fortunately for me, she'd forgotten to give me a timescale.

My first ever *Facebook* photo album felt like an achievement worthy of a diploma or at the very least a mention on my CV that I no longer wanted to think about. But I'd spent ages ferreting through old pictures that had been taken in the last decade or so – it had been far more entertaining than my study books. A few days after creating the album, I sat at the laptop flicking through it but stopped when I got to a picture I'd uploaded of Richard. His body looked good on it – strong and powerful. He had always worked hard to stay in shape. The fact he was wearing *Speedos* on the photo, had left it wide open for abuse from Maddy, Steve and a few other friends who had since left a string of comments, ripping it apart. I looked into Richard's pale blue eyes on the picture. The fact I'd still not spoken about my fear to him was still sitting heavily on my conscience. A month had now passed since I'd promised Maddy I would raise the subject with him.

I clicked onto some of my other pictures, as a means of blotting it from my mind. There were loads of William and Elyse, a picture of me jumping over a fence on my pony and a graduation picture with my friend Sophie from University, which reminded me of her recent email where she'd managed to drop in the lines: "…you're a Jack of all trades" her response to my accountancy exams, and "…we need to meet up before we're both grey." She would have been innocently clueless that her words were enough to make me want to pull my hair out when I read them. My other graduation photo was of me clutching a six-month-old William.

Making the most of my limited time, I casually browsed through the friends of an old colleague. I was looking to see if I could spot any more familiar faces or names; people were starting to feel like collectable items on the site.

And then I spotted him.

I must have searched around five-hundred Anthony Hope's on *Facebook* before and failed to find him…until now. To me, there was only one Anthony Hope in the world, and this was the one. I looked at his tiny profile picture. He was pictured on a sailing boat – part of it was slightly out of focus in the background. Even with his *New York Yankees* baseball cap on I could see it was him; there was no doubt whose cocky smile I was looking at. I quickly sent a friend request through, and then decided that I'd better send an email because I wasn't sure whether he knew me by anything other than my nickname – Little N. I sat looking at my screen, and suddenly I'd become electronically tongue-tied as I struggled to think of something appropriate to say. I waved my fingers over the keyboard like I was trying to dry my nails. Somehow it helped me think what to write.

To: Anthony Hope

Always wondered where you went to. Hope you are well... Love Nicole (But you probably remember me as Little N)

And...a few hours later...

Nicole is now friends with Anthony Hope.

CHAPTER FOUR

The phone was ringing and I ignored it. It had been ringing all day – four or five rings then it would stop. But this time Anthony Hope and his profile picture sat conveniently in the centre of my laptop screen, so there was absolutely no chance that I was going to pick up any call. Piles of clothes waiting to be dropped into suitcases also sat inconveniently around me. I could have waited until we got back from holiday to look at his page, but that would have been like going away and leaving a mystery parcel sat in the hallway. The phone stopped. A single click on his name and I was able to go away without giving him a second thought; my curiosity satisfied. So I did it and cursed *Facebook* for taking so long to load everything, and I was in. Shit! His page felt strangely like I was snooping around someone's house, even though they'd given me the key to get in.

The first thing I honed in on was his Relationship Status: Single! I didn't even want to question why this was the first thing I noticed. But then I'd expected him to at least be engaged by now. Politics said Democrat – this was my first reminder that he wasn't English. Employment said 'The RocX' – that sounded like a band name, which meant he was probably still making a living from singing. I planned to check out the band's website using *Google* later.

I was desperate to read his Wall so that I could piece little bits of his life together from his Status Updates. I told myself I would browse for ten minutes and then get on with the packing.

There was rather a lot of activity; he'd been quite busy with his Updates. I'd got hours of reading material ahead of me, but a few jumped out:

Anthony has quit smoking...again – that was from 2007.

I found another posting from early 2008 saying pretty much the same thing and I thought of Maddy...for some reason.

Anthony is hating the navigation exams – I only want to sail a goddamn boat around for a bit and not circumnavigate the world! That one explained his profile picture.

Anthony is back in New York with his folks for Thanksgiving – another reminder that he wasn't a Brit. Where was he living when he wasn't in New York? I wondered.

Anthony is thinking about sleeping in the parking lot as there's more room in the truck – these digs are absolute shite – and that post definitely sounded like he was still in a band.

Anthony is jamming – made me think about his attachment to his guitar.

Then I spotted: *Anthony's got the zipper stuck on his pants dude.* For a few seconds I completely got the wrong end of the stick – language barrier – I shook the first image from my mind. Obviously he meant the zip on his trousers.

Time wasn't on my side: I had gone way over my ten minutes and I really needed to be getting on with the packing, so I left his Wall and moved on to his photos. There were loads where people had Tagged him in and they showed him singing at various venues. There were also many of him looking hammered in bars and clubs.

The thing I really noticed was his hair; it was still deliciously dark but he'd chopped it off at some point. It was now angled into his neck but longer on top around the fringe – it suited him better. On one hand he looked older, but on the other hand his new hairstyle softened him. I suppose it was a bit like looking at a dog after its coat had been trimmed off – it showed the same cute effect.

I could feel myself frowning in concentration and lapping up the information in front of me.

The phone started again – I ignored it.

I moved onto the albums he'd created – I knew these would be more personal and give more insight. There was an album on a "fishing vacation" as he called it, in Madagascar. There was one of him skiing, but obviously he'd typed the wrong place on it because it said New York. Since when could you ski in a city full of skyscrapers? There was another of him sitting nonchalantly under a tree with a white, colonial-type house in the background – that said New York as well, but the typo error wasn't what interested me – it was the photo. I found myself lingering on it – he looked so bloody sexy in it - in an understated way. He was wearing jeans and a blue v-neck sweater. He was leaning against a tree with his guitar resting on his lap. Next to him was a can of beer and what looked like a white note pad. I thought back to the times he used to scribble words down. Maybe they were the song lyrics he was singing nowadays? His long legs were stretched out it front of him – one resting on the other. The camera had caught him with a half-smile, as though someone had asked him to look up, but he'd failed to raise anything but his eyes. His fringe had fallen forward, catching the corner of his right eye. I wanted to brush the stray hair out of his way and kiss where it had been, working my way down to his mouth.

I sighed. The phone started again, this time it was more persistent.

I looked at my watch, sighed again, and clicked onto another photo – in this one he looked like he was in a rickety rowing boat moored at the end of a jetty. He was holding a fishing rod and only wearing shorts – I'd never seen his naked chest before. I could see a few dark hairs scattered across his torso. He had a flat stomach but no real signs of muscle. I was starting to wonder whether adding him was actually good for my health. I scrolled to the bottom of the picture. This said New York too – but I could see it wasn't a lake in Central Park. No skyscrapers anywhere. I concluded that he must have been pissed when he wrote the captions on his pictures.

The next picture was a family one. It said: Dad, and Big Sis Alice, at the bottom. His sister took after his dad, except his sister was blonde and Anthony's dad was dark like him. But his dad looked thicker set than Anthony. Presumably his mum must have taken the picture. I recalled someone once telling me that Anthony's dad was a conveyancing lawyer but Anthony rejected the same career path – to his dad's despair. I didn't know how much truth there was to the rumour.

I came out of the album and opened up another he'd called "work 'n' stuff". There was a promotional shot of him with his band mates – they all looked similar ages, and the photo was pretty much like every other band shot out there with the guys all striking different poses. The band logo *The RocX* was in large letters in front of them. The X extended downwards – like a firework exploding across the picture – the graphic designers obviously had a field day with it. Most of the other stuff looked pretty much like the pictures he'd been tagged in so I closed it down – I could always go through those another day.

Over five hundred friends! He'd got five times the number of friends I had. I couldn't help but wonder how many had been ex-girlfriends. That was one of the things that did strike me about his page – there was no evidence of any specific girlfriend. Loads of females – but no one female dominated any part of his *Facebook*. But I never did grasp what his type was when he was at *Opus*. The other thing that struck me: no Big Apple pictures – I was expecting to see inside a city apartment, roof-top living, yellow taxis and Broadway.

I picked up the phone and dialled 1471; the caller has withheld their number message played. Anyone who knew us well would have either mine or Richard's mobile.

I logged out of *Facebook* and went to *Google* his band. The first hit that came up had a '.co.uk' web address but...surely that would mean he was living in the UK? I clicked on the site and went straight into the Contact page. I was right. He was in London and not on the other side of the Atlantic like I thought. I closed my laptop. It didn't matter that he was still here...his addition to my *Facebook* was harmless.

I called Richard to see if he had been trying to get hold of me.

He said no, but the calls were probably connected to the banks – most likely calling from India.

The plane landed at Larnaca airport and we stepped out into a heat wave. The extreme heat at the early hour was nothing to the extreme heat we went on to experience during the day.

Two days into the holiday and I was trying to get more comfortable on a sun-lounger as my towel had started forming criss-cross patterns on my skin adding to the appeal of the white sun-cream smears. The overall effect meant that my black all-in-one, slashed to the waist swimsuit was a waste of time.

I lay down, but then jumped back up again to lower the parasol some more. Richard had definitely found a good spot at the sloping end of the pool, so it was safer for Elyse and it was slightly more shaded. Half the guests were like us, parents with young children, the other half were young clubbers, so they didn't get up until lunch at the earliest. It also looked like a lot of people had gone home and this was a bit of a change over day anyway. If the previous night's evening entertainment was anything to go by, Alcatraz was going to look appealing. We couldn't go for romantic meals, and we couldn't go clubbing in one of the Meds biggest clubbing resorts – Richard's too old anyway, even I'm on the borderline.

We were trapped for two weeks with no air-conditioning, as the air-con in the room appeared to be for aesthetic purposes only. I was seriously starting to think that we needed to re-consider the whole holiday thing. Try different things.

Richard's wife was on the sun bed next to me. She'd chosen to holiday with us and the rest of Richard's family this year. She still has the formal status of wife because she is still his wife. They never divorced. Richard being prepared to divorce her was good enough for me and possession of the ring meant more to her, than it did to me – I prefer the cage door open. When Richard initially walked out on her, back then, relations were very hostile, but time has healed and over the years I have grown to really like and respect her.

She was a hardened sun worshipper though, and never showed any visible signs of sweating in the intense heat, and as a consequence her hair didn't fall flat like mine, or her make-up slide off. She had all of her sun creams neatly organised in a cute little zip bag and she kept her pocket fan with her at all times.

I watched her get herself comfortable – she switched on her *iPod* (her grandkids had downloaded songs on it for her) and relaxed like a pro. She had already raised her kids a long time ago, so she had every smug right to sit in peace looking glamorous and relaxed. I on the other hand, in my ghostly, smeared state was fidgety, spending my time hopping in and out of the pool like a yo-yo with Elyse.

'Do you want a drink?' Richard asked.

'No I'm fine,' I said, as his wife confirmed the same from the sun bed next to mine.

'So you don't mind me going and having another pint then? They're not very strong. In fact, I think they're watered down.'

'No, I don't mind,' that was my attempt to help ease his guilty conscience. It worked as he happily wandered back over to the bar.

'Blast. That's my phone, where is it?' I chaotically tipped everything out of the beach bag to find it before it stopped. 'Oh…it's Maddy,' I said, as I flipped down my phone and then gave Maddy a quick rundown on the place before asking how things were her end.

'We're fine. I left you a few messages on *Facebook*,' she said.

'Have you? It looks like there's Internet access here, so I'll have a look at some point.' Opening messages was like opening presents, pleasurable. I was now itching to get on the Internet to see what she'd put. Something had amused her, I could tell, there was a smile in her voice.

'Oh…and I added that Anthony Hope. He's such a *Facebook* whore, doesn't even know me and he added me. I saw *you'd* added him,' there was devilment in her voice, a note of one-upmanship, her watchful eye letting me know that his addition to my *Facebook* hadn't passed by her. Bugger…she had remembered his name. My instincts had been right – I should never have mentioned him to her and Lorna. There was no way that I was going to give her the pleasure of asking why she'd done it.

'Anyway,' I continued, in the best *casual not disturbed by it* voice that I could muster, 'he's in a band called T*he RocX* which is based in London. He's not in New York like I thought. Have you seen all the female friends he's got, there's hundreds, obviously still a player; life's still one big party for him,' I said, while not condemning him for this. It's a matter of fact that men get a much better deal. They can take as many as twenty years longer before deciding to settle down as they don't have to worry about the biological clock, and they become distinguished – not old. But his lifestyle was helpful as a means of flippantly dismissing him to Maddy as an insignificant addition to my *Facebook*.

'No, I haven't had a look, I just added him.'

'Have a look,' I said, with contrived disinterest.

'Will do, well just a quick call, to check you are all okay. Enjoy your holiday and speak soon…got to go sorry,' and she'd gone before I got in a bye. I wondered if Richard's wife had listened to the conversation and if she had heard enough to mention anything to Richard.

The hours slowly drifted by, punctuated by lunch, then quiz time – I would have happily taken a gun to my own head each time we had to sit through a banal quiz, and then we went back to the room, showered and change only to then get wet through again with sweat in the restaurant. Then the whole process was then repeated the next day and the next.

Richard and I had a rule that one of us stayed sober for

William and Elyse, and this night was my turn to have a drink…or two. I was egged on for the Karaoke and sung at best an interesting version of *Living La Vida Loca*. I love singing, but usually only in the confines of my home, car or Maddy's playroom on the *PlayStation*. A few cocktails down and *what the hell* I thought, I was never to see these people again, and I was up and away. I could feel the alcohol kicking in fast and my usual natural grace that Richard found so attractive was probably somewhat lacking. I handed over the microphone and tip-toed off to the Internet with my cocktail and straw now firmly in my grip.

Getting your bearings at a strange PC while your head is spinning is not the easiest task in the world. But, somehow, through sheer determination, I managed to type in the hotel reference number that Reception had given to me, and I navigated myself straight to *Facebook*. A tiny envelope icon at the top of my screen was showing I had one message. Expecting it to be from Maddy, I went straight for my emails.

From: Anthony Hope

Of course I remember Little N. Hope you're well. XX

God…I could still hear his voice and I quickly closed down my email and read Maddy's messages, which I found on my Wall. Clearly William's two teachers having to share a box of chocolates as their end of term gift had smugly entertained her. I will never know how Richard managed to cock that one up. My instructions were clear enough: buy two boxes of chocolates. I took another long sip of my drink; then I checked my *Facebook* notifications…

I'd been tagged in a photo. Maddy had tagged me necking wine, and here I was feeling drunk again.

I then fumbled my way around the site until I found the photo that Sophie Morreti had commented on. It was the graduation one with us throwing our caps in the air. I read her long message but that took a while because the effect of the alcohol was making it difficult for my eyes to read in a straight line.

I'll never forget our uni days – hot chocolate and faces stuffed with cheesecake in our spare time. Now twelve years on and you're still only 5ft 2! he he. Need to meet up squirt before we're both too wrinkled and past it! X

I added a comment below ...

No intention of growing old, got Botox for that. I think I've just typed this on the wrong bit and now everyone will see it on the Newsfeed, but I am too pissed to care. X

And then I somehow found myself back in my emails again.

Hi Anthony

Nice to hear from you. Currently in Cyprus but slightly not sober at the moment. I hope you appreciate tje effprt to tyope. X free dprnk here.

'Here you are, what are you doing?' It was Richard. He had come to find me. 'Elyse's looking for you. Are you going to get off that and join the rest of us? You're being anti-social.' Even slightly drunk I could detect annoyance. Why did he hate me being on the computer lately?

'What are you looking at anyway? Bet it's that *Facebook*. It is, isn't it? Can't you take a holiday from it?'

'I'm not looking at anything. I'm coming. Maddy told me she'd left a message. I just need to log out,' I wasn't drunk enough to slur my words, or at least I thought it was clearly said. I took another long, noisy sip of my drink through the straw, getting the frothy bits from the bottom. I then logged out and was back watching the entertainment, until Elyse wet her pants, and then I escaped back to the room, passing all of the teenagers and twenty-somethings in miniscule dresses on their way to the clubs.

I failed to get anywhere near a PC for the rest of the trip.

CHAPTER FIVE

Once we were safely back home, the holiday felt like it had been a million years ago, and the Botox comment had now been removed from my *Facebook*. It didn't matter that the Botox had been justified. *Ilex Drapes* had stressed me out, and I kept reading about stress being a big ageing factor. The crush on a 21-year-old could also have had something to do with it, but I didn't want to consider that possibility and I didn't really want everyone knowing that much about my private life. But it was too late for that stupid email to Anthony Hope – it would be like trying to retrieve a ring after lobbing it off the edge of a cliff – it had gone. At least he'd the decency to ignore it, which was a good thing because I was too embarrassed to apologise. I was far happier to pretend it didn't exist. It wasn't like I was going to have to speak to him ever again anyway. I hadn't added him to communicate with; my life was complicated enough: we still had the financial shit hanging over us and school holidays to contend with. This is what I tried to tell myself on the ninth of August, my 38th birthday and the day after the 2008 Olympics had kicked off.

I sat at the study desk. The study was the only room that felt closed off; it was the smallest, cosiest room in the house and the only room downstairs we'd carpeted, everywhere else was more or less open plan with either wooden flooring or stone tiles, which worked well with the solid Spanish oak doors and kitchen units and worked even better with kids and a dog.

In front of me was the old PC and it was infuriatingly slow. The screen went to black every so often then froze before loading up the next page, which meant that sometimes the text ended up jumbled up on the search bar when typed in too quickly. As long as it continued ticking along, I didn't bother replacing it or getting it repaired – it simply required a lot of patience.

While it was loading I sat thinking about some of the things said earlier around the table over dinner. Maddy, Steve and

Henry had joined us for my birthday – to stay at home had been my choice, but it had got a little uncomfortable after Mum and Dad also popped in with my presents. They were still miffed over the three grand my dad lost for some engineering work he'd done for one of Steve's companies that had been seized in the dawn raid. So all of them together in the same room was always a little awkward until they surmounted the hurdle until the next time they met. Mum and Dad had taken to calling them Bonnie and Clyde – not to their face of course. But that wasn't what had bothered me about the evening. It was the word 'bankruptcy' flying round the table like it was as insignificant as the naan bread being passed over our heads. Steve had told Richard that he thought bankruptcy was the route he should go. Steve was forced into it after the dawn raid – he didn't really have a choice. But Richard didn't say things like: I don't think it is necessary. Instead he said: 'I'm mulling over my options with lawyers right now.' I was starting to feel deceived by Richard. I'd always felt cheated that he was actually a couple of inches shorter than the 5ft 11 he had at first claimed. It still bugs me because he has as a consequence cheated my children of those same few inches. But this time I felt cheated over our financial security and I didn't know how to deal with the emotions that came with that.

While the PC was still on a go slow I looked down at the curry stain on my white brorderie anglais shirtdress. It was a few years old but I loved it; it still fitted perfectly. It was a dress I could only wear when I had a tan, which usually meant the occasional spray tan, but the Cyprus tan was still lingering. The egg timer on the PC was still static and I thought about the withheld-number phone calls which Richard still insisted on being the banks. On the rare occasions I did bother with the phone, I discovered he'd been right: it was usually someone from the bank. Always a foreign accent, always asking for Richard. I'd reached the stage where I no longer bothered to pick up the phone until I'd done the 1471. But then caller-withheld-number messages meant I had no idea who it was. How serious was our financial predicament?

Facebook was at last open and I read through some birthday wishes that had been left. Before I logged out I took a quick look at Anthony Hope's Page. He hadn't sent a birthday message – but then with 500 or so friends on there I was sure he wouldn't bother with those that he barely knew. I clicked on a video clip he'd posted which was filmed at a gig in Newcastle. The speakers didn't work on the study PC so I couldn't hear what song he was singing. It didn't really matter to me – it was his speaking voice I loved most. The camera went close-up and he played to it with his eyes. I loved his dark eyes; they had an upward slant and always looked like they were fighting for space with his cheek bones. I noticed his slightly chipped front tooth – for some reason this flaw made his face more interesting.

I logged off and picked up the heart-shaped memory stick that Maddy had given as my birthday present. I slid it from its small velvet pouch and held it for a moment. It felt like a smooth, cold pebble in my palm. I turned it towards the light, watching it bounce off the crystal's sharp edges. Then I pulled it apart – you had to break the heart in two before you could get to the memory. I put the two halves back together, dropped in back in the pouch and put it safely in the desk drawer.

A few days of William and Elyse back at school and life on the surface appeared to be calm and orderly again. The lack of noise gave a false sense of security. I walked into the study to pull one of the textbooks off the shelf and noticed that the study PC was still open on *Facebook*. I hit refresh to see if the connection was still live, as usual the screen went to black for a moment, but then, right before my eyes, at the top of my Newsfeed was Anthony Hope, along with gossip on the big bang experiment that had taken place that morning.

I wondered if the smashing together of tiny particles in a 27-

kilometre tube on the French Swiss border would create another one of him, in their miniature universe. Anthony had loaded some pictures of India. His Status said *Anthony loves Nepal*. I looked through the album – it appeared to be one of those walking adventure type holidays where you *slum it* in tents and guesthouses. I looked at a couple of pictures of him white-water rafting, and riding on the back of an elephant.

Richard and I should go there, I thought.

I decided to send Anthony an Instant Message.

Was this trip organised or did you plan it yourself?

It was a perfectly reasonable thing to ask. But I waited and there was no reply. He may have missed my message – there might have been no room for it to pop up along the bottom of his screen. It was either that or he didn't consider me worthy to even speak to because of that bloody email, I concluded. Then I thought that I could always look up Nepal holidays on the Internet. Because Richard was in the house I decided to get him to have a look at the pictures while they were still on my mind.

'Richard, come here a sec,' I yelled up to the third floor. He was sorting through some paperwork before going into his office.

'Why?' he shouted down.

'Come and look at these pictures.'

'What…now?' he shouted back down again, sounding mildly irritated by the interruption.

'Yes, now, while they're on my screen.'

Eventually he made his way back downstairs; luckily his reading glasses were already on.

'Look at these India photos,' I said cheerfully. For some reason I found myself being selective over the ones I lingered on, as in no close-ups of faces.

'Yeah…it looks like good fun.'

'It's Nepal…we could do something more interesting with our holidays.'

'Yeah...where you got those from?'

'They're on my *Facebook*.'

'Who are these people?'

'They're in Anthony Hope's photos,' I said, after thinking that there was nothing I should hide about him being on my *Facebook*.

His eyebrows raised, this was one of those situations where Richard would have benefited from a dose of Botox too.

'Anthony Hope as in *Opus*, that Anthony? Why is he on your *Facebook*?' he asked.

I managed a smile whilst telling him that it was me who added him as a friend.

'You added him? Well...who else have you added, have you got any ex-boyfriends on there? Is Loopy Luke on there?'

Why was he being so arsy?

'One ex-boyfriend is on there, but no Loopy Luke,' I said, thinking that Richard was being a complete idiot.

'Who else then?' he pushed.

'Nik,' I told him.

'As in Nik?

'Yes...as in Nik,' I reconfirmed.

'Fine...yes...Nepal looks fun, but I not sure it would be suitable for William and Elyse. Do you speak to Anthony Hope a lot then?'

'No, we have not spoken since we last saw each other – all that time ago,' I said, now glad he'd ignored me, so I didn't have to lie.

'So why is he on there then?'

'Because I added him as a friend as I've just told you.'

Richard looked at me strangely but seemed like he hadn't got time to go round in circles any longer; he had more important things on his mind so I let him get back on with his work, me with my studies.

I could hear Blue trying to let himself out of the kitchen French doors. Sighing, I put down my pencil and went to get the key to open the door and let him out. He was whimpering so no doubt he had spotted the neighbour's cat daring to venture into his territory. While I was waiting for him to return, I put all the keys into the plastic pot rather than leaving them lying around untidily next to the microwave. The phone rang and I waited to see if Richard would pick it up upstairs where I assumed he was working. It rang for a long time, so after it did stop I went to the study and did the usual 1471. It had been Maddy calling so I decided to call her back once Blue was back in. I returned to the kitchen and stopped dead. My hands and fingers tingled from the sudden shock. All the keys were once again scattered across the worktop as though they hadn't been put in the pot at all. I looked out of the kitchen window. There didn't appear to be anyone around.

I shouted Richard and he quietly emerged from the downstairs toilet with a newspaper.

'Have you moved these keys?' I asked aggressively.

'No. Why would I move the keys?' he said casually, but he was looking at me like I was crazy.

'I put them in the pot a few minutes ago, went to get the phone and when I came back in to the kitchen they were spread all over the work surface again.'

'Well you obviously didn't put them in the pot did you? You're always thinking you've done something when you haven't. Look at that incident with the window the other week. You're too disorganised, you're left hand never knows what the right hand is doing. You spend too much time with your head in the clouds.'

Maybe he was right and I had merely thought about moving the keys, but hadn't actually done it. I wasn't convinced though. The recalled sensation of the keys having been in my hands was too real. And just like Richard I also thought about the day that the lounge window had closed on its own. I'd never bothered to mention to him the fact that the cushions were still plumped up.

Were the two things connected? I checked the keys, but I couldn't see that there were any missing and neither could Richard. Blue let himself in and I locked the door, not bothering to put the keys in the pot again.

I put my foot down on the accelerator enjoying the long, free stretch of road whilst listening to the radio. It was still stuck on some intellectual station that Richard liked, and I'd not bothered to switch.

The news readers words filtered through my thoughts, "…the US Federal Reserve has stepped in with an $85 billion rescue package to save insurance giant AIG."

Relief washed over me but I still couldn't get my head around the global financial chaos that was emerging. The previous day Richard had been on a round-the-clock vigil, waiting to hear if the US would bail them out. He was clearly edgy and I didn't dare ask what it meant in terms of us and money. I hadn't even heard of AIG until that point. But Richard had said that they'd got a lot of customers' placed on risk with them which would have been a nightmare to get cover elsewhere because premiums would soar and they could lose clients as a consequence. But it looked like AIG had been insuring a lot of the banks toxic assets. I couldn't understand why the government wouldn't bail them out – they always bailed out the big companies. But Richard had pointed out that the American's let *Lehmans* go to the wall only last week. The US banks seemed to be falling like a stack of cards. I still couldn't get my head around a bank being bankrupt. It's as though the whole world was one big board game full of cheats who were slowly holding their hands up and saying "…sorry but we are in fact skint".

But applying logic, the financial services side of Richard's business was dwindling. People were cashing in, not investing, so that was few hundred thousand down this year, and the latest banks collapses were only going to make that worse. Financial services had until recently been one of the world's biggest growth sectors and Richard, even as one of the industry's highest-qualified advisors said even he didn't know where to tell people to put their money, and would rather not advise them at all. But if the insurance side was to become affected too – I knew it wouldn't be good. That would be hitting the largest chunk of our household income – it was like everything was hitting us at once.

I'd sensed that there was more to come when I had closed the doors on *Ilex*, but that didn't mean it made any more sense. For the last part of the journey I changed the radio to a pop station – *Cold Play's* Viva la Vida was playing. I turned the volume up.

I slowed down and pulled into the drive. It was then that I spotted something that looked like a package on the doorstep. I got out of the car and went to check what it was before getting the food shopping out of the boot. I picked up the little plastic bag that looked like pale cress, turned it over, and on the front it said Alfalfa Sprouts. On my doorstep, as if by magic, was the Holy Grail of anti-aging. I knew this couldn't be from Richard because he would have put them in the house. This had to be Maddy's idea of a lovely gift. A quick call to her and I found out that she'd found them in the local *Co-op* of all places. I'd been searching far and wide, and they were available only five minutes down the road. I couldn't believe I'd never spotted them in there. I put them in the fridge, along with the rest of the food shopping, and logged onto *Facebook* to update my Status. Status Updates were now starting to feel like a compulsory task, rather like brushing your teeth twice a day – it simply had to be done.

12:34 Nicole is feeling a little more relaxed now that the US government has bailed out AIG

After typing it in, I hit the Share button, launching it into cyberspace, and while I was on I scrolled down the Newsfeed, then stopped when I spotted a Status Update from Anthony Hope:

Anthony is lovin' Ireland...and has found a very beautiful fish in the sea...not throwing this baby back ;)

He made it sound like he'd caught a girl. It wasn't fair – his life appeared so carefree. Unlike mine that felt like it was crumbling around me.

'What now?' I asked as Richard re-entered the house with William trailing behind him. 'William just get back in the car and wait there.'

'But I...'

'But nothing, get back in the car. Where's his red socks?' Richard now turned his attention to me.

'Red socks?' I asked puzzled.

'Yes red socks, he says he needs *red* socks today.'

'Why?' I was still confused.

'I don't fucking know, but he's just checked his bag and says his red socks aren't in there. Where are they?'

'How should I know? They could be anywhere,' I said trying to rack my brain. Why red socks today, last week it was white socks for PE? But regardless, red or white, I was sure I'd put both in there. Shit! They could be in the wash basket, ironing basket, or any of his drawers, or even on the landing in that pile of stuff that still needs putting away.

'Will you hurry up! William...I told you to get back in the car.'

'But I'm going to be late, Daddy,' William was now starting to fret.

'Mummy will have them in a minute, please get back into the car and get your seatbelt on ready. Have you got them yet, Nicole?' Richard was starting to get really wound up, and I was flying from one end of the house to the other in my unsexy, unflattering but incredibly warm fluffy floor length dressing gown that was now making me sweat like a jogging Sumo wrestler wrapped in polythene.

'I'm just checking all his drawers.'

'Why can't you just have a same place for everything, you are such a disorganised person. You'd be useless in the Forces. You'd never know where you left your fucking gun.'

I felt my blood starting to boil, if I was a saucepan my lid would have been on the brink of rising before falling over the edge with an almighty clatter, 'This is not my fault and, lucky for you, I wouldn't be able to find my fucking gun, wanker!' I felt the word graze the back of my throat as I spoke. 'They're here!'

I hurled the red socks at him. Richard picked them up and proceeded to slam and lock the door behind him, leaving it to shake in its frame. Every night I got everything ready and I still didn't get it right, there was always something I missed. The new computerised school-letter thing was starting to do my head in. I'd not bothered to log in again because it was like getting into Fort Knox, it really has got more security checks than a bank account. *Facebook* was far easier to get in to. Maybe I should have looked lately? Maybe they'd put something on there about the socks. But there was no way on earth I was admitting that to Richard.

Where's my iPod? It had been in my hand just before Richard came back for the socks. I retraced my steps and eventually found it next to the ironing basket in the utility room. I then made a smooth, cat-like transition, to the treadmill and I managed forty minutes on level fourteen without it feeling too strenuous. *I will have thighs of steel,* I thought as the rapid club-beat vibrated through my body. When the muscles have relaxed and the heartbeat in a rhythm, exercise was the closest I got to flying with my feet still on the ground. And then, without warning, the *iPod* made a funny squiggle noise in my ear and started to belt out *Abba's,* I Have A Dream. But the lyrics held me from switching it back to my usual music. Instead the words increased my motivation as I blissfully sang along. Singing at full belt, while on the treadmill is what Richard calls painful.

Dripping with sweat, I pulled the earphones out, drank a pint of cold water before jumping in the shower. It had struck me as strange because I would never have thought of exercising to *Abba* in a million years. I put it down to some technical glitch on the *iPod* and hoped it wasn't going to pack up because that would mean that I'd got to suss out setting up a new one. The song remained in my head all day. It's as though my brain was split in two halves, one side was busily singing away, while the other was functioning on the tasks at hand. I found the lyrics uplifting and optimistic.

Maybe that's what I needed – some optimism, the wine Richard brought home later that evening helped too. I allowed myself to log onto *Facebook* before I sorted out William and Elyse's uniform for following day. With a gulp of wine and the lyrics still swirling around my head I updated my Status...

Nicole thinks there is good in everything I see...I believe in angels, fairy tales and the future.

By Sunday bedtime my future felt like it was going to be very short-lived.

William and Elyse were asleep upstairs. Richard appeared to be asleep on the sofa. I contemplated getting my laptop and logging back into *Facebook*. But then I heard a bang, like the sound of exploding glass. It made me jump like I had been hit with a thousand volts and it woke Richard.

'What the hell was that?' he asked.

'I've no idea. But it sounded like it came from our bedroom,' I said still feeling jittery.

'It must be one of the kids messing around and broken something up there,' Richard said.

We both sprinted upstairs, taking two steps at a time. We checked William and Elyse but they were asleep in their beds, so we rapidly made our way down the landing to our bedroom. Bits of glass shimmered on the window bottom.

Richard pulled up the blind and we stood aghast at the window. It was smashed from the inside. The outside panel of double glazing was still intact.

'Richard, there is someone in this house.' My legs felt wobbly with nerves. I need to get William and Elyse out of their bedrooms.

'You know all the doors are locked downstairs. All the keys are up here for the night.'

'How do you explain this then?' I asked picking up a piece of the broken glass. 'It's smashed from the inside, not outside,' I said as though he couldn't see what I could. I ran my finger along the edge of the glass and cut it. 'I suppose you're going to tell me this is not happening. Tell me that I'm asleep again are you?' I sucked my finger. It hurt.

'No. Don't be ridiculous.'

'Richard, what the fuck have you gone and done? Have you pissed people off in business, is this what this is all about? Is someone out to get you, me, our kids? Is this what all the phone calls are about? I need to know Richard.'

'You are being paranoid; there is no one in the house.' He pulled down the blind again as though hiding it from me would make me feel better.

'You don't know that for certain, what if someone stole a key that day they had been tipped back out the kitchen pot,' I spat.

'No one took any key from the kitchen that was your stupid head – just like the closed window, just look at your disorganisation with the kid's uniforms – you do stupid things all the time.'

I knew I was annoying him, but he eventually relented and told me to wait in our room while he woke William and Elyse and brought them to me. I made him check the wardrobes before allowing him to venture out with one of my exercise weights. I hid with William and Elyse in the en-suite with the door locked. I'd taken a plaster from the box on the shelf and wrapped it round my finger. The cut was quite deep and dripping blood. Elyse was still half asleep and leaning against me. William repeatedly asked what was wrong. I tried to stop myself from visibly shaking to keep him calm while we huddled in a corner. The oak door was too thick for me to hear anything that was happening downstairs.

The bathroom door handled moved. Someone was trying to get in. What if Richard was dead? *I should have called 999 before locking us in here, I had stupidly cornered us.*

CHAPTER SIX

I thought about the computer printout I had found sitting on the kitchen island. I had surmised that it must have been printed by Richard's daughter or something because Richard didn't know how to use our printer. What I couldn't understand was why he hadn't bothered to show it to me, let alone mention it. It was about imploding double-glazed windows, a relatively rare but baffling phenomenon attributed to the inside panel being warm from central heating and the outside temperature suddenly dropping. I thought back to my reaction the other night. I still felt such a fool for screaming at him when he tried to get the en-suite door open. It did make me wonder whether my over-the-top reaction was a legacy from when we were actually burgled: the large kitchen knife left in the middle of the floor did still haunt me, even though the police had said that it was probably only there to be used to cut through TV wires to get them free.

But why hadn't Richard bothered to show me the article? He'd not forgotten about getting the glass replaced.

I'd now put the paper in the drawer with the intention of stubbornly waiting to see when he would get round to mentioning it. I thought about the cut on my finger and removed the plaster to see how it was healing. I ran my thumb over it. Apart from it looking a strange grey colour from the plaster I was surprised that there was barely a sign of anything there at all. I smugly attributed it to my healthy green-tea and nuts and alfalfa sprouts.

I switched my focus to something else that had been troubling me:

Anthony Hope is listed in a relationship

The words sat in the middle on my *Facebook* Newsfeed.

It appeared on the day that I was going to a lap-dancing club for the first time in my life. It was Maddy's somewhat strange birthday choice for later that evening. So it was a day I was unlikely to forget for lots of reasons.

I sat staring into my laptop in the garden room with a mug of green tea and a bag of nuts beside me. Elyse was busy playing in the lounge, *Nickelodeon* was belting out on the TV; William was outside kicking his ball at his goal post as usual, and Richard was somewhere inside, I don't know where, I didn't care at that moment because I was still hacked off with him for not mentioning the computer printout on imploding windows.

Anthony Hope is listed in a relationship, it was as though the words were in a different text to all those surrounding it, drawing my eyes with the power of a magnet. Some of his friends had commented on it, as they invariably did on his Wall. If he so much as posted a full stop, someone would pop up with a silly remark about it or tell him how wonderful it was; Anthony was far more sociable than me. One friend had asked what she was like and he wrote back, "very spirited" with a wink on the end. The conversation reminded me of my Status the other week: angels, fairy tales and the future. Was this new girlfriend his fairy tale; his future?

This new girlfriend couldn't be the red head in a recent photo, because he'd only just decided to change his Status. I knew it wasn't really any of my business who the girl was.

Even so, I couldn't help myself. I wondered how many times he'd changed his Relationship Status since he'd signed up to *Facebook*. I was annoyed with myself for even giving it headspace. If I didn't know better I would say what I was feeling was jealousy. But jealousy wasn't something I normally felt. I was living with a man married to someone else for God's sake! I was even proud of not being a jealous person.

Curiosity was killing me and I found myself entering his Wall and found three photos from his Ireland trip. Was this new girl the fish that he wasn't going to throw back?

The long dark hair, pale skin and blue eyes of the girl staring back at me made her look Irish, somehow. She could have been anything from eighteen to twenty-eight, definitely younger than me; her face still had a youthful roundness, but her features were more grown-up than mine, making it difficult to guess her age from a photo. She looked slim, but could be tall or small. She was definitely pretty – as I had expected – but in a sophisticated way, rather than cute or overtly sexual. She was not prettier than me, just completely different.

Anthony had tagged her in the photos. I clicked on her name to see if her *Facebook* page was open. But it wasn't. She had privacy settings on. Her Location said London, but most of her friends were on the Ireland network. She appeared to be Irish, but living in London.

I suppose he could have been with her for a while, and only now changed his Relationship Status because he'd become seriously involved – I pondered all of this as I sipped my green tea; my eyes fixed to the laptop screen.

'Mummy…I want my Pwincess jigsaw, can you do it with me? Pweeeeease.'

'Yeah, in a minute, Elyse, I'm busy at the moment, I'll be with you soon.'

'But Mummy…'

I continued to scroll down Anthony's Wall.

'Can't you get off that thing? Elyse wants you to do a jigsaw with her,' Richard had made a miraculous appearance.

'Yes, *I know*, and I will be with her in a minute.'

'That bloody *Facebook*, I bet you're on that thing again!'

Oh…God – he likes to draw… – I heard my own sigh.

Someone had asked him if he'd drawn anything recently and it's not the sort of question you would generally ask someone unless you knew they liked drawing. I loved to draw, but probably, like him, didn't get the time.

I still continued to work my way down his Wall.

Perhaps I should delete him for my own good.

I spread the pieces of Elyse's jigsaw over the coffee table for her. *If only Anthony Hope was as easy to piece together as a jigsaw for three-year-olds.*

I glanced at the utter mess surrounding me. Elyse seemed to be taking the lounge over, with her dolls, pushchairs and kitchen set scattered across the floor. Elyse's toys supplemented Blue's diet with a least one piece of edible plastic a day. I'd lost count of how many massacred dolls we'd come home to since having him. I made a mental note that I needed to tidy up at some stage. I didn't consider it fair that Richard's sister should be made to look at the mess as well as babysit. But instead I found myself back on *Facebook*. My attention had drifted away from tidying up. I only wanted to see if any more comments had been left about the new girlfriend. While on there the red notification icon popped up in the bottom right of my screen:

Claire is getting to know his / her friends better

A friend had done one of those quiz things. I wondered what she'd answered about me and accepted the App.

Did I do that wrong? I wondered, as I now found myself working through questions about my friends, taking pot luck on my *yes* or *no* answers. It came to one on Maddy's brother – has he ever been arrested? Was it a loaded question? Like I really was going to put in "yes" to that one.

Does Anthony Hope believe in ghosts? Oh shit…No, not that question. Not after the spirited comment left on his Wall. *Yes* or *No*? Hmmm…*yes*. Well…lots of people do. Shit! He was going to get one of the notification things now that I got from Claire. A notification connected to me wouldn't have been so bad had I not sent that stupid bloody email. But why could I take part in quizzes about my other friends and it not be a problem? Why did it have to be different with him?

Once again, the presence of this man on my *Facebook* was causing me to question my every action in relation to him. Had it not been for him, I know I wouldn't have bothered to leave a generic apology on my Status Update for everyone to see; I would have simply forgotten about the quiz. I could still feel myself cringing as I continued picking up toys and placing them into plastic tubs. Once I'd cleared the floor, I stacked the tubs up behind the oak door in the garden room and started laying out my clothes for later. I'd opted for my purple Greek-style dress because I knew from what Maddy had said earlier that she was going for a little black tasselled number.

We arrived at the lap-dancing club too early, so we decided to head into the city centre for a few drinks first. Rather than taking two cars we all crammed into Steve's people carrier and managed to lose Maddy's older brother in a multi-storey car park – deliberately; he was already hammered from drinking all afternoon. Maddy could sense that trouble was looming and considering she was still on bail, the last thing she needed was to be dragged into a brawl with him or anyone else he got tangled up with. They both had the same hot temper, so throwing alcohol at him was like hurling it at an already raging fire. We passed some time in a swanky wine bar, and eventually drove back to the club.

It wasn't quite the Moulin Rouge-type venue that Maddy and I had imagined. Where was all the magical lighting, glitz and glamour? Not to mention the lack of sparkly, diamond costumes. It was dark, tatty, and had a fusty smell of stale alcohol emanating from the carpet. It's a smell you only notice when a club is empty. Apart from the scary-looking male staff that were obviously recruited to protect the girls, a few bar staff, and a couple of ogling lads in the far corner, we are the only ones in the club. The girls were heavily made-up; their angular, slightly wider faces indicated that they were probably Eastern European. They took it in turns to perform at the pole. Their underwear looked cheap and was badly fitted. They were clearly low paid and worse, probably exploited.

We all sat in a row on one of the faux leather curved sofas overlooking one of the dancing areas, clutching our drinks, as though we were watching a theatre performance. Steve, as expected, looked embarrassed and was attempting to look elsewhere. Richard said he wasn't that impressed with the place but was mentally critiquing the girls' bodies – like he did to women on a beach; he somehow always managed to hone in on every flaw. Steve's friend didn't look that interested and was deep in conversation with his girlfriend. I wasn't entirely sure but they actually looked like they were bickering with each other. He'd probably forgotten to mention where their night out was to be.

'I need a pee, you coming,' I said to Maddy. It was partially so I could find a temporary way out of the room.

Even walking around the empty place to find the toilets made you feel conspicuous. I pushed my shoulder against the door to open it and was pleasantly surprised: contemporary floor-to-ceiling stone tiles in black and beige, strategically placed spotlights and white sinks with stone surround. All it needed was a few neatly rolled-up hand towels in a basket, and expensive-looking soaps.

'I really can't believe that this is where *we've* chosen to spend *your* birthday. Whose idea was it again?' I said with a teasing smile, as I looked at her through the mirror and washed my hands.

'I know, but you have to try these things...here, do want to top your blusher up?' She handed her blusher over and then proceeded to re-apply her lip-gloss.

'Why? Do I look pale?' I asked, looking at my reflection again.

'No, just thought you might want to, I don't think the rest are enjoying it very much.' Maddy had a laugh in her voice.

'No shit, Sherlock.'

'Right being though it's my birthday let's take a picture of us together. Where is your camera?' Maddy asked.

I flicked through the images we'd taken, there were loads of them but I spotted something intriguing on all of them. My camera had been playing up a few weeks ago when I was trying to capture William and Elyse on the first day back at school – that day every photo was blurred. This was different. Clearly Maddy hadn't seen what I had seen as she continued to look at them.

'Some are okay, but if they're good of you, they're bad of me. You wouldn't think it would be that difficult,' she said.

'Errr…yeah, I would. But never mind that, look at the beam of light touching our heads, it's on every single one. We've got one each. We look like we've been kissed by angels.' I'd obviously got angels on the brain.

'Oooh…yeah, spooky, but I hardly think that angels would touch us!'

Laughing, I had to agree with her 'It'll be the reflection off the mirror, but it looks cool though,' I said, giving a more logical, but boring explanation and dropped the camera into my handbag.

'Come on, we'd better get back in there, they'll be wondering what we're up to.'

As she pulled the door open, a moaning Richard greeted us.

'You've been gone ages. What the hell were you doing in there?'

'Taking photos,' I said, as we walked back to Steve and the others.

'Photos? How long does it take to take a photo? Anyway it's crap in here, why don't we go home?'

'What? I encourage you to come to a lap-dancing club and you want to go home – I can't do anything right.' I couldn't argue with the crap comment, but the irony struck me at that moment that we were in a lap-dancing club, and he was the one wanting to go home.

'Actually, I'd rather have a kebab.'

Steve had seen his escape route and was jumping through it with both feet. Steve's mate looked half asleep as we all turned to him.

'He's been working long hours and he's knackered,' his girlfriend said. I almost believed her until he confessed that he was bored too.

'Right...why don't we all get a kebab then go somewhere else?' Maddy offered a compromise and everyone but Richard agreed.

'No, I'm going home, you coming?' he said, turning to me.

'What do you mean you're going home?' I was now feeling pissed at him for being so rude in front of the others, and on Maddy's birthday.

'I'm going home, are you coming or not?'

'I don't want to go home yet,' I said stubbornly.

'Well I do, so you either come with me or go with Maddy and Steve.'

'Fine, so I have to go home when you want to go home?' I was now feeling like a feisty teenager; furious at my parent's unrealistic demands.

'No, I said that you can stay with Maddy and Steve if you want to.'

'But that's not quite the same...*is it*?' If this was a contest – I was going to win.

'Do what you want, I'm going home.' We were still arguing as we moved down the stairs to the exit.

'What's up with him?' Maddy was speaking to me, but aiming her question at Richard. She knew exactly what was going on.

'Says he's going home.'

'What – is he leaving you here?'

'Yep.'

'What, abandoning you like he did on your birthday the other year.'

'Yep.'

Steve was convinced that Richard wouldn't do it; I think his logic was that surely he wouldn't dare do it twice to me. I don't think that Steve would contemplate leaving Maddy somewhere even once.

Richard started the engine of the car, as we all stood watching in the entrance of the club. Steve was still convinced he was bluffing until he saw him drive his silver *Mercedes CLS* through the exit and disappear from view. At least he'd exited in style, but once again he'd left me on a night out without any cash.

I stood there trying my hardest to make light of it, but my anger was simmering away. He'd made me feel bad for choosing to stay out, over going home with him, and if that wasn't good enough reason, I now felt bad that I'd been drinking and he hadn't, but he agreed to that one so that Maddy could have a drink. Richard and I on nights out just weren't suited: cinema, restaurants, meals at friends' houses were all fine. But bars or clubs, that's where the age difference revealed itself and caused a rift. Some things were just best done separately as this occasion once again proved to me.

The night was ruined after Richard's departure; everyone had lost steam and Maddy had started to stress about her brother – he wasn't answering his mobile and she was convinced that he'd been arrested. So we stopped off for a kebab before heading back home. I walked through the door a little after 2 am.

Richard's sister had gone and William and Elyse were asleep. Richard had gone to bed but had left the lights on for me, so I knew that his temper must have dissipated. My anger had subsided too. If anything, it had been replaced with sadness. Even Blue couldn't be arsed to get off the sofa to greet me; he'd barely managed to raise his head as I patted it on my way past him to switch the laptop on in the garden room.

I logged onto *Facebook* as I was still feeling wide-awake. Anthony Hope was online. In fact, he was the only friend showing as being online. It was strange that the space felt as quiet as the real world - the Newsfeed was static; it wasn't continually changing like it did during the day. Anthony must have been out for the evening too, or maybe he was always on this late?. But then I wouldn't know because it was rare that I was ever up at this time.

I wondered where he was, where he was sat, what he was wearing and whether he was with his girlfriend? Thinking of his new girlfriend, no one had added any more comments to his Relationship Status change since earlier in the day, I noticed. I then clicked back onto the Newsfeed again, just as Anthony's Status popped up at the top of my screen. It made me jump; like someone had secretly hot-wired my heart and then sent a jolt through my body.

2:15 Anthony wishes you were with me...

It was 2:15 – my watch confirmed when I checked it against the laptop.

He'd just that second posted it, then strangely logged off immediately. God… it felt like it was aimed at me. I log on; he updates his Status within seconds, and then instantly logs off after posting it. I replayed the last few minutes of events in my mind. Obviously, the message was meant for his girlfriend…I tried telling myself. It irritated me that I'd even allowed myself to think that it was aimed at me. I couldn't even face my own secret thoughts or had I just faced them but was still trying to deny them? It was too early in the day for self-analysis so I turned my focus on to my own Status Update.

02:19 Nicole is thinking: 3 males, 1 Lap-dancing club...one wants a kebab, one is bored and the third falls asleep... Maddy we are just too bloody good.

I knew Maddy would find it amusing when she next logged on. Thinking of Maddy reminded me of her brother. I thought about my *Facebook* quiz earlier in the day, and hoped that Maddy was wrong about him getting arrested. I said goodnight to Blue, switched the lights off and made my way upstairs.

The en-suite light stirred Richard from his sleep and he managed a weak, 'Hi, you're home.' I brushed my teeth, but couldn't be bothered to take my make-up off and slipped out of my dress; lazily dropping it on the floor in a heap. I climbed into the bed, pulling the quilt snugly around me. Richard's hand reached over to pat my thigh.

'Did you have a good time after I left? Where did you go?' he still sounded sleepy.

'For a kebab and then back here.'

'So you didn't go on to another club?'

'No.'

'So…I didn't miss anything by coming home then? Are you still angry with me?'

'No and no.'

'Okay, night night Little N, love you,' and he patted my thigh twice again before rolling back onto his side.

'Love you too…night.' I said. I fell asleep thinking about Anthony Hope.

The mere fact that we'd spent most of the night driving around in a car, rather than getting hammered, paid off tenfold the next day as William and Elyse were particularly hyper. The rift between Richard and I seemed to be forgotten, but lap-dancing clubs, he decided, weren't for him. Maddy had been right about her brother – he had been arrested. It wasn't his fault though – he'd been ripped off by a taxi driver, who drove off with his cash while he was standing at a hole-in-the-wall trying to get enough money to cover his fare home. As he kicked off at the side of the road, a police van happened to be passing and picked him up. Maddy brought him back around lunchtime, but the whole thing made me think again about the timing of the questions on that stupid *Facebook* quiz.

This was one of those grey, miserable days and even my skin looked grey. Richard had gone to see his mum at the nursing home; she had a form of dementia, which meant that she was permanently mixing up reality and imagination. Sometimes it seemed quite a nice state to be in; on the occasions where she thought that the Queen had been to see her, or her late husband had popped in – Richard's dad had died when Richard was only nineteen. But sometimes she would tell you that she'd just had a lovely dinner with him, but now he'd gone back to base – he'd been an RAF man. Other times the confusion was too painful to see.

I found a moment's peace to upload the pictures that I'd taken with Maddy onto *Facebook* and, when I logged on, I spotted a friend request. It was from Richard's wife who'd obviously decided to sign up. I agonised over whether to add her as a friend or not, but then decided that it was just plain rude not to. I noticed that she'd set her Relationship Status to 'It's complicated' It was probably the most accurate description for both of us. I had a quick look at her page; she hadn't really started to embrace the *Facebook* culture. I, on the other hand, was starting to feel like a real diehard pro.

I'd managed to upload the last five years' worth of holiday snaps on over the last few months and this latest album I decided to call 'Nicole & Maddy Lap-Dancing In The Toilets...200 pics later' – as just eight out of the whole lot were considered decent enough to be posted on there. The accidental beam of light slicing through the corner and the golden rays above our heads struck me again because it did make them look really mystical; in stark contrast to the depravity of our location. I thought about all the all strange and spooky things that had happened recently.

I finally got around to getting dressed when Mum, Dad and Grandmama popped in to see William and Elyse, before they set off to see Lysander. He was our horse that we kept in livery at the stables in the next village. He lived in our field at the top of the garden until last year, but Mum decided to move him because he wasn't weathering the winters without a stable very well and she was fretting that Elyse would get kicked now she was running about and not strapped in a pushchair anymore. But Mum and Dad always tried to tie both visits in together whenever they could, and, by including Grandmama, they managed to kill a staggering four birds with one stone. I could feel mum's glare from the leather sofa at the far end of the garden room.

'What are you doing on that laptop? Are you just going to sit there all afternoon?' she said irritably. 'Are you on that *Facebook* thing again? Tammy says you're on there a lot,' she added. Tammy was my brother's girlfriend and worked in Dad's office with Mum. As usual I was the odd one out, being the only family member not working in there. So I had a lot of egg on my face when my company failed and theirs was still ticking along. But that meant that Tammy got ample opportunity for harmless chitchat with mum and clearly my *Facebook usage* had cropped up in their conversations.

'No...it's okay – I'll get off in a minute,' I said, without looking at her and continued with my important research on Anthony Hope's Wall. I was intrigued, because Anthony's Relationship Status had changed from 'in a relationship' to 'it's complicated'. Why is it complicated? Is it because his girlfriend is married, separated or already got a boyfriend? I felt like a detective trying to solve a clue.

But there it was again, that ugly pang of unwanted jealousy. It would have been so much better if I'd added him and he'd got married to someone in New York, or at least engaged; even a long-term relationship in this country would have been preferable to this. Unable to reach any further conclusions, I read through a long conversation on his Wall with one of his friends. He was chatting about his dad and the fact that his law firm was struggling with real estate being in such a mess in the States.

I pulled myself away from the laptop in an attempt to be more sociable.

The next day, at 19:00, my Status said:
Nicole has changed her Relationship Status to It's Complicated
And the emails from Friends flooded in, wanting to know if

everything was okay with me and Richard. Damn...I hadn't thought it through properly. Do I say we've had an argument or that I changed it to be the same as his wife's Status? I thought about it and went with argument, a petty argument but we're fine, and I told everyone that. It was partially true, as we had had a little fight earlier in the evening over Richard saying that we didn't need our cleaner anymore now that I wasn't working.

A few hours later...

Anthony is thinking that 'complications' are something you throw in your own path :-)

Oh no...shit! Had his girlfriend coincidentally in less than one day left a husband, got a divorce or ditched another boyfriend? Or was it that he'd seen straight through me and was taking the piss? Oh shit, shit, bugger. I ran my hands through my hair. It could have been a coincidence or bad timing – I knew that. But what if it wasn't? I was going to have to leave mine that way now – I couldn't change it again, not now, not after that had just happened.

Anthony was starting to make me suspicious.

CHAPTER SEVEN

Sundays in our house were utterly boring. Mind-numbingly so unless you included the occasional imploding window of which Richard had still not bothered to show me the explanation he had. It was like the whole thing wasn't even open for discussion. But this particular Sunday, appeared at the time to be no exception to the boring rule.

Richard, as usual, had spread the newspapers right across the kitchen island; they spilled over onto the tall stools. For some reason he always prefers to read them standing up, with his reading glasses on, and football text on the television behind him. I walked into the kitchen to fill the water jug back up for the iron. As I walked towards the sink, an advert in one of the newspapers caught my eye. It was the *Sunday Times*, which had been folded in half and placed on the stool.

'Is that for real?' I asked as I picked it up for a closer look. 'Have I missed something and its April Fools today?'

'Missed what?' Richard obviously couldn't see what I was looking at, and was upset that I had interrupted his reading.

'Look at this job advert. The Bank of England is looking for a new Deputy Governor who will be responsible for financial stability. They are offering a nice little salary of £240K, how funny is that?'

'I hadn't seen it. Yes – that is certainly funny,' but Richard still wasn't sounding half as amused as me.

'Oh come on – you have to laugh at the irony of it all? Anyway…how come you've bought the *Sunday Times*, you don't normally buy it?'

'Don't know... just thought I would. I picked it up when I got the bread and milk from the shop...besides I do occasionally buy it for the financial news.'

'I've got to show Maddy this, I'm gonna load it onto *Facebook*,' I told him, as I walked back out of the kitchen to the study PC.

The ironing had fallen by the wayside and the plastic jug had been left sitting empty on the kitchen island.

I posted the advert as a photo on my *Facebook* and, as usual, I opted to share with all. I left a comment beneath it; offering it as a job if anyone was remotely interested. I hadn't spoken to Maddy yet. I'd sent her a text earlier on, thanking her for dinner at her house the previous night, but I had no idea what she was doing. By early evening she'd spotted the advert and left a comment on the photo. I clicked onto it to see what she'd written and I found myself in dialogue with her.

Maddy: *I could SO do that job. With my arms tied behind my back!!! Well at least be able to do a better job than the last wanker!*

Me: *I know…me too…*

Maddy: *Not to mention I could do something with the £240,000!!!!!!*

Me: *To pay back the Bank! LOL!*

Maddy: *God…you think so differently to me! More along the lines of new Prada, holiday, car…oh and a donation to world peace x x x*

Me: *I am trying to appear ethical…x*

Maddy: *Ethical????????? Oh er…yes me too!! xxxx*

I spent the next week or so flicking *Facebook* on and off all day long. I was starting to regard each hit of the refresh button as a treat for completing another study question. Maddy had been busy finalising arrangements for us to take the kids to a sleepover at a science museum for Halloween, which was in a few weeks' time. The whole arrangement of the event had started off as a tit-for-tat-style banter on my Wall. We had written a staggering eighty-five comments.

I was making a start on dinner; Richard didn't tend to get home until gone 19:00, which made evening meals in our house quite late, but I stubbornly preferred us to all to eat together. I'd moved the laptop onto the kitchen island to amuse myself on *Facebook*, in between chopping up the veg. With hindsight, this sort of behaviour should have probably flagged up as an early sign of *Facebook* addiction. Maddy hadn't posted her comeback on my last comment, but I knew it would appear, because she always had to have the last word on things; it was just a matter of time. But that's when Anthony logged on, the green light at the bottom of the screen indicated this. And his Status popped up at the top of my screen.

Anthony Hope wants you...

The words startled me, just like they did before, then he logged off again – also just like before.

I could hear his voice behind the words, pitched at the perfect masculine depth: the clarity and teasing naughtiness with the soft but colourful American accent – I guessed it to be the equivalent of an English *posh* accent. I remembered how his voice made my ears tingle, as though they couldn't absorb enough of the sound to satisfy their hunger. It's strange how some people's voices become locked in your head.

I knew the message was for his girlfriend; that made perfect sense. But why did he have to post it, when I was on and then log off again so quickly? But then again, I'd been on the site so much; posting something when I wasn't on would have been a challenge. Once I'd rationalised it as a coincidence, I hated myself for feeling disappointed that it wasn't for me.

But the next day, I wasn't so sure...

Anthony says that the heart rules the head...don't ya think? ;)

It was like he'd punched me in the heart with a boxing glove. Was that how he saw me? As someone who made choices with my head over my heart, only to later discover that the heart invariably overrides you in the end anyway.

It was a good job that I'd had my energy boosting birdseed, as Maddy called it, as my brain needed it today. She was forever taking the piss about my nuts and alfalfa sprouts.

My mobile rang and vibrated on the table right next to the laptop; I jumped then I picked it up, keeping my eyes fixed on the laptop screen.

'Hi, it's only me,' Maddy said in her upbeat voice. 'I know that you are studying, you don't need to tell me, but just to let you know in advance that William can have a sleepover at the weekend, if that's okay with you?'

'It's okay,' I said half-heartedly.

'Erm...right, you're not really listening to me are you? What are you doing that is so important that you can't speak to me?'

'Errr...it's that Anthony Hope,' I finally blurted out. It was the first time that I'd mentioned his name to her since I added him.

'Yeah, well? What about him?'

'It's his Status Update today.'

'So what? You don't speak to him do you?' She wouldn't have seen my Instant Message about Nepal, so I was able to confirm that I wasn't speaking to him, which however, did lead her back to why I was so bugged by his Status today.

'I think it relates to me.'

'How? That's not possible.' Maddy was as direct as ever.

'Where are you?'

'Home,' I heard her exhale cigarette smoke before she answered – she was probably sitting in the lounge, curled up on the sofa.

'Okay, then log onto *Facebook* and his Wall.' I waited while she logged on. 'Right, look at his photo.'

'Yeah, so what?'

'He has a can of *Diet Coke* in his hand.' She could now see the same as me which was a close-up of his face; he was holding the *Coke* against his cheek.

'Yeah...?'

'Think back to our conversation at the beginning of last week on my Wall.'

'Which conversation?'

'The one where I mentioned your addiction to *Diet Coke*...'

'Oh yeah...I thought that was funny...what was my comeback?

Well the alfalfa sprouts aren't doing you much good are they?'

'Yeah…that's the one. But Anthony posted this Status a few hours ago and immediately changed his profile to that picture you are looking at now. Not only has he made it his profile picture, but then, clearly not satisfied with it, he's cropped in closer and re-posted it so the *Coke* can is more noticeable. It looks like he wants to emphasise it.'

'Well yeah, but surely that's just a coincidence?'

'Yeah, but there's been a couple of other weird coincidences over the last few weeks that now makes this feel less of a coincidence,' I quickly moved on before she got me to elaborate on these. 'When you link that photo with his Status: "heart rules the head", I think he's aiming it at me. I think he's seen through me. He's got a girlfriend, they're already together, dating or whatever they're doing, so why would there be a choice between the heart and head? Why would you even post it as a Status Update? You've got to admit I've got a point.'

'It's all a bit much for me, surely he wouldn't be that deep?'

'I don't know. Maybe he's always known it, sensed it, oh…I just don't know. But, yes, I do think that he would be that deep, I really do.'

'Then I just don't know what to say…' and with that she hung up.

I wondered if she thought that I was going slowly mad with all of the analysing that I had been doing.

I pulled a piece of blank paper closer to me and started to write:

1 Drunken email – but in my defence, he never replied to it and I never sent anymore (that was 4 months ago)

1 Instant message regarding Nepal – genuine interest in the place and he never replied and I didn't send any more messages. I did ask Richard to look at them, but Anthony couldn't see that. That needs to be taken into consideration (1 month ago)

1 Poke – this was true, I had poked him once, but I'd also poked everyone else on my *Facebook*, male and female while I was bored one day. It wasn't until I was sitting in the hairdressers, cringing into a magazine article discussing "poking", that I discovered "poking" on *Facebook* was practically code for: I want to poke you! Maddy and I had been innocently poking each other for months. And my problem was that Anthony Hope wouldn't have seen that I'd been happily poking everyone on there.

1 Quiz – ghost question not my fault (recently)

1 Change of Relationship Status to 'It's complicated' – okay that was stupid (recently)

100 Times (approx) looked at his Wall, but he cannot see that – thankfully, so not relevant; simply an issue on my conscience.

I'd not really done very well on the passive observer front. It wasn't that it was excessive, but I had gone over my *just being nosey* rule. I moved on to my list of coincidences from Anthony...

1 wishes you were with me...(timing)

1 'Complications' are something you throw in your own path :-) (timing and smile on the end)

1 Wants you...(timing)

1 Says the heart rules the head...don't ya think (wink) (timing) (All recently)

Maybe it was my drunken email that had given me away? Maybe it confirmed what he'd suspected all those years ago, and instead of replying to that email, he'd just sat and waited for the right moment to strike. There was now a conversation on his Wall about 'complications' being him solving the problem of fitting dates with his girlfriend around his gigs – but that explanation didn't ring true with me.

My conclusion? I was none the wiser.

Status Updates...

12:22 Nicole... Okay my head is screwed now!!

16:15 Anthony Hope is laughing... ;)

He was laughing at me! This made me feel good and yet

stupid. My cheeks felt flushed with embarrassment and from my long-hidden desire. I could almost see him throwing back his head with his chesty laugh. I wished I knew where he was when he posted it. I felt like I'd been caught red-handed, and was heading straight for trouble without the will to stop myself.

17:57 Nicole likes cat and mouse.

CHAPTER EIGHT

'Noooooo!' Richard screamed at the television as he jumped up from the sofa, causing his beer to fly out of the can and land on the floor.

God, I hated football, the moronic sound of chanting and cheering with incessant commentary of the ball being passed around a rectangular piece of grass. I *especially* hated it on Sundays. But this particular Sunday I was hating it even more than ever. Every time he jumped up and cheered with that can in his hand I wanted to bat him one, William could be forgiven at seven years of age, he knew no better, and neither was he drinking *Special Brew*. Fortunately Maddy threw me a lifeline and invited Elyse and me for a stroll around the country park behind their house.

She had a tiny wooden door set in a crumbling stone wall at the bottom of her garden. I loved it because it always reminded me of entering the *Secret Garden*. It's as though this was our space, and all others were intruding. On this particular day, the air was still, and the temperature cold. We'd wrapped up warm and strolled around the edge of the lake; there was barely a ripple. The old trees had interwoven over the years, creating an endless archway above the path that looked more like a trellis in the autumn. I kicked the gold, yellow and russet leaves against the spongy ground as we walked. My head was so full of Anthony Hope that I felt as though I could run around the edge of the lake forever, while my head was left to work things out.

The previous day I'd spent an hour on the treadmill and Richard made me get off in the end, I could have kept going.

My Status Update on *Facebook* now said:

Nicole is Forest Gump...might do a marathon.

Maddy couldn't figure out whether I meant I couldn't stop running, or I wanted to eat a chocolate bar.

But while I was moving I could breathe. When I stopped, I was hit with pain. The pain of knowing that I was allowing myself to open up to someone who was out of my reach, and that someone was probably having a jolly good time right now in Paris. I knew that I should simply have removed him, so that there was nothing there for me to interpret or read into. But no matter how long I sat with my cursor hovering over that tiny *x* to remove, I just couldn't do it. I was still waiting for something.

We stopped off at the little cafe for a hot chocolate with whipped cream and arrived back at Maddy's house, rosy-cheeked and refreshed from the clean air. I let my feet warm on her heated floor in her hi-tech kitchen. Her highland terrier, Tia, was sat optimistically wagging her tail with her ball conveniently placed for me to repeatedly throw. Unfortunately, it wasn't Tia's lucky day, because on the glass island, to the right of the extractor fan housing the suspect police bug, was Maddy's laptop.

I'd opened up *Facebook* and on the screen was Anthony's sister's photo album. Anthony had commented on it, which meant that it had now pulled it onto his Wall – that's how *Facebook* works. I forced Maddy to reluctantly look at the images on the screen while we sipped sweet, hot tea.

'Right,' I said, as I placed the mug back onto the glass island surface and pulled up exhibit A. 'You see...*there*...a picture of a bee. That's what you called me the other day – a busy little bee,' I was almost singing my words as I swiftly moved onto exhibit B: a photo of a bird; eating bird seed.

'You also wrote...had our energy-boosting bird seed...that is what you put on my Wall, the day before these pictures appeared.'

'Yeah, but so what? Just a coincidence, loads of people have bird seed hanging in their garden,' her top lip was almost curling as though she was thinking that she couldn't believe she was being made to look at them.

Undeterred I continued. 'You also said on that day same day:

"William is always chirpy first thing in the morning...and there's *the bird*...and birds chirp,' I said as I clicked on the image of bird – to back me up.

'It's just a bird...if you've got bird seed you're going to have birds.' She reached for a cigarette, needing that kick of nicotine before I forced her to swallow more of my theories.

I could feel my frustration building. 'Yeah, it is just a bird, you're right, but the bird is sitting in the album with the busy bee and bird seed picture...and it's an exotic bird. Come on, they're weird things to put on *Facebook*, unless you relate them to my Wall,' I argued. Exhibit D this time: '...what about the frog then?'

'What? Oh go on then.' She was starting to sound exasperated.

She was almost succeeding in making me feel like I was going completely mad, but I was determined to make her see them as I saw them. 'Right, I reckon he's been through my "Brief History in Time" album and his got his sister to help him flirt with me. Just think of the words I wrote on my girly holiday photo where I had a dig at my ex. I wrote: "...most satisfying moment, dropping a bed on his head after he tried to catch his stupid bull-frog", and here before us is the little frog,' I said, as I went for a zoom-in on the frog picture. Surely she could see what I was getting at now?

'Look I can see they're weird coincidences, but surely no one would be crazy enough to even think this up, well apart from you that is. Perhaps a frog came in the garden... I saw some pictures he'd posted myself of his parents' house. They have a lake. Frogs like lakes.'

I understood her reasoning and I'd seen the photo of the house myself; typically American with dormer windows and an overhang – it was what made me Google New York in the end and established that New York was a vast state, not just Manhattan. But I couldn't see the photo that way.

'Yeah well, how ironic is it, that I have a severe issue with frogs, and a photo of a fucking frog pops up on his Wall, just as I think he's playing some sort of game with me.'

Maddy took over the laptop while still laughing, 'Well what about these images, what are these about?' and she clicked on a picture of a sparkler, another of his sister looking into an old mirror, and finally a tray of cupcakes, some of which were themed for Halloween; orange and black icing with plastic spiders stuck on top, and another tray with pink and white icing – underneath was a caption that said Eat Me.

'Go on, hit me with your explanation…?' she said, shaking her head.

'Sparkler…sexual fireworks? Maybe? I don't know and I haven't figured the last two out yet,' this was the best I could offer her.

'I guess a plate of homemade cakes would look strange to you.'

I opened and closed my mouth.

'Can I throw another one in for consideration? That if he wants to communicate with you, why doesn't he just use a more straightforward conventional method. One we can all under-stand – as in email? Just a thought. Don't know if that's something you've considered *maybe*?'

'I don't know.' Defeated, I closed the laptop.

He was certainly giving me the game of cat and mouse and I cursed myself for noticing everything. But I think that all of the police accusations thrown at Steve had more logic to her than the summary of evidence I was currently producing with bees, bird seeds, and frogs. I hoped to God that Maddy was wrong about her extractor fan as my eyes swiftly glanced at it. I thought about a group of CID officers tapping their headsets, disbelieving their own ears. It probably could have been enough to have us all committed! I finished my tea, rounded Elyse up from the playroom, much to Henry's relief, and we made our way home.

That night I tossed and turned, seeing the photos over and over in my mind, then it hit me – *Alice in Wonderland* and *Through The*

Looking Glass. I couldn't believe it had taken me so long to figure it out – but sleep or even half sleep is often clever like that.

In the early morning I crouched on the study floor, flicking through an old copy of the book that a relative had given to William when he was a not much more than a baby.

Anthony's sister's album made sense now: my computer screen was my window or looking glass that saw directly into Anthony's world and vice-versa. And Alice is the little girl who falls down a hole and emerges on the other side of the world and has to take a bite from the cake with Eat Me written on it, so that she can grow tall enough to reach the golden key to open the locked door.

Should I be having my cake and eating it? Was I like Alice...the little girl so reluctant to grow up that she disappears into another world? I was certainly reluctant to grow up and grow old.

I'd been trying so hard to live in the real world with my accountancy exams, and now, after weeks of barely leaving the house, I'd gone and bloody well fallen down a rabbit hole. And instead of graciously, sensibly, climbing back out of it and retrieving my disregarded, moral compass on my way back home, I was always drumming my fingers against a keyboard; waiting patiently for the magic key to open that tiny door into the world of the Mad Hatter, Queen of Hearts, Cheshire Cat and Mr Anthony Hope.

It did make sense that Anthony Hope was using his sister and that story to lure me in.

As expected when I ran this theory past Maddy, I was greeted with a: 'you're a complete fucking nutter.' But, as a consequence of trying to smoke Anthony out with something more solid and less cryptic – both our Walls were starting to look like the workings of the insane dedicated to the love of *Alice in Wonderland*.

As a consequence of my theory I'd been ashamedly continually hitting the refresh button on my permanently open *Facebook*. It could have been rain or sunshine outside. I had no idea as I hadn't bothered to open the shutters in the garden room. The real world was holding less and less interest.

Anthony was in Paris with his girlfriend. So my heart felt like it was in a slow state of twisted torture. I was still allowing it to open up, only to find it contorting in confusion.

I imagined him with me, but like one of those scratch edits in a movie, my dream was continually being knocked sideways by the thought of him laughing, holding and kissing his girlfriend in a way that only new couples do. I imagined them sitting in one of the many Parisian cafes, climbing the Eiffel tower, taking a taxi through the Arc de Triomphe, discussing pictures in the Louvre and generally strolling round a city I'd never been to.

I thought of Anthony's long, fluid strides covering the ground effortlessly.

I remember watching him walk. Despite his height, he was very erect, and his pace fast and purposeful. He had natural grace. For some reason, my thoughts turned to his hands. I remember being fascinated by them when I saw him playing his guitar. Unlike Richards's square powerful hands, Anthony's fingers were long, but the smoothness was broken by a callus, caused by hours and hours of playing his beloved guitar. My thoughts lingered longer than they should on his fingers.

I hit the refresh button once more on my *Facebook,* just in case he had finally returned. But, for once, it wasn't Anthony who had grabbed my attention – it was Maddy with her Status Update.

15:44 MD Maddy is so MAD!!!! May explode in to a million pieces!

I sat and laughed at that before I posted a comment...

15:47 Madd'y'onna Madd'y'onna...tick tick tick...Steve fucked up then? ;-)

A few minutes later she'd added another comment...

15:50 WHY CANT HE LEAVE MY STUFF ALONE!!!!!!!!!

I could hear the rage...

15:53 Might just leave you to sort this one out...bye x

15:57 BOOM!

I gave her a call.

'Okay, what's wrong?'

'What is wrong? That *fucking twat* has taken my car keys, fucked off to London all day on a job and I can't go anywhere, because he can't remember where he's gone and put the spare keys. I've been stuck in the house all fucking day. GOD I'M SO MAD.'

'Erm...' I said, trying very hard not to laugh. The thought of Maddy being trapped in the house all day was enough to send her over the edge. It was a wonder she'd not smoked herself to death. 'Do you need me to collect Henry for you?'

'No, my brother's doing it. Seriously I'm going to kill Steve when he gets home.'

I was silently glad that I wasn't in Steve's shoes – his evening was going to be miserable. 'Well...if you need anything, call me, but I need to go and get William and Elyse, it's already late. I'll speak to you later once you and your car keys are lovingly reunited,' and I disconnected the call thinking that had Richard driven off with my car keys today, I wouldn't have even noticed until teatime.

At 17:34, an hour or so later, I was pondering over Anthony's latest Status...

Anthony says there is always some madness in love. But there is also always some reason in madness ;)

He was back from his break.

I pulled a quotation book off one of the study shelves behind me, making a mental note that I needed to sort them all out. Half of the books had been pulled off by William and Elyse and were scattered all over the floor. I flicked through the pages, thinking that the book would come in handy one day – I was sure I'd heard these words somewhere before.

I started with *Love Quotes* and couldn't see it there, then moved onto *Madness,* and still couldn't see it. I was just about to type it into Google, which is what I should have done in the first place, when Maddy popped up with an Instant Message on Chat.

Have you seen your little friend Anthony Hope's status?

Yes… I think it relates to our postings

I posted my reply, thankful that the smug tone behind my voice didn't translate on IM.

Yeah me too…it's a quote by Friedrich Nietsche. German guy – think he's dead. I Googled it for you.

Coincidence that mad or madness crops up between us and turns up on his page…don't you think?

Tis a weird coincidence…must admit x

Thank you x

Having got the answer I wanted from her that meant she was at last starting to see things my way – I needed now to sit and think because, once again, Anthony Hope appeared to be tangling me up with his girlfriend. Why did it have to have a wink on the end? It seemed like he'd taken something off Maddy's Wall – the word 'mad' – to acknowledge my most recent Status which had said that there were more than two players in this game. So it now appeared as though he'd gone and pulled the extra player into the game.

What is he trying to do to me…other than turn me into a screwed up ball that is crippled by unleashed sexual tension.

My head screamed.

I heard Richard enter the front door, jumped off the PC and sheepishly followed him into the kitchen, making a point of asking him about his day, but I barely heard his words as I struggled to mentally pull myself out of Wonderland.

The next day I found myself flicking through the photos Anthony Hope had added within a few hours of returning from his Paris break.

I closed them down quickly – I didn't need to see them, they were exactly how I'd imagined they would be.

It was his lean long arms around my waist I wanted, and to be the girl in his photos. I also mentally noted that his girlfriend was very tall, standing probably only four or five inches below him. It was also bugging me that I didn't know what she did for a living. If she popped up as a doctor, vet or lawyer at that point, I think it would have been more than I could stand.

Despite the photos, my gut instinct told me that he was watching me closely; studying my every move on *Facebook*. If I posted a lovey-dovey album of me and Richard, would that have meant that I wasn't closely watching Anthony Hope? The answer was no…so I was still determined to drive Anthony out from his cover.

Even if that meant my measures were starting to feel like the actions of that the psychotic bunny boiler in *Fatal Attraction*.

I had spent most of the day freezing in our local Wonderland with Maddy and the kids. The whole place had been themed for Halloween and the final straw came after I got off the carousel and walked straight into a bin full of slime and frogs. At that point I left.

We drove home and I let William and Elyse into the house, before unloading coats and empty chocolate and crisp wrappers off the car floor. No matter how many carrier bags I put in there for them, they never use them. I stood warming my hands on the radiator in the kitchen, facing the glass dining-table, which I noticed was still covered in smears from breakfast. The car journey had been too short to thaw my hands and I wanted them to warm quickly, because I was itching to tackle the pumpkins with my newly acquired pumpkin tools.

However, I got really upset when I couldn't find the *WWE* pumpkin templates. I rummaged through all the kitchen drawers, making another mental note that I really needed to clear them out at some stage. I accused William of moving them, called Richard and accused him of moving them, and finally located them at the back of the oak unit that surrounded our American-style fridge freezer. I didn't even remember putting them there.

William and Elyse were standing excitedly either side of me as I stuck the template to the pumpkin. At that point, I remembered Maddy saying how difficult it was to cut into pumpkins, but I wasn't too concerned about it.

William looked on impressed as the *Undertaker* started to take shape.

I then cut out the last piece and we all stood back in admiration of my skill. I felt quite pleased with myself – clearly I wasn't as dumb as Maddy! Then I set about cutting out *Ray Mysterio* for Elyse.

My fingers were starting to feel sore, but Elyse's *Ray Mysterio* was starting to look good, if not better. I only had the outer edge to complete and fuuuuuck! I'd mixed up the black with the white and in my hand was a perfect intricately carved out face; in the pumpkin was a perfect round hole. William, protectively clutching his own pumpkin, fell about laughing. I told him off then explained to Elyse that hers was a very special lantern.

'We just need to find a candle and it will be perfect,' I futilely tried, but she wasn't buying into my vision. Her little, perfect, kitten-like face, looked up at me, just as it started to contort with the tears running down her cheeks.

'Where's the face? I wanted a face,' she wailed in a heart-broken sob, her little head barely reaching above the island as she looked at my huge mistake. William cracked up once more and Elyse lunged at him in a red-faced rage.

I stood, fingers throbbing, and took a deep breath.

'Right...shoes back on and get in the car.'

'Why?' William, despite being reprimanded, was still unable to stop giggling at Elyse's misfortune.

'Just get your shoes on please.'

'I can't, I can't undo my laces,' and I took the trainers from him and examined the string of knots that more resembled a master-piece created from *Scooby* string. 'Just get in the car as you are, we haven't got time to undo them, and we haven't got time to find the others.'

'Can I have a *mazagine*?' Elyse asked, through sniffles.

'Mag a zine...say mag a zine.'

'Mag a zine.'

'And again...'

'Mag a zine.'

'Good...now say Magazine.'

'Mazagine. So...can I have one pwease.'

'Elyse, I give up. And no...we are getting you another pumpkin. Now get in the car quickly...please.'

Having got a replacement from the veg store in the next village, I decided to show my hands some mercy by playing this one safe, sticking to the less intricate, conventional pumpkin face. I carved out tiny triangles to form the cross of the eyes, a triangle nose, and then that was when I had the brainwave. I hurriedly emptied the plastic toy boxes in the garden room, all observed by a puzzled William, and then I triumphantly pulled out a tiny plastic frog, perfect for Halloween. I grabbed the camera off the top of the freestanding unit in the kitchen and placed the frog in front of the mouth-less *Ray Mysterio*.

'Mummy, why are you taking a picture of my pumpkin and my frog?'

'Move your head William – it's in the way, good boy, you'll see what I'm doing in a minute,' I said, as I pressed the camera button down. 'Right then Elyse, let's cut the mouth out of Ray.' I said, as I picked the tools back up to create a simple wide smile.

'Can I have it, can I have it now Mummy?'

'In two secs, Elyse. I just want to take another picture. Right here...hold the frog' I said, as I handed it to William.

I then placed the now smiling *Undertaker* next to *Ray* and took another shot, minus the frog.

'There...done,' I said satisfied, as I finally handed Elyse her pumpkin. 'Right...do you want to see the pictures? ... Ready?' I asked. 'There is *Ray Mysterio, The Undertaker* and little froggy. And now... *Ray* is now smiling because he's eaten the little froggy,' I smiled as I explained it to them, thinking this was no worse than anything they watched on *The Simpsons.*

Elyse didn't really get it, but happily wandered off with her pumpkin. William liked it so much that he took the camera and flicked through the pictures several more times. The next day I loaded them onto my *Facebook,* with a little caption on the one without the frog:

Oh dear :-)

My ridiculous theory, using an equally ridiculous method, was that if Hope was watching my posts, and he had picked up on my fear of frogs, then this album would strike a chord with him, and yet another manufactured coincidence would pop up on his *Facebook.* And if nothing appeared that related to it, then, well, I would be proven wrong and he would be none the wiser as to what I'd been doing.

Blue jumped on the sofa, accidentally caught the remote and switched on the TV. I watched a body being removed from a Victorian terrace cordoned off by the police. It was old news footage from 2005 and a male voice spoke over the images: "A 22-year-old man has been arrested after Charlotte Hadley was found stabbed to death at her home in Manchester." The clip ended and cut back to a studio shot of some daytime chat show I'd never heard of.

"Obviously the Charlotte Hadley case was extremely tragic, but Jane, can you tell us how wide the definition of stalking extends?"

The presenter, an immaculately dressed middle-aged woman, spoke to a younger dark-haired lady on a sofa. The words Dr

Jane Tondal, Psychiatrist appeared at the bottom of the screen. She had obviously been warned not to slouch prior to going on air and appeared uncomfortably straight and rigid. I was about to switch off – but then decided to listen to the psychiatrists answer instead.

"Basically...a stalker is someone who watches you all of the time, and who phones, texts, turns up at your workplace or home uninvited; even communicates with you through social networking sites," she went on.

"Why do they do it?" The presenter asked.

"For lots of different reasons. The Love Obsessed Stalker, for example, may not have a relationship with their victim, but, like their description, they become obsessed with them. They have a fanatical love for them and will go to great lengths to obtain information on their target; they'll even get friends to help them. They may believe they are destined to be with their victim, if only their victim could see it. Very often this type of stalker suffers from some mental disorder as was found in the Charlotte Hadley case. Her killer was later diagnosed with dissociate identity disorder or better know as multiple personality disorder. But the stalking began after Charlotte broke off their relationship."

"I once remember reading something about stalkers believing that their victim is communicating through some kind of special coded communication. Have I got that right?"

"Yes...that's the Delusional Stalker you are referring to. Very often this type will stalk celebrities or people generally out of their social reach. The relationship doesn't really exist beyond the stalkers own mind. Their imaginary world is a far better place. Even things like the victim's choice of car registration can be bizarrely read into as being coded communication to acknowledge their secret love. In 2006, FTAC, the Fixated Threat Assessment Centre was set up to help deal with this type of crime. It's a combined mental-health and police unit."

"Are most stalker's dangerous?"

"They're not all dangerous... The problem is some stalkers don't realise what they're doing is intimidating or threatening. But then there are some who set out to be precisely that...they want revenge – they

intend to cause fear to their victim and they believe they've been wronged in some way. It can often feel like slow rape for the victim or in Charlotte's case result in death."

"This is all very fascinating and worthy of more discussion. But unfortunately we have to go to commercial... After the break we'll be..."

I turned the TV off. The psychiatrist's comments left me feeling uncomfortable.

CHAPTER NINE

Status: 31ˢᵗ October 2008 09:01

Nicole feels like a dream child moving through a land of wonders wild and new.

'While we're over this way, do you want to call in to see the new signage on the showroom?' Richard asked, as he turned his face to me, before focusing back on the road ahead. He'd taken the day off work, because it was half-term and we were on our way back home after spending the morning buying new sleeping bags for the Halloween sleepover at the steelworks, which was to take place later that night.

'Why? Have the new occupants moved in then?' I asked this because I thought Richard must have forgotten to tell me that the new tenant was finally in our old showroom.

I did know that he'd at long last sorted out the ongoing issue with the lease on the premises; the lawyers acting on behalf of the proprietor wanted Richard to still be the guarantor for the new tenant. Richard had flipped out in a meeting with a bunch of lawyers at the twelfth hour. He told them that they could do what the fuck they liked, but he would go bankrupt before he would agree to pay someone else's rent on the place – if it turned out they couldn't afford it. In the end, the new tenant agreed to provide the underlying guarantee; the way it should have been all along. The whole thing was ridiculous and yet another sign of the current lack of confidence in the business world. How great it would be if Richard could get the bank and other legal issues off his back with such petulance, I thought. But Richard wanting to show me the signage was why I'd assumed the new tenant had already opened up shop.

'No, they're about to though, that's why the new sign writing went up yesterday. They'll be opening up any day now. So it would be like kissing a frog, if you like?'

'Kissing a frog? Why have you just said that?' It now felt as though Richard was even in on all the madness around me. It is peculiar, how strange words feel even *stranger*, when you're in a moving car with rapidly changing scenery. It's as though it's all too much for the senses to take in.

'What? It's just an expression – have you not heard it before? To kiss a frog. It's like saying goodbye.'

'No. No I have definitely not heard of it, not used like that.'

But obviously, thinking about it, in the fairy tale, the princess kisses the frog goodbye, and the frog is then replaced with a prince.

But the last thing that old showroom felt like was a fairy tale, so I didn't make the connection.

I wasn't meaning to sound short with him though, it wasn't his fault that he chose those words. And it wasn't his fault that the new tenant was selling designer wedding dresses. All of my hard work, hopes and dreams for the place had been replaced with different kinds of fabrics. Curtains were now satin, silk and beads woven into beautiful gowns, designed to make a woman feel, ironically, like a princess. Each one of those dresses would eventually be filled with a soul full of hopes and dreams. 'No I don't want to see it. It's history. I've already kissed it goodbye,' I said.

'Okay, just thought you might have wanted to, that's all. I'll head straight home then.'

'I hope it works out better for them than it did for us, though,' I said, while thinking that they couldn't screw it up any more than we did, and my attention then drifted back to the text Richard had received the day before.

'What are you doing?' Richard asked, as I picked up his mobile.

'Looking at your phone. I want to see that text from yesterday.'

'I've deleted it now, I've told you it doesn't matter,' he said.

'Why didn't you take it to the police?'

'An isolated text? Don't be ridiculous – they'd laugh me out of the station. Don't bother about it.'

But it *was* bugging the hell out of me. He could pass all the other withheld numbers off as the bank, but this certainly wasn't from a bank.

Are you sure someone hasn't got it in for you? What about ex-*ILex* customers who lost deposits? Employees who lost their jobs? We're too easy to trace thanks to laws on directors' transparency. Credit-check companies are picking up data everyday on us. I keeping emailing them saying the company closed down but they don't remove things. We're easy targets for someone who wants revenge.'

'I think you are overreacting,' he said.

But if I thought logically it had to have been sent by someone who was on my *Facebook*. It couldn't have come from anyone else. So who the hell was watching me on *Facebook bar Anthony*? Why had someone got it in for me...and Richard? And...how had they got Richard's mobile number? No ex-employees or clients were on my Facebook either which blew my first theory out of the water.

'How can it not matter?' I said sulkily, while still staring at the phone. I think I was hoping that the text would magically reappear.

'It doesn't matter. I don't know who sent it. You've told me there is nothing to worry about, so I'm not bothered.' His tone was final and his eyes were fixed firmly on the road ahead, so I couldn't read his face.

'But the text is just evil, it could have caused trouble,' I tried again.

'It doesn't bother me...how many times...'

'That's not normal,' I said and grumpily placed the phone back into the console. I turned the radio up and focused on the depressed-looking buildings as we made our way back out of the city. I was sure that knocking them down and replacing them with the huge, metal monstrosities that keep springing up everywhere is only going to make it worse in another fifty years. Then I wasn't an architect, I wasn't anything. So what did I know? Nearly all of the buildings had massive "To Let" signs plastered across them.

Once home, we pulled everything out of the car and dumped the new sleeping bags in the hall. Then I retrieved the chewed up mail, along with Elyse's mangled shoes, from Blue.

'Mummy, can we play with the sleeping bags.'

'No. They're for later. Leave them alone please,' I pleasantly warned them as I headed upstairs to pack mine and William's overnight bags. Elyse was going to stay with my mum and dad for the night; I considered her too young for the Halloween event. I eventually came back down to see William and Elyse lying on the sofas in the new sleeping bags. Sometimes it felt like I was completely wasting my breath.

'I thought I told you both to leave those sleeping bags alone,' I said.

'They're only playing, they're not causing any harm.'

Richard was right, so I left them to it while I tidied the mess in the kitchen, which had been left after breakfast. But this turned out to be another one of those moments where I should have stuck to my guns.

My sheer frustration with the sleeping bags was temporarily reduced by Maddy calling, she had noticed Anthony's latest *Facebook* posting. She was even the one who mentioned it first on the phone. So after I placed the phone receiver back in the cradle in the study, I had a beaming smile on my face as I walked back into the garden room for another attempt to get the sleeping bags back into their ridiculously small carry bags. Richard shrewdly noticed my change of expression, probably because five minutes earlier I'd been on the verge of kicking a hole in the wall.

'What's with the smile?'

'Nothing, no reason,' I lied, attempting to wipe it from my

face.

'But you're smiling. What has Maddy said?'

'She's was just giving me the time to meet up later for the Halloween sleepover.' I lied by partial omission, because that had been part of the conversation – just not all of it. Richard thankfully left it at that. But I was smiling because Maddy had just confirmed what I had willed myself so hard not to see first thing that morning. Anthony was now a Fan of the band *Buzzin Fly* whose latest listed single just so happened to be *My Angelic Demon*.

So, okay, I had to admit that he may have simply liked *Buzzin Fly*, but to become a Fan of them just hours after my pumpkin pictures appeared? Once again it was safely subtle of him. But I was smiling because he'd spotted them, and also because Maddy had spotted the connection between mine and Anthony's Wall again. This meant that I wasn't going insane, or that we both were – so at least I wouldn't be lonely. But it would be even better if I could coax him into posting something that lacked subtlety; like the text sent to Richard's phone.

I turned my attention back to the sleeping bags, whilst wishing I'd been a fly on the wall when Anthony had spotted my photos. Did they make him smile?

'I need to get more air out of those bags,' I said. 'We need to roll them up a tight as possible,' I instructed, as Richard and I slowly rolled the first one up, only to get to the end to find that it was still like trying to squeeze a cushion into a plastic sandwich bag. 'This is fucking stupid. Why would anyone make the bags that small?

'William, Elyse...' I yelled at them in the lounge. 'I told you to leave these sleeping bags alone? Why didn't you do as you were told?' As soon as the words tumbled from my mouth I felt bad – it wasn't their fault, because the problem would have presented itself sooner or later anyway. The problem was with the idiots who designed them, not my children.

'This is a waste of fucking time, why can't you just take them as they are?' Richard finally said. He had no patience with un-cooperative, inanimate objects.

I glared at him and stomped into the kitchen to grab a couple of bin liners from the kitchen drawer; I shoved the sleeping bags in and tied a knot to form a handle. I stood looking down on what had now become ludicrously impractical camping equipment.

'That's fine. What's wrong with those? You'll be able to carry them with no problem.'

The two full bin liners before me reminded me of Anthony's Nepal camping trip – and I stood foolishly in the garden room, imagining myself on a similar trip, struggling to keep pace with his long stride – trailing behind him with William and Elyse. All three of us with our sleeping bags bobbing about on our backs like large, black *Space Hoppers*, severely cramping his style as he lobbed his cigarette stub in sheer annoyance.

I bet his girlfriend wouldn't have a problem with her sleeping bag.

And then I thought about my family holidays.

Could I really see him staying poolside all day long in an all-inclusive resort? I couldn't. His head would have been exploding on a sun-lounger with sheer mind-numbing boredom.

I didn't really fit in with his life as it was, I could see that. But it didn't seem to stop me from imagining kissing him on a beach.

I calmed down and piled everything we needed for the sleepover by the front door, before dressing William and Elyse in their new Halloween costumes. William had chosen a skeleton outfit and Elyse a black and lime-green witches dress with long green plaits for her hair. Once again, I grabbed my camera to catch the moment, and, like their first day back at school photo, the camera was capturing them in a blur. It was fine in the lap-dancing toilets other than the mystical lighting, and it was fine with the pumpkins the other day. But then William and Elyse scarpered when they heard mum and dad in the hallway; they'd come to collect Elyse for her sleepover.

I quickly flicked through the photos I had managed to capture; the results being the most angelic Halloween photos I'd seen. Like the lap-dancing photos, they looked like they'd been touched by angels and the *really* blurred one of Elyse standing by herself made her look like a pixie or a fairy – not exactly scary-looking.

I made a mental note to hunt down the camera manual at some stage, then placed the camera on charge for later, and made Mum and Dad a drink.

I'd just put the milk back in the fridge when I heard William's football smash against the garden-room shutters.

'William! Right that's it.' I'd practically flown into the room yelling my words, not entirely sure what I meant by my ultimatum at that point, but I was sure the "it" would come to me. 'William, I keep telling you...you need to use the inside of your foot, not the outside, it'll give you more control over the ball. Like th—'

For about the second time that day I was on the verge of exploding at Richard.

I could mentally see myself going for the three-move combo – jab, low kick, reverse punch.

Christ! Was there any wonder my head was happily dreaming of snogging Anthony Hope on a beach? Richard noticed the rage on my face and quickly backtracked.

'You know you shouldn't play football indoors as Mummy doesn't like it.'

Richard's discipline was second to none.

William could smash up five thousand pounds worth of shutters and Richard would critique his ball control. William's attachment to a football was like watching a person with Tourette's Syndrome; no matter how many times you told him to stop, he still found his foot kicking it.

I returned to the kitchen, my feet slamming against the stone tiles, cursing the fact that the "it" in my discipline never managed to materialise.

Mum raised her eyebrows, she wasn't saying anything – she didn't need to, the look said it all, as in "...I would never have let you, your brother and your dad behave like that".

Dad's way of diffusing things was to leave with Elyse pretty swiftly. Richard and I watched Elyse animatedly walk over to dad's truck, pulling her lilac suitcase behind her. She'd packed everything a whole week early in over-excited anticipation. I'd sneakily re-packed, as her skills needed some fine honing to say the least.

She clambered in, her legs barely able to reach the footrest, and Dad threw her bag onto the seat next to her. We waved them off but I couldn't see her little face through the blackened glass.

Richard then helped me load everything into our car. The sleeping bags being so cumbersome in their current *Space Hopper* state meant that the equally impractical boot of the *CLK* was full with those alone; so the overnight bags and snacks were put on the front seat of the car.

'Okay, I think that's it,' I said, and climbed in.

'Have a good time both of you, drive carefully, love you...are you sure you've picked your phone up?' Richard was shouting over from the front door while holding Blue by his collar.

'Yes, I've got my phone. I'll call if we have any problems. Love you too and enjoy your peaceful night,' I shouted over to him and closed the car door, before starting up the engine.

The long journey to Magna wasn't as uneventful as it should have been. I'd opted for leaving my car at Maddy's and hitched a ride in Lorna's instead. Maddy had taken her car because she was worried she would need to leave at any point because of a sick relative.

It was very dark by this stage, and we made a quick stop for a *McDonalds* and a fuel top-up. But somehow Lorna managed to reverse into Maddy's car at the petrol pump, smashing the bumper and number plate. It was yet another one of life's more awkward moments, which managed to silence the conversation for most of the journey; Lorna was obviously pre-occupied with her thoughts. Henry, with his seven years of wisdom, had estimated the damage at about a grand's worth. Richard had clearly told the wrong person to drive carefully.

We pulled into the side road with the monstrous Magna building facing us. Magna must be one of the most intimidating buildings I've ever seen, and at night with poor street lighting it was even more so. I think it was the combination of sheer vastness, cold dark metal, and no windows. It was like staring at a rusty metal container blown-up so big that your eyes couldn't digest it in one take. Even inside the place it was dark. From past experience there, one felt blinded by the daylight afterwards and that was part of its appeal to kids.

This was the first time we'd ever been at night though.

We dragged all our stuff out of the cars. The *Space Hoppers,* along with carrier bags containing my food stash, practically cut off my circulation after twisting tightly round my fingers as I carried them inside. Lorna, as usual had way over-catered, right down to proper camping beds and a large bottle of *Bacardi.* We effectively signed our lives away on the Health & Safety forms on reception. I was praying that we were not going to be spending the night on the steelworks' floor; a tiny detail that Maddy could have conveniently forgotten to mention. It would have been like kipping on Dad's factory floor; waking up covered in oil and grease.

Thankfully this was not to be the case.

A witch with Alice Cooper eyeliner led us to a conference room. This was to be our communal bedroom for the night – not ideal, but more satisfactory than the alternative I'd imagined. We marked our territory using Lorna's camp beds and our sleeping beds. I noted that I was the only one to forget pillows and that

Henry had a cute child-size sleeping bag.

After settling ourselves in, we entered the main room. Halloween themed pop songs were playing in the background and, in contrast to the darkness of the main museum – this room was overly bright with fluorescent lighting. The boys and Lorna's daughter Mae had familiarised themselves with everything available, and had started to work their way round the themed creative activities laid out on different tables.

'Do you think they'll let us open that fire door?' Maddy asked. I wasn't sure whether the comment was aimed at me or Lorna.

'Why? It's not hot in here' I said, answering anyway, thinking that I wasn't particularly warm, even in my coat.

'No...you prat...so that I can have a cigarette. It's miles to the main entrance.'

'I'll go and ask. I'm sure they will,' said Lorna and she wandered off to sort it out. Although not quite as bad as Maddy, Lorna needed her fix at regular intervals too.

'They'd better do, or I'll kick off big time.' I didn't doubt that Maddy would kick off for a second, and prayed to myself that they didn't tell Lorna that the door was linked to an alarm.

'It's fine, we can stand out there,' Lorna confirmed. 'You coming, Nic?'

'No...I'm going to colour with Mae...it's okay – you two go off and slowly kill yourselves.' And with that I went over to the colouring table, grabbed a Halloween-themed picture and set about colouring in. I'd always found colouring with new felt-tips relaxing.

'Very good. Well done...would you like a gold star?' Maddy patronised.

I nodded and then shivered as the cold air that she had let in reached me.

'What are the boys doing?' she asked.

'Still making disgusting bug-filled gunge,' I answered, without losing focus on my colouring.

'Anyway...have you established who sent that text to Richard?'

'No. He deleted it. Says he's not bothered who sent it,' I said, whilst finishing the cauldron's flames.

'What text?' Lorna was clearly intrigued as she grabbed a picture to colour too.

'Richard got a text yesterday saying, "...cuckold. Always the last to know", can you pass me the green please, Mae?' and I started work on the witch's face.

'What's a cuckold?' Lorna asked, as she picked up a felt tip.

'The husband of an adulteress is the dictionary definition according to Richard. Don't worry Lorna, I'd never heard of it either – it's an old-fashioned word,' I reassured her, while wondering which part of the picture Lorna was going to colour purple.

'No, I hadn't either,' Maddy confirmed. 'Do you think Richard sent it, or has he made out it's been sent to him?'

'But why would Richard send a text to himself?' Lorna was struggling to keep up, having only just heard the story.

'Because she's hardly talking to him at the moment, so he thinks it's because she's having an affair, so he's sent it to test her reaction; see if she reacts guiltily.' Maddy swiftly brought Lorna up to speed with her theory.

'I am speaking to him,' I defended, noting that my colouring was becoming intense; all of the talk was ruining my picture.

'No, you're f—' and she stopped herself swearing in front of the kids '...errr...like you should be,' she added.

My eyes involuntarily glared at her. This was her manipulative way of making me confront things head on. As usual she'd got me cornered in a public space and she was doing her male peacock display; when she did this I wanted to pull her feathers out to get the other, calmer Maddy back. Maddy would sooner die before losing an argument in public. I was sure that the women sitting at the far end of the table were absolutely loving this; I did my best to avert their eyes.

'I think that the text has come from someone older, because of the word choice, but Richard insists it's not from him. I've confronted him with that one already, and he just got mad with me.'

The word used in the text was certainly baffling me. What I'd reasoned so far was that the more upmarket media would use the word cuckold, because it was precise if it was appropriate to a story. But most normal people, the sort of people we knew who had a grudge, would probably have sent a text which said something like: "...your missus is a slapper". There was something older or more sophisticated about this text – which made it feel even more sinister and carefully plotted somehow. But then, on the other hand, it was grossly inaccurate as I was not Richard's wife. So did that mean someone had tried to be clever, but had not really known the precise definition, or that this person didn't know us well enough to know we weren't married.

'But who would do something like that?'

'God knows...beats me, Lorna. Anyway, I've blocked my *Facebook* Wall from everyone who has Richard's mobile number, or would at least know how to get hold of it.'

I'd also left a message on mine and Maddy's Wall that said: "...words are open to interpretation and can be easily miscon-strued."

'Why *Facebook*?' Lorna was baffled by *Facebook* being brought into the conversation; I'd forgotten that she never signed up to it.

'Because the silly girl thinks she's playing a game with someone on there, that's why *Facebook*.'

'What? Who?' Lorna was even more intrigued and her eyes flashed with greater interest.

'Can I have the green back please, Nicole?'

'Yeah, sure, here you go, Mae. It doesn't matter, Lorna. It's obviously only an imaginary game,' I said, staring at Maddy. She was still standing and not joining in with the colouring.

'The key thing, Lorna,' I continued, 'is that my *Facebook* is the only place where any of my actions could possibly be construed as affair material. But even then, I can't for the life of me think how.'

And it was true I couldn't.

Everything was done so subtly, to pick anything untoward on my *Facebook* you would have needed to see both mine and Anthony's *Facebook* page together. Only Maddy knew about that game, but Maddy had never heard of the word. I knew that for a fact because when Richard had shown the text to her, she'd asked what it meant as well. Richard had taken the piss out of the fact that neither of us had heard of the word. But again this made me think that I must have been right about the word being old-fashioned; otherwise we were the three thickest people on the planet. And considering I wasn't the *most* of anything – this was highly unlikely.

'Well, you're just a tw...err...idiot and you need to sort it out with Richard. I still think it's Richard...why else wasn't there a number shown?' Maddy said, as her final word on the subject, and then busied herself fetching us a coffee.

I was stumped on that last point – I wasn't entirely sure why there wasn't a number, and I had no idea whether it was true that a text could be sent without leaving a number trace. But both Maddy and Richard had raised this issue, and now the text had been deleted so I couldn't examine it. But again the choice of word couldn't have been Richard. Richard liked precision with words – he was the one who finally decided to quit the Air Force over the fact that the word "invitation" was being used as a substitute for "order". He'd been called in to see the Commanding Officer for refusing an "invite" and swapping it for a shag in London.

The next hour passed swiftly and with fifty or so children and parents floating about the large space, the noise levels had a soporific effect. Unable to decipher one sound from the other, I was easily able to disappear into my own thoughts. It's as though my eyes were watching the games, but, in reality, they were seeing nothing in front of me. My vision was internalised seeing only Anthony Hope as I sat there.

It was the sheer impossibility of him, yet the fact I couldn't help but think that he was where I should be. He was somehow in my past, but also my future. What were the chances of him still not having got into a serious relationship, of him still being in the UK, and of him having noticed me among his five hundred or so *Facebook* friends? It felt like I was being given a second chance. But the second chance felt as cruelly impossible as the first time our lives crossed. And…why do I want to kiss him so much? If I kissed him, would I no longer crave him? Would it finally break the spell he had over me?

'You're quiet, Nicole,' Lorna stated, breaking into my thoughts.

'What? No...I'm just watching the kids,' I lied, as I still blankly stared at them. 'What time is the ghost walk?'

'After we've eaten. Which should be anytime soon,' Maddy informed us.

The food had been an unexpected feast, rendering our copious supplies unnecessary. After eating, we left the brightness of the conference rooms, and made our way to the main museum. A chain of people walked down the maze of stairs, and back through the voluminous reception, then through the double doors into the familiar darkness.

My eyes adjusted to the change in light relatively quickly, but the sudden drop in temperature as we entered the vast hollow space wasn't such a comfortable transition. I zipped up my jacket as far as it would go.

Our guide was a young-looking Count Dracula; in fact, he was probably still in his teens and like a colt, he was tall, but still had some filling out to do. But being a young male, our boys had taken to him straight away, hovering and craving his attention.

He stopped the group at the edge of the long, metal suspension bridge. The smell of steel travelled through my nose as I looked around at the old metal workings below me. It was as though, some years ago, someone would have shouted "down tools" and those tools would never be touched again.

'William was a worker here in the steel works...' instantly my William was hooked by the ghost story.

'Mummy, the ghost is called William, just like me,' he whispered, with a big grin.

'Yes, I know... that's cool. Concentrate on what he's telling you then,' I said, smiling back at him.

Count Dracula told us that William was a good man who worked hard for his family. And I already knew, before he said it, that he came to a tragic ending, which was why the poor hardworking bastard was stuck in here for eternity. I tried to stay focused, like the kids, but I've never really bought into the whole ghost thing – even a psychic night had been unable to dispel that belief. Staff at the factory always said it was haunted, but I never saw any evidence of it. I even worked many Sundays alone in there, and nothing strange ever occurred.

I could still hear the young man's voice recounting the tale but he drifted further into the background, as I once again turned my thoughts back to Anthony Hope. What if *Ilex Drapes* was always meant to close? If it hadn't closed down I would never have signed up to *Facebook* and tracked him down. Even the thing with James...had I not had that crush on James, Anthony Hope may not have hit my radar again. In all these years, I'd never so much as had a crush on anyone, and then I close *Ilex* and develop a crush on its Administrator. What if Anthony Hope was always my fate? What if there is such thing as fate?

Through my jumbled thoughts I sensed the group starting to make their way across the suspension bridge. All of their different shoes made unique sounds as they hit the metal walkway. I felt myself hang back, subconsciously preventing them from disturbing my daydreams. In my mind I could see the sand, the sea, Anthony's white shirt and jeans. As though to breathe life into one of his pictures I imagined the sea breeze (the cold circulating around me probably helped with this) then I imagined kissing him on the beach.

Then, as quick as that vision vanished, a new one formed and I saw myself walking towards him. It was as though my footsteps across the bridge were my footsteps towards my vision of Anthony Hope; I was aware of the bridge's gentle vibration and metallic echo with each of my steps. This time I felt that I would be able to touch him, hold him and feel him; he was the keeper of the missing part of my soul.

I finally reached the end of the bridge, only to enter the empty, painted black room with high ceiling and dim lighting. It was at that moment that I felt three sharp prods on my right shoulder.

'Yeah, what?' I spun to my right as I spoke. Maddy must have fallen behind too I thought to myself. 'Eh, where *are* you?' I said again, confused and resentful that I'd been pulled from my thoughts.

I instinctively turned my head one hundred and eighty degrees from my right to my left and back again, to find myself facing Maddy who was about seven or eight feet in front of me.

'You're there! What? *How did you just get there?*'

'What on earth are you going on about?'

'How did you just get from here to there?' I asked, still baffled.

'What are *you* going on about?'

'You're asking me? You just tapped me on the shoulder and I turned round to find out what you wanted and you're standing over there, not here.'

'I didn't tap you on the shoulder!'

'Yes, you did. I felt it. You prodded me three times,' I said, indignantly.

'Are you calling me a liar? How could I possibly tap you on the shoulder and then get all the way over here.'

'I *don't* know. But I know what I felt and someone did it.'

'There's only us here and it *wasn't* me!' she said as we both took another glance around the still-empty space. The source of the mystery text flashed through my mind. But we were in a secure building full of parents, kids and staff far removed from my ordinary life.

Logic alone said no one could have gone back over the bridge. We would have heard them and spotted them before they could reach the far end. The faster you moved on the bridge the more noise it made.

'I'm very aware of the fact there's only us here, which is precisely why it must have been you. Are you playing games with me?'

Why wouldn't she just own up to it... how long was she going to keep this up for?

'For God's sake! I didn't tap you on the shoulder, I swear to it.'

'On Henry's life?'

'On Henry's life, on everyone's life, look – no fingers crossed.' She held her hands in the air. 'I didn't do it!'

'Well then – who did?'

'You must have imagined it.'

'I did not – I can still feel the finger...'

Continually thinking about it had provoked a burning sensation beneath the thick padding of my jacket. The prodding was so firm and decisive that it was as though the finger was extended as it hit the top of my shoulder. I knew I couldn't possibly have imagined it.

'Well...I suggest that you forget about it. Come on, we'd better catch up with Lorna and the others.'

Resigned from reasoning with her any further, I trailed with my thoughts still working through the last few minutes. I was, by this stage, feeling unnerved but there had to be an explanation and now this was going to bug the hell out of me until I'd solved it.

Just as we headed for the room to the right, the rest of the group returned to the large space. I stood in a trance among the children and parents; still replaying in my head what had just taken place. I knew what I had felt; there was no disputing it. It was the rest of it that wasn't making sense.

I knew deep down that Maddy couldn't have done it, as it wasn't physically possible, but she was the only suspect I had. But if she was prepared to swear on Henry's life, then she was definitely not lying.

CHAPTER TEN

The rest of that evening passed in a haze, interspersed with personal disasters. My new plain black pyjamas turned out not to be so plain – they had the words: "mirror, mirror on the wall, who'll be fabulous at the ball", written across them in tiny silver lettering, fine if you're four.

Henry had out-manoeuvred me on the toilet run and, as a consequence, I'd spent that last part of the night in a pint-sized, pee-soaked sleeping bag, while he was curled up next to Maddy – in mine. But while necking the *Bacardi* I had established that "William" the ghost didn't exist. It turned out that the staff had made up the ghost storyfor the kids. So despite Maddy virtually putting a ban on any further discussion on the matter I was still bugged as hell by the whole shoulder-tapping thing, and was glad to get back home. William was more intrigued about it than bugged though.

'Daddy, Daddy guess what? Mummy got tapped on the shoulder by a ghost.'

'Did she?' Richard said, clearly not sure what to make of William's tale, considering we'd been on a Halloween adventure for kids. 'So you all had a good time then?'

'Yeah, it was brilliant, Daddy. Can I have some cereals?' he said going off on a tangent.

'Yes, in a minute. Let me just help Mummy get everything out of the car.'

As we pulled the bags out, I filled Richard in on the shoulder tapping but, like everyone else, he didn't really take the incident seriously. He appeared to put it down to either my head being the only thing tapped last night, or someone living did do it. My attempt to explain that that theory was impossible failed to register with him, but that was because he wasn't there to see the space we were in.

'Your dad phoned and said that he'll drop Elyse back off in a few hours. She's been fine over there.'

'Yeah I know, I've already rung them, I want to take a shower now because I feel yucky.' I said, then gave him a summarised version of Henry's sleeping-bag saga.

'Do you want some breakfast?' Richard kindly asked whilst sorting William's cereal.

'No, the food there was amazing, already had a good English breakfast. Did you enjoy your curry last night?' I practically ran upstairs, not waiting for his answer, because I was desperate to get clean, but I was equally desperate to get on the computer, and with Elyse not due back for a while, I knew I was able to get on there without any bother.

'Yes...it was very nice...thanks for asking,' he shouted up to me.

Having showered, I quickly threw on my combats, grabbed a top, and left my hair to dry on its own with the intention of tying it back later. My skin felt tight, so I dipped my finger in the jar of moisturiser on the bathroom shelf and patted it into my skin on my way back downstairs, before disappearing unseen into the study.

'Do you want this tea in there with you? I take it you're going on *Facebook*?' I felt my neck tense and my face scrunch up. I paused momentarily, having been caught red-handed.

Yes...and yes, please,' I shouted back, sounding as unperturbed as possible. Suddenly logging onto *Facebook* was the lesser of two evils.

I waited for the PC to fire up. Richard put my tea on the desk, sliding a pile of books and papers out of the way in the process, which reminded me once again, that like everywhere else in the house I really needed to sort the study out.

'Do you fancy a shag later?' he said casually. 'If the kids go to bed at a reasonable time, obviously,' he added.

'Dunno, I'm not at later right now, so I don't know,' I said, thinking that it wasn't one of my *pencilled in his diary rota* days, and by asking for it, he'd just put me right off. Besides my focus was heavily on my PC.

'Okay, well see how you feel later,' and he disappeared back into the kitchen, leaving Blue behind who was curled up on the corner armchair creasing William and Elyse's school uniforms, which were draped over it. I was too impatient to move them elsewhere and instead I tapped my fingers on the desk as I waited for the search engine to appear on my screen.

When it did, I typed in the words:

Three taps on shoulder + meaning

And within seconds, my screen was full of results, but when I actually looked at them most were offering definitions of tap and shoulder. I was *quite* sure even I knew what a shoulder was and what a tap was in several different contexts, so I tried again...

Tapped on the shoulder three times

This time it pulled through different pages from the web.

Other people had posted messages on forums wanting to know exactly the same as me. It seemed quite a common phenomenon and always three taps, same finger. But I'd never heard of it before. But neither had I heard of moving keys, windows having a mind of their own and text messages without number traces. As for taps on the shoulder, those who had experienced it seemed as freaked as me, though, which was obviously why they'd written on the forums. I sipped my tea intermittently as I read through posted replies. Some said it was a *possible muscular twinge*; a nervous twitch, that could need medical attention. But there was nothing wrong with my shoulder, and anyway, it wasn't even a twinge, it was a prod; a purposeful, unmistakable, finger prod.

Some entries said: *friendly ghost or spirit*, but more said *Guardian Angel*. A tap on the right shoulder is your Guardian Angel trying to get your attention. *Try meditating to communicate,* I read. *They want you to pay attention to something.* To what though? What am I supposed to be paying attention to? No idea.

I couldn't believe that I was even buying into this.

But the right shoulder? Guardian Angel is on the right side. So what if the tap was on the left, I curiously wondered and typed more key words into my search engine. I scrolled through the results until I found something: three taps on the left is the Devil, the Fallen Angel. Thank the Lord, quite literally, that mine was on the right. But an angel on Halloween? Were there angels on Halloween? That didn't make sense either. Since when have there been angels with their wings and halos alongside witches, pumpkins and ghosts? Angels are linked to religion and spirituality: Halloween is more commercial and about the wicked. God knows, again quite literally. Wasn't there supposed to be a drop in temperature with ghosts as well? Not that I would have noticed in there – it was already too cold. At least I wasn't the only nutter on the planet it had happened to, if nothing else.

Thinking of Halloween reminded me that we had entered November. So keeping with my *Alice in Wonderland* theme, I posted a quick Status Update on Facebook...

11:45 *White Rabbit White Rabbit White Rabbit*

I kept the PC logged on, because I intended to spend more time on it later looking at Anthony Hope's Wall. I picked up my mug, and after three failed verbal cautions, grabbed Blue by the collar, pulled him off the chair and went to see what Richard and William were up to.

I sat chilling with them in the lounge, watching some crap show that William had put on TV until Dad arrived with Elyse, who came through the door still insisting on pulling her suitcase herself. She looked like a *Polly Pocket* air stewardess and gave me a quick hug, wrapping herself round my legs – she'd obviously missed me.

After releasing me she joined William on the sofa. William once again filled Dad in on my ghostly experience, which was greeted with a mocking laugh from Dad and Richard.

'Yes, well for your information. It's an angel. Three taps on the right shoulder is an angel wanting to get my attention,' I said, not quite believing that I'd let those words fall from my mouth. But it was too late.

'Where have you got that from? Is that what you were doing in the study...looking it up?' Richard asked, still laughing at me.

'Yes,' I said defiantly.

Dad made me run through the whole story, because he could clearly see that I had been affected by it.

'It could have been a member of staff – they'll have set you up,' he finally said.

'Dad!!' I almost screamed at him. 'There was no member of staff around.'

'They would have been on a pulley, were winched in to tap you on the shoulder and got heaved out of the way again,' he suggested.

'Are you being serious?' I said incredulously. 'Dad this wasn't some multi-million-pound stage performance of *Chitty Chitty Bang Bang at Halloween*...this was just a few members of staff, doing a few extra hours to entertain kids. Plus, from where I was stood, there wasn't the mechanics to have a pulley system with some silly twit flying around above me. Your theory is impossible...utterly ridiculous,' I said, feeling infuriated by an explanation which could only have come from the mind of a design engineer.

'Oh well. Must have been a ghost or angel then,' he said, backing down and leaving me to stew in my own insanity. 'Well...I'd better get back to your mum. I'll leave you to the madhouse, Richard,' he said, as he made a retreat to the front door. 'Bye you two,' he shouted over to William and Elyse who, after being reunited for all of two minutes were already in an almighty bust up over the lounge television. Why does Elyse have to scream when they fight? The noise was adding to the cacophony around me.

'Yeah, thanks for bringing Elyse back, Bill,' Richard said.

'And…thanks for having her last night. Thank Mum for me,' I shouted after him, then remembered to make Elyse thank him too.

'Thank you Gwaaadaaaad,' she shouted, before going for another sly kick on William who went into an *Oscar*-winning performance of a slow, painful death.

'There will have been someone there, you just didn't see them, that's all it is,' Richard said as he closed the door on Dad. He meant well, but I wanted to punch him for it.

'Look, I'm telling you, no one could have moved that fast,' and, to prove my point, I forced Richard and William into a shoulder tapping improvised role-play session in the kitchen; if nothing else, it separated William and Elyse. Both eventually agreed with me – you couldn't tap someone on the shoulder and move fast enough into a position without being seen. So at least we'd cleared that point up.

'So, are you going to let it drop for a bit,' Richard asked; now sounding like Maddy.

'Okay, I will. But…you don't think that something bad is going to happen do you? Am I being warned about something? What about that text? Do you think they're connected?'

'No!'

Yep, he was definitely sounding like Maddy and so I went to fetch William and Elyse's uniforms from the study chair instead. *So much for being organised,* I thought to myself as I re-ironed them, but this time placed them on the chair in the hall. I then slid myself in front of the laptop in the garden room – I did not want to creep back into the study. My theory was that if I was sat only a few feet away from the lounge door, I wasn't exactly excluding myself.

I logged on to *Facebook* and left a few notes on my Wall about the shoulder tapping, and effectively forced Maddy into a written declaration, on Henry's life, that it wasn't her who did it, and within four minutes she sworn on her Wall that it wasn't her.

I then clicked onto Anthony Hope's Wall.

Just clicking on his Wall had my tummy in fluttering knots. I could see a link he'd posted for some event he was performing at that weekend. I clicked on it to open it up fully so I could read all of the text. At the very bottom it said: *Catch the flippin' frog – Next Time 13th Dec – log it.*

'Catch the flippin' frog.' I said the words back again.

This statement only seemed crazy if it *wasn't* directed at me. It had me wondering whether he had just given me an opportunity to meet up with him in a few weeks' time. He'd given me a venue, a date, and ample time to organise getting there. Why else would he use such a stupid line to forward sell an event?

But merely thinking about seeing him sent a sexual wave through my body as I imagined the venue and thought about what I would wear for the occasion. But then reality kicked in because how the hell would I sneak off to some venue in London unnoticed by Richard? Even something five weeks away wasn't remotely possible – he may as well have been in New York for all it was worth. But then could I do it, if I really tried to engineer it? I didn't know.

But why would he be interested in me? Why would a man who could take his pick from any twenty-something groupie be remotely interested in me. But then why wouldn't he think it easy for me to get somewhere on a particular date – my *Facebook* made me look like a socialite from my pictures. How was he supposed to know that I'd only stepped foot in a lap-dancing club once in my entire life, and yes, I did have photos of two other clubbing nights with the Maddy, Lorna and a couple of other friends. But their timing had been unfortunate, in so far as, I had barely been in a club since having William and Elyse and both occasions were since signing up to *Facebook*. All in all, my *Facebook* gave an unintentional edited version of my life.

I wrote a message on my Wall.

It would be lovely...if only I could escape at the drop of a hat...

Again, this was a message that would only make sense to him *if he was watching me.*

I felt Richard slide into the bed next to me and his hand wandered onto my thigh, as he moved his head close to my ear. I felt his warm breath which was minty from his toothpaste.

'Do you fancy a shag then?' he said.

Ugghhh! My head screamed.

'No, I'm really tired. Sorry...night – love you,' and I turned my back to him.

'What is wrong with you,' he said, annoyed.

'Nothing. I'm just tired. Go to sleep,' I replied, and somehow I don't know how, I managed to sleep dreamlessly that night. Like a boxer knocked out for nine, I came round the next morning on ten, fighting fit and desperately biding my time to get onto the laptop for a slightly longer run than a few minutes. However, having William and Elyse around, I knew I was probably going to have to battle for this one. I also knew, at the very worst, that William and Elyse were back at school in a couple of days, having finally got to the end of half-term. But the angel thing was still bugging the life out of me.

I wanted to know what I should be paying attention to. I guess I was hoping that it would lead to an overall explanation for everything strange that had happened. At this point, I had a theory about which direction I should be aiming at. I hadn't even got the patience to get showered and dressed, in case I missed a quiet, harmonious moment away from William and Elyse. I was like a junkie waiting to get hold of my fix.

Richard eventually disappeared into the garden with William for a kick around. For once, I was grateful for the overzealous approach to what should be a hobby. But William and Elyse being separated meant that Elyse would play happily without tormented interruption.

I put the soft broom back into the utility room and brought

the laundry basket into the lounge and sat sorting socks into pairs, whilst watching Elyse play with her dolls for a bit. After a while I disappeared into the study and hit the search engine on the PC.

I typed in my words:

Anthony Hope + Bible + Angels + Nicole

The old PC was playing up again, so I had to delete my words and start again. But it then turned to black. I cursed it and had to patiently wait for it to return to normal. But this was my theory: angels are biblical, and one way or another they had started cropping up left, right and centre in my life recently, which had started after my *iPod* had that funny glitch. So I was starting to wonder whether there was anything in the Bible, any passage that referred to an Anthony or even a Nicole, which would give some kind of link to us. Perhaps there was something in there that was relevant to me at this point in my life.

I was fully aware that it was a crazy thought, but everything I had ever considered to be the norm was getting turned on its head.

A few moments later my screen was full of cached results...

A Hope's novel: Anthony Hope

Simon Dale by Anthony Hope

Anthony Hope author of Simon Dale

I laughed. My search enquiry had pulled up some book by an author with the same name as my Anthony.

I looked at the words in my search bar...

Anthony Hope + Nll

This is what had been left on my search enquiry after it started to play up; most of my letters were missing.

It wasn't quite the tiny cryptic message in the Bible I was hoping for. But, out of curiosity I decided to click on one of the cached results.

Buy this book online: An historical novel written in 1898 involving the Actress and Courtesan Nell Gwyn.

I felt myself shiver.

This was weird, very weird: a man called Anthony Hope wrote a book about an actress and courtesan.

I had trained as an actress, and technically, I was a courtesan, although I was not living in the court of a king. But like "cuckold", "courtesan" isn't a word used nowadays. The fact that Richard was still married to his wife made me a *courtesan*, well sort of, as a *courtesan* is a woman who takes the place of the wife and Richard was in the top two per cent of the UK earners, so he could be referred to as a person of high social standing. So…that fact qualified me as the modern equivalent of courtesan as much as it shamed me to admit.

I was starting to think that my computer had played up deliberately. It was like having a ghost in my laptop. My life had taken a crazy turn. I didn't know about Halloween – but I definitely seemed to have bats in the belfry.

It was as though I was no longer in the driving seat. The way I saw it was: you just didn't get tapped on the shoulder by Mr Nobody, and then go and discover a book written by a man with the name Anthony Hope that was about a courtesan and a trained actress; life didn't happen that way.

I knew Maddy would love my latest nonsensical shit and this was yet something else I couldn't discuss with Richard. I probably should have set up a box-file labelled "issues requiring discussion with Richard", along with another, labelled "stuff I can't get my head around". I didn't want to hedge a bet on which would end up the fullest.

CHAPTER ELEVEN

After discovering the Anthony Hope novel I needed to know more about the story which I considered as natural curiosity. All I wanted was a short summary of the plot; a synopsis. I wanted to see if the only coincidence was the author's name and Nell Gwyn's profession. But it was easier said than done, and all I'd found were links to sites that enabled me to purchase the book and the odd site, which would allow me to read it online. I couldn't be bothered to wade through those; I wanted to know quickly. If there wasn't a synopsis, surely there must be someone in the world who had reviewed this book at some point? I stole my eyes away from the screen for an instant and caught a glimpse of William through the shutter-slats, climbing over the field fence, he was obviously nipping to see the neighbour's little boy.

I turned back to the screen and decided to just search for Anthony Hope – the author's name. I'd finished typing that in as Richard walked into the garden room with one of Elyse's dolls perched on his shoulder.

'Ooh…look, I have an angel on my shoulder,' he mocked as he held the doll in place.

'Piss off – it's not funny,' I said dryly.

'God…lighten up! Where's the carefree, happy, smiley Little N gone? Anyway, what are you looking up now?'

'Nothing,' and as quick as a flash, I'd hit the minimise button at the top of my screen.

'Nothing?' he repeated, but I knew that he didn't believe me.

He disappeared into the kitchen to read the papers and I clicked on the maximise button to pull the full screen back up and I headed for an encyclopaedia article.

I took a few seconds to look at an old black-and-white photo of Anthony Hope, the author; it must have been taken while he was anything from late twenties to his forties. He had a distinguished face and had lost most of his hair, but what was left showed that he had once been dark-haired.

Died in 1933 of throat cancer at the age of seventy.

Throat cancer? I touched my throat. I'd had a bad throat since Halloween – it had started late afternoon that day.

So was I being haunted by the ghost of Anthony Hope and not an angel?

I read about Anthony Hope being the son of a vicar; he'd received a knighthood, and was clearly a clever man having been educated at Oxford. But I still couldn't find the synopsis.

I was sure I'd heard of Nell Gwyn so I typed in Anthony Hope + Nell Gwyn.

Loads of entries for Nell Gwyn came up, so many that I almost felt foolish not knowing anything about her. But then I wasn't much of an historian. After skim reading a few articles I found out that she had been the mistress of King Charles II. Considering that the book was "an historical novel", as in a story mixing historical facts with fiction, I took it that the character, Simon Dale, was a fictional man, on the basis that he failed to be mentioned in any historical articles on the Internet in connection with King Charles II and Nell Gwyn.

I took a break, and made myself and Richard a mug of tea. While the kettle boiled I pondered whether in this book Nell was the King's mistress, and the protagonist Simon Dale was some kind of fictional extra-curricular love interest. But I couldn't tell from the bits and pieces I'd found whether I was right to assume that Nell took the role of both the actress and courtesan in the story. I poured the milk into the tea thinking that really I needed to buy the book which would be far easier than attempting to scrape bits together online. But then, owning a book with Anthony's name slashed across the front probably wouldn't be such a good idea.

I put the mug of tea on the oak coffee table, within reach of Richard, and gave him a prod. He had taken one of his catnaps and was flat out of the sofa with his jaw slackened. Blue was in the same sleeping position. They looked like a pair of corpses and here I was *Googling* dead people. Elyse was sitting at Richard's feet, brushing her doll's hair.

I sat back at the laptop and re-typed *Anthony Hope* one more time, just see if there was anything else I could find and then stumbled across one of his famous quotes:

Economy is going without something you do want in case you should, someday, want something you probably won't want.

I found the words arresting and as I was about to read on I felt a draught behind me.

'Why have you just crept up behind me, you made me jump?' I said, annoyed. My nerves were still jangling from the other day without Richard peeping over my shoulder.

'I didn't creep up behind you, I just wanted to see what you are looking up now and what has you so engrossed?'

'You did creep up - you've even got your reading glasses on,' I argued. 'Anyway, I'm looking up an old novel called *Simon Dale.* Have you heard of it?'

'No... Why on earth are you looking that up?'

'Just am. I think it's pretty much a long-forgotten book about a fictional man and an actress stroke courtesan.'

'So why are you interested in it?'

'Told you, I just am...no reason.'

'Strange. Look, Nicole, you have been acting really odd lately, are you okay?'

'Yes, I'm fine,' I lied again; this was starting to become a habit.

'Are you going to get off that thing soon?'

'Yes in a minute...I am nearly finished' I said, thinking I'd definitely slipped into *Wonderland*. The plot was different but the madness was all there.

Richard left me to it and I logged onto *Facebook*. After the comment I'd left only the day before about not being able to escape at the drop of a hat – I wanted to see if the living Anthony had left anything at all since then which acknowledged the impossibility of anything happening between us.

If only he would speak to me, not in the cryptic way, but in the way two humans should communicate.

And then, I typed a short message in the small information box on my Wall. It was a space which didn't filter through the Newsfeed; it was a summary of how I was feeling at that moment.

My life is as mad as a hatters. Ilex Drapes showroom had new signage put up yesterday and it is now a bridal shop. Richard asked me if I wanted to "kiss a frog"

Who is writing???

I noticed Anthony was online too and within minutes his Status Update appeared at the top of my Newsfeed...

09:10 Anthony doesn't know...

He managed to make me jump for the third time. I posted my own Status Update.

11:47 Nicole is thinking shit?????

Within in two seconds of posting my Status I realised what he'd done. He'd been onto my page and he'd read my note. He was responding to my words: he wasn't sure who was writing either, that's what he must have meant. If crazy things were happening my end, maybe they were his end too? Or was it that he had simply done what I wanted him to do and posted a Status Update that was more obviously connected to me.

I felt such an idiot for not thinking before I updated my Status and I logged off in a huff, took a hot shower, busied myself emptying the washer, put another load in, helped Elyse dress her doll for a bit, but an hour later I'd finally succumbed to my urges and was back on *Facebook*. I felt relief wash over me as I read his next Status Update.

12:36 Anthony KNOWS he wants THAT though!

He knows he wants me. The words almost made me want to cry with joy. It amazed me how his words, when isolated from all other senses, had power over me. I was unable to hear him, unless from inside my head, I couldn't touch him, smell or taste him; all I could do was stare into a photo of his eyes – the irony was that I almost felt like I was at the mercy of a fictional man.

Thinking about "who was writing", I decided to use the About Me section on my *Facebook* page to try and steer him towards the old novel. I had no idea whether he knew I'd trained as an actress, I think he knew I wasn't married to Richard. There was always the possibility that he'd stumbled on the author who took his name years ago. He may have already known about this book, which was why he'd considered it fun to toy with me. But then it dawned on me: what if the ghost of Anthony Hope was trying to warn me away from the living Anthony Hope? What if the fictional man he created in his novel doesn't end up with Nell Gwyn?

There was definitely something strange about the sequence of events as in they were all connected with two common threads: *Facebook* and *Anthony Hope*.

I retraced the string of events in my mind and came to the conclusion that the whole thing was utterly crazy; yet, when laid out, it seemed to make sense if you accepted the paranormal. Even the strange incident with the keys and windows fitted if you accepted the idea of spirits. And that explanation was more palatable than isolating the text message as the work of an evil *Facebook* stalker.

But it was as though I still missing something – some vital link.

CHAPTER TWELVE

I didn't realise what I was doing was considered a dangerous practice; I didn't even have a name for it at the time. I knew it was a weird thing to do, but then again I'd no intention of telling anyone I'd tried it; the same way as you don't bother telling people you had a go at trying to bend a metal spoon after watching Uri Geller on TV. I think it was more a case of what the author, Arthur Conan Doyle once had Sherlock Holmes say: *Once you eliminate the impossible, whatever remains, no matter how improbable, must be the truth.*

So I continued to sit and stare at Anthony Hope's face while I mulled things over. Just looking at him made my eyelids feel heavy; as though my pupils had dilated so much that the lids were compelled to close to protect them from taking in too much light. I stared more into his rich eyes. The laptop cursor turned into a hand when my finger scrolled across the mouse pad and I used the tiny hand to trace the outline of his mouth, his head, his neck; the places I so longed to touch. Just thinking about him sent soft, tickly electric pulses through my body, it make me shiver like someone had brushed by skin.

I put my hand to my mouth, with my elbow resting on the table, and took a deep breath. I so wanted to feel his hands gently pulling my hair from my face as he tenderly and slowly kissed me, making me feel even smaller in his arms, and then the unwelcome sound of my mobile interrupted me.

'Hi…it's me – how are you?'

'Fine. How's the bump on your car gone down?' I suddenly remembered that I'd not asked Maddy about it since Saturday.

The car she was driving at the moment belonged to one of her relatives; her own car went back to the finance company after the dawn raid.

'I'm letting everyone else deal with it as I can't handle it…too awkward with it being Lorna and them being in so much financial shit at the moment,' she said.

'Probably a good idea to stay out of it,' I agreed.

'Anyway, they've got to get a couple of quotes for repair, so I think they'll decide what to do once they're in. Thought I might pop in for a bit tomorrow afternoon before I pick Henry up from school. Will you be in?'

'Yeah sure, it's fine. Where are you now I asked?'

'I'm at Steve's mum's. Anyway what are you up too? Richard says your acting weird.'

'Does he? Have you heard of Nell Gwyn?' I asked, while doodling flowers on top of the notes I'd made on her life history.

'No, why...should I know her? Hey, what's the noise in the background?'

'It's Mick-The-Cleaner. He's vacuuming. Anyway that doesn't matter, back to Nell I have been looking her up. She died in 1687, when she was only thirty-seven, so no, you don't know her as such, just may have heard of her, that's all. I'm piecing bits and pieces together since my shoulder taps.'

'For fuck's sake. Richard's right. So...do you think she's your ghost? Why is she your ghost?'

'I just think she may be connected to this whole thing somehow,' I said, omitting to mention Anthony Hope's novel.

'Do you now think you were Nell Gwyn in some former life?'

'No, I don't mean that.'

'Have you ever been regressed to a past life then?'

'As a matter of fact I have been – well, sort of, it didn't work. The whole event hadn't been my idea...think I was too uptight...they couldn't get me into the hypnotic trance thing and the imaginary door I had to get through was locked. Mine wouldn't open.'

'That figures. So, tell me about Nell then.'

'Nell Gwyn was an orange seller turned actress and courtesan, she was the mistress of King Charles II in the 1600s. Hers is a bit of a Cinderella rags to riches fairy story really. They called her

Pretty, Witty, Nell.'

'Very interesting...if you are into to that kind of thing...but so what?'

'I'll explain more tomorrow.'

'Fine...have it your way...I'll see you tomorrow – unless, by some fluke, I see you on the school run later.' This was her dig at me because she always insisted on getting there earlier than I did.

'See ya...bye,' and I put down the phone, and continued to chew at my already battered pencil.

I tried to re-focus on my textbooks for the next hour or so, but my head wasn't taking things in very well, and it needed to be working at full strength because my next really big exam was looming.

I headed for the kitchen with my textbook, piece of paper and pencil in my hand so I could double-check my textbook answers while the kettle boiled. I then recalled something I'd read on Saturday: *try using a meditation to communicate with your Angel.*

I wondered if you could do this with ghosts or spirits? I still wasn't entirely sure what I was dealing with here, if anything at all. I then grabbed my pencil, closed my eyes and completely blanked my mind, well almost, as the thought of this being crazy flashed into my brain first, but then I forced myself to breathe deeply for a few minutes until my head was entirely clear – no thoughts, just calm, and I let the pen do its work.

There were no voices with verbal communication coming through, nothing but a feeling. A feeling of where the pen should go, but I had no idea of its direction. Eventually, the sensation stopped, the pen no longer felt compelled to move and I opened my eyes. On top of all my workings out for the text questions was now an incomplete number eight.

Why wasn't the eight finished off? I wondered. *Had I opened my eyes too soon?* What had also intrigued me was that I wasn't looking at some aimless squiggle, which was what I'd expected to see when my eyes opened. Again, spurred by curiosity, determined to leave no stone unturned, I wanted to know more, and besides this was far more interesting than my textbooks.

I left the unmade tea and jumped back on the laptop, strumming my fingers on the keyboard while I thought through a method of searching an incomplete eight. I couldn't think of one so I simply typed in number eight + meaning, and as usual, the Internet had it covered.

But, once again, I felt like a dumbass, because I'd completely forgotten that number eight is the mathematical symbol for infinity. I continued clicking on and off different sites that looked interesting. I read that number eight was the number of cosmic balance, victory, karma and money, and that in the Bible it is the eighth day (the resurrection), it is seen as a transfiguration and beginning of a new era or order; which follows the seventh day, the day of rest, and the sixth, the day of creation.

Then I found loads of articles with references to the Beijing Olympics which opened up on the eighth day, of the eighth month, 2008 at eight seconds, eight minutes past eight p.m., all because the Chinese believed in the lucky power of number eight, and in typical Chinese fashion they'd embraced this to the full. In fact, it would take another hundred years before they could do it in such style again – as in the year 2108, and that was providing they won the Olympic host bid at that point – so 2008 really was their lucky year.

This was all very interesting, but how did eight relate to me and what eights are relevant in my life?

William James, my little small wonder, was to turn eight in February. But that one little precious thought then sent my thoughts snowballing – thinking about William turning eight reminded me that it was eight years to the month since I'd last seen Anthony. I'd left *Opus* in November 2000. It struck me as strange that in the year we pass through 08/08/08, Anthony Hope is back on the scene. It felt like us working together had been the day of creation, the seven years of separation had been the days of rest, and eight was the resurrection. It was silly, but for some reason I found it logical.

So…were we destined to be together forever? Or did I write an incomplete eight as in forever not mine?

The one thing I did know for certain was that I'd never have noticed the significance of the number eight between us if I hadn't just drawn what I had. My thoughts then turned back to the Olympics; the eighth of August was the day before my birthday. That meant that I was still thirty-seven on the day it opened. On the eighth of August, 2008, I was the age of Nell Gwyn when she died.

Was there something in this spiritual communication, or just many coincidences? I pondered and then gave Richard a quick call on his mobile, before vowing to get on with my text questions. He picked up on the third ring.

'Hi…is there a problem?' he asked, confused by the fact I was calling him for a change.

The lack of noise in the background told me that he was sitting in his office. His mahogany desk was in the centre of the room and other than files it was relatively bare; quite bland really. He always said that clients went there for his brain, not to sit admiring accessories and artwork – Richard had an air of confidence, which only comes with a superior brain. Sometimes talking to him on the office line reminded me of the days where I would make excuses to take files to the upstairs offices, just so I could drop in his room on the way – our relationship had been exciting in the early days. Sex had been the tool for breaking through the enigma he was. He'd propositioned me at his work Christmas party and pretty much offered me a financial arrangement for sex which I had taken as a joke until he mentioned it again the next time we were at work together. After the initial shock I declined the money and took the uncompli-cated sex with a man who told me he would never leave his wife.

He did eventually pay the mortgage on a house for me – it made financial sense and was better than sneaking in and out of hotel rooms.

'Problem? No. One thing though...do you insure any buildings which used to belong to Nell Gwyn?' I asked.

'Why on earth do you want to know that? I've no idea...are you sure that you are okay?'

Just as I was about to confirm that I was fine, I heard Maddy's voice in the hall talking to Mick-The-Cleaner, and I explained that I needed to go.

I was a little confused because I was sure that she'd said she was calling round tomorrow, but she bounced into the kitchen, looking sleek in her fitted black dress, leggings and what looked like new leather boots, and suddenly I felt self-conscious in my mismatched outfit: tatty *Dr Who* black/grey cardigan, grey T-shirt and khaki combats which reminded me that one trouser leg was still caught inside the *Ugg* boot as I went to free it. I hadn't even bothered to put a brush through my hair after the shower and it had dried with unflattering kinks, which was the nearest it ever gets to a curl. To top it all, my skin looked pale from no make-up and lack of sunlight.

In fact, as I flicked the kettle on, a quick glimpse in the mirror told me that I looked strained. I had the look of a mad scientist, who had just been pulled out of his lab after getting close to discovering the secrets of the universe.

'I thought you were coming tomorrow,' I said pleasantly, because I was genuinely pleased she'd popped in – I was dying to tell her about my discoveries.

'Yeah. But I thought I'd call now because you're acting really strange.'

'I know. Well I am, and I'm not...it's just all this weird stuff,' and I told her about Anthony Hope's novel.

'So you now think your Anthony Hope is the reincarnated author Anthony Hope, is that what you're saying?'

'No...'

Instead I told her about all the other bits of information I had unearthed, including the unfinished number eight. Then, after considerable and expected verbal abuse, she finally humoured me by taking a look at my drawing.

'It's not an incomplete eight you idiot, it's a fish – you've drawn a fish... I can't believe I'm even having this conversation,' she said and I took another look at it, seeing it with fresh eyes. She was right; it was a fish.

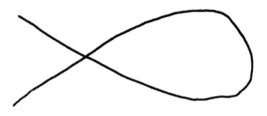

'You do the insane thing of drawing with your eyes closed and you don't even see it's a fish,' she added cockily. 'It takes me to see it.'

If she'd managed to get any more enthusiasm in her voice she would have convinced me that it was perfectly normal to do such a thing.

'Well, maybe I was supposed to see eight first. That is a number that is relevant to me. I'll look up the meaning of a fish later,' I said, feeling more stupid than ever.

Perhaps I saw it as a number first because I'd spend all morning looking at numbers. My head was full of numbers – that was the only rational explanation I could think of and, by this stage it had really started to feel as though it was how I should have seen it.

'But the book, how weird is that though? It's almost like that Jane Austin thingy on TV I watched a few months back where the woman from today's world got caught up the classical fictional book and ends up falling for Mr Darcy, isn't it?' But as I said it, I knew there was a vital difference: one was entirely made up and the other was my life.

'I don't know...I didn't watch it. Look, I admit that all the coincidences are *really* weird. But you are starting to worry me. And where do you really think this is all going? You don't seriously think you're going to be running off with him and living happily ever after, do you?'

'No, of course I don't think that,' I said, whilst thanking God she couldn't see my fantasies. 'It's just...he's playing games with me, I can't help myself, and now on top of all else, I can't get my head around all the weird Nell Gwyn stuff.'

'Well...if you want my opinion, he needs to get a proper job at his age instead of having time to play silly games with you,' she said, in a superior tone.

'Proper job?' I raised my eyebrows but held my tongue. If I'd held back any further I swear I would have choked on it. It was the precise definition of "proper job" which had instantly sent a snapshot of one of Maddy's so called proper jobs into my head: one day in a call centre which turned out to be promoting sex lines – she didn't even have a dirty voice! But I really didn't want to get into the career choice debate, and besides, Anthony Hope wasn't the one on police bail.

'Yes, proper job. Being some singer in a band no one has heard of isn't exactly a proper job; not exactly *JLS* are they? Anyway, I'll have another drink with you and then I need to nip to the shop before getting Henry. Have you got any chocolate or cake or something sweet in?'

Maddy left shortly after making do with nuts, because other than a jar of *Nutella*, raisins or a bowl of cereal, I'd nothing sweet to offer. But her swift departure allowed me just enough time to get back at the laptop to see if I could find anything relevant connected to a fish; which I knew wasn't going to remotely help me through my next exam, but was far more interesting.

I headed for the study PC because Mick-The-Cleaner had started cleaning the stone floor in the garden room.

The study PC hadn't been shut down properly, which was convenient. I pulled the cord to open the wood venetian slats, then I typed in: *fish + symbol*.

Once again, my screen was full of results.

After opening and closing several sites, I finally settled on one that looked quite straight forward and to the point. I studied the image on the screen. It was coming back to me that the fish was the Christian symbol, along with the cross or crucifix. But it was also known as IXOUS, which was Greek for fish; ichtus was an alternative spelling for the same thing.

But I wondered why I didn't see my drawing as a fish straight away. I glanced back at the drawing on my paper on the desk, next to the keyboard, and then I looked back at the screen. My fish was facing the right, but almost every one I'd clicked on so far were facing the left – they were effectively swimming in the opposite direction to my fish. Perhaps if I'd drawn it the other way round, I would have seen it as a fish – who knows?

I scrolled through some more articles all about the origins of the fish in Christianity. I read about the fish symbol pre-dating the cross, although one article spoke about the cross forming part of the fish's tail. I looked at the fish image again, and could see clearly what the writer of the article had meant.

I then read that each letter in IXOUS formed the first letter of a Greek word which translated to: Jesus Christ God Our Saviour. But it was the second letter I was taken with, the "X", which was the first letter of the word meaning "Christ", but alone that letter was Chi, the twenty-second letter of the Greek alphabet pronounced "chee". I stared at the Chi or X, long and hard, because it was strange that "Chi" was also linked to the Chinese philosophy of circulating life energy, inherent in all things, and what is an eight if it is not a continuous circulating path? Even the Yin Yang symbol looks like two fish. I wondered if this was merely coincidental or evidence that of one belief drawing inspiration from another over time.

Then I read about the miracle in the Bible connected to fish; the loaves and the fish story.

Suddenly I thought about my fish swimming in the opposite direction again. But then I'd drawn mine with my left hand and the left is supposed to be the sign of the Devil, just like the left shoulder was the Devil or Fallen Angel. That's why they used to chop the hand off left-handed people in the past.

Eventually, I managed to find an article discussing the relevance of the direction of the Christian fish: my fish was swimming away from evil to the righteousness.

So that was good, wasn't it? But then I was interrupted by the phone; this time it was Richard calling me.

'Just checking you are okay. Maddy said you're drawing fish now.' I was starting to feel that they'd got me under close surveillance.

'Look, I'm fine. I did draw a fish earlier. I closed my eyes, blanked my mind, drew a fish... well an incomplete eight that looks like a fish, but they're linked anyway. I'm busy looking up what it all means now,' I said, knowing that it sounded completely bonkers. 'The fish is the Christian symbol. But did you know how Jesus is spelt in Greek?' I said enthusiastically.

'No...bu—'

'Well it's IOTA, ETA, SIGMA, OMIGON, UPSILON, SIGMA and added together, numerically they equal 888. The value of the first letter is ten, the second is eight, the third is two-hundred, the fourth is seventy, fifth is four-hundred and the last one, sigma, again is two-hundred. Those numbers, added together make 888,' I continued, as I made my way through the notes, which were thicker than my study notes for the day.

'It's a bit like the Devil being known as 666; Jesus in Greek, using the Gematria system converts to 888. And guess what – we passed through 08/08/08 this year – the day before my birthday and it only comes around once every century. It won't happen again until year 2108,' I said, but I was also slightly aware that I'd probably blown Richard's head with too much information. Even for someone with a brain like Richard's, it was a bit much over a telephone when you're not expecting it. It was the sort of thing better presented in a full indexed report which could be digested before opening it up for discussion.

'Er…yes, that's all very interesting, but why on earth are you interested in it. What is going on in your head?'

'Well eight is…an important number this year, that's all. The Chinese are quite hot on number eight, supposed to be lucky. Did you know that the Bible is supposed to be encrypted with numerical codes as well? There are tons of articles about it on the Internet.' Well saved, I thought.

'No, I don't really know much about numerical codes in the Bible. Talking of numbers – you have noticed the time haven't you? You need to leave in a minute to get William and Elyse. Don't get carried away with what you're doing and forget them will you?'

'Of course I'm aware of the time,' I lied, having only just glanced at the clock on the computer screen. 'But, anyway, the Bible is crawling with numbers. 111 is supposed to be something to do with Jesus too, as in 111 multiplied by eight is 888, the whole thing is fascinating. Numbers aren't just numbers they all have meanings. Number eight is the resurrection and transfiguration.'

'So…what are you saying, that 888 means Jesus is returning this year?' he said, laughing at me.

'How the hell should I know, I'm not the Pope? I'm just telling you about the stuff I'm reading. It's interesting that's all. Oh…and did you know that we are supposed to be moving into the Age of Aquarius, which is the sign for water.'

'No.'

'The changeover is supposed to happen every 2150 years. The problem is no one seems to know the start date for the Age of Pisces, which means that they can't calculate the precise date when the 2150 years is up for Aquarius to then take over. There are all sorts of online debates about it. But, basically it's the end of one era, the fish and the beginning of new era – water. Aquarius is supposed to be the coming together of science and religion. But even that all ties in with the importance of number eight; if eight is supposed to signify the beginning of new era or new order. The whole lot makes sense in a wacky kind of way, if you believe in all that stuff. By the way, William's an Aquarius.'

'If you say so, look you'd better go. I'll see you later...love you.'

'Love you too.' I placed the phone back on charge, let Mick-The-Cleaner know I was off to do the school run, while quickly plonking the pocket dictionary on the garden room table with all of my papers and textbooks; for some strange reason it had been left open on the kitchen table, with the front cover and back page being the visible part. I'd picked it a few seconds earlier to see which page it had been left open on. It had been the one with words beginning with "qua". I knew this couldn't have been anything to do with Mick-The-Cleaner, because he was always careful not to move things around, or if he did he would fold them or place them with precision. Richard regularly went berserk that he was paying to have his loose change stacked in neat piles. So if Mick had picked it up off the floor or something, he would have left it closed, not open – surely?

I did take a quick scan down the pages to see if there was anything Richard could have been looking up. But nothing on the page struck me as anything he wouldn't already know or be remotely interested in. William had his own dictionary with pictures in, and Elyse couldn't read yet. With all the other stuff buzzing around my head, I hadn't got headspace or time to give the dictionary any more thought.

CHAPTER THIRTEEN

I walked into the dark club around 23:00 and *TheRocX* still had half an hour to go. I worked my way to the front and watched him. The place wasn't that busy. The band obviously performed to a slightly older audience and light rock had never really been my thing. I admired the fact that he could sing, in fact I admired anyone who could sing, but it was his speaking voice that really got me.

I felt good in a gold, shimmery dress, which complimented the golden highlights in my hair.

The dress finished above my knee; short enough to show off my toned tanned thighs, but not short enough to be considered tarty. It exposed my arms and dropped at the back; the fabric was so fine and delicate, I was afraid it would tear if I caught it with my nails.

After the last song, I rushed backstage to find him; he was still in a corridor and my eyes locked onto him. For a second he had a look of confusion, then a wide grin made its way across his face. He said something to his band mate then walked towards me, hugged me, then wiped my hair from my face, before kissing me with the longest, most delicious kiss I'd ever experienced.

The whole thing happened so quickly I hadn't seen it coming. His skin tasted salty with perspiration. I then spent the next eight hours in a place that could only be described as my own heaven on earth.

I slept blissfully, re-living the whole experience, once again feeling his damp skin against mine, it was intoxicating like fresh blood being injected into my veins, seamless and un-spoken, mad but complete. It was like finding a home for my soul. I rolled onto my other side and stretched my arm towards him, ready to snuggle into his body. I patted the bed to find him. Why couldn't I reach him? I opened my eyes. He was no longer there. There was a folded note on the pillow, my eyes scanned the room

– his clothes had gone, his jeans and boxers were no longer on the floor, or his navy shirt thrown over the TV – all evidence of him had gone and the room was silent. I opened the note, which had been written on the hotel's stationery.

The writing looked hurried:

Thank you for last night, it was special, and great to see you again after all these years. But sorry I have to go, I'm meeting my girlfriend this morning. Take care. X.

My heart sank; I read it a second time.

I felt used and conveniently disposed of.

I tore it into tiny pieces and threw them to the bottom of the bed. The tiny squares floated down onto the white sheets and floor like confetti. I stepped from the bed, feeling the cold against my naked body. I grabbed my clutch bag, which I'd bought especially for the occasion, and jumped back in the bed pulling the sheets around me. I switched on my mobile to call Richard, but the phone repeatedly beeped to alert me to recent text messages. I opened them up sequentially.

Where the fuck are you? I saw Maddy in the supermarket earlier. Clearly she's not in London with you. So who the fuck are you with? And incidentally…you might want to take a look at a few other messages sent to my phone last night.

As with all Richard's text messages, it had been carefully typed in full. I started to shake, and my head felt as though it had been hit with a brick, I was trying to think through thick fog and my heart was pounding in my ears. I opened up the other five messages starting with one from Maddy, that had slipped in before Richard had managed to forward the other messages onto me.

Sorry didn't know what 2 say 2 Richard. Pretended not 2 know anything call u l8r X

I stared at the eight in the middle of her abbreviated "later", then I read the next four messages, I could feel bile rising:

Cuckold

Cuckold

Cuckold

Getting the message? Courtesan finally showing her true colours is she?

Tears streamed down my face, I'd made a mistake, a big mistake and who the hell was sending the text messages? Who was watching me? The messages scared me, but at that moment the fear of Richard's reaction gripped me far more. I'd betrayed him and there was no going back. I closed the last text message, wiped my eyes on the bed sheet, leaving traces of mascara, and then selected Richard's number. He picked up, his familiar voice was icy.

'I'm sorry,' I said and I tried again. 'I'm sorry,' but no sound would come out. 'Sorry, sorry, sorry,' I said repeatedly, but still no sound; he still couldn't hear me. I started thrashing around the bed, and then the sound of my own voice echoed back in my ears as I yelled out:

'sorry,' and my eyes opened.

I had broken through the dream.

My pillow was damp from tears, and Richard's side of the bed was empty, he had obviously taken Blue for his normal morning walk. Relief washed over me, but the nightmare haunted me for the rest of the day. I knew any expert would say that it was my conscience playing out my longings, my guilt and my fears all neatly wrapped into one scene.

At around 16:15 William and Elyse jumped out of the car, flinging the doors wide open, and stood impatiently at the front door, while I loaded myself up with all their things. I got William to take the keys I'd gripped between my teeth, so he could open up. Blue came racing through it to greet us, then, as usual, he ran straight to his dinner bowl.

I tipped the beaker of dried food into his bowl, which made the usual loud clatter against the metal, busied myself cleaning out congealed yoghurt, and crusts from the lunch boxes, pulled out of the school bags what seemed like a dozen party invites. I pinned them on the fridge door with magnets; I intended to deal with them properly the next day, which meant, like usual, they'd be dealt with twenty-four hours before the deadline. Then I successfully negotiated my way through William's union-representative skills on reasons why he thought he shouldn't be doing homework at my command, and by 17:03 I was back at the study PC; and back on *Facebook*.

Despite my nightmare, I still desperately wanted to speak to Anthony Hope – communicating with him was a million miles away from hopping into bed with him. And he was clearly at the root of all the madness. But, as yet, I was still not one hundred per cent certain he was even communicating with me at all; I just had to know, and I had a plan.

I pulled up the photo of me and Sophie at our graduation; the one that I accidentally left the Botox comment on a few months back, and I typed in a message at the bottom of it, as though it was for Sophie, but really I had aimed it at Anthony Hope. There was method behind my madness, even though the message was loopy...

Currently wrapped up in my own Wonderland and thought about you writing your dissertation on Lewis Carroll – wished I read it now.

Having really strange experiences at the moment for one with an open mind and no particular religious views I'm finding myself trying to reach the shoulder tapper.

Closed my eyes let the pen draw...opened my eyes and result looked like no. 8 incomplete, or a fish symbol.

Even Mad Maddy is starting to think I'm crazy but there are too many coincidences.

At 17:08 I suddenly remembered what had provoked the Botox comment in the first place and typed in another message below it...

Just a minor correction...I am a fraction under 5ft 3! Not 5ft 2!!

Now Sophie was going to think I was barking, so I blocked her from viewing the photo.

In fact, the only people who could now see this photo was Anthony Hope and me; this message was intended for his eyes only.

It was a whole day later that he spotted it, or rather he responded to it. At around 17:00 I logged into *Facebook*. I'd snuck into the study as a means of escaping the head pounding I was getting from William and Elyse since they'd got back from school in unrelenting, demanding moods. At the top of my screen were Fan pages I'd added earlier in the day: Nell Gwyn, Peace, Ichtus Festival, and Eight to Infinity. I added them knowing that the additions would also filter through to Anthony's Newsfeed, or he would spot them when he viewed my page.

Within in a few minutes of me logging on Anthony had posted his Status Update:

17:06 Anthony's favourite Lewis Carroll quote: Everything's got a moral...if only you can find it.

I read and re-read his words.

And after opening and closing my eyes, a Lewis Carroll quote was still sitting at the very top of my screen. I was finally proven right.

The fact it had appeared only a matter of hours since I'd made reference to Lewis Carroll meant this couldn't possibly be a coincidence. It was as likely as a Charles Dickens's quote popping up on N-Yo's blog if I'd left a quote for him lying around. So clearly Anthony had chosen this quote in response to my words on Sophie's photo. At least that part of my head wasn't going crazy. I'd finally driven him out of his hiding place with words. But why had he gone for that quote in particular? What did he mean?

'Can I have some cereal, Mummy?' William entered the study with his *Nintendo DS* in his hand, then tripped over Elyse's doll's pushchair and skidded on one of the books scattered across the floor. He looked bewildered for a second but straightened himself back up.

'No I've told you, your food is cooking. Get some milk. That will take the edge of your appetite,' I said firmly, after I'd make sure he hadn't injured himself.

'I don't want milk. I'm hungry.'

'Well it's milk or nothing until dinner,' and Elyse entered the room with her *Barbie*.

'Mummy, can you put *Barbie*'s shoes on, they keep falling off,' I took the doll off Elyse, and as I did so Anthony's Status disappeared from my screen.

I dropped the doll on the desk and scrolled all the way down my screen. Where had it gone? I kept scrolling. Nothing. Not only had that Status vanished from my screen, all of his old Status Updates had gone.

He was gone. I couldn't find him.

Everything's got a moral...if only you can find it. Find it? Where was he?

My heart was thumping. Had he just deleted me from *Facebook*?

But why would he delete me now? It didn't make sense. He'd finally revealed his hand, only to disappear. Why would he be watching me closely if he wasn't interested in me? If he wasn't interested in me, I would be invisible to him. This game required two willing participants.

'Mummy, my dolls shoes...now.'

'Elyse just shut it a minute,' I snapped, as my fingers trembled over my keyboard, my eyes being dazzled by the shocking pink nail-varnish that Elyse had put on me a few days earlier. 'Oh God... I can't lose him... not now.' Suddenly the guilt of my nightmare was forgotten, or was this another nightmare? I scrolled down my list of friends. He was still there. His tiny photo was still sitting there. But my trembling continued. He must have done something with his privacy settings, blocked me from viewing his Status Updates or something. My face had flushed with panic, my cheeks were like a furnace and I ran my hands through my hair several times, as though that would help.

'Mummy, are you going to get me some cereal, and where's my *DS* charger? It has gone flat, look.'

'Mummy, my dolly's shoes…' and they both keep going, one being scratched in with the other, punctuated by the sound of fireworks exploding nearby which were sending Blue into a tiz.

Someone was obviously making a whole week of Guy Fawkes celebrations and I could have done without it at that moment.

'Shut up the both of you. Give me a minute…please,' and without really thinking, my head in a flat spin, I sent an Instant Message…

Anthony,

I am really sorry. I thought you may have had feelings for me and I really didn't mean to offend you.

Nicole.

Instantly an email bounced back

?

I sent another email back

You've just blocked me from your Wall?!?

He instantly replied

Erm? ;-)

I sent another.

Very funny (no wink on mine) I've nearly ripped the heads off my children as a consequence.

Mine was the last message and then his Status Update returned to normal within a few seconds.

What the hell was he doing?

Then it dawned on me. I had spent the last few weeks trying to get the snake out of the grass, and he had me walk right into my own trap. I felt like I was foolishly dangling from a tree in my own planted mesh. He'd outmanoeuvred me; outsmarted me. Damn, I cursed. I may have humiliated myself, but at least my instincts had been right, my suspect was guilty, I just didn't know his motive.

CHAPTER FOURTEEN

I sat with a towel wrapped round me, dipping my toast soldier into my boiled egg while flicking through the newspapers. Richard cooking breakfast post-sex had become a ritual over the years.

The papers were full of Barack Obama's election as the 44th US President, which had taken place in the early hours. Richard had stayed up to watch the historical moment, but I'd fallen asleep in Elyse's bed and missed it. America's first African-American President was now having his acceptance speech played over and over on the television. 2008 had certainly proved to be his lucky year.

'Tell you what...if it was a beauty contest, Barak would have got my vote over Palin anytime,' I said to Richard, having left a similar comment on *Facebook* the previous night.

'What are you saying that you'd do him?' Richard said, with a cheeky smile.

For a moment, everything felt back to normal.

'No, of course not, no more than you would Kylie,' I said. Then I stood with a devilish grin on my face, watching his expression register what I'd just said.

I deliberately didn't hang around long. Instead I wandered out of the kitchen with my mug of tea, also thinking about my words; what was the difference in fantasising about a man on my *Facebook* who was out of my reach, and a man on television also out of my reach? Was there really a difference?

'Where are you off now?

'Study...for a minute.'

'You need to call Maddy. I did the 1471 and it was Maddy who called while we were at it. So don't forget. Anyway, I'm off to work. I'll see you around half five.'

'Oh...talking of Maddy...don't forget that on Friday night you need to finish early. School bonfire and a chilli round at Maddy and Steve's afterwards...and don't arrange to see your mum on Sunday, Steve's got us tickets to see WWE...'

I heard the front door slam behind him as and I logged onto *Facebook* and clicked onto Anthony's Wall. I felt almost dizzy with anticipation; I wanted to see if he'd left anything else since the embarrassing incident with Lewis Carroll. It looked like he'd stayed up to watch the Presidential results come in too.

00:45 Anthony is rooting for Obama, guys!!!!!

I remembered his Status saying he supported the Democrats so I should have guessed really. I clicked on his Status to view a conversation between him and his American friends about the results. Then I looked long and hard at Anthony's Comment...

Bells ringing...5 missing?! No it's 8

Suddenly, I was feeling a band of gold sliding onto my finger.

There were several postings, each giving the election results at various points, but his comments were way out of sync with the other results.

Did that mean that he was cleverly referring to my fish drawing? And...number eight with the diagonal line missing becomes a five. Surely this meant he'd acknowledged my drawing. One side of me felt excited that he was taking in what I was trying to tell him, the other side of me was more than slightly concerned that the lunacy of my recent postings could be causing him alarm as in *psycho woman alert!* I continued to read a couple of other Status Updates he'd left first thing.

Anthony feels alive...great result :-)

Reading his words had me imagining him walking down somewhere like Oxford Street with one of those half-baked, silly grins, which always have a tendency to make complete strangers involuntarily smile back at you.

This vision was relatively short-lived, because then I spotted a note on his Wall saying that he was going away to New York for a few days with his girlfriend. I just didn't get it. Why play games with me, when he had her? I sulkily went and grabbed the jar of *Nutella* from the kitchen cupboard, suddenly craving something sweet, and sat eating it with a teaspoon, while searching for a better example of the infinity symbol.

This time I found a Fan page which showed the eight turned onto its side – the correct position for it.

He *is supposed to be mine forever, not hers*, I thought as another spoonful of *Nutella* entered my mouth.

'Right you... in the car now,' Maddy shouted to me from across the school car park.

This wasn't a friendly invitation to catch-up on things that we hadn't managed to since *WWE* wrestling on Sunday night. So, I did a U-turn with a feigned smile as I passed a few other parents chatting and slowly made my way to Maddy's car. I've always hated the drawn in nights; it makes it feel much later than it really is. The air was cold and there was a damp, earthy smell from the wet leaves on the ground. The school mini-bus should have been back at 18:00 after the swimming gala, so it was already ten minutes late and William being on school transport always made me feel anxious.

'Hi,' I said tentatively, as I climbed into the passenger seat to be hit with hot air blasting out of the heater; it was stifling.

'You have got to stop playing these games. You are making yourself utterly miserable. It's never going to go anywhere and you'll lose what you already have if you don't stop.'

I kind of knew what she was going to say before she said it really, but it still cut deep, I didn't need to tell her that I'd had the nightmare. 'Do you want a *Coke*?' she added, before opening a can. She always said that she gets as much of a buzz from the crisp sound of the ring pull being released, as she does from the *Coke* itself.

'No, thanks, and I'm not miserable,' I said weakly, because I couldn't deny it. My *Facebook* looked all cheery with flippant lighthearted comments, but inside I ached, every part of me ached. And I hated the jealousy that I was feeling.

'You bloody well are miserable. I just watched you walk from over there. It's all to do with that stupid game you're playing,' she said, as she acknowledged another mother who had tapped her car window in a friendly gesture.

'I'm just confused, that's all. Anthony's definitely playing games with me, but he's fucked off home to New York with his girlfriend, and I just don't get it.'

'That's not the point. You shouldn't be playing the games. Delete him off your *Facebook* for your own good, and for Richard's sake. Richard knows something is wrong with you. You're bothering him. I still think that text a few weeks ago was set up by Richard.'

'I've no idea about the text – it baffles me. Richard doesn't even think it merits discussion. And I can't delete Anthony. I swear I've tried, but I just can't do it. It's not just about him now, it's all the other weird stuff as well that I can't get my head around, like the Anthony Hope novel. I almost feel like I'm caught up in my own book; everything is very weird.'

'You don't even know for sure that he's playing games with you.'

'I'm telling you he is. I found some stuff on the Internet the other day about his sister. She has a website listed on her *Facebook*. I was trying to find Anthony's exact year of birth. But it turns out that his sister is a children's book illustrator, and does other bits of drawing. So it would make perfect sense that she would use images to help Anthony communicate. Just think about it, she spends most of her working day using images to convey messages. I still think that album with the birds, the bee and the frog was carefully fabricated. Look, using images may seem strange to you, but it doesn't to me and it wouldn't to either of them...they both have an artistic streak.'

'Well yeah, you're right, it is strange to me. But why did you want his year of birth, what's that got to do with anything?'

'Oh...that was...well,' I stammered, wondering why she had to ask me that question. 'That was just because I was looking at the numbers we all have in our birthdays, and I didn't have his birth year to work it out. Anyway, I posted a load of text as a photo on *Facebook* with all of my recent discoveries, including references to the deceased Anthony Hope's novel. Look, it all makes me look completely bonkers. So you needn't worry, he probably won't play games with me again now. He'll have concluded that I'm a freak after that lot,' I said.

'You did what?' And she made me explain the excruciatingly, embarrassing details again.

Even now I still don't know what made me do it. But as for finding his date of birth I got nowhere. I found his sister's, and took a good guess that if she was born was born in July of 1967; Anthony was most likely born in January of 1969, which would make him slightly older than me.

'When the fuck did you do that? I've not seen it on there,' Maddy asked.

'It was a few days ago now. But no, you wouldn't have seen it. It was aimed at him. Everyone else was blocked from viewing it. Anyway, it was on the morning he went to New York.'

'Actually, I can't even be bothered to discuss that – it's ridiculous and irrelevant anyway. I've told you it can't ever go anywhere. Do you seriously think he would take you, William and Elyse? Where would you live? Fucking hell, you'd even have to get a job. How the bloody hell would you survive on a normal wage?'

'Ha ha...very funny.' I said, hearing the sadness in my own voice. 'I do realise that. I just can't delete him...the thought hurts too much.' I knew deep down everything she was saying was right. In my head I had even role-played family life with him; William and Elyse being at their worst. I pictured them pulling his books of his bookshelf and mixing up all of his DVDs and accidentally snapping the strings on his guitar.

Thrusting William and Elyse on a man who appeared to have spent most of his adult life as a bachelor would be like hitting him with a tornado fuelled by plutonium. It wouldn't be fair. And if I left Richard, where would I live, if I didn't live with Anthony? In reality, you don't just move in with someone you have never even dated, just because of a gut instinct. But I had very little money of my own. My long-term stab at providing myself with independent wealth had catastrophically blown up in my face. I wouldn't want to move William and Elyse into council accommodation, with us living off State benefits. I would also be forcing them to change schools, because I couldn't afford private education on my own. And, more than anything, I wanted them to have the education I didn't have and when they are young. I didn't want them to have to educate themselves in their mid-twenties, like I did. I wanted them to grow up with the confidence to believe they could be whatever they wanted to be at the age they should be thinking it. And, on top of everything, Anthony was in London, and London was a place for the ridiculously, obscenely wealthy or the career singleton's who eventually got married and moved to more suitable rural areas. It would be selfish and cruel of me. My life was no longer just about me, and Richard had done nothing wrong to deserve such treatment by me. Never in my life had my head felt so confused.

'How can it hurt...you've said yourself you've not seen him for eight years?'

'I don't know. It's just how it is. I told you before that I always felt like I belonged with him, and that book hasn't helped me now. I need to get hold of that book to find out what happens in it, but the other part of me can't face it.'

'Look – book or no book, you need to stop it.'

'Yeah I know, and I will. Just give me a little more time...I think that's the mini-bus just pulled into the drive.'

'Fine. Come on, we'd better go and get the kids.'

Maddy's words weren't lost on me. They replayed in my mind along with my own thoughts almost continuously for a couple of days afterwards. But I just couldn't delete him. He was still in New York and hadn't been on his *Facebook* at all, so he was either avoiding it, or was somewhere that didn't have Internet access. Wherever his was, he was still slowly eating away at me.

Every day he was away I looked at his *Facebook*. It was like staring at a house when the occupant was away and you can sense the quiet. I felt like the busy little bee (me) was futilely trying to wade through its own sweetly created honey, but was stuck in one place.

Then Maddy left me a message on my *Facebook*:

To BEE or not to BEE......that is the question!! The only question!!

And that's how I spent the next few days, feeling like I was slowly dying with each Status Update...

13 November 19:59 BZZZZ

14 November 10:33 BZZZ

14 November 17:30 BZZ

15 November 08:17 BZ

Richard walked into the kitchen, catching me staring at a mug that I'd placed on the kitchen island.

'What on earth are you doing now?'

'Seeing if the string on the tea-bag flaps around,' I said, attempting to be nonchalant, while I continued to stare at it intently. I'd deliberately got William and Elyse off to bed early, so I could take another look at it in peace.

'Why?' he asked puzzled.

'Please don't make me explain, because I know you already think I'm going crazy and this will only add to it. Trust me.'

'No, seriously, I *do* want to know. You are obviously staring at it for a reason,' he said, as he crouched lower down to take a look at it from my level.

Blue had joined in and so all three of us were staring at a mug of hot, green tea with the string hanging down the side. It was definitely not moving with the same level of momentum it had done earlier in the day, even with disturbance from Richard and Blue. I stood up straight, and, once again, found myself not knowing where to start with my explanation of events.

'Right, here goes,' I took a deep breath. 'Earlier on, I made myself a drink of tea and plonked it on the desk in the garden room and then I got on with my studying, while it cooled down a bit. After about five minutes or so, I was distracted by the tea-bag string flapping. But no windows were open, and you know it's draught free in there. Anyway, it was flapping towards that dictionary.'

'What dictionary?'

'The small pocket one. It was left open in the kitchen...the other day, you must have been looking up something...'

'I haven't,' he said.

Clearly like everything else in the house the dictionary had the ability to move on its own.

'Well, regardless, someone had taken it down and I moved it onto the table in the garden room the other week. But I was working from several textbooks today and they kept closing, causing me to lose my page. It was annoying, so I picked the dictionary up, and I used it to weigh down my textbook pages. Anyway, because the flapping string on the tea-bag was in the direction of the dictionary – I picked the dictionary back up, wondering if this was a ghost thing again. I know...it sounds crazy. You don't have to interrupt,' I said, as he looked like he was about to interrupt. His mouth shut again. 'Anyway...the dictionary was still on exactly the same page that it had been the other day, the day I was looking up fish and Infinity symbols and my eyes kept going back to the word "quadratic" which gave the definition: "Equation in which the variable (X) is raised to the power of two, but nowhere raised to a higher power".'

'So what?'

'Let me go and get the dictionary,' I walked back into the kitchen and handed it to him and he had put his reading glasses on ready.

'But, I don't get the significance, it's just the definition of a mathematical equation,' he said, putting the dictionary back down and taking his reading glasses off again.

'Well *obviously*, it's related to maths. But the wording also sounds religious. A variable raised to the power of two (as in two people), but nowhere raised to a higher power (as in God). The variable "X", the cross is raised to the power of two,' I said, explaining with an overuse of hand gestures, which now looked like I was directing traffic.

'Well yeah, if you want to look at it that way. But I still don't get it.'

'Maybe this will be easier for me to explain. I looked up quadratic equations on the Internet... and found quite a straight-forward example of one, look I'll show you how it works,' and I grabbed a pen, scribbling down the equation for him.

'That's the equation without any numbers...you could write it like this...

$$X (x^2) - XXX = O$$

'Any numbers can be inserted into the equation as long as both sides balance. Basically X multiplied by X squared is equal to the number, which sits on the other side. So, when I put the three eights's in; based on the fact that eight is somehow relevant to me, I found that eight multiplied by eight squared $8 \times (8 \times 8)$ is equal to 512. So the equation then looks like this...

$$8(8 \times 8) - 512 = 0$$

'And 512 is William's birthday – February 15th when you reverse the numbers, as in 2/15, you know like 9/11, the American way of writing dates. Look, this is how you would solve the value of X, if it was presented as a mathematical sum.

$$8 (x^2) - 512 = 0$$

'Divide both sides by eight which will then leave you with:

$X^2 = 64$

'The square root of 64 is 8, So X equals 8:

$888 = 512$

'There, see', I said, after frantically scribbling the workings down.

'Yes, very good, that's very clever of you.'

'Thanks, but you're not getting it. What's weird is how 888 just so happens to balance perfectly, mathematically with William's birthday, and he turns eight in four months' time. And if William hadn't been born, I would never have got involved with *Ilex Drapes*. And William was never supposed to happen. You know what the clinic said, that a child conceived naturally would be highly unlikely. For God's sake we never even bothered with contraception for years because of that report you had done. But William was the entire reason I got involved with the company, so I could work flexible hours, and that company just so happens to have gone down this year – the year the world has passed through 08/08/08. The company collapsed the 14th of February, the day before William's birthday. Don't you think it's just amazing?'

'*Ilex* closed on the 15th,' Richard corrected.

'No it didn't. It was the 14th remember?'

'It was the 15th,' he argued back.

'It was not. I signed those papers in the offices on the 14th and I remember thinking what a shitty Valentine's Day it was.'

'Yes, but they didn't go to the court until the 15th of February. I went down there first thing while you got the train down to London,' he said defiantly, and then the penny dropped, he was right. I was in London on that Friday with Mum, Dad and Grandmama for William's 7th birthday; Richard stayed with Elyse. I'd spent that entire weekend in a daze. The only kick back to reality was my mum's sharp tongue (never great with sympathy) and William's humour as he dashed through the Tube turnstiles at such lightning speed that I got knocked a foot back as they slammed shut on me. How could I forget all of that?

'Well – that just goes and makes it even weirder,' I said, thinking that a whole damn equation balanced my life.

William's birth took me away from Anthony Hope, and *Ilex Blinds*' closure had brought me back to him as consequence of events which occurred on one precise date – 15th February, or 2/15; if digitised and reversed.

I'd always considered William as a small miracle who had saved me from a childless, empty pursuit of a career at the cost of what really mattered in life.

'The numbers are merely coincidences, and coincidences are weird things. So, why are you staring at the mug now?'

'Because I'm still wondering whether it's due to a ghost or an angel. Look, there is no way on earth I would think of some random equation, that just so happens to balance with the number I drew the other day, and two significant events in my life.'

'You drew a fish!'

'I know, but I saw it as an eight first, and, like I told you, the fish and the three eights are connected. But, never mind that, did you know what a quadratic equation was? Would your head even be drawn in that direction? And just what are the odds of the dictionary being left open on that page, when neither of one of us recalls using it recently?' I picked the dictionary up once more. 'Look 632 pages in this book, and it just so happened to be open on that page – page 442. See...it doesn't even open up naturally on that page, that's not where the spine is weak,' I said, with increasing frustration, as I wafted the book beneath his nose.

'You need to calm down. Yeah, I can see it is strange and no, I wouldn't think it up. But—'

'You're the walking computer and if your brain hadn't gone there, my head certainly wouldn't think it up, and I'm crap with dates, you *know* I never even remember the date we got together, you remind me every year. I just don't pay attention to dates – my head just wouldn't travel in that direction. By the way…did you know that Lewis Carroll was a mathematician as well as a writer, he even loved photography, and my camera was playing up just before all this weird stuff started,' I said, trying to breathe deeply at the same time.

'No, I didn't know. But what has he got to do with anything? Is he your ghost now? I thought it was it Nell Gwyn, or Jesus Christ? I'm losing track.'

'You're not as confused as me. But my *Facebook* is covered in references to *Alice in Wonderland*. Doesn't it strike you as strange that all the other spooky things that have occurred recently have been to do with windows and keys? And why doesn't that text message bug you – it had no number attached to it and the wording was so old-fashioned. Not normal.'

Richard shrugged his shoulders and dropped the corners of his mouth. 'Just doesn't, no point wasting energy on things you don't have answers for.'

Fortunately Richard's complete lack of understanding of *Facebook* meant that informing him of my references to *Alice in Wonderland* on there could have been perfectly normal online behaviour for all he knew. I decided to let the flapping tea-bag drop, and filled him in on the genius of Lewis Carroll instead.

'Lewis Carroll wrote a fair few maths books under his real name: Charles Lutwidge Dodgson. He got a double first from Christchurch at Oxford – a bit above my former polytechnic degrees – he was a logician, and he *loved* wordplay. He'd even been groomed to be a priest from being a boy. Just how do some people manage to cram so much knowledge into their heads?'

'Well…your head is certainly funny, Little N, crammed full or not. Anyway, are you now going to drink your green tea?'

'No. I didn't make it to drink it, you can have if you want…' and with that I wandered off with William's endless Christmas wish list.

CHAPTER FIFTEEN

Pomona, the Roman Goddess of fruits and orchards, despite her great beauty, had no desire for marriage.

She had turned away the most eligible suitors, preferring to spend her days pruning and nurturing blossoming trees in her own Garden of Eden.

"If a tree stands alone, a vine has nowhere to grow and the grapes will wither and die," said the old lady as she re-adjusted her dark cloak. Then she spoke some more, telling Pomona that Vertumnus loved her like no other and he would love her gardens as did she. Pomana's heart softened, as she listened to the wise words. The old lady then shed her cloak, revealing her true self to Pomona.

Now stood before her was the persistent Vertumnus, whose trickery and charm had finally seduced her. Pomona and Vertumnus married and lived happily, tending the orchards together.

A naked bronze statue of Pomona, standing in the Pulitzer Fountain of Abundance can be found in a small park area, close to the Plaza Hotel in New York City. The sculptor, Karl Bitter, was killed after getting hit by a car on the day he completed the mould for Pomona. The work on the statue was completed by his assistant.

* * *

A video had been embedded into the online article, and I clicked on the small triangle to play it from my laptop.

The establishing shot was the entire statue of Pomona, who was naked and holding a basket of mixed fruit; water was flowing from the mouths of rams at her feet and the sound of it cascading into the six basins beneath her could be heard above the sound of people passing by.

The clip then cut to an arc shot, so Pomona could be seen from 360 degrees, and finally, the short clip cut to a tilt; starting from the lowest basin moving up. Then it finished on her behind; and that image dominated my laptop screen. It had to be an unfortunate technical glitch – or it could have been filmed by a man.

I sighed. So why does Vertumnus remind me of Anthony Hope? Perhaps it was the man's cunning trickery I wondered, as I scrolled back up to the article's opening paragraph for a second glance:

The Roman's celebrated the harvest of apples each year with 'Pomona Day.'

'Pomona Day' is one of the cultural influences which helped to shape what we know today as 'Halloween.'

'Halloween...' I whispered to myself, and hit the "X" to close down the site.

Everyone had congregated round the kitchen table and we helped William and Elyse fill Mum, Dad and Grandmama in on their exciting day at the country park; my attempt at dragging Richard into a family day out, rather than us wasting yet another Sunday. Elyse climbed onto Grandmama's knee, and William, after completing the tale of his adventures wandered off into the lounge to watch some TV.

Mum asked how Bonnie and Clyde were, wondering if there was any sign of a trial yet, which there wasn't, and Dad and Richard talked business for a while. Dad was finding it a struggle at the moment: he'd expanded just before the credit crunch, moved into bigger premises, and now sales had fallen, so every month was becoming a battle. It seemed that even those who had grown their company steadily for years were at risk from potential decimation; companies' cash reserves are soon wiped out. I hated to hear of Dad struggling, it seemed so unfair, because after three heart attacks and a quadruple bypass, he could have spent the last fifteen sitting on his rear, claiming benefits. He could have easily played on his health like thousands did after the ancillary mine industries went down, following the pit closures. But he didn't, he used his engineering skills, set up on his own and kept fighting. With his small frame, and energy you'd never even guess he'd suffered the heart attacks, they were like silent ticking bombs that had gone off periodically since I was fourteen, leaving us all with a dreaded fear of unexpected phone calls at obscure hours.

Richard opened the fridge door, clearly he was peckish, but he held up one of my alfalfa sprout bags.

'Why do I keep finding out-of-date bags of these in here, why buy them if you're not going to eat them?' he asked, before lobbing them in the bin.

'If I didn't think I would eat them, I wouldn't buy them, would I? For someone so intelligent you sometimes ask such stupid questions,' I said, but I didn't want to say that I wanted to eat them, but was finding them increasingly difficult to incorporate into food without it actually ruining the taste.

'Is she still on some faddy diet, you're too thin as it is,' Mum said.

'I'm not on a diet, nuts are *actually* fattening, but I keep forgetting to eat the sprouts,' I defended myself, but my weight *had* dropped. It was nothing to do with a faddy health diet, it was called being too miserable to eat and I knew I couldn't afford to lose any more weight; my skinny jeans were starting to fit like loose fit, and when my weight dropped too low my face became gaunt.

'Well…you're just too thin,' she repeated.

'Anyway, I think she's about to join one of those religious cults,' Richard craftily added.

'I am not! I am merely trying to make sense of weird things, and I'm trying to be open-minded about everything that is happening around me and rule out the impossible. That does not make me a religious fanatic.'

'She's not still banging on about getting tapped on the shoulder is she?' Dad asked.

'Yes, she is, and now she's drawing things and reading the

Bible,' Richard said and I saw the tension travel through Mum's body.

She could cope with us ill in a physical sense – just about, but odd behaviour on top of weight loss – she wouldn't know how to deal with it. The problem with Mum is that she cares too much.

'What ya been drawing Little N?' Dad asked, holding back a smirk behind his mug of tea.

'I'll show you,' I said, as I grabbed one of Elyse's magazines from the far end of the table.

'That's my mazagine,' Elyse said.

'I'm only borrowing it, you can have it back in a minute,' I didn't bother correcting her because I was too eager to scribble things down for Dad.

I felt like a teenager again and like Dad was helping me make sense of my homework.

I started with the fish, explained that the Greek word for Jesus converted to 888 using Gematria along with all the other interesting facts about number 8. I then ran through the quadratic equation with him, the fact that the three eights balanced with William's birthday and the day the court closed down *Ilex Drapes*. Dad's lips remained in a pout, forcing the dimple in his chin to reveal itself. It was the expression he always had when he concentrated.

'So, after the flapping tea-bag incident, and the discovery of the quadratic equation, I tried the automatic writing again. It was more a case of wanting it to throw up something that would rule everything else out as nothing but a coincidence. I was trying to prove a point to myself,' I justified.

'I keep telling her that coincidences are strange things Bill, but she won't have it,'

'But where does the eight come in, if you drew the fish symbol? Tell me that again.'

'The fish and the 888 are closely connected. But there is a perfectly good reason why I saw the fish as an eight. Take a look at these three drawings,' I said, as I scrawled them down on the page. Tell me what you see.'

$$\triangle C \sqcup$$

'A triangle, circle, and a rectangle,' said Richard, as he peered over dad's shoulder.

'Yeah, same here,' said Dad.

'Not a pyramid, beach ball and a plasma TV then,' I said smugly. Both of them looked at each other confused, not knowing where I was heading with this.

'The reason that you both see a triangle, circle and rectangle is down to gestalt psychology. None of those drawings were complete shapes. I missed a section from each and your brain completed them for you; it's called "closure". A familiar shape can depend on your own understanding of the world. So the reason that I saw my drawing as a number eight was because my brain completed the image to form a familiar shape; just like it should do. The Christian symbol of the fish wasn't familiar to me, and if I was to draw a fish, mine would have an eye and fins, basically the whole works. I believe I saw what I was supposed to see at that point in time.'

'Who is Gestalt anyway?' said Dad still looking at my drawings.

'Gestalt isn't a person, it means seeing something as a whole rather than organised parts. You must have seen the famous gestalt photo of the young girl and old woman where it is very difficult to see both simultaneously?' I said, as I filled in the missing section on the three shapes.

'Oh yeah, I think I have seen it somewhere,' said Dad.

'There is only one difference between a young girl and old lady,' said Richard grinning through his long pause, ready for his punch line. 'And that's time. Isn't that right Bill?' And both Dad and Richard chuckled like two schoolboys in front of four generations of females.

'Okay. So what else have you been drawing then?' Dad said, curbing his chuckles.

'The letter 'D' and a dot, as in a ".." or full-stop,' I said, as I used the pen to re-create a tiny dot on the paper.

Dad looked puzzled. 'Surely that can't mean anything?' he said, as he pulled the magazine towards him, so that he could see it better.

'Oh yeah?' said Richard and I glared at him again. Fortunately Mum and Grandmama were still being distracted by Elyse as we were doing this.

'Like you, Dad, when I first looked at it, it looked entirely meaningless. And I'll even admit that I was a little disappointed, because it meant that everything else must have been a coincidence. But after a few minutes I looked at it again, and played around with it.'

'How can you play around with a dot and the letter D?'

'Wait for it,' said Richard. 'This is Nicole, after all.'

'It was easy. All I did was convert the tiny dot into the word 'dot.' So then it became either DDOT or DOTD,' I said and pulled the colouring book back towards me so I could write both versions down. 'But DDOT didn't look right, and the other thing is that the fish I drew had been in reverse, so my instinct was to do the same with this and put the dot before the D to make the DOTD,' I added.

'But what is DOT, D,' he said. 'Or even D, O, T, D.?'

'This is where it got interesting. What day did I get tapped on the shoulder?'

'Er...Halloween, when Elyse had the sleepover at ours.'

'Yes, exactly, and DOTD is the official abbreviation for Day of the Dead. It scared the crap out of me when it came up on my computer screen – I thought it meant either William or I was going to die because it was William's birthday, which was in the quadratic equation.'

'What is the Day of the Dead? I've never heard of it,' Dad asked, before finishing off his mug of tea.

'Apparently, "The Day of the Dead" translates to "Los Dias de los Muertos". It's an event which has evolved with influences from the Celtics, Romans and Aztecs. It's a three-day festival held in Mexico at the same time as Halloween, All Saints Day and All Souls Day.'

'I know about All Souls Day,' said Richard. 'It is the day that you remember and pray for those in purgatory; to help them enter through the Pearly Gates.'

'You're right and it's celebrated on the 2nd of November. But All *Saints* Day is celebrated on the 1st of November and it is also known as Hallow's Day, or Hallowmas, which is the day after All Hallow's Eve, otherwise known to us as Halloween. So are you starting to see the connection? I get tapped on the shoulder on Halloween and then I go and draw something that turns out to be the vital link between religion, spirituality and Halloween. That can't be a coincidence, surely?' Neither Richard nor Dad came forth with an alternative, more rational explanation.

'It turns out that there is a serious religious belief that around the Halloween period, the spiritual veil between our world and the *next* world is at its thinnest. So that could possibly be why the shoulder tapping occurred when it did. There appears to be far more to Halloween than all of the commercial crap.'

'Life is strange,' said Dad. 'But you know my theory of alternative dimensions, and that spirits could be where one dimension crosses over another.'

'I'm not saying I'm right about all this. All I am saying is, drawing the DOT and the D at that point was hugely significant to me. But even if this came from my subconscious, it took my conscious brain to translate it. Have you heard of Jung's theory on synchronicity? It is from the 1950's.' Both shook their heads. 'Synchronicity is the idea that life is not a string of random events, but rather that there is some kind of deeper cosmic order and that our minds have a kind of psychic access which enables us to see the present, past and future events. It's a belief that says that our minds can tap into a whole wealth of information; like some kind of database. Jung believed in things like ESP, telepathy and spirituality. But Synchronicity is when…,' I said, whilst trying to think of an example, '…it's when you think about someone, and within seconds your phone rings and it's that person on the other end…'

'Ah, I get it,' said Dad and Richard continued to busy himself with topping up the tea.

'Good, so at what point do you accept concurrent events as more than coincidental? How many times does the dice have to throw up a six before you are picking it up to see if it's because the weight is unevenly distributed. And then, at what point do you say it's something more than a coincidence,' I asked.

'I don't know…I'd probably smash the dice open,' said Dad.

'Take a look at this,' I said, as I drew the infinity symbol on the paper. 'Look at what happens when I use simple gematria to convert the letters of DOTD into numbers. It makes D equal 4, O is 15, T equals 20 and D is 4 again.'

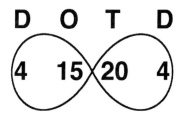

'Each loop of the symbol is weighted at half of 8, the cosmic balance, and where "X" sits at the centre of the symbol, there is

152 – February 15th – the very same numbers in the quadratic equation. The zero doesn't really count because it's nought or nothing.' Dad took the drawing from me.

'Can't you see how strange this is? Since the tap on the shoulder, everything I have drawn or have been led to is connected only to a very specific set of numbers. And not only that, there are literally billions and billions of things I could have drawn from my subconscious brain. But I swear there is something about these numbers: 8 and 512, or 152 whichever way it runs. There is something about the 8 multiplied by 8, or "X" squared; or raised to the power of two. This is because when the quadratic equation is written as an unsolved puzzle, it is the "X" which has to be solved. Only, in this case, I already know that "X" is 8 which is to be raised to the power of 2.'

'I must admit it is strange. The probability of this happening must be pretty high. But finding meaning in numbers is pseudo-mathematics, you can try to find number patterns and meanings in anything,' said Dad, who spent his days using proper maths in engineering.

'I agree with you up to a point; there are lots of people offering to tell people what their life means in numbers, and I'm aware that numerology is very popular, but this little lot makes perfect sense to me – and I am untrained in all of this. These numbers are connected to my past, but something tells me they're also connected to the future; otherwise, what was the point of being made to pay attention to something?'

By now, I was starting to feel quite smug that I'd managed to explain everything without including any reference to Anthony Hope, and the feeling that whatever all this was, he was the ultimate connection.

'I want to show you something from the Bible. I was reading it yesterday.' I said and went and pulled it off the study bookshelf; it had finished up sitting somewhere between *Being Jordan* and an encyclopaedia on the world's greatest philosophers.

'It's the Vine and The Branches. You need to read it from here, Dad,' I said now back in the kitchen. I pointed to 15:20. 'Read it all the way to the bottom, and then tell me what *you* think it means.'

'See, I told you...she's going to be off to join some cult or other,' Richard said, laughing.

'You're being ridiculous even saying it,' I sniped.

'Do you need Valium, are you depressed?' Mum finally joined in the conversation from the far end of the table.

'No I don't need a Valium. I am not depressed at all.'

I couldn't believe my own mother was telling me to take Valium. The whole scenario would have been funny if I wasn't for the fact I was feeling so sad. But longing for another man is not the same as depression, stress or anxiety.

'You're spending too much time on your own. You need to get back to work or...something,' Mum said, which opened up the whole debate of my not being able to work, the study I was doing for nine exams, and the care I gave to William and Elyse. I could add a job to that workload, but William and Elyse would be paying the price. I fought back with positivity.

'Anyway, the two tax exams I've got to take, I'm going to do through a place in the City that runs professional courses. I start studying for them in January, and I'll sit the exams in June. So that won't be in isolation – I'll be with other students.' Grandmama agreed that it was a good idea as Dad put down the Bible.

'Well?' I said, raising my eyebrows; the Botox had all but worn off.

'The Bible is open to interpretation; the passages can mean lots of different things to different people. Here...you read it, Jackie,' and he slid the Bible to the far end of the table.

Mum pulled it towards her, took two glances at it before virtually tossing it aside; another indication that I was stressing her out. But her dismissal also landed her at the wrath of Grandmama's tongue.

'You're not like our Nicole. You're not a deep thinker.'

Mum's face was a picture. Clearly she didn't know whether to defend herself at the risk of insulting me.

But Grandmama was my saviour. She let no one, not even mum attack me. Even Maddy with her mouth was wise enough to tread carefully around her, when it came to me. So I safely offered my interpretation. 'God cuts off every branch of the vine that bears no fruit, the others he prunes to make them more fruitful. So my current interpretation is that it is, like the credit crunch, the greed was no good for us. The world money tree has severely had its branches cut off, so efficiently it could have been done with a chain saw. But we still have to keep faith in God. We (mankind) need to have faith that he knows what is best for us. What is best for us is to love each other. Like it goes on to say in this bit at the bottom:

My command is this: Love each other as I have loved you. Greater love has no one than this, to lay down one's life for one's friends. You are my friends if you do what I command. I no longer call you servants, because servants do not know their master's business. Instead, I have called you friends, for everything that I learned from my father I have made known to you. You did not choose me, but I chose you and appointed you to go and bear fruit – fruit that will last. Then the Father will give you whatever you ask in my name. This is my command: Love each other.

I put the Bible down on the table.

We were a non-churchgoing family. As a child, Sundays had always been Gymkhana day, topped off with a Chinese takeaway in the evening, so reading the Bible out loud around the table had just rendered my family entirely speechless. The silence brought forward the sound of the lounge television.

Richard smugly raised his eyebrows; Mum definitely looked like the one in need of Valium. Grandmama broke the silence.

'What led you to that then?'

'Pomana...Vines...15:20,' I said, knowing that the tenuous link would make little sense to them, but it definitely made sense to me.

CHAPTER SIXTEEN

I rested the weight of my body against my thigh as I knelt, taking pleasure from the hot water bouncing off my back. Richard always moaned about the length of time I spent in the shower. But it wasn't just the shampooing, conditioning, exfoliating and whatnot, it was also one of my favourite places to think.

Using my right index finger, I cut through heavily formed steam on the glass panel to trace an eight. Droplets of water burst to form straight lines of water that ran down like teardrops on a face. New steam formed over the eight and it slowly vanished. Then I wrote the full equation: $8(X)^2 - 512 = 0$ Underneath I wrote X cross, X Chi.

I whispered to myself: *"X" raised to the power of two, but nowhere raised to a higher power – nowhere or is something trying to tell me that the no. as in 'number' is where something is raised to a higher power?*

My scribbles vanished again in the newly formed steam. Lewis Carroll Christchurch, I then wrote. Was my ghost Lewis Carroll? Was that such a mad thought? And why does it all equal "zero?" This time I traced a large zero. Was "zero" the hole I had gone and dropped myself into with Anthony Hope? On the adjacent panel using the index finger on my left hand I wrote cuckold. What am I missing here? I whispered. I was still none-the-wiser. I turned the shower off and stepped out of the cubicle, then wrapped a towel round my wet body. Just as I grabbed my hairbrush off the shelf, my mobile rang.

Still clinging to the towel, I ran across the carpet, leaving behind wet footprints and dropped my hairbrush on the way. I heard Dad's voice. Dad on the other end of a phone on a workday had completely thrown me. *Something must be wrong with Mum*, I thought.

'Friendship,' he said.

'What about it?' I said, baffled.

'That biblical passage – it's about friendship. I read it again in my Bible when I got home last night.'

He said his goodbyes and left me to my thoughts: whether it is friendship, love or lust; these are nothing but emotions and feelings that we can rationalise. Yet, because we lack the resolve to brush them aside, emotions have the power to cripple us.

As I watched Elyse on her swimming lesson, being equally crippled by the poolside sub-tropical heat, I thought about Dad's words from the day before. The other mothers attempted friendly conversation, but their words and smiles were interrupting my thoughts; so I listened to them through a long, dark tunnel.

My eyes were so tearful and it felt like as though I'd got something wedged in the back of my throat. I could no longer bear the heavy brick sitting stubbornly on my chest. But I knew once Elyse was dropped off at school, I would sit at the computer and type a letter to Anthony Hope. I had finally taken on board Maddy's words of wisdom and accepted that I could never be with him, and I needed to stop reading into messages on his *Facebook* that gave me false hope of living happily ever after with him.

I hated the idea of removing hope in every context of the word, but more than anything, I hated the thought of him never knowing what I felt for him and the attraction I'd always held.

By just stopping communication, giving no explanation, I would effectively be dismissing him as insignificant. But I knew that the letter would be the end.

I dropped Elyse off at school and got back to the house in the late morning. I ignored the aftermath of the breakfast rush and entered the study to start typing. The moment I started typing the tears finally came, but I persevered through the blurred vision.

27th November 2008

Anthony

I am really sorry but cannot continue to play games with you, as they are slowly destroying me. Putting my feelings in writing is not something I have ever done before and it is smashing my heart into one million pieces by doing so. I'm not even sure whether you are still playing games with me.

I will openly admit that I was attracted to you from the first day I saw you – you have danger written all over you. You then had a string of girlfriends and I thought my instincts were right. Then one day you were sitting reading a book and the title took me by surprise – I felt myself fall there and then. It was something I fought hard to conceal and kept it buried inside.

Aside from my feelings towards you I was with a man (Richard) who had put himself through hell to be with me.

Fate also intervened and I fell pregnant. At this stage all of my choices were removed and I had to leave Opus and you behind.

I never forgot you and assumed you eventually went back home. It wasn't until my company collapsed earlier this year that you started to once again hit my consciousness.

I spoke to Maddy about you. This being the first time I had spoken to anyone about the feelings I'd fought.

I then joined Facebook, and found myself trawling pages to find you. I foolishly thought that if I added you as a friend, I could look at you without you ever knowing my feelings – I've truly blown that one! Maddy added you as a friend, not at my request, but I think as a means of watching over me. I have never asked why she did that. But in your crowded space I thought you would not even notice my presence so it was no big deal. But then some of your Facebook Status Updates hit me hard.

Over the last weeks I have fallen harder than ever and it is now causing me to withdraw from Richard. I cannot explain to him what is happening to me. He speaks to me and I don't hear him. It is like I am locked in my own world. He is continually asking me if everything is okay and wanting continual reassurance that I love him. Richard is a kind, loving man who holds my heart in a different way. We don't kiss; we haven't kissed like two people should for over ten years and he never questions it. I guess I love him like a best friend.

But now, I've allowed the floodgates to open to you and that's where my problem is. I am trapped here. If there were only me I would walk out of my front door now with just the clothes on my back. But there isn't just me. I have William and Elyse. If I left Richard my conscience would only allow me to walk away with nothing. To take my love and take financially would be too much.

This means I have no way of supporting myself and William and Elyse in a way that they are used to. Being with you would require money. Where you live, and the way you live. Without it you would be destroyed by domesticity. In short, without a miracle (lottery win) I am unable to go anywhere. Eight years ago it was just me, now it's not, but you will always have my heart.

You will always be my greatest love story; I could never bring myself to read the old novel by Anthony Hope, I stumbled across a few weeks ago because I am too afraid to read the ending. I just wish I could have had the fairy tale with you.

I made discoveries that all seemed to indicate that I should be with you. I was somehow guided to them. They have no meaning alone but only with you in the equation. My circumstances prevent me from being with you, so they must be for you alone. If you ever want them I will give them to you. Maybe my life is intended to be one of sacrifice. Who knows? But I do know this is a one-sided letter; making assumptions that you have feelings for me. I don't know whether you do or don't? Regardless, I feel I have had to send this letter because I would regret not telling you. I once again ask you not to remove me as a friend, and let me become the passive observer of your life. The last thing I ask is that you give me a truthful account of why you chose to play games with me. By the way, your Irish girlfriend is very beautiful.

Love you forever

Nicole x

It was going to have to be sent to his private email because *Facebook* inconveniently didn't accept attachments. My first ever letter to a man and the second time I'd let Anthony slip through my fingers, like he was a pile of worthless sand. I eventually stopped procrastinating, but the second I hit Send – I regretted it – I should have remained silent.

I sat motionless agonising over the word "love". I should not have used that word, but "...lust after you", wouldn't have been right either.

I was sure that my feelings were more than lust, but how could I really know? I'd never allowed myself the chance to find out. In a few hours, he would read it, and I would be swiftly removed as his friend. What had possessed me to send it?

There was a part of me that hoped he would listen to my words and not delete me, but deep down, he would have to be insane not to, after a confession like mine. There was no point him keeping me as a friend. It was like the "Game Over" had finally popped up on my computer game, all my lives were used up, and I'd made myself look an utter fool. I felt utterly wretched in the process.

The phone rang. I picked it up and hurled it against the desk, the battery fell out, but I swear it was still ringing in my ears.

The tears kept on coming for several hours, until I got into the car to fetch William and Elyse from school. I avoided eye contact with the occasional passing parent, because of my blotchy red face and puffed up piggy eyes. I listened to William and Elyse enthusiastically telling me about their day on the way home, and fired a few sums at William; mental arithmetic was his favourite pastime in the car – he had Richard's freaky head for fast maths.

My own head still had that heavy aftermath from sobbing, which always hits like a hangover. Suddenly William and Elyse stopped being jovial and started bickering over car space. 'Mummy...Wiwyam's legs are in my space, he's touching me.'

'William, sit up straight please,' I said, as I glanced at him through the rear-view mirror.

'I'm not doing nothing.'

'I'm not doing anything, not I'm not doing nothing. Sit up straight please.'

'Mummy…he's still got his legs in my space.'

'But I'm tired, Mum.'

'William, just move your legs please, and stay in your own space. Stop winding her up.

Elyse, I saw that, don't you dare pinch him. If I could reach you bo—' and then they kicked off into an almighty row with an insane level of noise that my head was not prepared to take.

'Just shut up the pair of you. Shut up!!! I'm trying to drive,' I heard myself yell.

It was like the yell of childbirth – like it had come from the mouth of someone else. At that moment I just wanted to stop the car, get out and kick in every panel of it in. I wanted to take every ounce of frustration out on the car.

'Mum, you need to take a chill pill,' William said calmly, as though they hadn't been making noise at all, and as if I was the only one losing it.

'William, just stop it…please,' I said, with remorse for being angry with them. My turmoil over Anthony was not their fault. Our numbers may have collided, but our worlds were simply too far apart.

One day, I vowed, I'll read that sodding novel.

But I didn't want some old book telling me that I'd done the wrong thing.

CHAPTER SEVENTEEN

An email from Anthony Hope sat in my Inbox.

It had come through while I was on the school run. I didn't know whether opening it there and then was such a good idea. I didn't want to allow myself to cry in front of William and Elyse, and I still needed the puffiness to go down before Richard came home from work, otherwise he would be asking what was wrong.

As usual, the sensible option wasn't the option I went for. I opened it up, read it, and it made no sense. So I continued to stare at it, as though it was an anagram that would eventually make sense. I couldn't understand why he had sent such a curt reply and then not removed me from his *Facebook*. I read it through once more:

Dear Nicole

I am really sorry but I think you need to re-read your emails. I was merely responding to an old acquaintance. I love my girlfriend very much. The story is all yours.

Take care

Anthony Hope

This was utter bullshit. What emails? Other than the initial email after he'd added me, and the emails following his prank with Lewis Carroll, there had been no emails between us. The game wasn't using email. Why the hell would he go to the trouble of reading the Lewis Carroll comment on my Wall then go and post one of his famous quotes on *his* Wall if he considered me as nothing more than an old acquaintance. He was the one who pulled the stunt with that quote.

If he wasn't interested in me he would have ignored me; I would have been invisible to him. And how can he be in love? He can't have known her two minutes, otherwise she would have already been on his *Facebook* months ago, the fact I didn't really know him and thought I loved him was beside the point. For the first time, since adding him, I wanted to punch him, kick him and scream at him until he did make sense, or until he at least confessed to deliberately messing with my head. I thought about his friends calling him Ant. If he was an ant then I could have stamped on him. The asshole.

The only thing I could feel from his letter was anger. Had I embarrassed him? Was he angry with me for simply telling him my truth? But then, what had I been expecting him to say? He wasn't even acknowledging the game. He was pretending it never happened. Well…at least he'd replied, and at least the reply had evoked emotion that didn't need tears.

I knew then that it would definitely have been smarter, more sensible, to have simply stopped posting things on my Wall that he could translate and respond to; I should have remained silent about my feelings towards him. But, as a consequence of the stupid way I had gone about things, I was now like some pathetically wounded animal waiting for the hunter to finally put the bullet through its head. I was waiting for him to finally hit the tiny "x" button.

Not allowing Maddy to read the email I had sent to Anthony was probably one of my rare wise moves. However, telling Maddy that I had sent the email, and telling her about Anthony's reply was definitely *not* a wise move, I concluded, when I saw what she'd put on her Wall a couple of days later.

Maddy says if you are going to play cat and mouse, make sure you are the cat.

OMG! I groaned out loud.

I am not a mouse, I am a lion.

A lion always lives to fight another day, even when feeling weakened. No doubt Anthony had already seen it, and yet he'd *still* not brought down the guillotine.

Maddy had got her friends wondering what the fuck she was going on about on her Wall. They were trying to decipher her Status Update. I kept hitting the refresh button to see what her friends were writing, cursing the fact that she was screwing the times of my mock paper I was supposed to be completing for my exam.

By early evening, Maddy was spitting feathers. Being slightly hacked off earlier at the fact she couldn't get Henry the life-sized dragon he wanted for Christmas, was now a minor issue in comparison to this. I sat at the laptop in the garden room, my fingers flying over my keyboard as emails emerged back and forth between us....

Maddy: Your little friend Anthony Hope has deleted me.

Nicole: What?

Maddy: He's gone. No longer listed as one of my Facebook friends. He's knocked me off. Why would he knock me off, and not you? You sent the letter not me.

I stared at her question, thinking about what I said in the letter to him about Maddy. He must have gone and removed the watchful eye, I thought. I couldn't tell Maddy that of course; she would have flipped even more.

Nicole: I don't know why

Maddy: Well I've got a good mind to leave a snotty message on your Wall for him to read. Give him a piece of my mind. I really don't like him. I don't know what you see in him anyway.

Nicole: No please don't do that. I accept that I can't play games with him, that's over. But don't leave a message on my Wall for him. Just let him stay on my Facebook where I can see him. He's probably going to delete me soon with or without your help.

Maddy: Okay

Nicole: Thank you. Lots of big kisses

I posted my last message then took another look at Anthony's latest Status Update with fresh eyes:

Anthony is playing AKON sorry, blame it on me!!

I watched the pop video on YouTube and then found the lyrics on some other website. I spent some time mulling them over to Richard's puzzlement. He walked over, looked at the screen, but

I could still sense him glancing over from the sofa while I remained in a trance-like state, leaning into the laptop with my elbow on the table and head propped in my right hand.

Bad Boys, Bad Boys...he's posted a song about Bad Boys.

The fact that he's posted this around the same time he's removed Maddy, makes it feel like his cryptic apology that he didn't want her to see. Or he's removed her, to show some kind of loyalty to me. Perhaps guilt has dealt him a hefty blow after he sent that email. Guilt has a powerful way of doing that; it sits heavily on the conscience. As I sat reasoning things through, my instincts were telling me that this was his apology and apologies make it very difficult not to forgive – I forgave him.

A few days later I found myself sitting and looking through what we had both written on our *Facebook* pages since my stupid letter.

The problem with forgiving someone, who also happens to be a person you have humiliated yourself in front of, as much as I had, is you tend to feel quite safe in the fact that there isn't really much else you can do to make matters worse. This time round though, I was trying desperately hard to view his Wall without decoding his words, and linking them back to my *Facebook* postings.

So, just because he'd gone and joined the group Derailed – it didn't mean that I'd derailed him with my words. And no, my Status hadn't been remotely connected to his when I wrote: *Nicole is sighing...really need to get my head back on track.*

Then I thought about the 'Vine and The Branches' and I quickly typed in...

Why don't I just beat myself with a stick...better still do the job properly with a branch...having an early night!!!!

I felt my fingers slamming against the keyboard like stamping feet. This was all bullshit, just like his email. I turned the laptop off and walked through the lounge.

'Where you off to now?' Richard asked, slightly slurring his words as he lay horizontal on the sofa.

He'd started calling in at the pub with Blue most nights, pretending that he'd taken him for an extra-long walk. It was his blatant denial that pissed me off the most.

'Bath,' I said and made my way upstairs.

After turning on the taps, I glanced at myself in the mirror; wiping away the steam each time it built up. But even the steam could not hide the evident truth. I was getting thinner as each day passed and my face looked so gaunt and pale, but I couldn't stop my treadmill workout or face the food that I should have been eating.

I leaned over the side of the bath, swirling the water with my arm, taking pleasure from it massaging my skin each time I reversed the direction. I spent a few more minutes idling; playing with William and Elyse's plastic yacht, which had been left in the bath.

After a while, I dropped my clothes into the wicker laundry basket which was noticeably over filled and climbed into the bath, sliding beneath the bubbles, closed my eyes and allowed the steam to penetrate my head. I allowed one hand to gently caress my breast while the other hand explored between my legs until the tingling became too much. I knew that if I forced myself to be relaxed I would sleep deeply, and then I would feel no pain.

I sat back up. My sudden movement caused the water to swish from one end of the bath to the other. I dropped Elyse's tub of foam alphabet letters into the water. *Tell me what I should be doing*, I said silently in my head. If there really was some kind of spirit or angel, then surely they could use these letters to spell it out to me. I sat and stared and stared at them floating on the surface. Nothing happened.

CHAPTER EIGHTEEN

Kanye West's *Love Lockdown* had been playing on *MTV Base* most of the week. I'd put the *Sky* channel on as an alternative to the *iPod*, since William had smashed the speaker with his tennis ball a few days earlier.

The thing about *MTV Base* was that it tended to repeat the same songs over and over, but even then I hadn't noticed the album title that the song had been taken from, because I never really glanced at the screen; I'd simply been listening to the ironic lyrics as they played in the background while I revised for my exam.

But Anthony had noticed. His Status read:

Kanye West's new album got a buzz...ZZing drum beat – check it out!

Had he used the emphasis on "ZZ" as in 'sleepy-head' because I'd gone to bed early the previous night, or as in busy bee, I wondered. I looked up the album. It was called *808s & Heartbreak*. It couldn't have been more fitting. Anthony was still definitely playing his game, and this time he was playing even harder than before.

He'd clearly picked up on the significance of number eight or the infinity symbol from my *Facebook* Wall, and I had said in my ridiculously long and cringeworthy email that I did have some numbers if he wanted them, so a day or so after Anthony had pointed me in the direction of Kanye West, I decided to type in the whole equation so he could see it. A quadratic equation appearing on someone's *Facebook* was probably as odd as a Lewis Carroll quote, but I didn't care, I simply wanted to pass the numbers on to him, I felt as though I was fulfilling some kind of duty.

I couldn't tell whether he'd picked up on the equation at the time. All I really noticed was a few more photos taken from his trip to Ireland several months ago. They showed him singing on the stage at what looked like a party. But I couldn't see how these photos related to the equation.

The game with Anthony continued in earnest as we hurtled towards Christmas.

I knew that I should have summoned up every ounce of my strength to stop myself playing the silly game, but Anthony's hold over me was like a drug. Perhaps we all have our own opium, capable of destroying us, but I desired so badly to smell his skin. Maybe there is something in the research that says attraction is down to a scent that we each have. I couldn't remember his, not like the way I remembered his voice, but I craved it as though another part of me remembered it dangerously well.

Each time Richard and I rowed, I immediately retreated to the computer to stare at Anthony's photos on *Facebook* or I would quietly sit and sketch the contours of his face as though they held the answers to everything. But that was also when the craving hit the hardest. For the first time in my life, I was facing up to the fact that I wasn't as strong willed as I'd considered myself to be. The pain of thinking I would lose him from my *Facebook,* after my letter, was far greater than the pain of him still being where I could see him. I couldn't take the opium; I could merely keep it close by. He sat behind the screen of my computer as though he had a sign saying In Case Of Emergency Break Glass. But I knew it was highly unlikely that the glass between us would ever be broken

The Christmas tree had been placed in the lounge and decorated with the collection of red and gold baubles, cherubs and jewels that I'd gathered over the years. Richard wasn't remotely interested in the tree, but for William and Elyse, it always had to go up early in December because it was a binding contract that Santa couldn't back out of. Our six-foot tree was, as always, overshadowed by Maddy's twelve-footer but I had no desire to compete with her over this.

Having got the December exam out of the way, I turned my attention to getting the Christmas presents sorted. William's had been relatively easy to get as I only had to shop online with *Chelsea Football Club*. Elyse was a one-stop shop at *Toys-R-Us*, but the rest required a trip into the city.

It had been a good few months since I'd been shopping in the city centre. The Christmas decorations had been put up, but somehow it felt like a quiet fairground that had all the flashing lights and music that continually changed as you moved around, but lacked the vital atmosphere to make it special; it had no pre-Christmas buzz. This could have been my own emotions casting gloomy shadows over the council's efforts. But I was struck by the lack of people; even parking hadn't been a problem this year. And I was passing far too many vacant premises. The government's plan of reducing the VAT down to 15 per cent to boost trade either wasn't working or it was saving it from being obliterated altogether.

While I wasn't too heavily laden with carrier bags I decided to take the five-minute walk to the large high-street bookstore. This was Richard's favourite shop, and as usual, I hadn't got a clue what else to buy him. I'd already got him a Swiss Army Knife, the nearest thing to a tool box he would possess and the shop assistant reassured me that 3-inch blades were perfectly legal. But Football was the only sport he was really interested in; he didn't care about things like the Arts, although apparently in his thirties he did go through a very brief spell of being a fan of *Painting by Numbers!* But he'd grown out of that one, so interesting books were always a good bet for stocking fillers, along with new socks and pants.

I wandered around the different floors looking for inspiration. The problem was that there was too much inspiration crammed on the shelves. But then I settled on a couple of Barak Obama books: *Dreams from my Father* having grabbed my attention first. I placed that and a couple of other books on the counter and got my credit card ready. A young, student-looking guy scanned them. .

'Is that it?' he asked.

'Yes. Thank y—', I began. 'No, actually...it's not...can you tell me if you have a book in stock, please?'

'Yes, but I would need to take you over to the other computer screen.'

I walked around to the other side of the counter.

'The book is old. The author is Anthony Hope and the title is Simon Dale.' I said, once he'd opened up the right screen. I felt a bit like the old man from the "fly-fishing" *Yellow Pages* adverts!

He typed the details in and then turned the computer screen towards me.

'Is that the one?'

'Yes, yes that's it...have you got it in?' I asked with a mixture of surprise and excitement.

'No. But I can order it for you. It will take about six weeks to come through. We can post it out to you, or send a note to let you know when it's in.'

He was merely trying to be helpful, but I stood looking at him while I considered my options: six weeks, and thud, the book lands on the hall floor and Richard picks it up, or among the mugged mail retrieved from Blue, Richard finds a postcard notification with teeth marks right through Anthony Hope's name.

'No. Thank you. I think I'll leave it. I'll just take the Obama books please.'

It was another week before I started to wrap the presents and, as I was doing so, my mobile rang. It was Maddy.

'You're not going to believe this...the school play has only gone and fallen on *X Factor* final night. Can you fucking believe it? We're going to be stuck there four fucking hours on a Saturday night. We're going to miss the X Factor final!'

'You're joking? Four hours. We've got to sit there through all of the kids' years, not just William and Henry's? And on X Factor final night? That's taking the piss. Why has the school made it on a Saturday night?'

'Fucked if I know...but I'm finding a way out of there. I can't wait to see Henry and William with their usual one line as sheep or shepherds, and that's it, after their play I'm off.'

'Yeah well...I'm not going to be far behind you. I don't think we are being selfish about this. I mean if you didn't have a child, would you seriously choose to go and watch a school nativity play on a Saturday night...regardless of the X Factor final?' I said, while I continued to wrap presents, balancing the phone on my shoulder.

'No I wouldn't...anyway, talking of selfish and stupid. What is going on with your Facebook?'

'It's Anthony Hope, he still appears to be following me through Alice in Wonderland with things he posts on his Wall.'

'I know what you are doing. It's the why I'm asking about.'

'Look. When I get to the end of Alice in Wonderland. I'll stop.' Considering I still hadn't fulfilled my last promise of talking to Richard, I avoided sticking one on the end.

'You'll stop. And then what? Are you going to start another book with him? What have you got lined up next? Are we going to be going through War and Peace? If so I can't wait for that one, should keep it going a bit...just wake me up when you get to the end though.'

'No more books...anyway you wrote on my Wall that you were going to book me in with a top shrink. I just used it as my Status... Nicole is going to search top shrinks. Feel like falling down large tunnel.'

'I did, didn't I? Sorry.'

'Don't worry. It turned out to be quite useful, so thank you. But that's why I was drowning in my own tears; then Anthony

Hope *wished he had a key to open all doors*!!!!! I wrote *twinkle twinkle little bat, how I wonder what you're at*, and that I was *curious and curiouser*. Apparently he wants to *have his cake and eat it* and he's been smoking on a video clip. And now I'm thinking of becoming a Fan of *Peppa Pig*.'

Maddy stayed silent. I don't think she could quite visualise the cartoon versions of Anthony and I in quite the same way as I could.

'Look, I know it is pretty immature stuff and a bit complex to explain, unless you really understand *Alice in Wonderland* and you relate it to the story with a modern twist. But basically he writes Status Updates relating to her, but really they're following what I write on my Wall, or at least that's how they appear to me.'

'Just hurry up and get to the end of your book and then stop it.'

'Okay, I will...so have we got a deal to get out of the school play early?'

'I'll find a way round it.'

I didn't doubt her for a second.

I lay next to Elyse on top of the bed staring up at the ceiling and thinking; I was trying to prevent myself from falling asleep along with her. Her skin still had a faint smell of lavender baby-bath.

I wasn't still thinking about ways to get out of the school play; that had taken place a few days before and had been easy in the end. I was not long behind Maddy and Steve who had simply scooped up Henry and left. But Elyse got bored sitting in the audience, so I took her out early to get back in time to watch Alexandra Burke beat JLS with her version of *Halleluiah*. Richard stayed behind with William, because he had no choice; his grandson was in another one of the plays. So, as I lay there, I was thinking of *Alice in Wonderland* and how Lewis Carroll hadn't simply thrown it together in jumbled chaos, like I'd always considered as a child; there was far more too it.

As I stared into darkness the penny suddenly dropped with regard to his Knave of Hearts. The Knave is judged in the court in the final chapter of the book. But it's not just a playing card who has run off with a plate full of jam tarts. The jam tarts are symbolic of tarts: prostitutes or courtesans. And the Knave who sits as a young prince in a pack of cards is also a rogue, a rascal, a scoundrel and a humble man. But the Knave is also known as Jack. Anthony Hope was both my prince charming and bad boy 'Jack.' He was the Jack of Hearts at the very heart of my equation. But how could he drop honey into hot milk...yet still crave the sweet tart? On my last thought I unintentionally dozed off and, over the next few days, I managed to weave my crazy thoughts into Status Updates, thinking at that point that the only person they would be remotely interesting to was Anthony Hope.

CHAPTER NINETEEN

It was the lull on Status Updates from Anthony, along with lack of access to my study books between Christmas and New Year that finally triggered me to read the Anthony Hope novel online. It was as though I needed the 'Anthony' substitute as a quick fix. I knew from messages left on his *Facebook* Wall that he was working through Christmas. I also knew his girlfriend was staying with him. And I guessed that two child-free people living in a capital city would spend their time visiting a whirlwind of glamorous parties.

It is true that we had a massive piss-up party at Maddy's, but I never bothered going to Richard's work party and even he didn't grace them with his presence this year. Christmas Day had been an endless round of visiting relatives: Richard's mum in the nursing home first thing, then over to Richard's wife mid-morning. That was the tradition, so that Richard got to see his children and grandchildren on Christmas Day. Then back to ours for Christmas dinner, which ended up more of a Christmas supper as the turkey was far too big and took far too long to cook. Dad turned up alone, leaving Mum in bed with flu, refusing to spread her germs; her present and dinner were sent back with Dad. Grandmama had escaped on a coach trip to Scotland and my brother and Tammy had been on the same rally race around relatives, managing to turn up to ours just as our forks dived into the turkey. Matt and Dad had an almighty row over Matt's piss-poor timing, so Matt and Tammy swiftly despatched William and Elyse's gifts and left.

Overall, Christmas was, as usual grossly over-rated and by New Year none of us could be arsed to do anything and spent the next day moaning to one another on the phone about how bored we'd all been.

Anthony Hope had posted a clip from the Rat Pack with Sammy Davis Junior singing 'She's Funny That Way,' at the Sands in 1963. So I played the video clip several times over, marvelling at the way he managed to find a clip which answered my question: "What was he playing at?" It was a heckled version of the song about a woman crazy for a penniless man, but she would happily live in a tent, despite being better off without him. I was also mildly irritated by the fact he arrogantly seemed to know that he was behaving like a love rat and was revelling in the attention.

My Status Update in response simply said: *You're such a card – Jack! ;)*

Mum finally got over her virus soon after New Year and had offered to come over to see William and Elyse as well as giving Richard and I the chance to escape to the cinema alone for the afternoon. Our plan was to see *Australia*, which had just been released.

The house was a tip with school holidays and new toys scattered everywhere. The overwhelming pile of ironing was the finishing touch, which made me decide to blank it all and escape to the Study before Mum and Dad arrived.

The search engine was still open on the screen and instead of typing in *Facebook*, I typed in *Anthony Hope + Simon Dale + Story + Plot + Synopsis* in fact anything that would pull up the dreaded but compelling book.

Chewing on the corner of my lower lip and leaning in towards the monitor, I scrolled down the cached results, and then finally clicked on a free version of the book, which had been uploaded in its entirety. *Perhaps I could slowly read my way through it each day?* I clicked the "next" box on the screen to get past the title page and was now faced with chapter headings.

My eyes slowly made their way down the long list – Chapter One: The Child of Prophecy, Chapter Two: The Way of Youth, Chapter Three: The Music of the World, Chapter Four: Cydaria Revealed, Chapter Five: I am Forbidden to Forget, Chapter Six: An Invitation to Court, Chapter Seven: What Came of Honesty,

Chapter Eight: Madness, Magic and Moonshine, all the way down to Chapter Seventeen: What Befell my Last Guinea and Chapter Eighteen: Some Mighty Silly Business. Even the chapter headings appeared to have some pertinence.

My eyes continued to read down all twenty-six chapters that appeared on my screen.

Just as I was about to enter Chapter One, I heard Mum and Dad enter the house. I paused but then decided to leave Richard to do the pleasantries, my absence was also masked by William and Elyse's enthusiastic welcome.

I double-clicked on Chapter One: The Child of Prophecy.

I found some of the language in the opening chapter hard work, and cursed myself for being so thick. It wasn't exactly *Jackie Collins*. The general gist of it was about trust, truth and God. But I felt my mouth fall and I heard my exhaled breath when I'd got to the end of the second paragraph:

I, Simon Dale, was born on the seventh day of the seventh month in the year of Our Lord sixteen hundred and forty-seven. The date was good in that the divine number was thrice found in it, but evil in that it fell on a time of sore trouble for both the nation and for our own house.

I whispered the opening line. The words echoed in my head. The odds of this just couldn't be. I leaned forward, resting my elbows on the desk and leaning my head into my hands. Anthony Hope had created an historical novel about a fictional man who just so happened to have a bit of a thing for divine numbers. But in this case the divine number appearing three times was seven, not eight.

But eight followed seven, and then I thought about six being the day of creation, seven the day of rest and eight the day of resurrection. For me, this long-forgotten book had been resurrected as eight in year 2008 which it had been when I first stumbled on it after Halloween.

As for "trouble for the nation and our own house", even that sounded familiar as I thought of the current financial shit we were all going through. This was too freaky. I shivered as though my blood had recoiled to safety.

'What are you doing? If you're going to the cinema, don't you think you should be getting yourself sorted?' Mum said, as she popped her head around the door. 'Ahh…might have known you'd been on the computer in here. Don't you think you'd be better off tidying up a bit, have you not noticed the state of the utility and the spare room upstairs?'

'I'm coming… I'll just be a few more minutes, and I've only got to put my coat on,' I said, dismissing her so that I could rapidly scan down page two.

Betty Nasroth, the wise woman, announced its imminence more than a year beforehand. For she predicted the birth, on the very day whereon I came into the world, within a mile from the Parish church, of a male child who should love where the King Loved, know what the King hid and drink of the King's cup.

So, this Betty woman was some kind of psychic who predicted the birth of Simon Dale. A man from humble origins with his destiny mapped out to fall for the King's mistress, Nell. So what happens then? Does he end up with Nell Gwyn? Does he manage to steal her from her King? I needed to get to the end of the book.

'Nicole, are you coming? We need to get going if you want to see the film,' Richard shouted through the door.

'Yes, I'll be out in a minute… I've nearly finished,' I shouted back, as the study PC had chosen now to go slow. 'Hurry up,' I cursed as I waited for it to open Chapter Twenty-Six: I Come Home. The screen turned black for a few seconds and then the chapter opened up. I repeatedly clicked on the next page icon at the bottom of the screen to get to the final page of the book. I scanned down to the very last paragraph…

'and have you utterly forgotten her?'

Her eyes were safely hidden.

I smiled as I answered, "Utterly"

'See how I stood! Will thou forgive me, Nelly?'

'For a man may be very happy as he is and still not forget the things which have been. "What are you thinking of, Simon?" my wife asks sometimes when I lean back in my chair and smile "of nothing, sweet" say I. And in truth, I am not thinking, it is only that a low laugh echoes distantly in my ear. Faithful and loyal am I, but – should such as Nell leave nought behind her?

So...the fictional man ends up with the other woman, not Nell – it's there in black and white.

If I am right and this book is trying to warn me away from Anthony Hope, then this latest girlfriend of Anthony's will be the one he will eventually marry, leaving the courtesan, me, with nought. The thought of Richard's financial shit popped into my head.

I quickly flicked back several pages, until I found the last reference to Nell – why had she ended up with nought? *Great,* I thought after eventually finding it. *Not only does she not get the man in question but she's drops dead after getting poisoned. That's it. I can't read this book, there is no point. The whole thing is ridiculous. I'm being ridiculous. How can an old book tell Anthony's or my future?* I went to grab my coat off the back of the kitchen door.

We barely spoke a word as we drove to the cinema.

Richard was listening to the radio, while I thought through the author Anthony Hope's words and my numbers.

It was like I was scribbling things down on a blackboard in my mind so I could see things more clearly.

Nell ends up with "nought" which is "nothing" which is also "zero".

The quadratic equation has "0" or "zero" after the equal sign.

But if seven has slid to eight, this time around the "zero" should slide to "one".

But "one" of what? I didn't know.

I still felt like I was missing something with the numbers. I instead turned my thoughts to his character marrying the other woman in the book. That last paragraph implied that Nell was still the one in his head. I was sure I was in Anthony's head. I felt his presence, or at least felt like I was being watched.

'You're very quiet,' said Richard. 'What are you thinking about?'

'Nothing,' I lied.

A couple of days later I lied again.

I had not long returned from an indoor sporting venue after spending the day there with Maddy and the kids. Richard had stayed home with Blue. As usual, I logged onto the laptop in the garden room to see what I'd missed while being out. But Richard came up behind me, placing an A4 sheet of paper next to me.

'What's this all about,' he said.

I looked at it from the corner of my eye, barely interested. Then I saw what it was and sat frozen for what felt like minutes, rather than seconds.

'Hold on a sec while the Internet loads up.'

My eyes slyly glanced down the page, checking that I hadn't been foolish enough to have mentioned Anthony Hope's name on there. Thank God I hadn't. I tried to curb the sigh of relief which made me cough. I couldn't believe he'd found my crazy number ramblings connected to number eight and the numbers in our birthdays that I'd posted on *Facebook* months ago for Anthony to see, just before he went away with his girlfriend.

'Where did you find it?' I asked, daring to look up at him.

'On the desk in the study. I needed a piece of paper and thought it was a blank sheet until I turned it over and saw that lot,' he said, pointing to my scribbles.

It was then that I remembered recently using the scanner in the study. I must have taken the sheet off there without looking what was on it, and then left it lying around on the desk. Thank God I hadn't found Anthony's date of birth when I typed it all out. *Oh no...what if he's looked up the title of the book on his mobile and discovered the link back to Anthony Hope? Is Richard letting me dig myself into a hole and then going to throw Anthony Hope in at the end? How should I play this?*

'So...what is it then? Is the question that difficult?'

'No...not at all...it's just that...I'm thinking of writing a book,' I said, while thinking what the hell possessed me to say that.

'A book? What about?'

'Erm...just stuff...you know...like...us lot, the credit crunch and life. I feel as if we are trapped in *Alice in Wonderland*.'

'So what's the relevance of all the numbers? Our dates of birth a—'

'I'm using the ghostly numbers in there somewhere... I'm not sure how yet and I just wanted to see all the numbers in our dates of birth...to see where particular numbers cropped up.' I said, still unsure why I actually did it myself that day. It was utterly crazy and I cringed as I wondered what Anthony must have thought about it when he spotted it all.

'So...what has that novel *Simon Dale* got to do with it? Why is that mentioned on there? Haven't you mentioned that book before to me?'

'The book. Oh...it...it's also set in dark and difficult times...I thought it would be useful that's all,' I said cringing, hoping that he wouldn't later look it up himself later as see Anthony Hope's name.

'Oh right...fine...whatever...write your book then. Credit crunch could be a good subject...it's certainly topical.'

Richard left me to it, I felt myself relax, sort of.

CHAPTER TWENTY

Given my obsession with a man on my *Facebook*, the worst thing that could possibly have happened in my life was that I would be unable to get online.

And, on the 18th of January 2009, I woke up to find we had no Internet access. I tried to refresh the connection. I unplugged the router, shut down the entire PC, logged back on again, all to no avail. I typed in the IP address, re-typed the router user name and password, clicked on Save and tried again – still nothing but the same message that said: Internet Explorer cannot display the web page.

I repeated the process several times over while also trying to get William and Elyse ready for school. I was reaching the stage where I had that overwhelming urge to hurl the computer through the study window. I couldn't believe out of all the days of the year it had chosen this day to do this to me.

Enraged, I called Maddy and I quickly explained my predicament and that I needed to send a very urgent email. In other words, could I pop round as soon as possible, as in, the next hour after Richard, William and Elyse have left the house? She agreed and freshly showered and bare faced, I grabbed the letter I needed, stuffed it into my bag, jumped into the car and raced over to Maddy's.

As I pulled through her iron gates the CD changed from *Love is Noise* to *Infinity 2008*. As usual, her front door was unlocked and she was standing in the kitchen still in her pyjamas, which was pretty normal for her around 09:00.

Without seeming too rude I made a point of first checking out her latest family addition – Bella the hamster; Henry's Christmas present from her brother.

This cute tan-and-white creature weighed in at practically nothing but was currently causing constant brow-beating in my own household; William and Elyse were working on acquiring their own tiny balls of fluff.

'She's cute, but I'm glad I've not got one to clean out every week,' I said, as I placed Bella back in the cage.

As we waited for the kettle to boil, Maddy fetched her *Apple Mac* for me. She'd bought a *Mac* because the shiny white colour-coordinated with her kitchen. Then, she lit a cigarette, while I sorted out my email.

'So...what's the urgency then?' she asked.

'It's Anthony, not an urgent email at all – sorry,' I cringed. 'He posted a Status last night that said he's got an important announcement to make.' I didn't like her expression. It was the narrowed eyes that did it. 'Look, I haven't been on my *Facebook* much this last week...I've been trying hard not to,' and I felt my face scrunching up, as I tried to justify my behaviour.

'I might have known he'd be the reason why you've raced over here so quickly without even bothering to blow dry your hair.'

'I know...I know...but I want to know what he means and he can't see my hair is wet...otherwise I would have.'

'Vain cow. And it shouldn't be of any interest to you what he means,' she said, with one of her superior Miss Piggy hair flicks, as *she* called them.

Sometimes I was never sure whether her moral high ground was the result of her coming from a broken home; her mum moved to New Zealand after being divorced from Maddy's dad.

'I am aware of that,' I said.

The laptop had been left open on the Proceeds of Crime Act. The lack of control over their situation had her spending hours studying the finer details of the Act so that she could try to stay one step ahead. This was all driving her mad. As a consequence, I was becoming as familiar with POCA as she was with a complete stranger called Anthony Hope.

'Can you get *Facebook* up for me please?' I asked. She pulled it up for me and slid the laptop back my way.

I signed myself in and pulled up Anthony's Profile.

Loads of people had left messages for him, wanting to know what his news was – just like me.

'Look at them all,' I said. 'If I'd left a Status like that, probably only five people would be remotely interested – one of which would be you.'

Maddy just laughed and handed me a mug of tea.

I sat and read every single message running over several pages while Maddy had a bit of a tidy up before her cleaner arrived. I left another message on my *Facebook* Wall, saying I liked the picture of the Jackass in a paper crown.

I took a few moments to ponder if he'd posted this picture to look like the prince, jack or knave on a pack of cards. I didn't really know for sure.

'He can't have gone to sleep at all last night,' I said.

Maddy raised her eyebrows.

Why doesn't he seem to sleep much at night? I silently wondered, as I imagined him in boxers and a loose T-shirt, sitting propped up in his bed playing on his laptop. I also imagined him with a couple of books by his bedside, like I always had.

'He's probably like you Maddy...gets midnight munchies and insomnia from all the nicotine.'

'I've never been able to sleep...it's nothing to do with nicotine...you ask my dad what I was like as a kid...Mum and Dad tried everything with me,' she said, while blowing her cigarette smoke out of the kitchen window.

'Why is he posting Status Updates in a weird language in the early hours,' I said, while still looking at them.

Anthony says he can't help but wonder...

Anthony says: Es gibt Grobe Macht in wortern, wenn sie zu viele von ihnen zusammen nicht festmachen.

It looked German to me, but I couldn't be entirely sure. It was as though he was trying to cryptically tell me something. But what? I scribbled the words down on the back of an envelope that was lying around.

'How's your German?' I asked, while taking a bite from the toast Maddy had now placed in front of me.

'Non-existent, why?'

'These Updates definitely look German to me. Do you have any German friends that I don't know about?'

'No but I have a Belgium friend.'

'Hmmm…right well – I'll find an online translator. God I hate your laptop. Everything's there but it's all in the wrong place. Where's the search bit gone?'

'God, you're ungrateful. I let you play on my laptop and you slag it off,' she took it from me. 'There…you're in now.'

'Thank you.'

'Any luck?'

'No…it's not going anywhere.'

The whole thing had frozen.

She took the laptop off me.

'Internet's gone down…keeps doing this lately…you'll have to wait a bit,' she said calmly.

I didn't feel calm.

'Why now? What is it with the bloody Internet today? I swear this Status is something to do with me.'

'You're mad,' she said.

'I need to know what it says…what if he's going home or…he's getting engaged?'

'Oh, what a shame that would be,' she said.

I pulled a face at her.

Maddy just shook her head and simultaneously closed her eyes. So I continued with my spoken thought-processing.

'It could just be a message to a German friend,' Maddy offered, as I sat frantically trying to get the Internet back up.

'No…because they would have replied to it…they wouldn't just ignore it…surely? None of his friends' names sounded particularly German either. I've looked through them already. But it might not even be German. I could be completely wrong. Oh...I don't know. I wanted to show you his New Year photos with his girlfriend as well,' I said.

The fact they had looked so good together had really hurt, which was why I'd been trying to stay off *Facebook* for the past week.

The Internet came back up.

I breathed a sigh of relief and quickly pulled the album up for Maddy.

'I still prefer him in casual clothes, rather than suits. Suits are definitely for businessmen,' I said, as I looked at the first picture.

But he still looked edgy, even in a suit. He was like the baddy in a movie: you should really be attracted to the good guy, but the more dangerous-looking bad guy just has that sexual edge.

'Here...look at them properly then,' I said, forcing her to look at the album taken at a Black Tie event in some hotel somewhere. They were posing like they'd been shot for *Hello* magazine.

'Yeah, they're nice typical New Year photos of a new couple. She's no prettier than you though,' Maddy said, while scrutinising them.

'Oh, come on. She looks gorgeous on these pictures and she's tall.'

'So what? Do you want to be tall? I know I don't. I love being small... Steve hates tall women, says they look like men.'

'I like being petite...most of the time,' I said, as I thought that now and since the arrival of this girl wasn't one of those times in my life.

'What does she do for a living?' Maddy asked.

'Dunno...her *Facebook* has privacy settings...besides, men don't care whether women have a brain or not...and she'll have a sexy Irish accent,' I said, changing direction to strengthen my argument.

Lately I was not only disliking being small, but was also hating my bland English accent, which was the result of hundreds of pounds spent removing an accent which was only useful if you planned to appear as a guest on *The Jeremy Kyle Show.*

'So what? She could have a funny voice...?'

'Yeah I know that...but...she's younger than me.'

'And... therefore lacks life experience and conversation,' she shot back.

'Funny, that's what older women used to say to Richard having never met me. Anyway she has long dark hair...look, you're just not getting it,' I said, laughing at her resignedly.

It didn't matter what negative comment I could throw at her, she would throw a positive one back to make me feel better. This was probably what I needed from her, because my own confidence was dwindling by the day.

'If he ends up back in New York we could both lose him,' I said, feeling a dull ache, which was staring to feel like an emotion attached to me like some clingy lapdog these days. But strangely it was as though I knew I couldn't have him and was getting used to him having this girl around. If Anthony Hope's old novel was to mean anything, then she had to be the one my Anthony Hope finally marries. I wanted it to be her rather than anyone else, even if I was insanely jealous. But until he did get married I considered it fair game to fantasise about being with him on that isolated beach, twiddling a wedding ring that had never remotely interested me until now. Lately, I'd also started daydreaming about us sitting somewhere quiet in the open country, and in between sensual kisses we were sketching the scene before us; comparing our work to see who had drawn it better.

Thinking of kissing Anthony and the betrayal involved also reminded me that I'd forgotten to tell Maddy about Richard finding the paper with all the things about number eight, our birth dates and references to the old novel. I filled her in on the whole uncomfortable tale.

'So, rather than tell the truth...you've now got to write a whole fucking book,' she said, after I'd finished filling her in on the details.

'Great…so we're all going to be in a book…written just to cover your ass. You could write a book on how to complicate your life with words. I'm pretty sure I would have come up with a far easier excuse.'

'Yeah…well, I might really write a book. I could write a whole fucking book on you and Steve alone,' I said, teasingly.

'Another good excuse not to get a job…that could keep you busy for another couple of years…probably take you into retirement if you drag it out,'

'Ha ha.'

'Anyway – so that was it? Richard just accepted that as an explanation?'

'Yeah pretty much.'

'No fucking way Steve would've.'

'Richard did. But anything is plausible with me. To suddenly announce I'm going to write a book is no different from me suddenly announcing I'm quitting my job to go to university. He's used to me.'

While I gave her every last detail on my latest debacle, her Internet went down again. I was reluctant to head home, because waiting for it to come back up was like Richard sitting and watching the football scores come in on a Saturday afternoon. I didn't want to miss it – I wanted to get that strange Status translated. But while I was waiting I decided to make use of my time and pulled from my bag the broadband letter.

I impatiently worked my way through the endless touch phone options, until I eventually got to a human being, only to be told that the account had been cancelled. A new direct debit (Richard must have set up, not me) had failed to go through before Christmas and delays with the mail meant the payment reminder letters hadn't reached us.

'A week?' I heard myself almost scream down the phone. 'You

are telling me that you have input the wrong account number into your system, cancelled my account without considering the effect of Christmas holidays, and now you're telling me you're going to take a week to sort your errors,' I said. 'I need my Internet. I can't do my work without the Internet, this is going to cost me money,' I lied, in utter despair but my lie got me nowhere. It was going to take a week and that was it.

I put down the phone with force and then looked sheepishly at Maddy, hoping she would understand why I was feeling so demonstrative.

'I want to kill Richard. Why did he have to change the bank?'

'I'll be seeing a fair bit of you over the next week, then?'

I eventually tore myself away from Maddy's laptop and went back home.

The day wore on and after tidying up, I noticed that Elyse's rainbow paints were still on the table. I picked up the sponge brush and ran it along three of the colours, drawing a sweeping eight on a piece of paper. Then I had an idea and pulled out the telephone directory from one of the kitchen drawers; we may not have the Internet, but we did have a fax machine.

Language Courses & Schools, Tutoring I read.

I dialled the number at the top of the list and a young girl answered.

'Is there anyone there who can speak German?' I asked. 'Or a language similar to German? I added in desperation.'

'No, sorry. There are no tutors here right now.'

I thanked her and then continued looking down the list of possibilities, until I eventually found a lady who actually spoke German, rather than wanting me to sign up for an entire course. She sounded mature and kind.

'I wonder if you could help me?' I began. 'I've received an email from a potential German client and I'm not quite sure if I'm translating it correctly. It is very short. I could fax it through to you...?' Fingers crossed she would say yes.

'No, problem,' she said and gave me the fax number.

I painstakingly wrote the words out:

Es gibt Grobe Macht in wortern, wenn sie zu viele von ihnen zusammen nicht festmachen.

Then sent the fax. I'd almost forgotten how to use one; it had been that long.

I had a reply an hour later:

Doing a literal translation word for word isn't possible and strangely it is as though it has been put through one of those on-line translators, from English to German. But in this case, reading between the lines, it appears to be a quotation by Josh Billings which I took liberty to check on the Internet for you: "There's great power in words, if you don't hitch too many of them together."

Strange thing for a potential German client to send to you?!?

But hope this helps.

Kind regards, Maureen.

Cringing at her comments, I sent anther fax back thanking her, and then looked at the words.

Great power in words – does he mean great power in *my* words?

If you don't hitch too many together – my letter was rather long – is that what he means?

So...my numbers may mean something to him after all? Perhaps there is power in my numbers?

But then, on the other hand, he's in a band and a band sings lyrics – what if he's leaving the band and finally going home? If a member leaves there won't be so many hitched together and he might be saying that they'll be better off without him...

I was no nearer deciphering the message even if I now knew what the German translated as.

15:30. He would be rehearsing now, if he *was* still in the band...damn, how the hell was I going to survive a week without my Internet?

By the time Richard came home from work I was pacing

around like an addict gone cold turkey.

'Why are you behaving so over-the-top about your Internet?' Richard said, laughing. 'Are you sure you're not having cyber-sex on there or something?'

'Don't be so ridiculous,' I said, moving the fruit bowl four inches to the left. Did you mess with my Internet account deliberately?' I finally snapped.

'Christ...no I didn't. Sometimes there's no talking to you.' he said and left me alone in the kitchen to stew.

I was totally incapable of sitting down and chilling out. If the pacing had been constructive it wouldn't have been so bad. But it wasn't – it was totally aimless. I was doing nothing more than moving things around from place to place. Even the reminder letter from the finance company, asking Richard for a fifteen thousand pound balloon payment went from the top of the fruit bowl into the drawer, where I couldn't see it.

The next day I was back at Maddy's, but being subjected to heavy cigarette smoke two days on the trot had started to block my sinuses, giving my head a heavy, underwater feeling – but I was happy to tolerate it.

The laptop was on the arm of the sofa. I was still waiting to find out what was happening with Anthony. I'd even checked the band website; but there was nothing on there about anyone leaving.

Maddy went to fetch Steve's laptop. She logged onto her *Facebook* and we posted messages to each other, whilst sat no more than two feet apart. Maddy's friend Ivana also logged on from her home and joined in with us to finalise arrangements for her birthday bash. I managed to lose the best part of the day at Maddy's, munching my way through chocolates and biscuits, as though I was on a stakeout! Just before I left I caught Anthony's next update...

Anthony's found out he's going to be an uncle...big sis is having a baby! Mom is going nuts with joy.

Was that it? I thought.

'Surely that can't be his big announcement?' I said out loud, but Maddy was too busy on Steve's laptop to notice what I was looking at on hers.

I felt glad that he was going to be an uncle, but his joy reminded me of yet another reason why I could never be with him: I knew that he would make a great dad someday but I didn't want any more children.

Anthony needed to be with someone younger than me.

I left a Status Update, which said... *f ANTastic news!* X.

CHAPTER TWENTY-ONE

On the day that Richard got his new car, I tried my best to think of something nice to say about it.

'It's got heated seats, and take a look at this Sat Nav...it's loads better than the Merc's,' Richard said, as William and Elyse bounced around on the back seats.

'Yep...it looks good,' I said, barely registering it.

'And now Blue will be able to come on days out with us...we can all go out as a family.'

I nodded, half-heartedly.

'I couldn't expect your mum and dad to take out a huge lease on a car...and I still think this is better...it's more useful...with kids you need a practical car,' he said.

Mum and Dad had to take out a lease on Richard's behalf, because of all the financial gloom hanging over him with the bank and legal case – he couldn't get finance on a new car at a reasonable rate and his Mercedes had been sold; the cash from it having been sent to the finance company.

A few days or so later I had to take my own car on a trip to the other side of the city, to sign a legal document. I followed a car with the Christian fish symbol stuck to the back bumper for the latter part of the journey. It struck me that I now honed in on them; even the AIDS and breast cancer awareness ribbons were in the shape of a fish.

At the solicitors I waited in reception and then was shown in to an office.

'I just need to explain all the legal ins and outs,' the solicitor said, from behind a stack of green boxes. 'You do know that the document is so that the bank can have the second charge on your house?'

'Yes...I do.'

'So, this form gives the bank the power to repossess and sell your house and they can do this without negotiation.'

I knew that if I refused to sign the form, Richard would be completely stuck. So...I signed the document, wondering how the hell I'd managed to get my life into this state. Everywhere I turned I had no choices and everything was so damn complicated.

I handed the solicitor the cash for his services and, once outside the building, I decided that I may as well sort out Richard's Valentine card while I was near some shops.

It was always hard to buy Richard cards, as he was not *My Husband*; he was technically still somebody else's.

In the end, I selected the same as usual, one saying: *To The One I Love*. It had two cute bears on the front, hugging each other and said little which was how I felt.

Getting closer to Valentine's Day also meant getting closer to the 15th of February – William's 8th birthday, and because of the crazy number thing I became increasingly edgy, in case it did all have something to do with him.

On the 13th of February, I'd taken William and Elyse to a roller disco in the evening. The drive back had been on poorly lit roads covered in black ice and driving with extreme care had left my eyes tired and gritty from the straining.

I had made myself a green tea and whilst at the laptop looking at *Facebook* I used the wet teabags on my eyes – it was pleasantly refreshing. I leaned back for a few minutes, resting my head against the chair then removed the tea-bags. Through my clouded vision I could just make out a Valentine's card posted by Anthony Hope. I frantically rubbed my eyes to get a clearer look.

It wasn't a romantic one. In fact, it was completely out of sync with the soppy way he carried on with his girlfriend. And besides all of that – it had been posted before it was even Valentine's Day which didn't tally with the fact his *Facebook* indicated he was to be spending Valentine's Day with her – it was unnecessarily premature as far as their relationship was concerned.

I studied the words: *Cat was on a mission...he was coming fast...he told pussy to whip her pants off quick.* There was a picture of a cat with an enormous grin, riding on the back of a silver bullet.

A huge smile crept across my face.

This card had to be aimed at me...it was obviously meant for me.

I looked to see if any comments had been left. There were none. There was no way that he could post a crude card like this and not have a single friend comment on it. It just wouldn't happen on his *Facebook*. That meant that only I could see this card. I felt myself smile again. I also felt the thrill of sexual secrecy.

I was in his head, which meant that I was taking up some space, however small, in his heart.

After sleeping on it, I came up with a better idea for a response to Anthony's card. Something that, in theory, would confirm I was right that his card had been aimed at me. I lifted the heavy plastic tub full of photos from my bedroom wardrobe and started sifting through them with the help of William and Elyse; they were marvelling at photos of themselves as babies. I was searching for a photo taken in Majorca, about a year before either of them even existed.

'Mummy, look at this one, I'm crawling,'

'That's not you. William, that's Elyse. She had your old baby-grow on.'

'Who's that?' William asked, again.

I took the photo from him. It was from an album I'd put together for Richard some years ago that had photos spanning his childhood, marriage, first children and then his grandkids. Our life was in other albums.

'That's Daddy when he was much younger, younger than I am now,' I said. 'Can you make sure you don't jumble them all up.

Put that picture back where you found it, please William,' I said, as I made an even bigger mess by frantically going through them all. I eventually found the photo that I was desperately looking for.

I tried to view it with external eyes. *Is this photo too suggestive? Would I be really embarrassed if anyone else saw it? Would Facebook remove it? Would Richard be upset if he saw it on my Facebook?*

In each case my answer was *no*.

In the photo I was in a diaphanous sarong, so it was not risqué, but quite suggestive – it had a hint of nakedness, as it was clear that beneath that black and white voile, I was knickerless.

As soon as I had a free moment, I posted it onto *Facebook*, ensuring that Anthony Hope was the only person able to view the picture. And then I waited.

But I didn't have to wait long. At 16:21 he typed in the words: *BEEeeautiful...somethings ya wanna do.*

I could hear his voice behind his silly words. So he really did want to "do" the "busy bee". I was right. He *was* watching me very closely. This proof was strong as the Lewis Carroll quote.

And I surely did want to *do* him too. My game with Anthony sometimes felt like the longest lingering, teasing foreplay you could ever experience.

Shaking myself, I quickly typed in a non-sexual response: *Nicole's head and heart are being held hostage...Beehave!*

A second later…

Anthony is behaving.

Is Behaving or is Bee having? I didn't know what he meant.

CHAPTER TWENTY-TWO

The 15th of February came and went without incident. In fact, it turned out to be the smoothest birthday party William had ever had. But the first piece of evidence I found that appeared to prove the numbers were somehow connected to Anthony Hope, materialised in early March, the same day that other things in my life were not adding up. The evidence also showed me how easy it was, to not always see every detail in front of you.

With my head tipped upside-down and blood rushing to my face, in a futile attempt to get volume in my hair, it wasn't the carpet I could see: it was a close-up photo of Anthony Hope standing next to his girlfriend. Behind them was the club where Anthony had met her. It was called "Infinity Club". The slogan beneath the logo said "For nights you want to last forever". What where the odds of him meeting her in a place that had the symbol I drew.

I continued to mull things over: I wondered if he'd posted the profile picture of him and his girlfriend so that I would notice the symbol on a close-up shot.

I should've spotted it on the other pictures of him in the same place that he posted after I left the equation on my Wall.

Still deep in thought, and deafened by the hairdryer, I didn't hear the voice shouting to me. Maddy's head appeared around the bedroom door, making me jump.

I grabbed my towel from the floor to wrap around me. Thank God I had underwear on.

'You scared the living daylights out of me,' I said, feeling shaky.

'Sorry, I was trying to call up to you, but I couldn't speak too loud, because I think you've got a bailiff at your door, I can smell them a mile off,' she said, with an air of confidence born out of experience.

'A what? I'm going to kill Richard. Good job he bought a

bloody estate car that looks like a hearse. At least his funeral will be on the cheap.'

'I parked my car out of the way, so he didn't see me come in. Then I had to jump over the side fence – thank goodness that the patio door was unlocked. I am quite impressed with my agility actually; I was like something from an action film.'

We waited until we heard his car finally move away from the drive, before venturing downstairs. He'd pushed an envelope through the letter box. Even Blue didn't seem interested in going near its poison. I opened it up, feeling sick and jittery, because I didn't really know what to expect. The letter was from the court, I could see that much from the stamp on the front of the envelope. My worst fear was that it had something to do with the bank overdraft and that they were now going to go for the jugular rather than agreeing to a reasonable repayment deal, like Richard wanted.

I thought about the effect on William and Elyse if they lost their home. I could feel my stomach churning.

'It's about twelve hundred quid,' I said, almost relieved, yet confused by the amount.

I put the letter down and then went through the palaver of getting through to Richard at his office.

'Why the hell have we got the court demanding twelve hundred quid? I shouted down the phone. 'Are things so bad that we can't afford to pay twelve hundred quid now? Why have we just booked a holiday to Egypt, then?'

'I know all about it. Don't worry. Calm down. I'm not paying them a penny. I'm still trying to get the solicitors to drop the case over the company I bought,' he said. I cursed it for the millionth time.

'Why don't you tell me these things. At least warn me,' I demanded.

'I didn't think it was necessary.'

'What like you didn't think it necessary to show me the

printout on imploding windows?' It was the first time in a while I'd thought to mention the printout. I'd been too engrossed in the game with Anthony.

'What printout on imploding windows?'

'The one in the kitchen draw.'

I opened the drawer that I'd put it in months earlier after finding it. It was no longer there. 'You've moved it now,' I said indignantly. 'It's no longer here.'

'I haven't moved anything. I haven't got a clue what you're talking about and as for the solicitors – I don't see why I should be paying out anything, when the solicitors should be getting my original ninety thousand back. But make sure you keep the doors locked.'

Keep the doors locked? I can't even make keys stay in a pissing pot and printouts stay in drawer.

'That is going to be impossible,' I said.

'It's just until things are sorted out.. If you don't lock the door and they just walk in, they'll have your laptop and your paintings.' Richard hung up.

'What's wrong,' Maddy asked.

'I don't know. Apparently the court thing is not a big deal. But sometimes it feels like either I'm losing my marbles or Richard is losing his and he is making it feel like it's me. I know I put a printout out on imploding windows in that drawer. I can still see it sitting there in my head.'

I thought about Richard's mum with dementia. What age did dementia usually strike? Because we both accepted that Richard had the superior brain, were we both falsely blaming his failings on my brain? I pensively chewed my lower lip. What if the tables were turning with age?

'Maybe William or Elyse moved it?' Maddy said trying to be helpful.

'Hmmm or too much stress,' I didn't say it but I realised I needed to keep a closer eye on Richard.

The Egypt holiday soon arrived but something didn't feel right about telling the house-sitters to make sure the door remained locked which struck me as daft because I was still convinced there was a rogue key floating about somewhere in the world. And it all seemed all the more ludicrous over twelve hundred pounds, although Richard said he'd definitely pay it to shut me up.

We were flying from Manchester airport, but we needed an overnight stay in the airport hotel. Richard had made the best out of it by calling in on one of his clients on the way. William and Elyse had nodded off in the back of the car; the anticipation of the holiday had finally worn them out. I spent my time switching between radio stations, cursing each time a good one lost signal.

We hit the winding Snake Pass and I stared at the bleak moors on either side of the road.

Richard started to question why I was so quiet.

'I'm bored,' I replied. It sounded a completely stupid statement to make when we were only a matter of hours away from a week of five-star luxury in Sharm El Sheikh with Maddy, Steve and Henry and we had more than enough stress in our lives to keep us occupied.

'What do you mean you're bored?

'I'm bored with my life, we don't do enough together as a couple.'

'You're busy studying. You chose to do those exams.'

'I know that. And I'm trying to get through them as fast as possible...you know I am.'

'So...are you saying that you're bored with me?' he turned his face to mine.

'No! I just feel like I'm not doing enough with my life. I've lost my way...other people that I know seem so happy and fulfilled and I feel like I've left my dreams behind somewhere.'

'What people? Are you talking about *Facebook* again? Do you mean that Anthony Hope is fulfilled and you are not?'

I felt myself tense when I heard Anthony's name fall from Richard's mouth. If I needed any proof that Richard's mind was still as sharp as a razor this was it. But did that mean he knew about my game and was staying silent? Was Maddy right about him being behind the text message?

'No...why did you say that?' I asked with feigned innocence.

'I don't know...it's just that he's on your *Facebook* and you worked with him. You don't regret being with me do you? Do you...fancy him?' he said, as he unnecessarily changed up a gear and back down again, still unused to the manual gears.

'Of course I don't regret being with you,' I said, as I deliberately continued to stare out at the uninhabited landscape. 'I just think that we should do more together. Oh and yes...Anthony Hope is doing a job he loves. Okay, it's not a conventional career choice for a grown man, but he loves it. And he always seems to be going away with his girlfriend. They go walking and fishing together, and skiing...I love skiing but never get around to it these days because you won't go. I love horse-riding but I haven't had a dressage lesson since I fell pregnant with Elyse.'

I took a pause to gather my breath, then continued, 'Do you know that I've never even been to Paris, because you've already been? How can you get to my age and have never been to Paris? We never seem to make anything of our weekends.'

'Look...we could go to Paris, if that's where you really want to go. You have been to lots of other amazing places though. Plus we do have children and we could have gone to more amazing places if we had left them with childcare – but we decided not to...'

Richard was referring to the free holidays we could have taken over the years to places like Australia, Canada, Nevis and Cannes – all first-class travel in world-class hotels. One of the perks that Richard had from a tie-in with a major financial company. But children were excluded, otherwise it wasn't allowable as a tax break.

'So is this why you're quiet – because you're bored?'

'I guess so...I just feel empty.'

'What kind of feeling is empty?'

'I don't know...I can't explain it. But that's how I feel.'

'Well…when we get back from holiday...we'll plan a weekend away together. Is that okay?'

'Fine,' I said, wondering if a weekend away could even remotely fill the void I felt.

'I just want my happy, smiley, carefree Little N back...'

'I know...and I'm really trying to find her.'

I'd been transfixed by the scenery as we travelled by taxi from the airport to our accommodation. I'd always been fascinated by the landscape in the Arab countries. The mountainous deserts on my left still looked untouched. It was the expanse of rich shades of orange, set against a backdrop of deep blue that made it feel like another planet, barren of complicated life. Palatial holiday retreats were on the other side of the relatively new road, facing the sea.

The hotel was everything Maddy had said it would be: seven swimming pools, log flumes, luxury sun-loungers and massive suites. The kids were loving every available second.

And, despite being bored with my life in general, I did at this point feel pretty good in myself – physically. I'd managed to regain the weight I'd lost, I had a spray tan and French manicure before leaving England, and I'd treated myself to a new string-bikini. In a way, I was clawing back some of my zapped confidence as a consequence of the game with Anthony Hope.

Things weren't going quite so well for Maddy though. She'd developed a painful abscess in one of her back teeth not long after arriving, and so far, it had been unsuccessfully treated by the hotel doctor with an injection in her bottom and a bag full of pills.

The pain from her abscess finally started to alleviate after a trip to a proper dentist, located in a village close to the desert. But she was still taking it easy and resting alone. I retreated to my suite with Elyse while Richard and Steve took the boys on a glass-bottom boat ride.

I sat on the bed next to Elyse, flicking through one of the magazines I'd picked at the airport. I read it from front to back, including all of the tiny box adverts, making myself feel rubbish again. It made me want to be followed around by an on-tap air brusher, and like I should have achieved everything by now. I wanted to shoot the twenty-something journalists for making a thirty-something like me feel like they'd failed. I placed the magazine on the bedside table and sighed.

Elyse blissfully slept on, making it impossible to even imagine the force of her incandescent petulance earlier on. I now felt guilty that she'd managed to pull me down to her immature level as we argued by the poolside before I'd finally dragged her back here.

I inspected the ceiling. It was high and arched and probably a real pain in the ass to paint. The mahogany furnishings looked more Moroccan than Egyptian, I thought. Then I thought I might as well read the book that Maddy had loaned me – *The Reader*. It was quite short, so it had a chance of being completed while we were staying here. I pulled it from the travel bag and helped myself to a bottle of Evian from the mini-bar. Three hours later, Elyse still slept on.

I heard a faint knock on the door and got off the bed to open it.

Maddy was standing there with Steve's laptop in her arms. She looked much better, the facial swelling had subsided and she was back to her normal chirpy self. She checked Elyse out and, like me, concluded in a low voice that she was suffering from sheer exhaustion.

'Anyway...I know you must be missing *Facebook* by now...so I thought I'd treat you,' she said, almost whispering as she plonked the laptop on the bed and unravelled the cable.

She pulled the adapter off my hairdryer, which had been left on the dresser, and stuck it on the end of the laptop power cable. She'd been dangling the laptop over me like an unreachable carrot since we'd arrived; I hadn't picked up from the brochure that the room had Wi-Fi, so I not bothered to bring mine.

After finishing setting it up she stayed and chatted for a little while longer, before leaving in her oversized straw hat which looked wider than she was tall.

I heard the door close behind her and didn't waste a second before logging onto *Facebook*. Their connection was faster than mine at home.

I read through some messages that Maddy had left on my Wall. She'd been happily amusing herself with the fact that she'd got Internet access and I hadn't. Then I went straight onto Anthony's profile. And smiled.

I smiled, because on his Wall was my window of opportunity to spend a day with him.

I looked into his eyes.

His profile picture was still the one of him in the Infinity Club on the day he met his girlfriend.

What if I take my chance to spend the day with him and end up totally humiliated by him? I thought, as I remembered the harsh words of his reply to my insanely long email..

I sighed and, feeling shivery, jumped off the bed to turn the air-con off. I then opened the patio doors to let in a less chilly, gentle breeze through the voile curtain instead. As I headed back to the bed, the door opened and William walked in, followed by Richard who dropped the beach bag on top of the pile of suitcases. I hushed them, pointing to Elyse.

'Get your swimming shorts and goggles...here's your towel,' Richard said to William.

And then he stood by the patio doors, watching him go and

find Henry, Steve and Maddy – they were sitting by the edge of the pool.

'I'm nipping to the loo. You can tell me how the trip went it a sec,' I said.

I walked back out to find Richard with his reading glasses on, looking at the laptop I'd left open on the bed.

'I presume this is Steve's laptop

'Yeah...Maddy lent it to me,' I said, while I attempted to slyly turn it away from him.

'Then why is Anthony Hope on the screen?'

I squirmed, 'He's just giving everyone a chance to go to some posh event at his boss's house somewhere in Surrey...it's all in aid of charity. I was just having a nosey at it...nothing important.'

Richard pulled it back in his direction and continued to stare at Anthony's photograph. The event was going to start off with champagne and canapés in the grounds of the house, and included a hot air balloon ride mid-afternoon, and then in the evening a formal sit down dinner, while Anthony and his band, and a few other bands, performed. The best bit about it was that a comment on his Wall had indicated that his girlfriend was unable to make it.

'He really does love himself doesn't he,' Richard stated after studying Anthony's photo. 'Are you *sure* you don't fancy him?' he then said.

'I don't fancy him. And he doesn't love himself, he's probably no vainer than me,' I said, while also staring at the photo.

He looked good on it – you could see the faint stubble which emphasised his jawline.

'Anyway...he's got a girlfriend – she's Irish. Look...I'll show you the pictures if you don't believe me,' and just like I did with Maddy, I forced him to view some of Anthony's photos.

'Why are they always posing together, do they think they're the Beckhams? God he really loves himself...just look at him pose...! But I still think you fancy him,' he said, in a teasing tone and definitely not the tone of someone suspecting an online game with another man. Unless it was a double bluff?

'Well, for your information, I don't fancy him. Anyway, what do you think about his girlfriend?'

'She looks quite attractive. Nice hair I suppose,' he said, before finishing off the last of my Evian.

'Attractive? You wouldn't like her...she's tall,' I said bitterly and slammed the laptop shut.

'Christ...why are you being so nasty?' he snapped.

I wasn't exactly lying to Richard when I said I didn't fancy Anthony. Because, technically, I didn't fancy him - I foolishly believed myself to be in love with him, and that by definition is different.

By the pool, I felt myself sinking into the thick cream mattress, shaded by one of the bamboo parasols. The soft breeze floating over my almost bare flesh made it feel like Anthony was delicately caressing my body. The tingling sensation of the air became the tingling sensation of his lingering kisses.

Should I take the chance and go to the event?

CHAPTER TWENTY-THREE

Early morning sunshine made its way through the roof light windows.

It was good to be back in my own bed.

I turned on to my other side and the red glow of light on my eyelids vanished once I'd buried my head under the covers.

The electric-blue dress scooped elegantly round my neck, dropped low at the back and fitted perfectly around the bodice area and was encrusted with tiny beads. The fabric was light and floaty and trailed slightly longer behind me. I caught a glimpse of my blue shoes as I strode past a few people that sat at different tables in the garden. I didn't really notice their faces. The house was a grand country estate, like the house of our former boss at Opus, and there was only me and Anthony – no Richard.

I walked towards the glass doors heading from the terrace. Anthony was wearing his sunglasses and grinned at me.

I continued to make my way towards him; head slightly lowered, eyes looking up. I was smiling and hiding my shyness behind my hair as it fell forward.

As I got closer to him, he appeared to get taller, and then he spoke: 'I can't believe it's you...you actually did it, Little N,' and he pulled me to him, holding me securely. I could smell his after-shave – but I knew I would forget the scent the minute the dream was over.

Feeling pressure from the mattress against my hip, I turned over again and pulled the quilt even tighter round my body, replaying the dream once more, only this time, when I got to the door, his girlfriend unexpectedly breezed through it and stood towering above me. Her presence engulfed me like an oppressive dark shadow and I was unable to break through it and reach Anthony. Her cascading dark hair and sleek black dress made her look elegantly gothic. Her force had left me weakened and damned. I opened my eyes.

A few hours later, I found myself at *Wonderland* down the road, trying to kill yet another day of the school holidays with Maddy.

I sat and watched Elyse play with the diggers in the sand pit and, for a little while, I crouched down next to her. I drew an eight with my finger and retraced it several times over. Then I wrote *cuckold*.

Why would somebody send a single poisonous text and then never bother us again?

Who on earth would have such a morbid interest in us?

I got up and sat on the bench where I was more comfortable, and discreetly observed all of the women around me watching over their own children – at least half were grandparents.

The sullen mood I'd managed to pull myself into followed me back home. I stood reading through William's rules that he'd recently posted on his bedroom door; painstakingly written in fountain pen.

READ BEFORE YOU ENTER

No girls allowed.

Boys rule.

Girls suck.

Boys rule the world.

Did you know that girls sob most of their life?

My mum can't sing at all

Neither can my little sister

I walked back downstairs, thinking about William's emphasis on boy's ruling; he'd listed it twice. As for girls spending most of their lives sobbing? I tried to think of the number of times William had ever seen me cry – it was very few. Surely he meant Elyse; she was allowed to cry, she was four. And does William really think my singing is that awful?

Richard having finished work early noticed the particularly miserable look on my face. He followed me through to the kitchen then asked if William and Elyse had played me up.

'No...they've been fine,' I said, grabbing an apple from the fruit bowl.

'So what's up with you then?'

'Nothing,' I lied and took a bite from the apple.

'Do you want tea, I'm having one?' he said as he pulled a mug down from the cupboard.

'No, thanks. Actually...I'm not fine. Have you read the notice on William's door?'

'Yeah, it's quite funny isn't it?'

'Yes it is but...Richard – I don't have any choices in my life – that is what is really bothering me.'

'What do you mean?'

'Even if I didn't want to be here, I have no choice in the matter. I couldn't support myself.'

'That's ridiculous. Thousands of women live as single mothers,' he said, pouring the hot water into the mug.

'Yeah, but their kids might suffer...'

'So...don't you want to be here?'

'I'm just saying that l feel trapped.'

'You're being ridiculous.'

'I've never married, because I like my door open. But my door isn't *really* open. The reality is that I am trapped. Even if I wanted to leave I couldn't. And it's that bit that eats at me. The fact I don't have a choice. All I really wanted was financial independence. And I don't have it.'

'You're just being stupid,' he said.

'I had a crush on *Ilex*'s Administrator...James,' the confession dropped from my mouth.

Perhaps I was offloading one guilt to help ease the other.

I'd suddenly gone off the apple.

'A crush? Did you have sex with him?' The unfinished tea was now left stewing on the side. His eyes had a look of fear and his brow had knotted.

'No, it was just a crush. A stupid feeling – like I wanted to kiss him, that's all. I'm over it now...the crush is long gone.'

Richard's face eased, 'Well, I guess a crush is harmless. Why didn't you tell me at the time? You didn't kiss him did you?'

'Of course not. But I told Maddy about it.'

'When?'

'When you were thinking about retiring. I promised her then I'd talk to you...but I'm a bit slow getting round to things and I'm sorry.'

'What's me retiring got to do with it?

'I was scared about you retiring.'

'But I'm not retiring...really. You know full well that if the court case doesn't get dropped, the bank doesn't behave reasonably, and the Inland Revenue continue to drag their heels over the tax scheme, then I might as well go bankrupt, walk away from it all and live off my pension funds that they can't touch, until I'm out of it. But I'm not giving up. I'm simply finding the most logical way through all the dross. So...this James thing, is this what has been eating away at you?'

'Perhaps. I don't know,' I said, still hating to hear Richard mention the possibility of bankruptcy, even though I knew it made financial sense.

'Well, perhaps the crush thing was my fault. I pretty much left you to deal with the *Ilex Drapes* thing on your own. I wasn't really there for you when I should have been.'

'But you're dealing with stuff that I'm not dealing with now. Yes, I admit it still does make me wonder why the hell you got us in so deep, and why you never saw the credit crunch coming,' then I stopped myself. I hated myself for throwing it back in his face. Because I knew he did everything with the best of intentions even if he did take risks I would never have taken. But then I could never achieve what he had.

'Maybe it was just the stress at the time,' he said.

Then he laughed before teasing me about wanting to kiss a 21-year-old. I think he was secretly relieved that he was dealing only with a crush.

'I think you're right – we need to get away together. Just the two of us,' he added.

'I'll speak to Mum about having William and Elyse,' I said.

'Good...all I want is you back. You're just so cold. You freeze when I go near you. It's like you've got an emotional wall around you,' he said.

'I know and I'm sorry. But you seem to suddenly want an affectionate lapdog – and I have never been that.'

'Yes, I do love that about you. But a bit more affection would be nice right now.'

'I am trying, but you can't turn a natural cat into a dog because it suits you.'

'Just give me a hug now and then,' and he grabbed me. 'Look, you've frozen again. You need to sort yourself out... otherwise you *will* end up as a single mother,' he said, suddenly.

I turned away then walked out of the kitchen, trying not to let him see me crying. I needed to sort out the rest of the things for a camping trip with Maddy. I took the list from my handbag as I walked upstairs. Most items had already been ticked, but I still needed a bottle opener. I didn't want to go into back into the kitchen so I got Richard's Swiss Army knife from the bedside drawer instead, that had a bottle opener on amongst other things. I put the list in my cream jacket pocket. I was still wiping tears away as I tried to carry on normally. How bad could taking just one day be?

Richard was shouting something up to me, so I hung my head over the banister.

'By the way the police were here earlier,' he said matter-of-factly.

'The police?' I questioned. It surely had something to do with the text message I thought optimistically. Why hadn't he mentioned it earlier?

CHAPTER TWENTY-FOUR

I'm not sure whether I was baffled or incensed by Richard. Baffled probably had the slight edge. He was quite right to point out that I sometimes walked around as though I had blinkers on, but as far as my car went, I got in and drove, I got back out and I locked it. I'd also been parked at *Wonderland* on the edge of a row which meant I didn't even see my car from the front or back, only the side which is probably why I hadn't noticed my registration plates were missing. The police had knocked on our door after the local petrol station had reported a drive off from one of the pumps. Apparently in the hours leading up to the fuel theft someone had nabbed my plates specifically for the job. Fortunately CCTV footage and vehicle registration documents proved we were not party to the crime. But the bugbear I had with Richard was the fact that there had been a police officer stood in our house, drinking our tea and Richard had been given the perfect opportunity to report, or at the very least quiz the officer about a text message being sent without a number trace to his phone.

And Richard had not taken that opportunity.

It was irrelevant to me that the officer had told him that there had been a spate of make-offs triggered by rising fuel prices in the recession.

'Besides, the police have got far more important things to deal with than isolated text messages of no significance,' Richard said while trying to change the batteries to William's remote-control Ferrari. I could see he was using the wrong screwdriver but said nothing.

'You know I care about that text. I don't care that my car is without reg plates,' I said petulantly. 'The two have to be connected – my car could have been targeted deliberately.'

'Don't be daft. Why can't you just forget about that fucking text?'

'I still think you were behind that text, Maddy is right.' I snapped.

'You can think what you want. You're wrong. I'm going out with the dog,' he said slamming down the screwdriver and disappeared into the utility followed by Blue. I felt bad, almost evil for even thinking ill of Richard and let out a helpless sigh before sorting out William's Ferrari with the right screwdriver. I drove the car at the wall in frustration and stopped before it smashed against the skirting board.

I shook my head as I stuffed the front page of the *Daily Mail* into the study drawer. The headline had read: "Curious and Curiouser." and it also featured a cartooned version of the Chancellor of the Exchequer Alistair Darling looking like *Alice in Wonderland*. It was the paper's response to the budget having a chance of pulling the country out of the mire. I saved it because it made me feel safe in that I wasn't the only one feeling like they were surrounded by madness. I looked at my watch – 9:30 and I needed to go, I was meeting Maddy in twenty minutes. I dragged Blue off our bed, checked that all the doors were locked and got in my car, heading for *Gossips*.

The door creaked when I pushed it open, and I breathed in the comforting smell of homemade cakes and pastries; my empty stomach rumbled. I could see Maddy at the farthest table; her hair was pulled back and her face was bereft of make-up, as she had just done the school run only one off from wearing her PJs which she frequently did. But she still looked a lot calmer and more fresh-faced that she had in a long time.

Steve had finally been given a June trial date. The charges, as expected had been dropped against Maddy. For most people this probably would have been a terrifying prospect, but it was the limbo that had been slowly killing them, and at least now they would soon be able to plan their life again.

I ordered my favourite cheese and mushroom omelette and a

pot of tea and made my way over to her.

'We might be off to some posh event in Surrey,' I said as I pulled the chair out. I had a big grin on my face.

'What?'

I explained the charity event to her and the way that I had booked the tickets.

'Let me get this right. You have paid Anthony Hope three hundred quid for three charity tickets just so you can spend the day with him. But instead of booking them as yourself...you've done it as Nell Gwyn?' she said, leaning back, as though madness was catching.

'That's right.'

'So...how the hell is he supposed to know it's you?'

'If my instincts are right, he will get that Nell Gwynn is an alias for me. I left a hint on my *Facebook* and I did mention the old book in that letter I sent to him.'

'And if he doesn't get it?'

'Then I'm wrong about him playing a game with me,' I said.

'So...when do you get the tickets?'

'They're e-tickets, so by email...the event isn't until late August.'

'You're crazy,' she said, as she tried to get a third cup of tea from her pot. 'Why are you so convinced that he's playing this game with you? I'm not,' she said with narrowed eyes.

'I accept I might not be interpreting everything right but there are too many coincidences...other than when he's promoting some gig or other, the coincidences are continual. Things like me recently calling his short Rome trip a bit of a *ROME-ance* and he went and posted a video of a skier calling it *taking the piste*. Get it?...I was taking the piss out of him.'

'I get it,' she said with a sigh and stirred the tea-bag around the pot.

'And when you called me a vain cow, he went and found a picture of a cow. And when I put Richard on the front of one of my photo albums he went and became a Fan of *your old man is an ass-hole,*' I said.

'Don't get that one,' she said, wrinkling her nose.

'You have to think about it... he was having a dig at Richard calling Richard old, sugar daddy...but what about when he got stuck in Scotland because of the snow? I put on my *Facebook* that I was at a loss for words. And within minutes of him logging on, he put that *Anthony forgot how much he loves libraries.* In other words, he'd pointed me in the direction of an entire building stuffed full of words.'

'But it—'

'Let me finish...there was the time recently when I'd picked up that his girlfriend is still at college. I put that German Status that said: *ha ha hatte es wissen sollen schulferien viel verngungen knutshe dich!!!* That meant *I should have known...school holidays...have fun, hugs and kisses.* He went and added a Lego rave. Get it? A Lego rave. Surely you get his humour behind that?

'Yes, but it's just so mad. Anyway, what is his girlfriend studying?' she asked.

I think it was her attempt to bring normality into the conversation as the elderly waitress placed cutlery and bread on our table. I grabbed one of the rolls and leaned back to give her space.

'I don't know...something to do with travel and tourism.'

'I just don't get why he doesn't speak to you properly,' she said, while shaking her head.

'I don't know either.'

'Yeah...so...these could still be nothing more than coincidences.'

'Christ... how many do you need? Okay, what about the hamsters then? Remember the other week when you thought you'd lost Bella and I was taking the piss on my *Facebook* that your hamster was only minutes from being declared a goner.'

'Yeah...I still can't believe I found her,'

'That was bloody lucky, but two days later Anthony posted a

video clip for the new film *G-Force*.'

'So what?'

'I now realise, the film isn't even about hamsters at all. *G-Force* is about Guinea-pigs. The only reason I thought it was about hamsters was because he said it was about hamsters. He'd manufactured another coincidence, but fucked it up without realising it.'

The waitress placed the food on the table and I let it all drop for a bit. I listened to Maddy talk – there never a dull moment in their house.

Back out on the street, we decided to take a browse round the boutiques. Maddy spotted a black padded jacket she liked in one of the windows, it was a bit of a twist on a *Barbour* – it would look great with jeans.

'Lets go in...try it on,' I offered.

'Okay – but I told myself that I wouldn't spend any money today,' she laughed.

Luckily the jacket was way too big for her but we continued talking as we browsed the rails.

'If Anthony does email Nell Gwyn, then you and Lorna could come with me...I bought three tickets and it will give me a reason to go to Surrey,' I said, holding a black dress against my body. I liked the sheer sleeves and the way it was tucked in at the waist.

'Steve really will kill me...you know his take on infidelity, ever since his first wife left him...would you seriously go?'

'I don't know...I really want to. Do you like this dress?' I said still holding it.

'Yeah, I do actually,' she took it from me for a closer inspection.

'But that's why I've bought myself time with an alias. This way, if he really does want me there he will email those tickets to Nell Gwyn...if he doesn't want me, then Nell Gwyn will never get an email with the tickets...the ball is back in his court so to speak.'

Maddy was standing in front of the mirror now holding the dress against her.

'It would suit you,' I said, while standing behind her, seeing it from the reflection.

'Hmm...'

'Do you fancy going fifty-fifty on this dress?'

'Okay – that's cool – we'll share it. So...when is this charity day again?'

'Late August.'

'This could be as interesting as Steve's trial day. Just the thought of it makes me wince.'

I considered this quite a good response to my actions. I was half expecting her to rip my head off, like she normally did, and start ramming the virtues of moral behaviour down my throat.

CHAPTER TWENTY-FIVE

Something had been bugging me all morning, ever since I'd double-checked the official entry form for my two big tax exams in June. It was still five weeks away, but there was something I was missing about the dates.

I sat at the table, grabbed the newspaper, and just as I was about to take a bite out of a sandwich, the phone rang. I debated whether to pick up.

'I only half-expected you to answer,' Richard said. 'Only ringing to see if you've heard about the MPs?'

'No...what about them?'

'They've been fiddling their expenses; ripping off the taxpayer with the looks of it. False accounting basically,' he said and I heard myself laugh with him.

Clearly the news hadn't hit the newspapers yet, or at least not the one that I was looking at.

'Fiddling the taxpayer...false accounting...it's a dangerous fine line between that and some of the stuff that Steve's been arrested for,' I said. 'When is Steve's trial again?' I snapped at Richard.

'I'm not sure...why? It's in my diary.'

'I need to know now.'

'Why is it so important?'

'Please...just get it for me,'

I could hear pages being flipped over. Then the sound stopped.

'It's on the 18th of June.'

'Oh noooo.'

'What's the problem?'

'It is the same day as one of my exams! I promised I'd be there for them,' I wanted to scream with sheer frustration.

'You don't have to miss the exam. Stop getting yourself in a flap over it. We *both* promised Maddy, and I will still be there for her. Her dad will be there, Lorna and Bruce will be there. I'm sure she'll understand. You're being too hard on yourself.'

'I did promise and now I'm going to let her down because of these stupid exams.'

'That's life sometimes,' Richard said calmly. 'Anyway, changing the subject, have you spoken to your mum yet about them looking after William and Elyse so we can have a weekend away? I was thinking of Paris via the Euro Tunnel.'

A flash bulb went off in my head...we'd have to go from London and that's where Anthony has his rehearsal studios!

I'd now completely lost my motivation. Thinking about letting people down I cared about made me think of the betrayal involved in spending a sneaky day with Anthony Hope. Would getting him out of my system be better for my relationship with Richard in the long term? I pondered this for what must have been the thousandth time. I wanted to know if my fate was to spend that day with him – how many times in your life do you get the chance to go up in a hot air balloon with the man of your dreams and get to wear a beautiful dress at the same time?

I found myself reaching out to the angel. I'd promised myself I wouldn't try the automatic writing thing again, but then I wasn't very good at keeping promises of late.

But it would either give me that answer I needed, or for my own sanity, prove everything else it had thrown up as nothing more than a coincidence – just like Steve's trial date landing on the same day as my exam.

I breathed calmly for a few minutes, until I felt light-headed, almost like I was floating. I let the pen in my left hand take over. It was only when it was no longer compelled to move that I re-opened my eyes to look at the squiggle before me.

I placed the paper down and leaned back, then leaned forward towards my laptop, minimised my study notes, and clicked on *Google*.

I typed into my search bar: *Greek symbols*.

I simply thought about the Greek Gematria which had cropped up before – at least it was a starting point.

There was a poster with a range of Greek symbols, I enlarged it, but none of the symbols looked remotely like the squiggle on the paper next to my laptop. I clicked back a page and clicked on a document showing the Greek alphabet. I scrolled down the letters but could see nothing which exactly fitted my drawing. But I looked long and hard at the sixth letter of the alphabet – Zeta.

I held up my paper again.

I flipped it over and used the light shining through the shutters to show the image in reverse through the paper. I looked back at the Zeta symbol on my screen, then back to my paper again. My drawing was like the Zeta symbol in reverse.

Why is everything I draw always in reverse?

Before dismissing it as rubbish, I needed to know if there was a link between Zeta and Lewis Carroll.

This seemed a pretty logical link in light of everything else that had happened in recent months. I quickly typed this into the search bar.

The word Zeta threw up tons of articles, most of which were on the actress, Catherine Zeta Jones, but there was one cached result that caught my eye.

42 (number) – WIKIPEDIA, the free encyclopaedia

Lewis Carroll made repeated use of this number in his writings.....A conjecture for the sixth power moment of the Riemann Zeta-

Function......

En.wikipedia.org/wiki/42_(number)-cached-similar

I wasn't sure which line of text to deal with first but opted for the Riemann Zeta-Function because I'd never heard of it.

I typed in *Riemann Zeta-Function + Lewis Carroll* this time.

My eyes were drawn to an article in *THE SEED* magazine. I opened up the document.

It was an article stating that mathematicians had found a link between prime numbers and quantum physics, and it had been written three years earlier. The mere mention of quantum physics meant I already knew this article was likely to be as clear as mud, but I forced myself to continue.

I was confused because when I was at school 42 wasn't a prime number. The article seemed serious enough, not some kind of intellectual joke flying over the top of my head – or maybe it was and I was just too thick to get it. I scribbled down the writer's name: *Marcus du Sautoy* and planned to check him out.

My eyes scanned the article searching for more references to 42.

I found a paragraph which basically said that the first two numbers in the Riemann Zeta-Function are one and two. But mathematicians now think that the third number is 42.

I scrolled up to the top of the article, trying to read it more closely, but getting no nearer to understanding it.

I scrolled back down to the bottom of the article, to see if the final paragraph summed it up in layman's terms. It wasn't layman enough for me. But still curious I typed in *Zeta + unsolved mathematical puzzle*

This popped up:

A million dollar prize for the unsolved Zeta Riemann hypothesis

If my ghostly, spirit visitor was Lewis Carroll, then he certainly had a very wicked sense of humour.

I'd been led from a simple little quadratic equation, straight on to the hardest unsolved mathematical problem in the world;

which could just so happen unlock the mathematical key to the universe – the so called Holy Grail of maths.

But it also had a much needed cash prize attached to it – considering I only had a GCSE in maths I had no chance of solving it.

I decided to read a little about *Marcus du Sautoy*. He is a professor based at Oxford University, just like Lewis Carroll had once been.

Realising that I was sending myself on another crazy trail, I folded my laptop screen down, and attempted to turn my attention back to my study. I pulled over my textbook and sat staring, glazed-eyed at the next exercise, but my head was still involuntarily ticking away at Zeta and the link with quantum physics.

I blinked hard, and then re-opened the laptop. This time I typed in *Zeta + planet.*

I amused myself with all sorts of cranky articles about Planet X, Nibiru and aliens called Sumerians and Anunnaki who were supposedly living a clandestine life among us. There was even stuff on the Net claiming that Jesus was an alien. Suddenly, what I was doing didn't feel quite so crazy in comparison to some of stuff posted online.

But then I found myself drawn to several references to the Mayan calendar and the end of the world in 2012.

There were literally thousands of different articles discussing things like polar shifts, black holes, solar storms, earthquakes, volcanic eruptions and tsunamis.

I sat back.

Mayans. DOTD is celebrated by the Mexicans at Halloween. I'd printed loads of stuff about it a few months back; there were two other symbols I'd drawn in there too: a spiral and delta. But still hadn't really sussed them because they were too vague like pieces from a bigger jigsaw I hadn't got.

I sat and re-read through some of the pages to double-check I was right and I was.

Next, I looked back at my laptop and typed in: *Mayan calendar 2012.*

The Mayan calendar ends on the 21st December 2012 at 11:11 after 5125 years.

5125, I whispered.

If that was rounded down it would be 5120 - the same three digits in the quadratic equation.

My head absorbed, then it computed - in 2012 I'll be 42.

I remembered something else I'd read on the Internet, on some site about biblical numbers.

I picked up my calculator and typed in 37 x 42, looked at the answer, that wasn't it, so I tried again, this time I keyed in 37 x 24, as in Zeta reversed, like my drawing was reversed.

888 sat in the window on the calculator. I stared at it. I couldn't believe it. Why is this number repeatedly cropping up?

Was the world going to end at 11:11 on the 21/12/2012?

Was this why the resurrection of the novel Anthony Hope had the seven moved to eight, and why the zero or nought, should move to one respectively?

I recalled previous articles I'd read on number 1 or multiples of 1 being master numbers.

But If I am going to die in 2012, along with everyone else, does that mean I might as well jump at the chance with Anthony now, while I still can?

Before I got myself ready to do the school run, I checked the email account I'd set up for Nell Gwyn – but other than a welcome to my new account there had been nothing else sent to it.

'Did you know William, that if you fall down a hole at any point, it takes precisely 42 minutes to fall through it,' I glanced at him in the rear mirror.

'What?'

'Whether you fall from England to New Zealand, or England to New York, or Canada to England, or England to Spain and so on...it's always 42 minutes, regardless.'

'Cool...did you bring us any chocolate?'

'Yes. You know the man who wrote *Alice in Wonderland*? His favourite number was 42. And guess what? He wrote about it taking 42 minutes to fall down a hole in another one of his books. That was way before anyone on the entire planet knew that 42 minutes was really how long it would take to fall through the earth. Lewis Carroll did it without any calculation. Isn't that amazing?'

'Yeah...can I play football before I do my homework?'

'My friend at school is called Alice,' Elyse chirped.

'Your grandma wanted me to call you Alice, but William and Daddy liked the name Ellie – so that's why you are called Elyse. It made us all happy.'

'Can I have a hamster...that would make me very happy,' said William.

'No...for the billionth time.'

'But Henry's got one.'

'So you keep telling me.'

'I want a hamsteeeeer,' Elyse wailed.

'Want, don't get Elyse,' I reminded.

I turned to Richard over dinner…

'Did you know that a rainbow always appears at an angle of 42 degrees?'

'No...did you ask your mum about the weekend break? And did you speak to Maddy?'

'Not yet...did you know that in Kabalistic tradition 42 means *ein sof* as in infinite or endless,' I said, while wrapping spaghetti round my fork.

'I don't really care. When are you going to speak to your mum?' he said, then took a sip of red wine.

'Well – did you know that I'll be 42 in 2012 when the world might end...?'

'No...I didn't, but if the world is about to end, can you get on with phoning your mother. Are you sure you want to us to get away together? And can you please get round to changing the light bulbs in the study – I would do it myself if you hadn't bought such ridiculous lights - they are too fiddly for my fingers.'

'I'll get everything sorted...I promise...and besides there are other views that say that 2012 is the end of the Mayan calendar and it will be the official start of a new improved world of transparency where our psychic abilities will increasingly develop. I found bits and pieces on the Net about angels and spirits supposedly working among us to help us through this transitional phase – that could be why I was tapped on the shoulder on Halloween...it's all part of some spiritual awakening and ascension or something...what do you think?'

'Just phone your mother.'

Those more than a mile high must leave the court – rule 42.

I decided to stay quiet about a discussion on Exodus 26, where the linen curtains made from goat hair covering the tabernacle have a length of 42 feet. The Holy of the Holies where the Ten Commandments were scribbled down on stone tablets...one of which I was contemplating breaking with Anthony Hope.

CHAPTER TWENTY-SIX

Steve's trial and my tax exam were soon upon us.

Guilt was still sitting heavily on my shoulders about not being there for them, even though Maddy had been really understanding about it. It must have been hard for her, considering her view on my studies.

I'd spent most of the afternoon floating round the house like the spare part in a play, waiting for news to come in from the court. I took a quick call from mum, who wanted to know how my exam had gone. I reminded her about Steve, her least favourite person.

'If he has done wrong...he should pay...had your dad done more work for Steve, he could have cost us our livelihood...' she said.

'I know that, but they're my friends and I don't like to see them suffer either. There's far more good in Steve than bad. And if people hadn't screwed him over he probably wouldn't have done it to others...'

'Two wrongs, don't make a right...if people don't pay for their misdemeanours, then it makes a mockery of everyone else,' she said. I could hear the other phone ringing in the background; she was obviously at work.

By late afternoon Richard called back to say that Steve had got three and a half years, a Confiscation Order hanging over him for about half a million and journalists busy working on their copy for the evening papers. He said Maddy looked crushed. I sent Maddy a text telling her to call me when she was ready to talk. She sent one back:

My heart is breaking. I'll call you when I can speak X.

I felt her pain.

Steve not being around felt strange, but time was travelling fast and July soon came round. Maddy was coping well on the surface. Financially, she was fine; she still had the income from the family business. It also helped that her dad moved in with her and Henry. But it was the loss of Steven that ate away at her, not that she would let us see this side – I just knew her well enough to know it. The weekly prison visits weren't enough for her, even though he would only actually serve eighteen months of the three-year sentence.

I felt bad about leaving William with Maddy, just so Richard and I could have our weekend away. But she'd insisted on having William and our new hamsters stay with her, because she wanted everything to carry on as normal as possible for Henry.

Elyse was with mum and dad, and Richard's brother was taking care of Blue.

We checked into *The May Fair Hotel*, conveniently close to the *Nobu* restaurant. Richard was impressed with my choice. The room was quite small, but furnishings were chic in shades of chocolate and muted fudge, with an Italian marble bathroom. We left the cases, not bothering to unpack anything other than the card I wanted but had sneakily hidden from Richard. We headed out onto the street.

'So...where do you want to go first?' Richard asked, as we both stood looking up and down Stratton Street. This was the first time I'd been in London since William's 7th birthday.

'I don't mind. As long as I get to Oxford Street at some stage this afternoon...I'm easy,' I said.

'Why don't we go there first? I don't think it's too far from here, then we could go to Covent Garden for something to eat later.'

'Okay, great, I love Covent Garden.' There was an outside chance my plan would work.

'Why do you want to go to Oxford Street anyway?'

'Buy a new bag with my birthday and Christmas money.'

'Taxi or walk?'

'Walk, although I don't know how far I can go in these shoes,'

I said, looking down at my black wedges. The plan was that they and my fitted black pencil-dress would take me right through to the evening, without the need to return to the hotel until much later.

'Would you mind if I shopped alone for a few hours?' I asked, praying he wouldn't say "no". I thought about the card in my bag. If he didn't want to be alone, then my plan was ruined.

'No…why?'

'I just want to – you put me off when you hover over me.'

'Fine…actually,' he said, looking at his watch, 'I need some new trainers, I'll go and sort those and I can find a bar with *Sky*…I think there's a rugby game on today.'

We made our way to Oxford Street and I found an *iPhone* store, and asked them why my new iPhone wasn't ringing out loud. A teenage sales assistant flipped down a button with an amused grin.

'And you call me a techno retard?' Richard said, before asking where I wanted to meet up.

'Dunno…how about in that coffee shop, we nearly stopped in?'

'I'll see you there in two hours…and be careful.'

'Okay,' I said and watched him wander off up Oxford Street.

I looked at my watch. I needed to find my way to Oxford Circus Tube Station, but I had no idea which way I should be heading.

The first road sign I passed said Davies Street, the second, Duke Street.

I checked them against the map.

I was going the wrong way!!

I eventually found the Tube station and made my way through the barrier with my day pass. Once on the other side I pulled out the address and directions that I'd scribbled down a couple of days earlier. I needed to take the Victoria Line from Oxford Circus as far as Victoria, then take the District Line as far as Earls Court, then change lines again, getting off at Fulham Broadway, all of which was supposed to take me around thirty-six minutes.

This was the most crazy, deceitful thing I'd ever done.

At last I ended my journey and fought my way off the train.

Fulham Broadway Tube looked surprisingly new; like a shopping centre, and Chelsea FC seemed to be mentioned all over the place.

Suddenly I felt guilty that I was now within walking distance of Stamford Bridge, the home of William's favourite football club, and I'd left him behind, while I went on a selfish mission.

Once on the main street I looked at my notes again – I needed to get on to Harwood Road, the recording studios were supposed to be just off there.

Then I found it!

There was a small gold plate on the stone next to the glass doors. My heart was thumping. Once again it hit me that this was a bad idea, a really *bad* idea. In the days leading up to this moment I'd fantasised about raw, in-the-moment sex with a man I was desperate to touch for real. Stood in the reality of the moment, that fantasy was far from my mind. I should have walked away at that point, but instead I walked tentatively towards the reception desk.

The place was quite bare. The only hint that it was a recording studio were the framed discs mounted on deep purple walls.

'Excuse me, I understand that The RocX are recording here at 4.30 today,' I tried not to sound nervous, but I could have ended up looking like an idiot if the arrangements had been changed since it had appeared on his *Facebook* page. It had appeared in a conversation with some kid who wanted to book guitar lessons with him.

'I have a card for one of the singers and wondered if it is possible for someone to pass it on,' I said, now feeling like some sort of weird, obsessed groupie.

'Yes...I can pass it on for you,' then she smiled sweetly.

She had a hint of an Eastern European accent and was very attractive. She made me feel a mess after being on the scruffy Tube. I could feel my heart pounding through my dress.

What if he turned up early?

I gripped the envelope and remembered I still needed to write his name on the front – I'd deliberately left it blank, in case Richard found it.

'Do you have a pen I could borrow please?'

The receptionist handed me a plastic biro. I wrote:

Anthony Hope,

The RocX

I asked the girl to make sure that Anthony got it. She gave it an inquisitive glance before placing it on her desk. As I was still stood facing her I heard the double-doors behind me swing forcefully open. I froze for a second not daring to turn around in case it was him.

'Hi there,' the receptionist said to the approaching figure, before turning to me. 'Are you okay? You look like you have seen ghost.'

'I'm fine,' I stammered 'I should go.'

As I pulled at the main door I picked up that the stranger behind me was called Peter. The receptionist asked if he was doing a coffee run.

Outside the building I leaned against the wall for a few seconds. My knees were trembling. What on earth had possessed me to do such a stupid thing? I had to get out of the area.

I found my way back to the Tube and thought about my card. I pictured Anthony staring at his name and flipping the creamy envelope over to open it up, pulling out the simple card.

I hobbled to Selfridges, to get myself a new bag and made it back to the tiny coffee shop just within my deadline. Richard was already there sipping a can of *Coke*.

'How was the game?' I asked while actually thinking about

my own game.

'Didn't kick off till five – so I had a few drinks and went for a wander round...did you get what you wanted?'

'Yes, do you like it?' I said, proudly showing off my new bag.

'Very nice. How much was it?'

'It's *Christian Dior*, so it did go slightly over my budget. I put the extra on my credit card,' I said, swiftly followed by my defence. 'But being black, I'll get loads of use out of it...and it is beautiful...feel the quality of the leather...it's so soft,' I was stroking it by now.

'Credit card?'

'Lets have a look at your trainers then...'

'I've got them on. Well what do you think?'

They were clumpy and awful.

'Erm, well. Are they comfy?'

'You don't like them – do you?'

'As long as they're comfy, they're fine. I can't walk to Covent Garden, because my feet are killing me,' I said, rubbing my feet.

'You shouldn't wear ridiculous shoes for walking. We'll get a taxi.'

We found a French restaurant and opted for one of the outside tables, so we could feel the benefit of the sun. I remembered reading something about Nell Gwyn spending much of her life in Covent Garden. I thought about Anthony somewhere in the city.

Richard told me how pensive I looked as he topped up my glass of wine.

'Why don't you just give him the paper with the name of the hotel written on it? Clearly he doesn't understand you,' said Richard. 'You can't say Champs-Elysees properly.'

'Oh fuck off...' and I handed the taxi driver the printout for the hotel.

The taxi driver, dropped us off on the corner of a busy road, pointing us in the direction of a side street. We spent ten minutes walking up and down the narrow street, being thankful for the shade cast by the tall buildings. We eventually found a tiny entrance, having missed the hotel sign above it probably four times.

The foyer was no bigger than the front room of a terraced house. There was a reception desk, small bold striped sofa, and a PC for guests.

Perhaps I should have skimped on the London hotel, and upgraded the Parisian hotel?

We made our way upstairs in a cranky lift and then walked into a beautiful, recently decorated room in white and pale creams. It had that perfect mix of contemporary with chintz.

The sumptuous pile of scatter cushions were now all over the floor. Richard leaned over to me.

'You really seemed to enjoy that.'

'I don't ever *not* enjoy it...' Richard had always been a considerate lover, in fact the most considerate lover I'd ever had.

'No, I mean, really enjoy it...a break from the kids must be doing you good.'

'Yeah...but my phone still isn't working,' I said dismissively.

'Why are you changing the subject? Can't you leave your phone alone for a bit? Why is it so important?'

'It's not. It's just bugging me,' and I picked the phone back up for another go.

'I can't check that William and Elyse are okay,' I said, while still messing with the settings.

'There is a perfectly good phone right there, next to you, and mine's in the safe.'

I looked at the phone on the bedside table, next to the crystal based lampshade. 'That's not the point...I want my phone, and that phone doesn't have Internet.'

'It's all about bloody *Facebook* again – can't you leave it alone for one weekend?'

I reluctantly abandoned my phone to the hotel safe, but flatly refused to stuff my new bag in there as well. We took a gentle stroll round the city. Richard, like me, preferred to see cities on foot.

We stopped off at chic cafes whenever we felt like it and I dragged Richard to Avenue Montaigne and Avenue George V; taking in the elegant buildings housing *Chanel*, *Christian Dior*, *Givenchy*, *Hermes* and *Jean-Paul Gaultier*.

Richard took me up the steps of the Sacre Coeur and back down to the Red Light District, and we finished the day in a candle lit restaurant – in many ways the day was like old times.

We eventually found our way back to the hotel, after far too many wrong turns, and my eyes instantly locked onto the PC on the back wall.

'Would it really bother you, if I spent a few minutes on that computer?'

'Okay – go on then...I'm going to get a brandy from that bar in there,' he said, as he pointed towards the archway.

I sat down on an antique chair and noticed that *Facebook* was already in the search bar.

Once the homepage came up on the screen it was all in French, but the format was the same.

I typed in my email and password then waited.

It was even slower than at home, but eventually a red box popped up.

I couldn't understand it, but I knew which box it was – it was the one where your password or email is incorrect. I tried re-entering my email once more. Why the hell was it rejecting my email? Had someone hacked my account? If I wasn't careful it would lock me out altogether.

I was going to have to wait until we got home to find out if Anthony had left a response to my card.

CHAPTER TWENTY-SEVEN

Maddy had said to pop round to hers so that we could have a proper "catch-up" on my Paris trip, but I stood waiting, like an idiot, at her electric gates.

She also wasn't answering any of her phones.

In the end, I jumped over her wall, scraping my knees and walked through the open front door. As I did so, I bumped into her temporary new cleaner but she had no idea where she'd gone either, so I sat in the lounge and waited for her.

When Maddy finally came back, she apologised; she had had to nip in to work to drop off some papers.

As she plonked herself into Steve's favourite chair, I noticed that her weight had dropped but, like me, she could ill afford to lose it.

I took another look at the ceramic dish on the coffee table; it was still full of cigarette stubs. Clearly the new cleaner hadn't made her way into this room yet to remove the evidence. Now was not the time to lecture her, I thought, as she filled me in on Steve's latest prison tales. The best news was that she'd discovered that you could buy a fast-track appeal, so she was going to try and get his sentence reduced. But he'd been moved to a Category D – Category A was the worst apparently.

'So he could order a *PlayStation,* if he wants too, but they get confiscated if you behave badly. All the TVs in the cells are being upgraded for plasmas,' she said then laughed. 'Can you believe it?'

We both agreed that the system was wrong.

'You need to take my mind off of all of this – can I see your new bag?'

She whipped it from my side.

'I love the leather...so how was it? Did you have a great time? She asked, handing the bag back to me.

'Yep,' I said, as I pulled my thank you gift out of it; a pair of earrings which were very similar to a pair she had once told me she wanted.

'I love them...they're like the Tiff...'

'Tiffany ones,' I finished for her, 'I know...sorry – I can't afford the real thing.'

'So how was it, then?' she asked, while putting them into her ears.

'I snuck a card into Anthony Hope at the recording studios,' I said, before I could change my mind.

'You did what?'

'I wasn't going to tell you...but what the hell,' and I gave her a rundown of the event.

'Jesus! What if he'd seen you? Shit! I would have died on the spot. Thank God I wasn't there with you.'

I smiled. I had said as much as I really needed to say about the whole thing.

'What did the card say?'

'On the front was a bumble bee with the words "Bee Lucky" and then, on the inside, I wrote "Hello Jack" with a little heart above the words, and, underneath I wrote: "Just passing through the City", and I'd drawn a tiny squiggle of a mouse.'

'That's all it said?'

She almost sounded disappointed.

'Yep.'

'Have you had any reaction to the card?'

'Can't tell... he posted a video clip of Michael Jackson's *Thriller*, later the same day. Jackson equals Jack... So maybe? Also he could have viewed what I had done as being thrilling...? He also became a Fan of *Deadmau5,* which does look like dead mouse, and fits in with our game of cat and mouse.'

Maddy had one of those expressions that a teacher wears when listening to an unbelievable excuse from a kid .

'Has he sent the email about that charity day through to your alias yet?'

'To Nell Gwyn? No, he hasn't.'

'He surely can't just ignore that. Will you go?'

'Don't know...but it's over the summer holidays, so it's a good few weeks away yet...but I really don't know. I might – but what if the hot air balloon crashes?'

'Yeah...that would be bloody typical of you, you selfish cow...you'd go and die, leaving me to explain it all. Anyway, I've been meaning to ask you, can William come on a prison visit sometime with Henry...say no, if you think it's not a good idea.'

'No. It's fine. A least I don't have to worry about him being sheltered in private education.'

I laughed and then picked up a call from Richard about having to do the school run later. I put the phone on the table.

'Your phone's working again then?' she acknowledged.

Yes – I had to re-set it. Apparently when you go through the *Eurotunnel* you are supposed to keep it switched off, until you get to the other side. Did you also know that the keys on a French keyboard are all over the place? It took me a day to realise why I couldn't get into my Facebook account over there.'

'No I didn't know that either. Anyway, how is Richard coping with all the financial shit?'

'Not well.'

'I reckon he will end up going bankrupt, but it's the best thing he could do,' she said.

I hoped she was wrong.

After Paris, nothing noteworthy happened for a few weeks – life ticked by.

On my birthday, I chose to go out for a meal with Richard – I couldn't hide away for two years on the trot. Because it had fallen on a Sunday, the city restaurant was virtually empty – as in us, and one other couple.

The meal was going pretty well, until a famous England football manager and his team walked in; and opted for the table directly behind ours. Richard's voice became louder and he tried to engage me in a conversation about football.

I took another sip of my wine, wondering why he didn't just pull up a chair at their table and leave me to sulk over the fact that Anthony hadn't bothered to leave me a cryptic birthday message. It wasn't like I was asking him to give me the world.

The next morning, I sat watching William and Elyse play on the trampoline through the shutters; their moves always made me wince – every second felt like a potential A&E visit.

While they were happy outside I decided to log onto *Facebook*; I wanted to delete Anthony because it was painfully obvious that he cared nothing for me.

I clicked straight onto his Wall and called it my "one last look", but I had not been entirely convinced that it would be.

When his page opened up, I could see that he had been busy; it took me a few seconds to digest it all.

1:52 Anthony's magical moment... "a celebration of life"... I'm an Uncle ;)

1:53 That's getting older...innit...missed it ;)

My first thought was how nice – his sister was now a mother – but why should I even care.

But then I looked at his words.

He'd incorporated my birthday message in with the arrival of his sister's baby: a birthday is a "celebration of life", and at each birthday, we get older – and he'd missed my birthday. The thought of deleting him evaporated. Instead, I ached for him to be real, rather than just words on my screen.

It was a day later when I realised how I'd missed the obvious. I could hear Maddy talking; she was sitting on her work surface, saying something about having to dial different numbers at the prison, only to keep getting the same person with a different job title. I could hear her, but wasn't really taking in what she was saying.

'Okay, what's wrong?' she asked.

'It's Anthony. This morning on *Facebook* he commented on his sister's photo album.'

'So what?'

'His sister posted photos of her new baby on the 8th of August. Anthony, commenting on them, has pulled them through to my Newsfeed. But this is what the "X" raised to the power of two in the equation was: 8th of the 8th month.'

'Actually that *is* weird...even I have to admit that.'

'It gets even weirder...they've called the child Simon, the name of the character in the old novel that I stumbled on.'

'Oh my God, that's spooky.'

'I know...that child hadn't even been conceived when I drew the symbol, back in October, and I was lead to the quadratic equation before then too. It's all there on my *Facebook*; locked in time. No one can dispute it. This isn't like one of those "...an angel sat by my bed" things, that no one can prove either way,' I said, whilst pulling one of her stools up to the island.

'No...it's certainly not that.'

'So, I've worked it out...that child must have been conceived around the 15th of November, 2008 – just about the time I sent him my letter. I wonder whether this is why he was freaking out in German...this must have been what he was trying to tell me. He would have known when the baby was due. It was nothing to do with him leaving the band.'

'Could be...who knows?'

'This is why my words had power. It all makes sense now,' I said, more to myself. 'I still can't believe they've called the baby, Simon. And...do you know what is even freakier?'

'No?'

'We are in the year 2009 now...'

'No shit...are we?'

'Very funny...the child was conceived in 2008, but born in 2009. And when you calculate two to the power of nine, it equals

512: the number sitting on the other side of the equation. I was right all along: the numbers were linked to the past and the future. This can't possibly be a coincidence.'

Maddy shook her head and shrugged. 'Two to the power of nine?'

'Yes – like 2 x 2 x 2 x 2 - until you get to 512. A two with a tiny 9 above it. That equals 512 and year 2009 is 2 to the power of 9.'

'I get what you mean when you put it like that.'

'Mmm…I don't think it could mathematically happen this way again, certainly not for thousands of years.'

'I honestly don't know what to make of it all,' she said, reaching for her cigarettes. 'Have I ever told you that some of my relatives are supposed to have psychic abilities; I sometimes get bad feelings about things. You should have seen me the week before we got dawn-raided. I sensed that something bad was going to happen. It was almost a relief when I found out what it was. You ask Steve.'

'Ask Steve?'

She laughed then said: 'Well…on your next prison visit, then.'

'I don't know…the whole thing has given me a splitting headache.'

'Well, unless you speak to Anthony properly, you're never going to know what he's thinking,' she pulled open a drawer. 'Here, have one of these,' and she slid a packet of painkillers across the island.

I swallowed the pills. I could feel them wedged in my oesophagus.

'And do you know something else? The novel *Simon Dale* opened with Anthony Hope's fictional character talking about his birth. The clues were there…I simply missed them.'

'I thought you hadn't read the book?' she said, while pushing the kitchen window open.

'I have only read the first and last couple of pages online. I still can't face the actual book, because the character of Nell dies in it

– I know that much.'

'I'm going to buy you that bloody book,' she said adamantly.

I continued to malfunction for the rest of the day. It was like I was running on autopilot, while my head ran over and over the sequence of events.

Later on, after having a horrid day at the country park, I walked into my lounge, removed several cereal bowls that William had slid under the sofa and then put on Elyse's favourite DVD; she was taking her moment to have complete control over the television, while William wasn't around. As she watched, she snuggled under her rabbit blanket and fixed her eyes on the screen. This was her idea of bliss.

My laptop was left open on *Facebook*, I refreshed my screen, but a prompt came up asking me to re-type my password. I did what was asked and then I clicked on the photo of baby Simon. A tiny new life, full of "hope" sat on my screen.

So much joy, so many good wishes from friends.

I kept on clicking my way through the album, looking for a precise birth date and time, but found nothing.

Then I wrote number 42 several times over on a scrap of paper with my right hand. Then I drew a circle around the last one; as I thought that time was irrelevant if it only takes forty-two minutes to fall through a hole from England to the other side of the Atlantic.

What really mattered was what I could see on my computer screen, and on the paper hanging out of the printer.

They both showed the album as being posted on the 8th of August 2009.

Nicole Hollis
11th August – Nicole is writing a book
18th August – Nicole has posted a video clip… .Lady Gaga's Love Game

23rd August – Nicole is not entirely clear but the 'X' factors....they want the money & fame!?! =)

Anthony Hope

25th August – Anthony Hope reckons Hasslehoff is a hero! He knows how to make a buck!!! That's cool in my book...

'So you are telling me that your permission to write this book is based on the thumbs up from David Hasslehoff, so to speak,' said Maddy, and she put on a cheesy grin and gave the thumbs up with both hands. 'I can see us all standing in court, trying to defend this one...this could be the best trial we have ever had,' and she leaned forward onto my kitchen island, cringing into her hands. I could feel myself cringing at the thought of it with her.

'I don't need you to tell me it's plain crazy. But Anthony's drawn a parallel with David Hasslehoff because Hasslehoff wrote himself into his own show, didn't he? And I'm writing us into our own book. Just think about it.'

'Even so...and not that I have anything against David Hasslehoff – but can't you get Anthony's proper permission to write a book rather than one based on drawing parallels with a complete stranger. Shit! This could be the first book that Steve ever reads.'

'We could send it into prison for him, page by page. Anyway, I'm running with the Hoff – and I'll deal with any legal angles later, if I really have to. I've got pages and pages of evidence printed off to back me up,' I said, while thinking of the sideboard in the garden room that was chock full of Facebook printouts, stored in blue ring binders that said accountancy notes. Nevertheless, I resisted the urge to show Maddy and there was no way I was going to approach Anthony again for anything. If I confronted him head on, I was sure he would lie again.

'So how does the book end?'

'I don't know, but my gut instinct tells me that the ending will find itself.' I hardly wanted to say that I'd got to figure out how to start it first. 'Anyway, this whole thing is your fault.'

'My fault? Her eyebrows shot up in surprise. 'Why? Not that I ever expect you to say that anything is your fault...but go on...I am intrigued...'

'Because it was you who got me to sign up to *Facebook*. You also arranged for us to go to Magna at Halloween and if something hadn't tapped me on the shoulder there I wouldn't have discovered any of it.'

She laughed.

In reality, Anthony was only half my problem – if I was to write about him, it meant confessing everything to Richard.

CHAPTER TWENTY-EIGHT

On the 18th of September 2009 I typed the following Status into my *Facebook*: *Nicole is glad that she bought the hamsters from the farm shop.*

In reality, it wasn't the E-coli outbreak on my mind – it was Richard going bankrupt. But, nowhere on my *Facebook* was there even a tiny glimmer of this truth.

Instead of a sad profile picture, I had a photo of David Hasslehoff wearing a leather jacket and skimpy underpants.

I watched Richard gather up his things, ready for the meeting with the bankruptcy court. He'd tried to book it for 9/11, but couldn't; too many people wanted to go down on that date.

In all the years that I'd known Richard, I'd never seen him like this and as he walked past the kitchen doorway to the lounge, my eyes locked onto the black-and-white photo on the hall sideboard.

Richard was a young boy on the photo, not much older than William was now, and he was pictured standing in front of the family car with his brother and sister. The car was an old, white *Ford Consul* with the number plate HK 7533. It had been taken in Hong Kong and you could see the mountains and the water in the background. His dad was working out there at the time as a code-breaker for the RAF, he had been exceptionally clever, like Richard, and had been educated by the Christian Brothers; the Catholic monks in Ireland.

His dad would never have approved of me.

As I looked at Richard, it was the boy within who looked back at me.

'Have you got everything?'

'Think so,' he said.

'Are you sure that this is the best way?'

I'd become immune to the demanding letters and phone calls but I could have lived with them, as long as we didn't get our door broken down. It was the anonymous text that ate at me more than anything else that had happened to us.

'It's the best way. It wipes everything out. No more messing with lawyers. If they'd dropped that legal case, then maybe there would be an alternative,' he shrugged.

I wanted to hug him, but I couldn't.

He left by himself and did not say goodbye.

Richard had been gone for several hours and I was starting to work myself into a frenzy. I selected the Send option on my third text message, asking him to call me. Then I paced for ages, finally finding myself back at the kitchen window, hoping that his car would come around the corner any second.

I was scared that he'd done something stupid; I tried to shake off the image of him sitting in his car, trying to gas himself. I was worried that I'd underestimated his despair. As Mum always said, women pop pills and men kill themselves, when they can't cope.

I should have insisted on going with him.

Then I heard the key turn in the front door and Richard walked in, still looking immaculate in his tailored suit. I exhaled a sigh of relief.

'How did it go?' I asked gently. I was expecting him to breakdown and didn't know how I was going to deal with it.

'Fine,' he said. 'I can't even begin to tell you how much better I feel, Little N. This morning was the scariest I have ever had, but now a weight has been lifted – it is really hard to explain. I would like you to read these pamphlets...'

I took them from him and thumbed through one of them.

'Nicole, the equity of the house will transfer to you, like the solicitor said. Because there is a charge from the bank against it and redemption penalties on the mortgage, there is no point in them going after it, and I could be out of it in six months, if they manage to sort their paperwork out quickly.'

'Good...that's a relief,' I said, as I spotted the title of one of the pages "Beating Bankruptcy". I put in down.

It felt like that whole cancer thing again, like when *Ilex* went down.

'Thankfully notifications no longer appear in the evening paper, they stopped that last year because too many people are going bankrupt.' he said.

Great I thought. For once our failings wouldn't find their way into print.

'It's not the money that's got to me.' he said shaking his head.

'I know...it's the feeling of failure,' I said. '*Ilex* going down was...'

'You can't even imagine how it feels when your job is to give financial advice.'

'You have never given anyone bad advice. You've made lots of people, lots of money. You just didn't take your own advice all of the time.'

'Like the cobbler and his shoes, the doctor and his health you mean.'

'Exactly...you took risks...you've always taken risks...most have paid off...but this one didn't. We have to look at it another way – we are better off now than when you left the house this morning. All of the debt has gone away, and your pension funds are still intact.'

'I know.' His brows were still knotted.

'And it's not like we have got to really suffer for the next year. Like you said, you could be out of it in six months. We're still better off than some others right now. I actually think that boredom will be your biggest problem.'

His face eased. 'Six months, or a year at the worst, and it'll all be over. Thank God I had the sense to put my money into pensions over the years. I've just remembered that I got you something while I was in town.' He ran back to his car before returning with a book. 'I got this to help with your writing.'

I took it from his hand. His kindness and support suddenly made me feel like curling into a small ball and sobbing. Richard was helping me to write a book, which detailed my attraction to another man. Just thinking about it made me feel sick with betrayal. I thought back to the words I'd written about Anthony in my opening chapters.

I would still want him even if I saw him today...

'Thank you,' I said quietly.

'The other day you said that you were re-tracing events as they happened, well...I thought that book would help you,' Richard said, as I stood clutching Alex Brummer's – *The Crunch: How greed and incompetence sparked the credit crisis.*

I was moving from a hole to an entire warren that I couldn't see my way back out of. Why was getting to the truth so complicated?

Richard nipped out again to get us some food; he'd already decided that he was taking over both the cooking and the afternoon school run for the next six months.

I looked at the book he'd bought again. The very least I could do was read it.

I saved my own incomplete book onto the heart-shaped memory stick Maddy had bought for my birthday, and moved over to the sofa. I lay on my back, holding the book in the air, and skimmed through it. After about half an hour I jumped up, paused, then ran to my laptop, logged on to *Facebook* and pulled up a photo I'd posted on my *Facebook* months ago.

I was right – Alex Brummer had written about the same H.M. Treasury job that I had seen advertised! That was round about the time when everything started to become weird around me, I recalled.

Brummer believed that the powerful new post had been created because the Treasury Select Committee considered Sir John Gieve to be incompetent in his role as Deputy in charge of monetary stability.

On the 9th August 2007, Gieve wasn't around, because someone in his family had died; an Act of God.

Richard came back through the door, with his eco-friendly shopping bags laden with food. I excitedly followed him into the kitchen.

'You're not going to believe this...guess which day the credit crunch officially started?'

'I take it that you are reading the book I bought for you.'

'It started on the 9th of August 2007. On my birthday! I turned 37 that day – and it's as though the moment I turned 37 my life was on a numerical path that I had no control of: so *Ilex Drapes* was never going to survive as a company! Once that freak rain started in summer 2007, our company was only going to go one way. And I'm sorry for ever questioning why you never saw the credit crunch coming...no one saw it, according to this book.'

'Well...that's nice of you to say, after all this time,' he said, sarcastically, as he put the salad in the fridge.

'Neither the FSA, Bank of England or The Treasury, had any idea that there was a problem until the 9th of August 2007. Alistair Darling really had been in *Wonderland*,' I said, as I thought back to him on the front page of the *Daily Mail* dressed as Alice on budget day. The article was still stuffed in one of the study drawers.

'I have told you over and over that there had been nothing from the FSA warning us about it.'

'I know, and I'm really sorry. I'll tell you something else; *Northern Rock's* collapse was down to Mervyn King,' I said, thinking I'd now tracked down the King in my own story. 'King refused to put any money into the banks when they froze on my birthday in 2007. When the banks stopped lending to each other, because they realised they were all holding a big fat nothing on their balance sheets, King refused to bail them out. Trichet did it for the French. King thought it was the wrong way to go... so it was King's decision which collapsed *Northern Rock*. If *Northern*

Rock hadn't gone down on that precise date, *Ilex Drapes* would not have been closed down on the 15th of February 2008. It may have still failed, but the dates would have changed.'

Richard continued to put away the shopping, while I voiced my thoughts.

'My quadratic equation wouldn't have balanced. But it was the 9th of August 2007, which set the chain of events in motion. Well, no, actually, it goes back further than that; it started from William's birth. But the real key was turning 37 and me remaining 37 as we passed through 08/08/08.'

'So the book's been useful to you then?'

'God, yeah...thank you. You know what, I don't feel guilty about the bank losing out on that overdraft, now that you've gone bankrupt.' I took a punnet of blueberries out of the fridge and started to eat them. 'The banks had us all building our lives on a false economy. All of the new builds, home renovations and conservatories being added – none of the money for them really existed. We were looking at sandcastles. The banks lent money for it all, only to disintegrate our castles in front of us. Then they went and pulled the plug.

'Hmmm...I don't know what to feel about this...'

'Just think about it – our bank encouraged two of its customers to merge their businesses and they allowed you to throw money in. Had they told the truth you would never have done that.'

'Well it's history now...and when this is all over, I'm going back in, fighting all the way,' he said, as he closed the fridge door.

'You sound like Steve, wanting to get out and rebuild his empire,' I laughed. 'Greed has put us all in a sort of jail-house, even Lorna and Bruce wouldn't be in trouble had they not blown their all their money on unnecessary things.'

'What you going to do now?' Richard asked.

'Write my book.' I said.

There was no way I could back out of writing it now.

After Richard's bankruptcy, I started to trawl through all of my research, and, as the nights drew in, I spent less time on *Facebook*. I was slowly facing the fact that Anthony was never going to email me in any form.

The last message I left for Anthony, said that the book will always be there for him, if his fairy tale ever ended; I was starting to think I could only write the book with his non-cryptic permission. I was still writing but morally no longer knew what to do with it.

I typed in his name at the top of my screen.

But he wasn't there.

My heart jumped to my throat and my head felt hazy.

He had defriended me, deleted me.

I wanted to climb into my PC and stand in an empty, black space, where he once was – and shout for him to come back; beg him not to leave me.

If only it was like a game on William's DS, where there was a button I could press to view from another angle, just so I could read his face.

He must have felt something when he did it.

I didn't know whether this made him stronger or weaker than me.

I repeatedly typed his name, hitting the refresh button, praying it was either my computer playing up or another one of his pranks, but he still wasn't there.

I managed to find his *Facebook* page, via his girlfriend's. His photo was sitting amongst all of her friends. I clicked on his name and could see that all his other friends were still there. It was only me he had removed.

I read his quote: *Make the most of what we have.* It felt like his parting words. I printed off the page and tears pricked my eyes.

'Mummy look,' I heard Elyse say.

'Yes, Elyse, in a minute,' I didn't even look at her.

'Mummy, look,' and I felt her small body by my side. 'I got you Daddy's torch,' I felt the tears trickle down my face. 'It's so you can see in here,' she added.

I hadn't found the time to replace the spent study light-bulbs, and had been managing with just the light from the PC.

A few hours later, I removed the privacy settings on my page and typed in a message.

Please add me back as your friend

It was pitiful and pathetic and, within minutes of me typing it, he was gone.

He had taken down his entire page. He had left *Facebook*.

It was as though he'd been sitting waiting for my response before he did it. Why had he singled me out first? Why had he taken down his page now?

That night I danced around my bedroom with William and Elyse. The music lifted my spirits and stopped me from crying and I knew that I would survive life without Anthony Hope. He'd gone but I was still living.

CHAPTER TWENTY-NINE

I stepped out of the bath, being careful not to slip on the tiled floor; it was still wet from William and Elyse having bathed earlier on.

I grabbed the towel off the rail and wrapped it round my body; I grabbed another and rubbed my hair as I walked into the bedroom to find Richard walking through the bedroom door.

'I came to see where you were...'

'Sorry...you looked like you were asleep on the sofa and I didn't want to disturb you,' I sighed. 'I need to speak to you...about my book.'

'What about it?'

'I haven't put you fully in the picture and things are eating away at me... I can't write it unless I tell you the truth.'

'The truth?'

'There's something I need to show you...' and I pulled the *Simon Dale* novel from behind a messy row of DVDs in the wardrobe. Maddy had done what she had said she would do and bought the book for me, but it wasn't until Anthony had deleted me that I let her give it to me.

The cover was charcoal grey, and if you looked closely you could make out a wooded area with a small boy sitting at the edge of water. The name Hope dominated the cover; Anthony was in smaller text beneath.

I saw Richard's eyes flicker suspiciously.

'Why have you hidden this book?' He sounded genuinely confused.

'This is at the root of what has been driving me mad... I've been playing around with Anthony Hope on my *Facebook*,' I blurted out, knowing this was not going to be as forgivable as my crush on James. I couldn't even look Richard in the eye.

'Were you...were you having cyber-sex with him? An online sexual affair?'

'God no – not online sex. Not even an affair. In fact, I don't really understand what it was. Plus you know Anthony has a girlfriend,' I said, finally brave enough to meet his eyes.

'You don't know what it was or what it *is*?' His eyes were on fire.

'He deleted me. It is all over now. It was just a silly game on *Facebook*,' I said, choosing to sit on the bed, making Richard tower over me. I deserved to feel small.

'What sort of game? I thought you said you didn't fancy him?'

'I lied. I've always been attracted to him. I can't even explain why, not really...but something draws me to him.'

'So, you're saying you want to be with him?'

'No! Yes...oh, it doesn't matter now. It was nothing more than a game, it wasn't sexual, we were playing with words. But I've told you it's over now...he's deleted me. Besides, I always knew I could never be with him. I'm just saying I have always been attracted to him...but realised eight or so years ago that he would be dangerous for me and there is nothing more alluring than what you can't have.'

'So...you can't have him – so you might as well have second best. Me! Is that it?'

'No...I'm saying it doesn't matter. None of it. It is all irrelevant. What I feel doesn't even matter. Besides which, he was too young for me and would not have wanted to take on the chil—'

'Oh my God! And what about your feelings for me? You've not once said that the reason you are with me and not with him is because you love me more!' Richard looked wounded.

'I'm giving you reasons of why I couldn't be with him...he is just a fantasy.'

'Great, so now I'm second place to a fantasy. Nicole...do you love me?'

'Of course I love you and I'm sorry, I'm really sorry. I only added him to my *Facebook* so that I could see what had happened to him, he then started playing a game with me, and I got sucked into it, I couldn't pull myself away...I tried, I even sent an email telling him I couldn't ever be with him.'

'You sent him a fucking email telling him that! What did it say?'

'It doesn't matter what it said, other than I said I could never be with him.'

'So is this why he's deleted you?'

'No...I sent the email over a year ago and he kept on playing this game with me. I couldn't stop myself from responding, because I could never really work him out; work out his motivation, and all this weird number stuff was linked to him.'

'So what did he say to your email?'

'He basically denied playing a game with me, but carried the game on regardless.'

'So why has he chosen to delete you now?'

'I don't know? It could be because of my book. It could be that he simply decided he really did love his girlfriend and was finally committing to her. I can't work it out. But he deleted me just hours before taking down his entire *Facebook* page.'

'Or his girlfriend found out what he was doing on *Facebook* more like it, and made him do it. He could have been playing games with loads of women on there, for all you know, and she's got wind of it.'

'I don't think so, not unless Anthony confessed to her. She couldn't see what I put on my *Facebook*.'

'Don't call him Anthony.' I could still see flashes of anger in Richard's eyes. 'Use his full name.'

'Look, if it makes you feel any better, Maddy reckons he wasn't even playing a game with me, but there were too many coincidences, right down to the day he deleted me,' and I tried to explain the bizarre game.

'So that old book, in your hand...what's that got to do with the real Anthony Hope?' he said as he turned off the main lights, leaving the soft glow of the bedside lamp.

'I found this book after I was tapped on the shoulder on Halloween night...it's connected to the numbers. This books starts with the three divine numbers of seven, whereas my book has the three eights...' I began and I explained the story to him. I reminded him about Nell Gwyn being an actress and courtesan but he got cross when I likened myself to a courtesan.

'I haven't read the whole book yet...but I know that Nell dies in it and that Anthony Hope's main character marries another woman. Since it's been in the house I've been terrified you will find it.'

'So, if you are saying that being with Anthony Hope is just a fantasy...are you saying you fantasised about him?'

'I can't believe we are even discussing this.'

'So...what did he do to you in your *fantasy*?'

'You're asking me ridiculous questions...you might as well ask me if he was better in bed than you...in my fantasy,' I added sarcastically.

'He'd probably be crap in bed anyway – I don't even get what you see in him. He loves himself; and he's just a rubbish singer. What would you even want with a singer?'

'Look I told you...I can't explain what it is that draws me to him; I don't even care what he does for a living. I feel another side to him, a much deeper, more complicated side and that draws me in.'

'Perhaps you should just fuck off with the wanker, it would be interesting to see how long he'd put up with you. A week, if you're lucky, but then you probably deserve each other.'

His words made me flinch. Then I felt a wave of anger.

'That's good coming from a man who cheated on and then dumped his wife for a younger model...and I'm not sticking up for him.' I needed to calm down, this wasn't helping my case. 'I'm trying to explain it all to you...but it's this book, this book feels like part of it. Don't you understand that I'm not fated to be with him, I never was...and he's not a threat to you.'

'Is this my fault...have I made you feel unloved? Is he why you won't marry me?' he said, calming back down again.

'No. But...when you first left your wife you kept going back to her and you killed a tiny part of me each time you did it.'

'And I still came back to you...you know, it was the guilt...the minute I went back to her the guilt disappeared and I wanted to be back with you.'

'Yes, but each time you did it, I became emotionally harder. I built a wall around me and threw myself further into my studies. And it was only a year or so after that, that Anthony came on the scene, and then within the next year I fell pregnant... All I'm trying to say, is back then it was never about me. It was all about you and your wife, and whether you and she were coping with the trauma of a break-up.'

Richard shook his head.

'I forgot about me. I didn't matter and I didn't deserve to matter because I was the other woman, and since running a company and looking after William and Elyse, I've never had the time to really think about me.'

'It's you I chose to be with. And if he really wanted you, he would have come after you.'

'Why would he have? Look at it from his perspective. I was with a rich, older guy driving round in a fifty thousand pound sports car. He'd arrived here virtually penniless. To him I probably looked like a gold digger. How was he supposed to know the car was partially financed and that I never tried to drag you up the aisle? When a woman is with an older man, people almost always assume it's about nothing but money... I fitted into a perfect stereotype.'

'Makes no difference, he still would have come after you. Anyway, he smokes and you hate smoking...cigarette smoke makes you ill.' He paused. Then a flicker of recognition. 'Ah... I'm getting it now. It's your ego – he has bruised your ego, so to hell with the fact that he smokes. He doesn't want you now. He has turned away from you and the game.'

Richard was right. Anthony had been destroying me, and now the last, tiny piece of my self-esteem was getting kicked away by Richard.

'I love you, I always have – no one will ever love you like I do; he would never love you like I do. Well, I suppose that fantasies are harmless. And… if you really want to write your book…then write it.'

I felt like even Richard was playing clever mind games with me now – he'd taken it so well. Perhaps it was the wisdom of age. I knew for a fact that I would have been sitting by the roadside by now had it been an ex-boyfriend that I had confessed to.

'Just thought you should know this fact – I now hate Anthony Hope,' I said, sullenly. 'Because of what he's turned me into – a selfish, deceitful liar with zero confidence; I also hate him for not being open and honest with me.'

'I wouldn't say you have zero confidence, but selfish and deceitful is probably accurate from where I'm standing right now. I'm seeing a side of you that I never knew existed. Look…write your book.'

'Sometimes I don't even know why you love me…you would have been far better off staying with your wife – she's caused you far less trouble than I have.'

'Well…I do love you, but you have hurt me very much. I don't really know how I'm supposed to compete with a fantasy man.'

As Richard started to undress he asked me if this was why I had felt trapped and, after thinking about how to answer his question without hurting him anymore, I replied: 'It's partly because sometimes I've felt as though I would be better off being on my own for a while – you know, to sort out my head and get things back in perspective. If I was on my own, Anthony still wouldn't be a possibility. I needed a reality check.'

Richard moved into the bathroom and started to brush his teeth. Sitting on the side of the bath I continued to explain.

'And…William and Elyse would have hated me for taking them away from you and dragging them into squalor. No one can live up to a fantasy, but no one can live up to *you* either. So, instead I've had to work things through differently.'

Richard spat into the sink and spun round. He had toothpaste all over his chin.

'William and Elyse? You are assuming I'd let you take them.' Richard's words left me speechless for a few seconds.

'You'd fight me for our children? I can't believe you would do that to me. But I really would understand if you didn't want to be with me anymore, because of the way I've behaved.'

He wiped his mouth and then spoke, 'Of course I want to be with you, I don't want you to go anywhere…but you must talk to me more, can't you see that?'

'I keep telling you that I'm trying to…but everything I have to talk about it so wrong and hurtful, so it has been far easier to say nothing and bottle it all up. I suppose, in one way, my book will be the best explanation you'll ever get!'

8th December 2009

15:00 and I sat at the kitchen table with my study books. The constant shifting between writing and studying was making my brain feel like it was being hit with a sledgehammer. But this was my last exam and I wanted to get it out of the way, so I could focus fully on writing.

The change from the garden room to the kitchen was helping slightly. I heard Richard's car pull into the drive and a few moments later, he walked through the door with his mobile in his hand and his reading glasses on.

'Have you seen this text?'

'What text? I can't see it from over here,' I said, reaching over to hold his phone.

Beware the knave of hearts, else the cuckold become
My blood ran cold.

'That text relates to my *Facebook*! That has to be from the same person who sent the other one. But that was months ago...why would they send another now?'

It infuriated me that whoever was doing this was trying to be smart with words. Just like the text before – it was sinister in style, only this time even more carefully constructed.

'Never mind that...what does it mean, beware the Knave of Hearts?' and he took the phone back.

'What do you mean, what does it mean? – did you send the text?' I snapped. I was tired of people messing with my head. Life was starting to feel like I was playing a game inside a bubble that was rapidly becoming starved of oxygen. If only I could have burst the bubble and let more air to my brain.

'No, I didn't! How could you think so? But what does it mean?' he asked again.

'It refers to the Knave of Hearts in *Alice in Wonderland* – he steals the tart. Jack of Hearts was my nickname for Anthony Hope – and I'm the tart,' I said, trying to make my explanation sound quite normal. 'Only me, you, Maddy, Lorna, Bruce and Steve even know about my game and only me and Maddy know about the significance of the Knave of Hearts, and you, if I did tell you that bit, I can't quite remember. Maddy wouldn't send it, because she was always trying to stop me playing my game with Anthony, in case I lost you.'

'That was nice of her at least she's—'

I cut him short. 'Lorna isn't on Facebook, Maddy would not try to stir this all up again, Steve is in prison without the Internet and… the wording of the text isn't Bruce's style…'

I turned to look at him. 'I still think you've sent this text...only you and the media would use a word like cuckold...' I said, holding up the phone. 'So what else are you lying about?'

He took the phone back. 'Nothing. Your talking nonsense and everyone knows that word! Personally…I think that wanker has sent this text,' he said defiantly.

'Anthony? Why the hell would he send a text to you? You said yourself that if he was really interested in me he would have made more of an effort, even Maddy's told you she's thinks the game was in my head.'

In fact, Maddy hadn't even skirted round with her words when she said to us both that Anthony hadn't got a clue I'd been stalking him.

'Anthony wouldn't have your number; my *Facebook* page has never revealed any telephone numbers. And my game had barely started when the first text came through around October last year. So…this can't be from him,' I argued.

'I'm telling you it must be him. He knew where I worked; he could have called the office for it months ago, he could even have got it from the FSA. I was talking to him about my work that day at your Opus work do,' He fired back.

'I still think you've sent it…that was such a convoluted theory. You sent it from your other phone.'

'I haven't got that phone with me!' Then he pulled it from one of the island drawers, and I stared at it with hatred, because it meant I still didn't have an explanation.

'So what telephone number has it come from? Try calling it.'

'I can't…there is no number,' he said.

'What do you mean there is no number? There has to be a number.'

'Look no number.'

I took the phone from him again, and studied it. 'It says no recipient.' I pushed it back into his hand with contempt this time. He obviously had no idea how fragile and confused my head was to play with me like this.

'You are being ridiculous…it beeped when it came through on my phone…I was driving so I picked it up and saved it.'

I thought for a second, then grabbed my phone, and typed in a text message; after I had finished, I sent it to Richard's phone and when it came through, I saved it.

'There see, that's how it should appear if it had come through from another phone...you've done this...why the hell are you playing mind games with me?' I spat.

'I'm getting so angry with you. In fact, why don't you just piss off with the idiot. I am telling you – I have done nothing but Save the text...send me another text.'

'Fine,' I sent another, and Richard's phone bleeped after about thirty seconds. He clicked on 'Save to Template' this time.

'There see. I've obviously hit the wrong Save button, I was driving and I hadn't got my reading glasses on, and I'd hit Save To Template in error. Now do you believe me?'

'I just don't get it,' I said.

'I do...this text is from that wanker...who else would send a text message like this?'

I took the phone back again and sent several text messages from my phone to his, saving to Template.

If you Saved to Template, it then gave you two options: create a message using the Template, or create a Template and Save as a Draft; which would sit like the message on Richard's phone saying 'no recipient.' So...Richard could have Saved as Template, like he was saying. But why wasn't the original text sitting in the phone? I was baffled.

'I'm telling you...that text is not from Anthony Hope. Whoever sent this text message must have been stalking my *Facebook* page for months. But they also have your mobile number so that would mean it was either one of your relatives or...'

'Why would any of my relatives do that?'

'Because I took you away from your wife...'

'You didn't take me away – I left...and surely they would just say something instead of hiding behind a text message.'

'Fine – have it your way. There are some ex-staff members from *Ilex* on my *Facebook* too, they would know where to get your number, but they wouldn't have a clue about Anthony Hope.

They wouldn't even know who he is.'

I didn't want to let it drop, because either Richard was lying or someone *was* stalking me, and had been stalking me for months. Suddenly, I felt like I couldn't trust anyone, and Richard still refused to contact the police.

Someone, somewhere, knew the truth about these two text messages.

CHAPTER THIRTY

18th May 2010

I explained my story to Juliet Taylor, an ex-national journalist who now made a living from selling real-life stories to newspapers and magazines.

I found her on the Internet – I liked her photo, she looked kind and like she would be sympathetic to my story. This was my brainwave to find a way to the top of the literary slush pile that gave me a less than one per cent chance of surviving the shredder. My theory was to generate interest in the story, prior to sending it off to a publisher.

Juliet was like I expected and gentle with her questioning. She was also massively switched on, without the condescending tone evident in many male journalists.

Her probing pushed me to the tears that I'd been holding back since Anthony knocked me off *Facebook*. For some reason I didn't feel as though I had any right to cry over him anymore. I'd been a willing participant in the game and always knew how it would end.

I finished my convoluted tale, putting the conversation back into Juliet's court.

'I have to say…' and she kept me hanging.

The bottom of my stomach felt like it could drop any second because I knew what was coming next. I'd heard it all before: my mind flashed back to a conversation with a down market tabloid newspaper journalist over the Christmas holidays. I'd had Razorlight's *Wire to Wire* playing in the background at the time and, while sipping a snowball cocktail, I answered questions like: '…did you have sex with him?' I had to say no. 'So…did you ever actually meet up? And the answer I gave again was, no. In the end he said, 'well in that case, I don't think we have a story,' and rudely hung up. There was another email in my Inbox from a news agency that said, "…sorry we don't deal with fiction." I didn't know whether to laugh or cry – they thought my life was fiction! Their rejections swirled around in my head as Juliet kept up with the suspense. I felt my hand gripping the handset tighter and tighter. Then she finally spoke.

'...I find this story truly fascinating.'

For one who had a tendency not to show tactile emotion, I wanted to hug her.

'You're clearly an intelligent woman and yet you embark on the fantasy that this man is playing with you on *Facebook*... and—'

She called me intelligent! This meant a lot because I was starting to feel as thick as a brick...and then my head turned to the fantasy bit.

'No, no it wasn't a fantasy, the game actually happened...it's the other weird stuff I have no explanation for, but I have a statistician in the USA calculating the probability, or rather the improbability as he's called it, for the sequence of events for those bits.'

'But, Nicole, the game, you don't sound convinced it happened when you're explaining it.'

'I swear that the game did happen, but you need to read my book, it's not complete, but it will help you to understand it better.'

I couldn't even begin to explain to her that I was starting to feel like one of those characters in a children's story who embarks on an adventure, but is left with nothing but a single object as a reminder that it wasn't all a dream. My papers, my book, were proof that it wasn't something I'd dreamt up. But it didn't help that Maddy kept saying that he was never playing a game with me. I suppose it was a bit like when you return from a holiday – you know it happened but it no longer feels real.

'Email the book, and I'll read it...but I only want to read it if you are certain you want to go ahead with publicity for the story...otherwise I will have wasted my time.'

'Yes, I'm sure I want to go ahead. I'll email what I've written so far.'

'Great, but give me a few days to get back to you. I think we will protect Anthony's identity; it's not really fair to expose him. And will I be able to speak to Richard at some stage?'

'Yes...he'll speak to you. I did tell him that I'd sent a brief email to your company.'

'How did he take it when you told him about your game?'

'I've hurt him and he feels second place to a fantasy,' I said.

I desperately wanted to ask why she wished to speak to Richard, but was too intimidated. I scribbled down her personal email on a scrap of paper from the study desk, then we said our polite goodbyes. I placed the phone back on the base with a satisfied smile. At last someone was listening to me.

Juliet called Richard on his mobile, before she called me about a week later. All she wanted from him was to make sure that I was strong enough to cope with the publicity. Richard told her that I would be fine with it.

Several hours later the home phone rang. For once I picked up the call like it was a hot brick. Juliet was the first person besides Maddy to read what I'd written so far. Her opinion was crucial to me and waiting for her response felt far worse than holding exam results in a sealed envelope.

What if she thinks I'm too thick to write a book...that I am not really as intelligent as she thinks?

'Nicole, I've read your book and...'

It's like being a contestant on a talent show, I thought.

Then she spoke again, 'I think you write really well, lots of interesting detail. Plus, you have good recall for conversation, and I love the link you make to *Alice in Wonderland*. I think this book has got a lot of potential, but...'

God she was killing me with her pauses, I'd almost completed a lap of the coffee table.

'Nicole, I'm still not convinced that he was playing a game with you,' she said finally.

So that was why she's said it's well written, she was softening her punch,

'I still think you imagined it.'

I couldn't speak, I'd been holding my breath while pacing and now I needed to take in air. I tried to avoid an audible gulp. I manage a weak, 'Okay.'

She continued to speak. I turned my mouth away from the phone, trying to regulate my breathing again.

'I think you were so unhappy and bored at the time. You had an awful lot of stress in your life, and I think you had a mental breakdown.'

'But you haven't got the whole story. You've only got a little beyond the Lewis Carroll quote. It's not until later on that the game with him becomes more evident,' I said, thinking how can she not possibly see that a Lewis Carroll quote popping up after my direct reference to him, was too much of a coincidence to be anything else? And the *Alice in Wonderland*…it wasn't me who even started with that theme. That's what I saw from his side of the Wall, so to speak. It was that dice thing again. How many times did it have to throw up a six – a million?

'I'm sorry Nicole; obviously I haven't got the entire story here. But based on what I do have, I really don't think he was communicating with you, really I don't. And obsessing about numbers – that is usually a sign of a mental breakdown.'

'Yeah, I'm sure I've read or seen something about number madness before,' I said, thinking that I wasn't obsessing about any old numbers, only these specific numbers that were all connected. And it wasn't the numbers driving me mad – it was the coincidences with them. Was that the same thing? I didn't know. I wasn't an expert in such matters. How could Deepak Chopra be held a hero by world leaders for writing about *Synchrodestiny* and I be hailed as a nut job for considering the same things as remotely possible?

'But, as I've said, I do think this story has potential, and I'm definitely interested in it. Would you be prepared to allow a psychiatrist to give an opinion in the feature?'

I almost wanted to laugh.

'Yes I would, all I want to do is get the story out there. I want to invite different opinions. That's the whole purpose of me writing the book. May be I'll go down as the craziest woman on the planet,' I heard myself laugh uncomfortably.

Juliet paused again. She was obviously thinking up a tactful response.

'You certainly have an interesting mind,' she said.

In any normal circumstances I would find being called bonkers in a serious way by a complete stranger offensive, but I liked her. I liked her because her mind was sharp enough to cut through my rambling explanation of a game and get to the crux of the story in the first place, and she had gone to the trouble of reading my book. The worst insult she could have thrown at me would be that she found my story boring.

I also had to accept, like Virginia Wolf once said: "…one goes down into the well and nothing protects one from the assault of the truth". A breakdown could be the truth – that could be what I'd written – the confession from the eye of a mental crash.

We finished the conversation with me agreeing to get back in touch, once I'd completed the manuscript.

I then ran up to the third floor to find Richard, who since his bankruptcy had taken to researching potential target companies, ready for when he could work again. Maddy had taken to calling him Saddam.

'Do you think I've had a mental breakdown?'

Richard swivelled round in the chair to face me. He removed his reading glasses.

'No why?'

'So you've never seen me behaving like I'm going completely

off the rails?'

'No...sometimes you do and say funny things, but you've always done that. Why do you ask?'

'Juliet, the journalist, thinks my numbers thing, and the game with Anthony was the result of a mental breakdown. She still doesn't believe he was communicating with me and that the whole thing was in my imagination. Richard, she even asked if I'd considered getting counselling for it.'

'Well...your game with Anthony was out of character for you – I always had you down as more loyal. Obviously, I don't know whether he was or wasn't...I haven't read your book yet. The numbers stuff is a set of really strange coincidences that defy reason...but no, I don't think you have had a breakdown. I don't think you need counselling.'

'Hmm...' and I hovered in the door way, silently pondering.

I was sure people who had breakdowns gave up on life; they didn't want to get out of bed, they let their appearance slide and wandered around looking like tramps, or they sat rocking back and forth in some corner. But I was none of those things. Then I looked down at my clothes I'd chucked on in a hurry: greying T-shirt, jeans with a hole in the knee, and a cardigan Richard called a rug, but it was warm, or rather it was making me sweat since I'd paced four miles on the phone with Juliet and sprinted up three flights of stairs. But these were like a dust sheet, because I was too busy trying to get my book finished and revise for my last exam, I considered. These clothes weren't indicative of a breakdown because my physical self was well-maintained.

'So...what else did Juliet say?'

'That's she's definitely interested in the story and she wants to travel from London to do the interview. She must seriously think it's got mileage because normally she only bothers to interview people over the phone. She wants to take pictures of us too. But now I've put the phone down...I'm not so sure about that,' I said. 'They might make me look very weak and vulnerable with the way they style the photo…it will make me look small next to you…make me look capable of being easily unhinged.' *Capable of being a stalker. For Christsake, I've even sent him a letter and called on him unexpectedly, all in innocence. But is that going to matter?*

'Well only you can decide that,' Richard said, not party to my thoughts.

I left Richard to it and wandered back downstairs to call Maddy. She found Juliet's opinion highly entertaining because she'd agreed with her; the game never happened. She did say that I had seemed a bit stressed out, so I could possibly have had one, but admitted that she'd been too busy stressing and obsessing about her own stuff and she may not have noticed what I was going through.

I called Mum and put the same question to her.

She said I did seem edgy after I was tapped on the shoulder, but no she couldn't see that I'd had an actual breakdown. Then I thought back to the day that mum suggested I take Valium!

The next few hours of my life were spent learning about mental breakdowns – I read all that I could about breakdowns from various Internet sites. By the time I'd finished my emotions had turned.

Richard had been station hopping on the car radio again.

It was stuck on his usual talk station, but I didn't want to mess with it while I was driving; I still wasn't that familiar with the entertainment system in Richard's car. Like some cruel twist of fate, the topic of conversation was stalking.

'…*the problem is that one type of stalker can very quickly turn into another…the once harmless stalker could become dangerous. Sometimes that stalker can become phenomenally angry with their victim. Rejection, or betrayal could trigger it, for example. It doesn't even have to be real – they could have an imagined wrong. What matters to them is that they feel like they've been victimised.*'

I'd had enough, heard enough. Richard had refused to go to

the police over the text messages, he'd advised me not to dump my manuscript on my doctor's desk bound with a ribbon that said "help me", and writing a book was clearly going to see me hanged like some psychotic crazy stalker if everyone saw the game in the same light as Juliet, the journalist.

All I wanted was to get to the truth, but getting to the truth was going to have consequences no matter which way I turned. I felt nauseated and wronged by the whole thing. But inertia was permitting slow mental rape.

And to do nothing was not an option I was willing to take.

CHAPTER THIRTY-ONE

Extracts from Police Witness Statement taken by London Metropolitan Police:

Signature: *A Hope*
Date: 7th January 2010

I am a musician and singer in a band called The Rocx based in London. I live at the address shown overleaf. But I am a US citizen.

I have been living at that address for 3 years (approx)

I have a smart phone and a laptop which I use when I am traveling to and from various gigs up and down the country to keep up with friends on social networks. I removed myself from Facebook and deleted my profile in October 2009 for reasons I do not wish to disclose, but I have never encountered any problems until now.

In 2000 I met a female through work who I knew only as 'Nicole' or 'Little N.' Her Facebook name of Nicole Hollis might not be her real name (surname.) We were both working for Opus Management at that time and I understand that Nicole was on temporary placement. We occasionally spoke but we were no more than colleagues. Nicole left the company a year later and I heard nothing more from her.

In July 2008, Nicole sent a friend request and brief email via Facebook which is private and not viewable to my contacts. Nicole asked me if I remembered her, calling herself 'Little N' and I did. I replied, more out of courtesy than anything else and told her that I remembered her. I received a further email from her but she stated that she was drunk and apologised for the typing. I ignored this email and did not reply.

On another occasion (I don't remember the date) she sent an email saying that she was sorry that she had been mistaken for thinking that I had feelings for her or something of the sort. I didn't know what she was talking about, or what had provoked the email. So I tried not to get into an email exchange with her.

In November 2008, out of the blue I received another email from Nicole which stated that she could no longer play games with me and that she was attracted to me but it was destroying her current relationship. Her letter took me completely by surprise. I replied and asked her to re-read the few email exchanges there had been. I told her I was very much in love with my girlfriend. She was no more than an old work acquaintance. I didn't really understand what the game was that she was referring to. But I respected her wishes to stay as a friend on my Facebook. I didn't consider her dangerous at that point, just irrational.

Sometime in July 2009, I was scheduled in for a recording session at the studios on Harwood Street, London. When I got there the receptionist gave me a hand written card. I opened the card and it simply read: "HELLO JACK, JUST PASSING THROUGH THE CITY". It was signed off with something that looked like a cat or a mouse. The note confused me to say the least. I did not know what it meant, or who it was from. The receptionist said the woman was small with shoulder-length blonde hair probably in her thirties. Because of my job I do get considerable amounts of female attention and the receptionist's description didn't help me. I left the card knocking around my apartment and forgot about it.

On the 7th January 2010 (today) several of my friends and relatives contacted me and asked if I had seen the book written about me that has a link from Facebook back to a website: (trueanthonyhope.com) The website has a free PDF download for the book. The book names me and was all about me and very true to life. It quoted information from my old Facebook account and used other information taken from other sources on the Internet. The book implied that I was involved in some kind of on-line game with this woman Nicole. From what I can tell she appears to have emailed it to over a thousand people connected directly or indirectly with me. The above-mentioned card she delivered to the recording studio on Harwood Street is mentioned in her book. But as I have already stated, I have had no contact with this woman since the email in November 2008.

The appearance of this book is quite disturbing and has threatened my relationship with my now fiancé who I am very much in love with.

The emails sent 7th January 2010 (today) have been sent from an account in the name of Nell Gwyn. I reported the emails to Facebook at 1pm on the 7th November 2010. Nell Gwyn is mentioned in the book which is why I know that the emails are connected to Nicole. I believe Facebook have now taken down the page. The Facebook page for Nicole Hollis also appears to have been taken down from what I can see.

I would describe Nicole as a white female aged late 30's to early 40's, between 501 and 504 tall, slim build, pale to medium complexion, mid-blonde hair. She has no distinguishing features. This description is clearly quite old as I have not seen her for almost a decade and I didn't pay any attention to her Facebook profile. The website does feature a photograph of a woman with blonde hair, but her skin has been painted gold and you can't see her face. I have no other contact for Nicole and have never known where she lives. Opus Management where she worked a decade ago was in Coventry, but I don't think she was local. Opus Management closed down several years ago after the owner died.

I cannot say if the book is an accurate portrayal of Nicole's life as I do not really know her or anything about her life of significance. But information in her letter of November 2008 seems to tally with information in her book.

At 14:01 hours on the 7th January 2010 I produced a copy of the email sent to me by Nicole along with the card which had been dropped off at the recording studio. I now refer to the copy of email as Police Item AH/01 and the card as Police Item AH/02. At the above time and date I handed AH/01 and AH/02 to PC 3072 Stafford.

I will abide by any decision the Police or CPS make with regard to this matter and I will attend court and give evidence if required to do so.

The victim Personal Statement has been explained to me and I wish to state the following:

I am in fear for my own safety as I now realize that Nicole has a fixation with me and as her advances have been rebuffed, she is now out to seek what she feels is revenge. She is clearly very clever and has found out many facts about me so it would not be difficult for her to find out where I live, so my property and my fiancé are also under threat. Everywhere I go I now have to look over my shoulder and I am turning into a nervous wreck.

Signature: *A Hope* Signature witnessed by: *PC 3072 Stafford*

RESTRICTED (when complete)

14:35 Details passed on a hand over to e-crime unit. E-crime to arrange court order to close down website and trace suspect. At this stage it is not known if Nicole Hollis is also a victim of a cyber-crime using pieced together information taken from her Facebook page and various other on-line sources.

FTAC unit notified.

PC 3072 Stafford.

I sat on the train with my head resting against the window. I didn't particularly like the reverse-facing seats but it was the only one I could book with a table. Reserved cards were poking out of the top of the other three seats around me. I hoped the other passengers wouldn't be joining until much later – a no show would have been preferred.

I didn't know what I was going to do in London when I got there; I had several hours to kill before I needed to be at the other side of the city. If Harrods stayed open late I supposed I could browse around there for a bit.

As the fields flew past I exhaled heavily on to the glass then drew an eight in the residue of my breath. I felt bad about leaving Richard with little explanation, but I knew he would have stopped me. I needed closure for my sanity.

I double-checked that my mobile was switched off and placed it into my cream raincoat pocket that was lying on the empty seat. As I did so, I felt the cold metal object in the pocket – it was Richard's Swiss Army knife I'd bought for him the previous Christmas. I played with it for a few moments feeling the sharp point of the blade.

I placed the knife back in the pocket, took my book off the seat and placed it on the table pushing it up against the window. Then I scanned the few fellow passengers: they were mainly smartly dressed business travellers, a couple of elderly people, some arty-looking types in need of a haircut, and a stressed-out mother with a stropping toddler I hoped would be getting off at the next stop.

In front of me was a businessman wearing a suit with a laptop resting on the fold-down tray I could see he had *Facebook* open and I continued to peep at him through the gap in the seats. He clicked onto the profile of an attractive blonde woman. He was obviously reading her comments. Then he clicked on the comments left by other men on her wall. He was not only checking her profile, but also those of the men she knew. He clicked on her photos lingering longer on some of them. Who was this woman? I wondered if he fancied her, or whether he was her jealous boyfriend. His behaviour fascinated me.

Then he closed his account and started typing emails in a foreign language. I could barely see the words let alone understand them so I turned away thinking *Facebook* usage was the same world over – its language was universal.

I tried sipping the tea I'd fetched from the café bar but didn't particularly fancy it as my stomach felt a little off. I put it down to butterflies. So instead I chewed the cardboard edges of the cup while staring trance like at my book that I'd put in a Tesco's carrier before leaving the house.

I wondered how many people had bothered to download the book – two, three, a hundred. It could even be none. The only one I really cared about reading it was him. I switched my mobile back on, logged on to the train network, and reinstated my *Facebook* page. I'd taken it down earlier in a temper. But now it seemed a better idea to warn Anthony that I was heading in his direction with my book. I didn't want to cause him a fright by turning up unexpected. At least this way I would be less of a shock. I typed in my Status: *Anthony Hope...Heading for Kings Cross Dead Man Walking!!!!!!!!* I put the phone back in my pocket and allowed myself to doze.

As the train passed The Emirates Stadium I knew that we would be arriving at Kings Cross within minutes.

I made my way off the train with the other passengers, pulling my raincoat as tight as possible around me. It wasn't the most suitable coat for January, but I'd left the house in a rush and it had been conveniently draped over the hall chair.

I focused on the tremendous arched window that reigned over the top end of the station. Unlike the grey pigeons I always associated with the place, I'd never really noticed the window's dominating presence before. But then, I'd never arrived in London alone before now. I made my way through hordes of zigzagging bodies to find a machine to purchase a one day, zone 1-4 underground pass.

I had been loitering about the city aimlessly for what felt like hours. There was an icy chill in the air as the night started to fall. I continued to lean against the brick work of a second-hand shop that sold collectable old toys and ornaments with handwritten price tags. I had already bored myself silly playing a memory game trying recall as many items and their price without looking, so I twiddled with the Swiss Army Knife in my pocket. I was glad it was there, as it made me feel less vulnerable as a lone female in an unfamiliar part of the city. The area looked relatively run down with tired looking one-man-band shops which were now closed for the evening and I still couldn't shake the permanent feeling of being watched. I thought of the unexplained text messages sent to Richard's phone – particularly the last one that had been different from the previous two. I had no way of knowing whether the threat in the last text would ever be carried out.

The poster for *The RocX* was stuck on a display board that was positioned next to the door of the *Devonshire Arms*. I'd checked it earlier, so I knew I was at the right pub, on the right day, but had resisted the urge to sit inside and draw attention to myself, which is why I was hanging around on the opposite side of the road.

I had no idea what time Anthony would show or how he

would receive me. I didn't even know whether he would be alone. I just wanted him to understand what he'd done to me, and how damaging his stupid game had been to me. And I needed to see *my* book in *his* hands.

Then I spotted him. I stopped leaning against the wall. His unmistakable stride was making fast pace down the opposite side of the road. He was wearing jeans with a shirt hanging loose. His guitar was strapped to his back and he was carrying his hand as though holding a cigarette, but he was still too far away for me to know this for sure. He was alone. I didn't know whether that was a good or bad thing.

I darted into the doorway and stealthily poked my head round the corner every second or so. My breathing was laboured and the increased oxygen made me feel dizzy. I resisted the urge to bolt in the other direction.

I was right about the cigarette. He threw it down and used his foot to stub it out. And just as his hand pulled at the pub door, I stepped out onto the pavement and shouted before I could change my mind.

'Anthony... Anthony Hope!'

He paused for a second then spun round. It was then that he checked the road before crossing and I could see his face was contorted and his eyes squinting. His body language said rage. He got closer. I couldn't move. I knew I wouldn't be able to speak.

He was a few feet from me.

'You fucking psychotic b...What the fu—'

It was then when I saw him reach for his pocket. I panicked, pulled my hand from my own pocket and lunged at him with the knife. I could hear the groan of my voice as dark red blood spurt onto the sleeve of my cream raincoat.

I dropped the knife, and the carrier containing my book, then ran without looking back. It wasn't until I reached the tube station that I realised he wasn't following. I had no idea if I'd killed him.

Running against cold air made my head and ears ache, and my lungs feel like they were spiked with icicles – I deserved to feel the pain. I felt feverish and it was then that I vomited with nothing to clear the lingering putrid taste. I had sick in my hair and pulled it back using the metal clip taken from my left pocket.

I don't recall how I found my way back to Kings Cross. It was as though I'd blacked out or something. It was only a matter of time before I would be taken by the police.

CHAPTER THIRTY-TWO

The arrest happened as I was stepping over the train threshold. I felt my arm twist back and cold metal slide around my wrists.

'...you have been arrested on suspicion of...'

The man's voice vaguely filtered through my senses in the same way that words do when you're coming out of anaesthetic. My head was heavy and I could barely keep it raised. But I was aware that I was surrounded by police officers and could see train passengers' feet clearing a path to let me through. I was disorientated and my legs buckled. All I remember is being pulled back to my feet then pushed into the back of a police car.

I didn't speak in the car. The last time I had been in police transport, I was a teenager – this was a much bigger mess.

I had no idea which station they'd taken me to, all I know is, I wasn't in the car for long. I was led to a small room where I was told to strip. I could see my clothes being placed into brown paper bags that were then marked and sealed. They emptied my raincoat pockets. Amongst small bits of screwed-up paper, I saw my hairclip. I asked for it. They refused. The *Fendi* watch that Richard had bought for my birthday a few years earlier was now in a polythene bag along with my iPhone; I wondered if I would ever get them back. I could also see the Swiss Army Knife also in a polythene bag. I felt sick from shock.

I vomited into my hands – my futile attempt to stop it – and it hit the floor where I was stood. My body began to shake involuntarily and my teeth chattered uncontrollably while the officers cleaned me and mopped the floor around me. The strong disinfectant failed to disguise the strong smell of vomit in my hair. They gave me a white forensic jump suit that was too big – a woman rolled up the sleeves and appeared to check my arms for some reason.

Then I was asked question after question: my name; date of

birth; did I have any illnesses? Was I on medication? My dietary requirements...they seemed endless...did I want a solicitor? I thought of Richard. I asked for my phone call.

Richard picked up the phone. He was shouting as soon as he realised it was me. He rarely shouted.

'What the hell is going on? I've got the police crawling all over the house, tipping cushions off the sofa, bedding off the beds, going through every fucking drawer. They've walked out with the computers, laptops, your blue study folders – why on earth would they want those? Your crystal memory stick that Maddy bought for you – they've had that. What have you gone and done now? All I know is they have a warrant to search the place on suspicion of Malicious Communication and that you've been arrested on further charges. Where the fuck are you?'

I closed my eyes. Tears rolled down my face.

I just wanted him to have the book.

They had my evidence. The evidence I'd saved to protect me, was now going to be used to hang me. And my memory stick – they had taken the heart that held my story. I couldn't explain it all to Richard.

'I'm in London somewhere – I'm sorry. I don't understand all the charges. Are William and Elyse okay?' My face screwed up with emotion.

'No, course they're not okay. William is distraught. He's scared and Elyse doesn't really understand what is happening but she's asking for her mummy. What am I supposed to tell them?' I could hear his voice was on the verge of breaking. 'Your mum and dad are on their way to fetch them. I want to know exactly what you've done?'

'I'm not sure. The police are asking if I want a solicitor do you think I—'

'Do what you like – but you can forget me forking out for one.'

'It's free,' I tried.

'You can go to hell for all I care.'

Richard hung up and I slid down the wall leaving the phone hanging. I wanted William and Elyse. I needed to hear their voices. I wanted to speak to Maddy. I thought about Steve, in jail. I needed my Mum, Dad and Richard. Even Grandmama couldn't help me now.

My emotions shut down.

The custody sergeant pulled me from the floor and then placed the receiver back on the hook.

'You do understand what is happening, Nicole? You are being detained overnight and will be interviewed sometime in the morning. You can make a decision about a solicitor tomorrow.'

'I'll take the solicitor.'

I didn't cry or sleep. I tried to clean myself the best I could with the few unexpected toiletries they'd provided, but then spent the night in a catatonic state staring at the cell's far wall. All I wanted was to be home and snuggled in bed with William, Elyse and Richard.

The cell door opened. I was muddled with time, not having my watch, but the wasted breakfast that they'd sent in earlier had indicated then that it was morning. A woman officer stood in the frame.

'Nicole. Your solicitor is here, could you follow me please.'

I was taken to a private room and was greeted with a Savile Row-suited man wearing shiny black shoes on enormous feet.

'Hello, Nicole, I'm David Trevellyn-Smith, duty solicitor, appointed to act on your behalf.'

I didn't take the hand offered. I didn't want to touch anyone or for anyone to touch me. He lowered his hand.

'Nicole. If I am to help you, you have to trust me. I am a duty solicitor, but despite what people say about us, I am independent from the police. Anything you say in this room is protected by legal privilege. Everything you tell me is in confidence. Do you understand Nicole? We haven't got long before they want to commence the interview.'

I nodded my head to confirm I understood. I then started to look around the room – it was empty but for a couple of chairs and posters on the wall, one of which was for an anti-weapon campaign launched only a few weeks earlier.

'Nicole, will you stop looking around you like the room is bugged and look at me please. I cannot emphasise enough how important it is for you to stay strong in this interview. Right let's see, I've got here some notes tha—' he began, but then he somehow managed to drop the papers on the floor. 'Oopsy daisy,' he said before going to pick them up. Obviously the notes he had were on me.

I spotted something I desperately wanted round a section of the pages.

'Can I have the elastic band?' I asked.

He was back to full height, he was well over six feet and had a kind, fatherly face with thick wavy hair that needed a good trim, but he looked in far better shape than I must have done. In normal circumstances I probably would have found him endearing.

'Elastic band?' he repeated.

'To tie back my hair – I need to get the smell of sick away from my face,' I was convinced it was still lingering in my hair.

'Right...right...of course. Yes, no problem,' he said passing it over. 'I think we should sit down.'

I sat a one of the chairs opposite him while tying back my hair. I had to force myself to listen for the sake of my family.

'Have you managed to eat or drink anything since being in here?'

'No,' I said. It was a ridiculous question.

'But, it seems they've declared you fit to interview. Nicole, I have a whole bundle of offences here, Malicious Communications, Harassment, Offensive Weapon in a Public place, Threat to Kill. So let's get the big question out of the way:

did you intend to kill Anthony Hope?'

'No...of course not.'

'That is good because you are going to need to hold onto that thought in the interview room.'

'I had a nightmare on the train that I had accidentally stabbed him. I was still dragging myself out of it when the police were pulling me from the carriage. It was the most horrific dream I'v—
'

'For heaven's sake, stop! Please...do...not...say...that in the interview. Have you not heard of *mens rea*? Guilty mind?'

'No. Yes. No. Probably. But it is ridiculous to say I would ever kill him. I'm not a killer.'

'I must say; you've not exactly made this easy on yourself by posting an entire book on the Internet.' He inhaled a deep breath then exhaled as he spoke. 'Dearie me! What ever possessed you?'

He turned and spoke to the window. 'It would have been so much easier for you, if you'd kept any revenge you felt necessary down to a simple little letter or email, like most would. But you haven't so...' then he stopped whatever he was going to say. 'That wretched *Facebook* destroys so many lives.'

He turned back to me, and continued: 'As a consequence of your book the police will know every one of your strengths and weaknesses, and will play you for all its worth – which could be a long time in prison if you foolishly say in there that you did "intend" to kill or even harm Anthony Hope. And you have involved an awful lot of police time and resources: e-crime unit, British Transport Police, Metropolitan Police. They're not going to be too pleased with you, Nicole. You've caused some chaos and they believe they've pre-empted a murder at the very worst. This is your first offence, isn't it? You have told the truth on the Risk Assessment forms that were completed yesterday?'

'I was arrested for shoplifting. But I was fourteen. I don't think it was even a proper caution they gave me.'

He thoughtfully chewed his lip. 'The other thing I have to ask is, if you didn't "intend" to kill – why in heavens name were you carrying a knife and why did you threaten to kill him on Facebook?'

'I didn't threaten to kill him on *Facebook*. I tried to warn Anthony I was heading his way with my book. And it was a legal knife; the shop assistant who sold it said so.'

'Based on the areas they want to question you – and I am reading between the lines here, as the police do keep their cards close to their chest with the notes they give us – but they seem to think they have *Facebook* evidence to the contrary regarding the death threat.

'They've misinterpreted my words.' I said. I knew exactly what the police had gone and done. 'They've not realised that "dead man walking" was a reference to the dead author Anthony Hope, it was my coded message to alert Anthony that I was heading his way. I can explain it to them,' I said hopefully. 'This is a big misunderstanding, they've misconstrued my words. I know I shouldn't have put my book on the internet and I know that they will probably try and charge me with something for it. But I was angry. This man had played me for a fool and sent my head crazy with his game. But I would never kill him or even harm him.'

'But you have given this man enough evidence, ammunition to say that he feels threatened by you. And with your book they have enough for a course of conduct as far as the Harassment Act goes.'

'I'm not threatening. I haven't done anything threatening. I've merely told the truth about what had happened and how it has affected me.' *Why didn't anyone care about the effect on me?*

'Let's get back to the knife for a minute, we're digressing. You are quite right, a three-inch blade is perfectly legal providing it isn't proven that you were intending to use it to cause fear, harm or kill. If you were then the law changes and it becomes an "offensive weapon". So why did you have the knife if you didn't intend to kill or use it to cause fear, Nicole?'

I tried to think. Why did I have the knife? I had no idea why I had the knife in my pocket.

'Self-defence,' I said, 'to protect myself.' Surely that was a reasonable excuse? I tried to explain it to him: 'Someone has been texting Richard periodically for well over a year. The last text they sent was on Christmas Eve and it looked like they wanted me dead, if you interpret "dog", as meaning "bitch". It said: "waste dog, duck out". And I constantly have the feeling of being watched. Lots of strange things have happened. We have a number for the last text to prove what I am saying, but no one has ever answered the phone – it permanently goes to answerphone.' This was the truth. But not the real reason I had the knife because I genuinely did not know why I had the knife in my pocket – it was just there.

'Okay, the text is a separate issue. Did Richard your partner, I'm presuming he is your partner, report the texts to the police?'

'No. He refused to.'

'Right, right...perhaps then, he should at some stage. But those texts are not the issue we are dealing with here and you're not quite grasping the legal concept of "reasonable excuse". There is no defence in carrying potentially dangerous items for self-defence. It simply proves that you intended to use the knife as an offensive weapon, if necessary. So given that, you still have no idea why you were carrying the knife?'

'No. It was just in my pocket.'

'Just in your pocket, and you didn't intend to kill him?'

'No,' I said resolutely.

There was a knock on the door, the same woman officer who took me out of the cell only minutes before entered. 'Sorry for the intrusion, but this is important. The situation has changed somewhat.'

'Camping trip!' I said. 'The knife was obviously still in my cream-jacket pocket from a camping trip. I remember. I mentioned it in my book. I have proof. It's just unfortunate it got left in my pocket.' *Surely this was enough to let me go home?*

The solicitor ushered the officer out of the door, obviously to move from my earshot. They had to be arranging for me to go home. He came back into the room.

'Nicole, it seems that the police cannot interview you as per PACE guidelines.'

'What's PACE?' I asked confused.

'It's an Act with guidelines that the police have to follow and failure to follow procedure in given circumstances can result in any statements you make not being admissible in court.'

I pulled a face. He still wasn't making any real sense. *What hadn't the police done that they should have? Was this good for me?*

He continued. 'Nicole, it seems you have said things in your book which will cause them problems getting anything through the CPS, Crime prosecution because of...,' he paused. 'Let's say your health for now. Nicole, you are who you say you are, aren't you?'

'Of course I am. So does that mean they're letting me go home?' I said optimistically. They'd obviously seen sense, my actions were justified, provoked.

'Not quite,' he said.

CHAPTER THIRTY-THREE

Patient number: Overleaf
Psychiatric Doctor: Dr Jane Tondal
Date: 15th October 2010
Provisional Diagnosis: ICD-10, F20.0 & 300.14

Patient was arrested 7th January 2010 by the Metropolitan Police. Her case was referred to FTAC and she was transferred by the police using powers under section 136 of the Mental Health Act for independent mental assessment.

Initially detained for 28 days (MHA S2) before conditions set for outpatient treatment.

Trigger for criminal activity: De Clerambault's Syndrome: phase of hope followed by phase of resentment.

JT: Are you happy to continue with this session now, Nicole?

Nicole: Yes

(As observed in previous sessions, Nicole picked up the Mind Maze puzzle. From this point in the interview she repeatedly guided the ball through the maze – avoiding all eye contact with me. She sat with one leg curled under and the other leg restlessly kicking against the armchair.)

JT: You do seem exceptionally edgy today. I can reassure you that Cognitive Behaviour Therapy has been proven highly successful when combined with medication. If you would at least try to let me help you, then we can manage this together – help you lead as normal life as possible.

Nicole: There is nothing wrong with me.

JT: That is the difficulty with this type of disorder, sufferers feel normal because for the most part they function perfectly normally in most activities. Can you understand that?

Nicole: Yes, and I'm sick of being told it nearly every time we meet.

JT: You do understand that we are trying to get you to explore the reality of your thoughts and perceptions. To help you distinguish between what is true and real, and what isn't. You remember having this explained to you, at the hospital?

Nicole: Yes. I remember. It is so that I don't react dangerously to my hallucinations or delusions. It is so that I don't harm myself or anyone else.

JT: Yes, Nicole. It is good that you are acknowledging that.

Nicole: Stop patronising me. And I'm not ill.

JT: Nicole, tell me why you attacked the doctor at the hospital?

Nicole: Oh come on, I didn't attack the doctor. I'd been unnecessarily sectioned for a month, or near as damn it. I had two choices, sit and do nothing while they did test after test, ask question after question, PET scans, CAT scans, basically treat me like a lab rat, or I could use the time they'd pulled me from my children to re-write my book. It was all fine until they started injecting me with drugs and the writing became difficult – I couldn't think and I barely wanted to move. I started to struggle. But I had a lucid moment and wanted to get something written down before they took me for more tests. All I needed was two more minutes, but the doctor tried to take my paper from me. I instinctively slammed my pen against the paper and accidently caught the doctor's hand. I didn't attack him. The hospital twisted the story.

JT: That's a matter of opinion. You were not sent to a writer's retreat. The report from the hospital does state that you were obsessive about writing the book and you had socially withdrawn yourself from the other patients.

Nicole: The place was full of nutters, and I had too much to do to bother making small talk with them.

JT: But this was a book that you had already written and posted all over the Internet. The hospital doctors' considered this as your way of ensuring that you were entwined with Anthony Hope forever. You were writing the book over and over again. It was another one of your symptoms.

Nicole: That is rubbish, I was re-drafting and editing. It was a balls-ache because I had to do it all long-hand. But I was re-writing the book to turn Anthony Hope into fiction, just like the character in the old *Simon Dale* novel. I decided that it was far better to be moral and protect Anthony's true identity. Who he really was only mattered to me and I didn't want to be a dark shadow hanging over his relationship. I was wrong to plaster it all over the Net in the first place – it made me weak. But I had twenty-eight days of being locked-up to revise the whole book. But yet again, the hospital has gone and twisted things.

JT: Finding it increasingly difficult to write would be the dopamine levels in your brain reducing to normal levels. You might be interested to know that excessive levels of dopamine occur from drugs use, smoking and stress. In your case, we think your company collapsing and the financial stress was the trauma that triggered the excess dopamine sending you into an acute phase of your condition. It makes you want to take risks and be sexually adventurous – a bit like adrenaline, your body craves the dopamine rush. You did show early signs of this with your crush on your company's administrator – that was before you fixated on Anthony. It was all part of the same thing. I'm sure you are intelligent enough to see that.

Nicole: But I haven't had delusions or hallucinations.

JT: Nicole, I know your experiences are very real to you. To everyone else they're not. We call the type you have experienced, non-bizarre hallucinations. This is because each one could be remotely possible depending on the majority population's held values and beliefs. I accept that different cultural values do make diagnosis of this disorder so complicated. But it is also what makes your condition so difficult for you to recognise.

Nicole: My so-called hallucinations and delusions all seem possible because everything I said happened – did happen.

(Words spoken in anger and the patient aggressively threw the Mind

Maze ball at the far wall. The force caused it to smash into several pieces. Patient sat motionless while I collected the pieces.)

JT: Nicole, why did you say you lived in a St Byrke-Crale, an anagram for cyber-stalker?

Nicole: Because I knew what would be thrown at me after I spoke to the journalist Juliet. I decided to put the rope around my own neck.

JT: Rope around your neck? Are you feeling suicidal?

Nicole: No, it was a figure of speech.

JT: Nicole if you have suicidal thoughts – you must tell me, because it will be another one of your symptoms, we can increase your medication.

Nicole: I am not suicidal.

(Patient having destroyed the Mind Maze ball, reverted to doodling more symbols and numbers on her piece of paper – still avoiding my eye contact.)

JT: Let's talk about the text messages and try to rationalise this together shall we.

Nicole: Fine.

JT: You said yourself that text messages aren't possible without a number trace. So those text messages weren't possible – they couldn't have been there – could they Nicole? That's why they were never reported to the police.

Nicole: Those text messages existed. It's the source that remains a mystery.

JT: Okay, let's move on to you being huddled in the corner of your en-suite bathroom convinced that someone was in your house. You remember writing about it in your book? But you also wrote in your book that you had a deep cut and when you removed the plaster there was nothing there.

Nicole: I said that there was barely anything there, there is a difference.

JT: And the printout on imploding windows was never there was it?

Nicole: The printout was there but it vanished. Sometimes I think Richard has been playing with my head, but I don't understand why.

JT: Nicole I want you to read this small paragraph I've saved it for you, it's taken from a medical journal. Can you read it aloud for me?

Nicole: Why can't I read it in my head? It's where you say everything else to do with me is held.

JT: Because I want to make sure you actually read it.

Nicole: "For people with paranoid schizophrenia, symptoms include delusions such as believing that they are being watched, persecuted or plotted against or even that a person is in love with them despite never having met them. Hallucinations will occur and are usually auditory, but can also be physical sensations such as being touched. They suffer grandiosity, jealousy or excessive religiosity all mixed in one melting pot."

JT: Nicole can you not see even a tiny glimpse of yourself in these symptoms? Your game with Anthony Hope is what we call Delusional Erotomania. It explains why you had intense sexual feelings for him. You did score quite highly on what we call first rank positive symptoms. When we put everything together, in one pot, can you not see how being tapped on the shoulder, being convinced that you are communicating with famous dead spirits or angels, believing you are being given glimpses into the future and convinced a man is communicating through special code are all your symptoms wrapped in one. It explains why you felt like you were in *Wonderland*. And it is perfectly normal for paranoid schizophrenics to find ingenious ways to explain things that otherwise don't make sense to them. You have managed to make incredible sense out of all your experiences and everything else that was happening in your life, even the world. Even your feeling of emptiness is symptomatic of your illness.

Nicole: So how did my brain think up a text using a word I'd never heard of? If those texts didn't exist, why did I quote the dictionary definition of cuckold to my friend Lorna? It was Richard who had given me the dictionary definition. But I eventually figured that it was how the book must have got from the study shelf to the kitchen: he had moved it to quote from it But if that first text hadn't been sent to his phone then I would never have found my way to a quadratic equation and I wouldn't even have had a story to get sectioned with. How do you explain that one?

J.T: We are doctors. We don't always have all the answers.

Nicole: What about the number I have from the text message that wanted me dead? Both Richard and I were sat in the kitchen when the text came through. You can't say that it didn't happen.

JT: We are still observing you at this stage for possible Dissociate Identity Disorder – alternate personality. It would explain the blackouts. You are one of the most intriguing cases. Nicole, tell me, where is Richard right now?

Nicole: He is with my children, where do you think he is? He got married you know, just like the old novel predicted.

JT: Are you talking about Anthony now? Nicole, you are aware that you have a restraint order against you. You still could be charged with the other offences, if the police eventually get your case through the CPS.

Nicole: Yes, I am aware.

JT: Good. But that old Anthony Hope novel was just a book; it didn't really mean anything, did it?

Nicole: I read it in the end – at the hospital. Anthony Hope wrote a love story of two people, Simon Dale and Nell Gwyn, who toy with each other and fight all the way through the book until he eventually falls for the taller, dark-haired woman and marries her, leaving the shorter, fair-haired Nell with nothing.

JT: But Anthony wasn't toying with you was he? He would have sent you emails. Made things clearer to you, wouldn't he? That is what people normally do. He gave a sworn statement to the police denying the game, Nicole.

Nicole: The statement wasn't the truth. By the way, Nell didn't die in the book. It was someone else who was poisoned, just shows how you can get hold of the wrong end of the stick when you skip read. Do you know what struck me the most about the old book in the end: a quote in the opening paragraph from Sir Francis Bacon, taken from his essay on truth. You should read it sometime.

Nicole: Perhaps I should. Nicole, do you still look for him?

Nicole: You have a crap view in here – what is the point of a window overlooking a brick wall?

JT: Why don't you want to answer the question?

(Nicole stopped doodling on the paper and for the first time in the interview she instigated eye contact.)

Nicole: Are you married?

JT: No, I'm married to my work at the moment.

Nicole: Don't leave it too late to have children. You have beautiful eyes – very dark. They remind me of Anthony's.

(Nicole shifted her gaze to my breast area and appeared trance-like for a moment.)

Nicole: I had a really strange dream last night. I've had it before.

JT: Tell me about the dream.

Nicole: It doesn't matter...shush... listen!

JT: What is it? What can you hear? Nicole, tell me what you hear?

Nicole: Not voices in my head if that's what you want me to say. It's *Rolling in the deep* by Adele. Don't you just love that song?

JT: Erm. Yes I do quite like it. Dr Webster must have the radio on in the next room. Nicole, you have called me several times this week, each time with nothing much to say.

Nicole: I just feel confused by everything that has happened. If I talk to spiritualists they make sense, if I talk to you – as much as I hate to admit it you also make sense, until I get home again. Sometimes it helps to hear your voice.

JT: Do you really believe in God?

Nicole: I don't know. I don't think we have all the answers.

JT: Would angels put you through what you have been through?

Nicole: I supposed that would depend on the angel and their purpose. Did you know fifty-three per cent of Britons believe in psychic powers and the afterlife? I saved a clipping from the newspaper.

JT: You are still taking your medication, Nicole? I've noticed your weight has dropped again.

Nicole: I don't like the drugs. I read on the Internet weight gain is major side-effect, I'd rather be insane than fat.

JT: Antipsychotic drugs do slow down the metabolism, I won't lie to you. But you need to take the pills. We believe you are still in the active phase of your condition. If you don't take the medication and your symptoms worsen, you do realise I will have to recommend that you are referred to other doctors for possible readmission to hospital, for your own safety. There are conditions set for you to be treated as an outpatient, you mustn't forget that.

Nicole: There is nothing wrong with me.

JT: If there is nothing wrong why do you draw these same numbers and symbols every week?

(I took the paper from Nicole. She didn't react.)

Nicole: Because I still don't know what the "one" rather than "nought" is that I should end up with, or what the delta and spiral mean.

JT: That is because they don't mean anything, Nicole. Try to see that you have created your own labyrinth. I'm going to recommend a switch to Aripiprazole – we can see how you go with that drug. But I'm calling it a day for today. My plan next week is to show you some random video clips, and song lyrics and we can look at them together and see how you would make these clips appear to be messages from Anthony, even though we know that they're not from him.

Nicole: Anthony doesn't play games anymore. There is no switch that has gone on or off in my head – he simply stopped the games. He's being loyal to his wife and if he's half the man I think he is, he will remain loyal to her. I am glad he has found someone he is happy with.

(Patient appears to have stopped taking the medication. A switch to Aripiprazole (20mg daily) has been recommended and for further examination by second independent doctor to take place. Personal recommendation would be for further hospitalisation to supervise medication, certainly until patient clearly out of the acute phase. Suspect suicidal symptoms, and also suspect patient/doctor fixation beginning to develop.)

<< End of Transcript>>

I turned the temperature of the shower up a notch and stood thinking about the computer printout for the imploding window. Not once had it occurred to me that Dad had left the printout in the house for me just after it had happened. It was only by chance after mentioning it to Mum that the matter had finally been cleared up. Mum said she recalled Dad saying that I never acknowledged it, but then he must have forgotten about it too, blissfully unaware about the confusion it had caused. But it made sense now that it would be Dad: an engineer would bother to investigate how a window could implode. Where the paper had disappeared to – I still didn't know.

Elyse tapped on the shower door.

'Mummy, I have a call for you.'

I silently cursed the inconvenience of the caller and opened the shower door instantly feeling the drop in temperature. I was about to say that I'll call whoever it was back in a minute but then I noticed she was holding a broken mobile, the screen was smashed. She'd obviously found it in the kitchen drawer and was role-playing with it. I went along with the game and asked who it was.

'It's a fwiend,' she chirped.

'And who...'

'Their number is zewo, eight, eight, eight, five, one, two,' she said and finished with a beaming smile.

My head replayed her numbers. With the water still noisily blasting out, I could have heard wrong.

'Elyse, what did you say?'

'The number is zewo...eight...eight, eight...five, one...two.'

I had heard correctly the first time. They were my numbers alright, but she'd put the zero at the beginning and not the end.

'Elyse....did Daddy tell you to say that?'

'No...it's a fwiend.' She started to giggle and left the bathroom.

'Elyse...who is the friend? Tell me...come back here now,' I shouted, but she ignored me.

I turned the shower off and trod carefully across the tiled floor so as not to slip. Once safely on the carpet I accelerated to catch her. I stood at the edge of the bedroom door, dripping wet and shouted to her once more. She still stubbornly refused to come back and I watched her skip the length of the landing, still giggling.

'Elyse come back,' I tried again.

But she disappeared down the stairs, leaving me no option but to return to the bathroom to get a towel. I decided to take one of the Antipsychotic pills stored on the bathroom shelf.

The paper ticket I had said thirty-four. The ticket dispenser fixed to the wall was still on twenty-five. That meant I was to be sat a fair while waiting for my repeat prescription for the antipsychotic drugs. I put my feet on the low table and slouched in the seat picking at my nails. The plasma TV was on but I couldn't be bothered to watch it as the sound was too low.

It always amazed me how busy hospitals were. It was only when you were in one that you realised how much illness there was in the world. I looked up at the OUTPATIENT sign. I supposed things could be much worse for me. There was an elderly man on the next chair but one. He looked a little like Goofy with his missing teeth – he was quietly working his way through a crossword. The date on his newspaper said 23rd February 2011. With everything that had happened to me, weeks and months were simply merging into one. The ticket dispenser moved to number twenty-eight.

Someone turned the volume up on the TV and I instinctively looked up at the screen. It was news on the earthquake that had tragically hit New Zealand.

'I dreamt this,' I said to Goofy while pointing at the screen. 'Well not this exactly, but I had a dream about an earthquake. It's horrible.'

The ticket dispenser moved to number thirty. The man just looked at me as though I was insane.

The report was focusing on the Chirstchurch cathedral and the damage to the stone spire. Thankfully no one had been hurt by the fallen stone. The journalist was calling it New Zealand's darkest hour, hitting the country's financial heart. Suddenly something switched in my head when I saw the date and time that the earthquake had hit – the text was rolling across the bottom of the screen.

'Excuse me,' I said to Goofy. 'Could I borrow your pen, just for a minute please?'

'Sure,' he said in a tone that sounded like he was happy to be of use to someone. He handed it over.

I took one of the NHS leaflets from a plastic display stand and wrote out: 21/12/2011, 12:51 42 seconds: the exact date and time the earthquake struck. Then I rearranged the numbers. On my piece of paper was 15/2, 42, and using the remaining '1' the date rearranged became 21/12/2012, the date the Mayan calendar comes to an end and a new era begins. That was it! All the numbers and symbols had come together. The delta and spiral symbol had finally fallen into place.

'I've sussed it,' I said to Goofy. 'Too late, but I've sussed it.'

'Good for you,' he replied. 'Good for you.'

The number on the dispenser had turned to thirty-two.

I took my mobile from my bag and clicked on Safari. I wanted to read about Christchurch cathedral. There were several pages to choose from, but I went for the first and tapped the small screen to enlarge the text. Certain facts jumped out at me:

Christchurch cathedral is located in Cathedral Square 8011, known locally as 'The Square'. The square, x^2, I thought.

The stone spire had been previously damaged in an earthquake in 1888 when approximately 8 feet of stonework fell. The 1888 earthquake was caused by the Hope fault. It was Hope's fault. And there staring back at me were the three eights and the one.

The Christchurch cathedral had been named and modelled on Christ Church, Oxford, UK.

The dispenser was now on thirty-nine. I screwed my ticket up and turned my attention to Lewis Carroll and pulled him through the search engine. I found what I wanted:

In 1882, Lewis Carroll, Professor of Christ church College, under his birth name of Charles Lutwidge Dodgson became one of the founding members of The Society for Psychical Research. The society still runs today and continues to investigate psychic and paranormal phenomena. In 1885 William James became the founder of the same society in New York.

The dispenser moved to forty-two.

I turned to Goofy. 'Have you ever felt like you are the only sane person on the planet?'

'Every day,' he said.

I left the prescription waiting and walked towards the hospital exit. I passed a woman with blonde hair carrying flowers and grapes. *The old lady shed her cloak, revealing her true self to Pomana.* The woman looked familiar and was walking alongside a man with silver hair. I heard her shout: "William James, Elyse Grace, come back here!" I turned around and walked back towards the woman knowing as soon as I reached her we would become one once again.

2012

The heat wave made it feel like summer but lingering daffodils were a subtle reminder of spring. Snow had been forecast next week along with an imminent hosepipe ban to conserve water. Maddy, Steve and Henry were on their first big family holiday abroad since Steve's release from prison, but her *Facebook* hadn't been updated with holiday snaps for a couple of days; so far she'd posted three hundred. With nothing of particular interest on my Newsfeed, I clicked on my list of friends instead. As a consequence of my game, I had less than fifty people left in the world I considered remotely trustworthy, others had loyally knocked me off after hearing about what had happened. Some people now considered me too scary to approach and a dangerous addition to their *Facebook* – scared they'd end up in a book, no doubt.

I casually scrolled down the short list displayed on my new iPad, but came to an abrupt halt when I spotted a familiar name, a name that had not been there for a very long time: Anthony Hope. There was no photo, just a *Facebook* blank face. He wasn't supposed to be there, it wasn't my fault he *was* there. Heart thumping and the restraint order swirling around the back of my mind, I clicked on his name. It said "deactivated account".

I then noticed several other friends who had closed their accounts for various reasons: fall-outs, bored with it, etcetera, but just like Anthony Hope they were once again listed amongst my active friends. Applying logic, it meant somewhere between 2011 and 2012 *Facebook* had changed the way that the site displayed an individual's deactivated account.

'Oooh shit,' I said out loud.

His presence could only mean one thing: he had not singled me out prior to taking down his page otherwise he wouldn't be listed amongst my other friends. I'd been mistaken. He'd never removed me.

How could I have got it so wrong? Time delay. That was the answer. A person's Facebook page must be traceable on the general search for an hour or so after the account's deactivated. The connection had been broken on my page, but not elsewhere on Facebook for some time. All my printout proved was how closely I had been observing him. How stupid was I to not have considered this months ago?

It took much longer for the full implication to hit home. So much longer that I'd disturbed Richard from his newspaper to tell him how thick I'd been to think Anthony had singled me out, then sat on the sofa licking my wounds for a bit because evidently, I hadn't been significant enough to Anthony to be singled out for removal. I wasn't special. His decision to leave *Facebook* had clearly been nothing to do with me. But I don't know why the most disturbing conflicting factor took so long to register. Perhaps it was the fact I was slowly being brainwashed into believing I was a psychologically disturbed stalker and forgetting to think of myself as the victim who had been made to question her sanity.

But the reality was, Anthony Hope could have been "activating" and "deactivating" his account willy-nilly still giving him full access to my *Facebook* page whenever and wherever he liked. Late at night, early morning, he could still be watching me or anyone else he chose. He may never have reactivated his account, not even once, but the option was there. The thought made me uneasy.

I clicked on his name once more; it gave me the option to "unfriend" Anthony Hope.

After months of pain and confusion I was the one who finally severed our connection.

Anthony Hope was now no more than someone that I used to know.

Forget not the past, for in the future it may help you grow.

E N D